MOST IMPRUDENT MATCHES
BOOK SIX

ALLY HUDSON

This novel is entirely a work of fiction. The names, characters, and incidents portrayed in it are the work of the author's imagination. Any resemblance to actual persons, living or dead, events or localities is entirely coincidental.

NO AI TRAINING: Without in any way limiting the author's and publisher's exclusive rights under copyright, any use of this publication to "train" generative artificial intelligence (AI) technologies to generate text is expressly prohibited. The author reserves all rights to license uses of this work for generative AI training and development of machine learning language models.

Angel of Mine Copyright © 2025 by Ally Hudson. All rights reserved. Printed in the United States of America. No part of this book may be reproduced in any form or by any electronic or mechanical means, including information storage and retrieval systems, without written permission from the author, except for the use of brief quotations in a book review.

Digital Edition ISBN: 979-8-9918384-2-9

Print Edition ISBN: 979-8-9918384-3-6

Cover design by Holly Perret, The Swoonies Romance Art

FIRST EDITION

For everyone who knows that love has no rules.

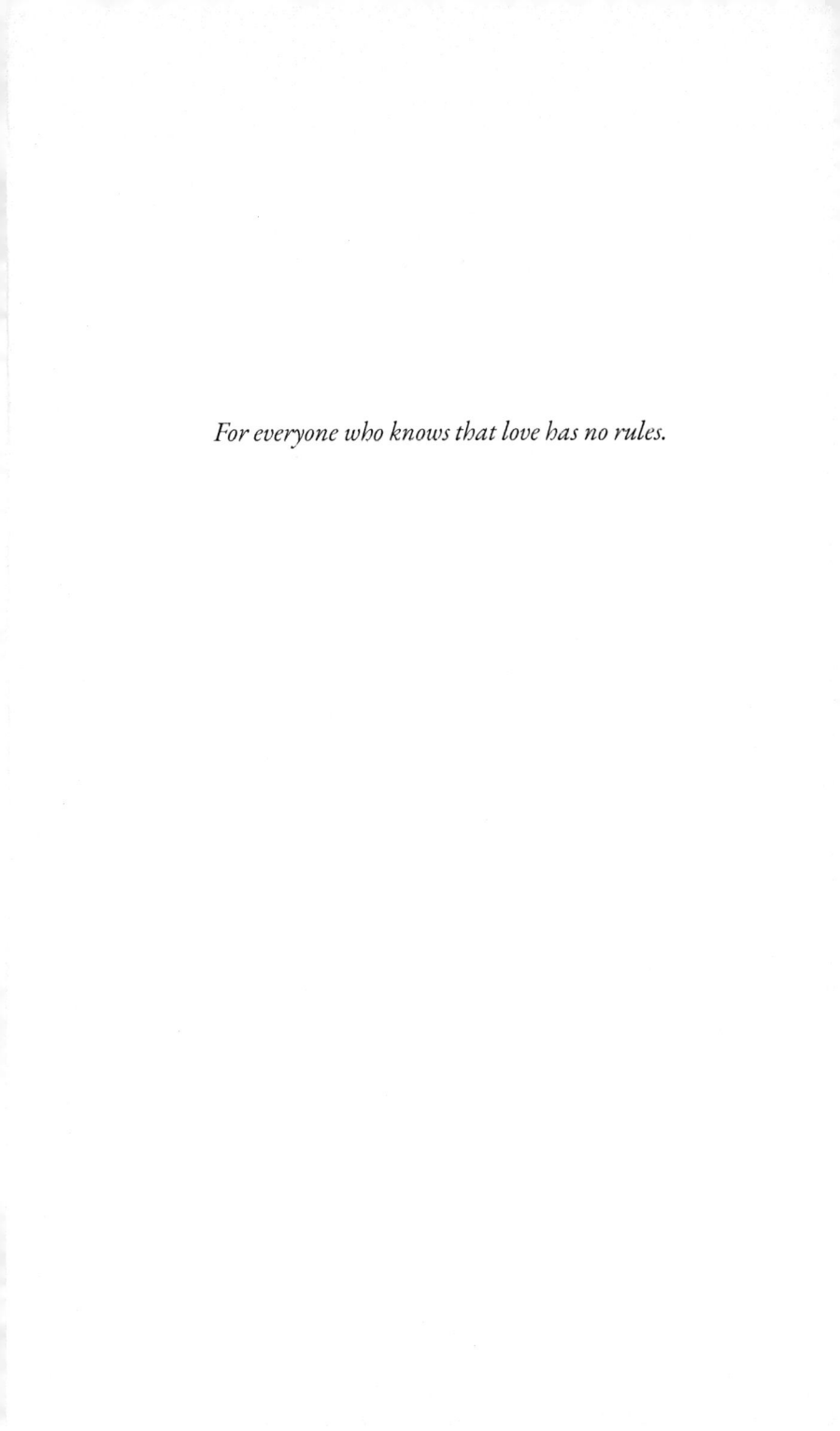

What is straight? A line can be straight, or a street, but the human heart, oh, no, it's curved like a road through mountains.

> — TENNESSEE WILLIAMS, A STREETCAR NAMED DESIRE

The Scottish Scheme

Prologue

SUTTON MANOR, LONDON - NOVEMBER 25, 1813

TOM

THE CEREMONY HADN'T BEEN beautiful. Nor was the wedding breakfast any sort of improvement. No, the best that could be said was that it was expensive.

My new sister recited her vows with barely restrained tears, a tensile note in her voice. I could not blame her for the reaction, not with the twisted set of my brother's mouth when he had deigned to glance her way—Hugh really could be an arse when he put his mind to it.

With the utter failure of Hugh's marital prospects, my mother's gaze had turned toward me. I was barely eight and ten—hardly in society at all—but she'd already thrust three frippery-covered misses in my direction that morning. Every single one had been as indistinguishable as the last.

The one presently seeking my favor had light hair with an oversized bow in it. Every time her head bobbed—which was often as she seemed determined to agree with everything I said—it flapped about despondently. Surely, it was intended to match the bow on her dress, but that had been severely starched and sat stiff like two peaks directly atop her ample bosom—which was almost certainly the intended effect.

The lady and I had already exhausted the readily available topics, the ceremony and weather. And no person of any taste could admire the decorations the Dowager Duchess of Sutton had chosen on the occasion of her niece's wedding.

"Your—um—your dress is very fine, Miss Kensington." It was a safe enough topic; ladies liked compliments and I knew little enough about her to compliment anything else.

"Thank you, Mr. Grayson. My maid said it suited my coloring, but I wasn't certain." Her voice could not possibly be that high-pitched naturally. Could it?

"Yes, it looks lovely with your—eyes."

Her eyes had been the wrong choice. Her head tilted to the side in puzzlement and her brow dipped low. "It does?"

"Yes…" Christ, I hated speaking to ladies. And why was my cravat so tight?

"My dress is orange. My eyes are blue."

"Yes…" Damn, I wouldn't have guessed orange on the dress.

It had taken years to recognize that my eyes worked—or rather, didn't work—differently from other people's. And even longer before I understood precisely how. Where everyone else perceived distinctive colors, I saw shades of what I now knew as brown. I could identify the tone, and there were a few colors I was better at guessing than others. But I could never be sure.

"You have unusual tastes, Mr. Grayson. If you'll excuse me, my mother is in need of me."

I bowed, resisting the accompanying eye roll. She was probably envisioning our future home—entirely too garish to abide.

This wasn't my first fumble with a lady, and I suspected it

wouldn't be the last. I couldn't lament my failure and I wouldn't miss her companionship.

My condition hadn't become a serious concern yet, nor was my utter inability to converse with eligible misses. I certainly hadn't found one I had any interest in actually impressing. But at some point, it might prove an impediment.

Mother had thrown a fair few ladies in my direction after Hugh announced that he, in her words *"meant to honor his fraudulently brought about engagement to the deceitful, scheming strumpet."* So she needed *"a daughter who wouldn't shame the entire family."*

It stood to reason, with the sheer volume of options Mother was shoving in front of me, that at least *one* would catch my eye. Thus far, such a lady had proved elusive.

Each of the ladies had been perfectly pretty in a rather bland sort of way. Their gowns were fine, decorated with laces and ribbons and baubles. They were tiny, delicate, fragile things with even temperaments and banal conversation. Topics were restricted to the recent weather, the present weather, the upcoming weather, recent balls, present balls, upcoming balls. The encounters were a slow, Sisyphean kind of torture.

I ducked behind a potted plant to extend my reprieve. Mother was in the center of the tulle-covered hell, too busy feigning a preening delight for all the guests to be occupied with matchmaking. She smiled and thanked as though she had not but two hours ago begged Hugh to leave the new Lady Grayson at the altar.

Her present efforts were impressive. If I hadn't caught each and every glower at the bride, I would have thought her pleased with the match.

She wasn't though. No, it seemed that our hostess, the Dowager Duchess of Sutton, was the only one pleased with this turn of events. The marriage was a fair victory to crow over. She'd secured a viscount for her unfortunate miss of a niece.

A bony hand grasped my elbow and yanked me forward. Somehow, I'd missed Mother's distinctive scent of lilacs and decay, and she'd found time in her schedule between artificial gratitude and seething, viscous glowers to return to her matchmaking.

"His Grace, the Duke of Rosehill," she hissed as she dragged me along. "He has an unwed sister and a widowed former sister-in-law under his charge. You met them once—last year."

"Mother..." It was a half-hearted protest. I'd learned long ago to choose my battles with her, and making nice with a duke's sister for a few moments or chatting with a lonely widow wasn't worth the argument.

She pulled me along, claws digging into the wool of my coat until she paused in front of—

Oh.

Dimly, under the rushing in my ears, I heard Mother prattling. "—Lady Grayson. Your mother introduced us at her annual ball a few years ago. It is a tragedy she stopped hosting."

The gentleman was clearly distracted. He offered Mother a brief glance before his gaze flicked back to the crowd. But he was... *beautiful.*

Dark hair swept off his wide forehead. Matching thick brows topped equally dark eyes. His skin was pale, and his jaw hinted at the ease with which he could grow a beard. He was shorter than me, shorter than Hugh, too, and stocky. But the cut of his crisp black-and-white waistcoat hinted at a muscled form beneath. Nothing about him was delicate; his expression, his appearance, his grooming, his apparel—it was all severe, sparing, and breathtaking.

This. This was what all the stories talked about. The

swirling, fluttering, tightening of my chest, the dampness blooming on my palms, the way the air had thickened to a soupy consistency that made breathing difficult. Somehow, when I inhaled, the air was still fleeting, insubstantial. There was too much of it in the room and not enough in my lungs.

"She's still—" he started. His voice was a musical tenor. And his hand gestured between us in a moment, flicking to one side before clenching in a fist at his waist. The gesture was enough to ensure I noticed sturdy, strong fingers beneath a white glove. "She is still mourning my father," he finished, his lips twisted all the way to one corner of his mouth by the end.

"Oh, and once again, please pass along my deepest condolences. I lost my dear Henry some years ago, but the grief is as sharp as it ever was," Mother simpered.

"I will. I'm certain she will be grateful." His gaze flicked about the room, still distracted.

"Your Grace, may I have the pleasure of introducing my youngest son, Thomas Grayson?" Mother followed the request with a proper curtsy, deeper than I thought her capable.

She then excused herself, slipping off with a significant look tossed back to me.

I was supposed to do... something. But what was anyone's guess. Because with Mother away, the air filled with an overwhelming, masculine, cedar scent. It shoved useful thoughts clean from my head.

"Pleasure," he murmured in my direction, still glancing uneasily around the room.

"The honor is all mine," I replied automatically with a bow.

His silence settled like a wall between us. Several gulps of his woody scent left me painfully aware that I was gaping like a dolt, but I was still too overcome for intelligent conversation.

"It was a lovely ceremony," I added, trying again. The

comment was inane and entirely false. I'd never seen two people less enthused with the prospect of wedded bliss.

"Yes, quite," he returned as his attention shifted back to me. "Remind me again of your relation to the bride?"

I blinked, head aflutter. "She is my sister. Of but a few hours."

"Oh, right. Yes, of course. So... you are not familiar with the layout of the house then?" he asked, gaze returning to the crowd.

I was fully gaping now. "Not any more so than anyone else. Are you looking for something, Your Grace?"

His gaze finally found mine and caught there for a minute. His eyes were so dark, I was absolutely certain they were brown—near black—and not some other color I only assumed was brown. For reasons I couldn't name, it was essential to me that I know what color they were, truly.

"No... yes..." he broke off, studying my entire form with a critical eye. "No," he finally settled.

Dismissed. Thoroughly, completely, unambiguously.

"Right... I'll just be on my way then," I muttered, a forlorn note creeping in. But I was unwilling to force my company on him.

Rosehill sighed as he shifted his weight onto his heels. Then his head tipped back to the ceiling, eyelids shut.

When he finished his ritual, his gaze found mine and pinned me in place. "You haven't noticed any... escape routes? Have you?"

"Escape routes?"

"Never mind. It's— Davina!" he called out to someone behind me, beckoning them forward with both hands.

A lovely girl in a fine frock of an indeterminate color stalked to his side, her arms crossed and expression unimpressed.

"You summoned?" she asked, mouth twisted into a pout. Then her gaze flitted toward me. "Who is this little cricket?"

I— What? *Cricket?*

"He's not..." His Grace said, trailing off before he waved away the thought with one hand. "Mr. Timothy Gregerson. Mr. Gregerson, Lady Davina." He gestured between us, not taking his gaze from the lady.

"It's Tom—"

"And where have you been?" His Grace demanded of the lady. *His lady?* My heart ached in pathetic agony at the thought.

"I was with Cee," she insisted. Then, she turned toward me. "Mr. Gregerson, it is an absolute pleasure to make your acquaintance." There was something flirtatious in her tone that had me stepping back.

"It's Mr. Gr—"

"No. Absolutely not," Rosehill asserted in her direction, once again ignoring my attempted correction.

"Xander! Don't be rude," she retorted with a petty stomp of her foot.

Xander...

He dragged a rough hand through his hair, mussing the perfectly coiffed strands enticingly. "Get in the carriage," he ordered.

Lady Davina grumbled but still made to follow his instructions and flitted past him. One step. Two.

"Freeze," he demanded.

Again she obeyed and paused mid-step without so much as a huff.

"Turn."

The pivot on her heels was slow, deliberate. When she finally faced us, her eyes were wide with false innocence and her lips were parted.

Rosehill's hand shot out in front of him, palm up. "Reticule."

She rolled her eyes in answer before plopping the beaded bag in his palm with the previously forgone huff.

He loosened the drawstring and pulled out a glinting decorative snuffbox. Xand—Rosehill sighed and held the box aloft for me to take. I raised a hand unthinkingly and he plopped it in—gloved fingers brushing against my palm. My heart tripped a beat or two.

"Can you see this returned to its rightful place? Thank you so much, Mr. Granger."

"I don't"—he was already shooing the lady, whom I was beginning to suspect, with some relief, was the sister and not a romantic prospect, toward the door—"live here. And it's Grayson. Tom Grayson," I called after them pathetically.

The snuffbox lay in my open palm, delicate gold flowers and vines wrapped around a refined agate lid and sides.

Without considering the implications, I wrapped my fingers around it, slipped it into my pocket, and thought no more of it. At least, not until later that night when I snuck it from my pocket and into my bedside table where it would remain for some time.

One

WHITE'S, LONDON - JUNE 4, 1816

XANDER

WHITE'S WAS a hell I was forced to visit on occasion for appearance's sake, a necessary inconvenience required to maintain the status required of my title. Nothing more, nothing less. To refuse to attend would be tantamount to a statement. One I had no interest in making.

Still, the effort was always a misery. I was not disposed to gambling, and the gentlemen there were prone to little else. At least Wayland's didn't offer a pretense of being anything other than what it was, a gaming hell, through and through. No, White's played at being a social club, but the wagers were every bit as outrageous.

My timing was strategic. On a late-afternoon visit, enough members would be present to notice me, but not so many that I'd be pressured into absurd long shots.

My stomach dropped as I approached. There, in his usual seat at the bow window—free to be admired as he felt was his due—sat Mr. Beckett Beaumont. Unfortunately, peace would be difficult to find. The sight of his fair hair and cruel sneer was almost enough of an irritant to have me skipping the club entirely.

But I hadn't been in months. And the Hasket men had always maintained membership at White's. Always. It was a matter of pride. One of the many rules for Hasket men my father had instilled from birth via drawn out, half-drunken lectures.

Except there was no pride to be found there, not truly. Last time I made the effort, the buffle-headed numbskulls had been wagering on raindrops clinging to the window—of all absurd things.

Steeling my nerve, I stepped inside and handed off my hat and coat. I made to slip past the dining area and go upstairs to the reprieve promised in the library. But it was not to be.

A cry of "Rosehill!" rang out from the window as I passed.

Damn.

After screwing my face into an estimation of surprise, I turned. "Beaumont, wonderful to see you."

"Come, come, sit with me. You know Parker, I trust." He gestured at the dark-haired man seated across from him. Wesley Parker had moved up in the world—to be afforded such a seat.

"Parker."

"Rosehill," he nodded with a poorly concealed sneer.

Beaumont was an unpleasant enough prospect, but something about Parker had always set my teeth on edge in a way Beaumont could never manage. Parker ran in my late brother, Gabriel's, circle, a world of secret dealings and ill-considered wagers I had never been admitted to.

I did as bid—there was nothing else for it. Beaumont was not to be cut. At least not by anyone wanting to avoid notice. And avoiding notice was my raison d'être.

Restraining a sigh, I settled beside him in the final chair

facing the window. I pressed my left hand under my thigh once seated. Only the right remained to be managed.

"How are you, gentlemen?" I asked.

"Better than Parker." Beaumont chuckled.

I raised a brow at the man in question.

He sighed performatively. From the ruddy flush of his cheeks to the glazed expression in his eyes, Parker appeared to be more than a few drinks into his afternoon. Slumped with his legs sprawled out to the side, he was well on his way to soused. The man had always *tried* for fashionable, though he usually came up short in some small way or another. Nothing anyone would notice save myself and possibly Beaumont. This time it was the fabric of his trousers; the buckskin was worn dark in the inner thighs. Low on funds then.

"I've a strumpet insisting to all and sundry I got her with child. As though she hasn't fucked every man south of Newcastle."

I resisted the urge to mention that there was at least one man south of Newcastle that she had not fucked.

"Is that why her father ended the courtship between you two, Rosehill?" Beaumont asked in a tone of false conviviality.

"Who?" I asked, only half listening as I signaled a passing barkeep for my usual drink.

"Charlotte James."

Damn.

I hummed. It was the sort of vagary I employed often in town, and my use of it now made my stomach turn. Lady James hadn't deserved my treatment of her years ago, and she didn't deserve the false implication now. But her father had caught wind of a rumor and that was the end of a perfectly acceptable courtship.

The barkeep brought my usual claret and a refill for the other men. Parker downed his in one swig. Christ, he was going to retch all over the floor. It was a wonder he'd managed a membership in the first place—they'd certainly revoke it for such a display.

"So, Rosehill, I haven't seen you in an age. How have you been, old chap?" Beaumont asked, apparently finished with Parker's predicament for the moment.

A comment about his—more advanced—age hovered at the tip of my tongue, but I swallowed it. "Oh, you know. There is always much to be done."

He hummed and opened his ever-present snuffbox, grabbed a pinch, and inhaled before offering it to me. Unthinkingly, I shook my head. Beaumont raised a suspicious brow, but he returned the box to his pocket without comment.

Today, he'd donned a simple navy coat and tan trousers paired with an elaborate cravat. Beaumont was often praised for his style, which emphasized the quality and cut of his garments.

I had always dressed in simple, elegant lines. My coats were impeccably tailored and made with fabrics of unmistakable quality.

When Beaumont wore fine linens and silks with elegantly considered designs that emphasized his form, it was considered fashionable. When I began doing the same, years before he did, the *ton* whispered that it was odd, off-putting.

"Such as?" He drew out the two words, enunciating. He always had an audience here at his table. And he knew how to play to them.

My sister is determined to drive me to an early grave, and my mother is one fabulous gown away from social ruin.

"Oh, the usual responsibilities that come with running several estates," I replied. My right hand had crept off the table, threatening to dance with the offhand remark. To occupy it, I snatched the glass again and took a sip. Out of the corner of my eye, I noticed his lip curl.

Another misstep. Beaumont wouldn't know about such responsibilities. And he wouldn't take that comment as the distracted nonanswer I'd intended. No, it was a slight.

His eyes narrowed. "I don't recall Rycliffe having so many demands on his time..." I sensed a trap there, somewhere. But I couldn't spot it. Parker shifted in his seat, tucking his legs back in properly. Lord, I hoped he didn't cast up his accounts on the table.

"Well, Gabriel passed before my father."

My brother hadn't had any demands on his time. At least not until Celine. And I very much doubted he would have described his wife as a demand. Or, perhaps he would have, but it would have been accompanied by a self-satisfied smirk and an innuendo about precisely how demanding she was.

"Still, he had a wife." There was something about his tone. I hadn't evaded his trap but I still couldn't name it. And I almost certainly couldn't avoid it.

"Yes." I fought to keep the trepidation out of my voice, but some must have slipped through because he straightened. Just a touch triumphant. No wonder he always had so many debts of honor due.

"Perhaps a wife would ease some of the burdens on your time. You should consider it."

"Perhaps I will."

"Though... I suppose you have." A self-satisfied tilt crossed his brow. That was it, the trap. My two failed courtships. The rumor that refused to die.

By now, the other gentlemen milling about had abandoned their pretense of conversation. They turned to watch. I could feel their eyes on my back, waiting eagerly for the killing blow.

I hummed with as little interest as I could manage.

"Why do you suppose a wealthy, handsome, titled gentleman such as yourself cannot catch a lady? They should be queued up and down the street for you. Do you need some advice on how to handle a woman?" The question was accompanied by a crude hand gesture. Parker snorted.

I knew what the trap was, but how he was going to spring it remained a mystery. He was unmarried as well—though he'd had more than one notorious affair. He could hardly use that as evidence of some imagined flaw.

"I can manage just fine. Thank you."

"The trick is to feast on the cunny, drives them wild. You know, the way you mollies do a cock."

And there it was. Worse than I could have imagined. My nails bit into my palms as my stomach churned with shocked fury.

I wasn't alone in my astonishment. Gasps from nearby tables served only to increase the drama of the moment. No help would come from that quarter, though, I needn't even look.

Never, not once, had I wanted to call a man out. But I did now. Desperately. More than I had ever wanted anything in my entire life. Bullet or blade, it made no difference, I wanted to pierce this man's flesh.

Not recognizing the difference between my present rage and the humiliation he'd intended, Beaumont continued. "I'd be happy to demonstrate the technique on your sister, if you need a practical demonstration."

I shot up, my chair screeching a discordant symphony against the wooden floor in the breathless room. It caught on a loose board and tipped over in a clattering climax. Dimly, I was aware of another chair dragging against the boards, filling the deafening silence.

My hand had knotted into a proper fist of its own volition and everything inside me wanted to deck him. Forget swords or guns, hang gentlemanly conduct. The only satisfaction I would have was fist on bone.

Ragged, like that of a taunted bull, my breath came and went in great, furious, heaving gulps through flared nostrils.

But I was a trapped bull, caged and impotent. I could beat him bloody and it would do nothing except add fuel to the rumors, turn them from a flickering candle flame to a raging inferno that left nothing but ashes. I might not care about myself, about the title, about the estate. But Mother and Dav would burn along with me and all the rest.

Between gritted teeth I shot the only pathetic retort available to me. "You'd do well to remember that of the two of us, I am not the one who would suffer the consequences of a duel."

Beaumont's eyes narrowed, barely perceptible, but I caught the twitch. He wouldn't make a scene, but my blow had landed. It may have been a glancing one, but tonight he would return to his let house where every single member of his staff would refer to him as *Mister*.

I tossed back the last of my drink before storming off, a furious parry regarding Beaumont's own familiarity with a man's cock trapped on my tongue. My shoulder knocked against that of the youngest Grayson brother, gaping in the aisleway on my exit. Nothing could have tempted me to stop, to apologize to the gawker. Instead, I threw the door open and stomped into the afternoon light.

Two

WHITE'S, LONDON - JUNE 4, 1816

TOM

How was it possible to go from elation to devastated fury in the space of a single breath? My knees were weak and jittery, and I was still frozen, half turned to the side where Rosehill's shoulder had brushed mine.

"Sit down," Hugh hissed under his breath. The order broke through the horror, and I collapsed into my recently vacated chair by the doorway.

One by one, patrons returned to their previous conversations now that the excitement had passed.

My eldest brother's club was always preferable to White's but Rosehill never went to Wayland's. Hugh favored White's —I suspected more out of habit than actual fondness for the place. And the hope of Rosehill was enough incentive to waste a few hours in the more fashionable club.

Hugh's attention had been thoroughly captured by the scene, but now his eyes were locked on me. "What was that?" he demanded in a whisper.

"What was what?"

"Do not tell me you were thinking of intervening."

"I do not understand why no one else was," I retorted.

"Damn it, Tom. It was a repugnant display, I will grant you that. But you are the second son of an impoverished viscount. Who are you to defend a duke? And Rosehill? You hardly know the man."

"I know him well enough."

"Damn it all, Tom. Rosehill can withstand powerful enemies. You and I cannot. Do not go about making any, I beg you."

"But—"

"Tom, please."

I bit back a curse and swallowed the remaining two-thirds of my scotch before signaling for another, glaring at my brother.

"Are you all right?" Hugh asked after an uncomfortably long pause.

"No, that was horrid."

Hugh's nod was subtle as he turned to the bow window. There was a self-satisfied set to Beaumont's posture. But something in the line of his mouth, the tightness around his eyes—something Rosehill had said hit a mark. I could only hope his parting jab hurt—if only a little.

When Hugh finally turned his gaze back on me, it was with too much consideration. In general, marriage and fatherhood had improved him greatly. But it had also left him more observant. A few years ago, he never would have noticed that I was seconds from casting my accounts all over the floor. That he read me now as well as he could was an irritant.

"Why did you agree to come with me? You hate it here."

"So do you," I pointed out.

"Habit. Appearances. It keeps doors open, doors I made need some day." He shrugged and finished his own drink just as the barkeep brought mine. Hugh snatched the fresh drink from the man's hand before it found mine. "You're finished for today."

I would die before I admitted that he was likely right and I couldn't handle any more.

"Do you really wish for help from *these people*?" I asked, unable to hide my disgust.

"Not at all. But I have little Henry. I won't have my choices limit his."

My fingers caught in my curls as I ran a hand through them. I wasn't willing to give deeper consideration to Hugh's comment.

A raucous laugh spilled out from behind me. I glanced around at all at the arrogant, lecherous drunks, the idle louts, the prideful gluttons. Sinners, all. And they'd be the first to condemn me to hell if they knew what lay in my heart.

Turning back to my brother, I was struck with the realization that at some point he'd become a man, and a good one. Quite without my noticing. Sometime between the beginning of their love story when Kate spilled lemonade on him and when he first held his son, he'd grown into his responsibilities. He was a man who would make sacrifices for his family. He hadn't always been that man.

"He's lucky to have you for a father."

Hugh scoffed.

"I mean it. You've changed. A lot."

"I know," he said, glancing down at his drink. "I'm sorry I couldn't be this way when you needed me."

"Hugh, you were eleven."

"And your elder brother," he added, though I wouldn't have. The four years between us was nothing.

"I had Michael." And I did. At times, Michael had been more father to me than my actual father. But he'd done it in his own quiet, unassuming way. It had taken years to appreciate the full extent of my natural half brother's sacrifices.

"You did. And I wish so often that I had allowed him to be there for me. Perhaps I wouldn't have been quite so doltish when I met Kate."

A chuckle broke free at the memory. I was pleased he and his wife could jest about the early days of their marriage now.

"I don't think there's an expiration, if there's something you wish to speak with him about," I said.

"That is true for me, as well. If you wanted to discuss something."

I considered it for a moment. Here in this ridiculous club full of evil people. Just confessing everything to Hugh. A small, naive part of me that could see it, Hugh clapping me on the shoulder and asking what I was still doing here, instead of chasing after Rosehill.

But that wasn't reality.

I shook my head.

"Are you sure? There's no lady you've taken an interest in? You've been busy lately."

While he was right that I'd been avoiding family gatherings, his guess at the reason could not be more wrong. I loved my new sisters; they were each clever and kind. But watching my brothers so in love—it left an uncomfortable ache in my chest where only joy should be. I was delighted for them, truly I was. But at some point Michael and Hugh had left me behind. They had found a life where I could not follow, a life of wives, marriage, and children. If I ever had those, I could not imagine I would be filled with the same happiness my brothers enjoyed, the same love.

The bitter laugh escaped without permission and I forced a smile to soften it. "Nothing like that," I assured him.

He caught his lower lip between his teeth, studying me in a way that had me shifting in my seat. "You have not met a lady at the theater? There is no one... serious? That is not why you are always there?"

"No, Hugh. I'm not about to run off with an actress." I still wasn't entirely certain where Hugh had gotten the idea that I spent all my time at the theater. The man had hardly listened to a word I'd said for nearly a decade, but mention an evening out once and he never forgot it. It was a notion that served me well and I chose not to disabuse him of it.

"Because I would understand. The heart does what it wants. But of course you know such a thing would be impossible." He was tentative there, looking up at me with wide, sympathetic grey eyes.

"There are no ladies, Hugh. I simply cannot stand the sight of you and Kate *sneaking* into every closet in the country."

That earned me a smirk and seemed to satisfy his concerns.

He settled back, switching to more concrete concerns. "So what do you think about replacing the carriage house at the dowager house this year? Should we wait another season?"

"Can you afford not to? Do you really want Mother coming up to the main house to borrow the carriage for another year?"

"She has improved... somewhat. Now that she has Henry to dote on."

"Better you than me," I muttered, snatching the drink out of his hand and savoring a hearty sip, desperate for the oblivion it promised.

Three

HASKET HOUSE, LONDON - JUNE 5, 1816

XANDER

I'D BEEN DREADING this night from the moment I received the invitation. It had all the makings of a disaster—the kind that would be spoken of in hushed, warning whispers for years to come.

"Tell me more of the venue for this evening, darling boy," Mother demanded in her usual over-enunciated manner. She and her poor lady' maid had delved so deep into the depths of her wardrobe room that I wasn't certain they would ever resurface.

"I've told you, Mother. It's a gaming hell. There are gaming tables. They've promised dancing, so I imagine they've set up some sort of floor. And there is alcohol—though not enough." I muttered the last bit under my breath as I inspected the decorative hair feathers Mother had pulled from somewhere.

"And this couple—the Waylands. They are fastidious in their hosting?"

"You've met Lady Juliet, Mother. We nearly wed."

The vanity Mother used for her toilette was an ominous sign. I hadn't seen that many pots and powders since panniers went out of fashion.

She humphed from the depths of her wardrobe. She'd taken over Father's room after his death and had her own converted entirely for the purpose of storing her many garments. Row upon row of gowns hung from the converted shelving. The majority of them were the stark black and whites she favored, but the older gowns, the ones she was examining at present were as bright as they were ostentatious

My stomach sank with the sneaking suspicion that she was going to choose something from before the turn of the century, and I could feel the humiliation bubbling up in advance.

Mother considered fashion to be an art form. Each piece of her ensemble was carefully considered to achieve a truly magnificent effect. The problem was that no one else shared her vision. Oh, they were polite enough to her face. But behind her back, laughter followed her every move.

My mother was beautiful, but it was an odd, discomfiting beauty if one wasn't intelligent enough to look for it.

She hadn't always been this way—so vain. I rather thought my father's callous disinterest in everything to do with his wife had something to do with her wardrobe statements. Every time he wandered off while she was mid-sentence, every time he failed to return home, every time he ignored her every word, my mother had found a newer, bolder, louder piece to add to her collection. She had spent her entire life screaming in perfect silence. And I was the only one who noticed, who heard.

I fussed with the ornate sleeve of my coat as I finally made my way to the settee. The sounds coming from her dressing room weren't overly promising—I suppose I would *oomph*, too, if I were being laced into one of her court gowns.

A silver thread had loosened in the seam of my coat, and the temptation to tug at it until the entire garment disintegrated on my body was nearly impossible to resist.

A rustling sound interrupted before I could enact my destruction, and Mother slipped out of her wardrobe with her haggard lady's maid in tow. I bit back a sigh at the overwrought expression on the girl's face—probably ought to put the notice back out. This one wouldn't last long at all.

I couldn't entirely fault her. Mother had chosen a robe à la française that I strongly suspected was from her debut season. The gown was beautiful, truly, and impeccably preserved. I was certain it had been admired by all in its time. But now it was so dramatic that I could hear the snickers already.

The skirts were too wide Mother had to turn sideways to escape the confines of her wardrobe. A lovely viridian, the hem was decorated with burnished pewter lace nearly a foot wide. It almost certainly cost more than the annual income of a small German principality. The dressmaker had carried the pewter detailing up the skirt in exquisitely embroidered swirls and leaves. The entirety of the stomacher was stitched with intricately detailed vines and flowers; it was truly breathtaking. And the pièce de résistance was the enormous grey wig with matching ribbons, jewels, and ostrich feathers woven throughout that the maid held clasped in both hands.

"Well, darling, shall your mother rouse the *ton* to raptured awe?"

I rose and sidled up to her with a sincere effort not to crush the skirts and pressed a kiss to her cheek. "You look beautiful."

"Yes, but will it inspire the proletariat and patricians alike?"

"I cannot imagine how you could do anything else."

"Splendid. Now, leave me and Marie to our ablutions and see to your sister."

I nodded and left to find Davina, ignoring the maid's quiet, "It's Marianne, Your Grace." She could sort that out herself.

Dav was already in the drawing room bedecked in massive peacock feathers that splayed out from the embroidered bird on the center of her gown. Her matching mask hung from her wrist as she distractedly plucked at the tassels of the pillow she had plopped across her lap.

"*Cacaw*," I muttered at the sight of her.

"Peacocks do not caw," she informed me in a pert huff.

"How would you know?"

"They scream. It's sort of an angry *mah-mah* sound." Her impression was absurd and almost certainly based in reality.

"When have you met a peacock?"

"Irrelevant," she said, then set the pillow aside and rose to smooth out my cravat. "When is Cee to arrive?"

A ludicrous story was almost certainly associated with the peacocks. One I had no interest in learning. Often, as long as Dav was unharmed with her reputation more or less intact, it was best to remain ignorant of such things.

I waved away my worries. "Any time now. And Mother should be down in an hour or six."

"How is she?"

The fireplace called to me. Once I reached the brick hearth, I knocked the coals about with the poker before setting it back in the rack. "No one will be impressed by the height of your plumage, I can promise you that."

"If she's already dressed, how much longer can she take?"

"She had yet to begin her ablutions."

"Ablutions?"

"She meant *toilette* but the common vernacular was lacking."

Dav sighed as the butler announced Celine's arrival. She swept into the room in a flurry of elegant mauve silk, delicate beading, and metallic threads catching the firelight. She was, of course, the picture of elegance.

After a quick greeting, she joined Davina on the settee. The ladies chatted amiably about something or other. It was impossible to maintain my seat as the minutes ticked by. Nervous energy stretched into my extremities, refusing to yield, and I strode to the fire again, repeating the previous exercise.

Dav snapped at me for my pacing before, as always, wandering down the most infuriating path. "Do you suppose they'll play hazard tonight? I find myself in need of funds."

Dread spread through my chest and I rounded on her. "Davina, you cannot—you must behave with decorum tonight. These people will be playing for real coin. And what could you possibly need funds for? Your pin money is more than generous."

I willed her to understand me, to recognize for once that she could not do precisely as she wished the second that she wished it.

"What on earth else would they play for? And it is hardly your business," she snapped as she crossed her arms over her chest. Her feathers rumpled with the effort.

"Davina—" My voice had reached an unholy pitch.

I cleared my throat as Cee jumped in to salvage the night. "Davina, darling, perhaps you might go see if your mother is in need of assistance?"

Dav sighed but rose and wandered off to find mother. Or trouble. There was no way of knowing.

I collapsed into the chair across from Cee, my head hinged back in exhaustion.

"What has a bee in your bonnet?" she asked.

My head lolled to the side to shoot her a glare. "We're taking my mother and my sister to a gaming hell. To a masquerade, no less. Mother will certainly expose herself to ridicule and Davina to ruin—and I shall be left with nothing but the scattered pieces of my dignity.

"Surely it will not be so bad as all that."

I sat up properly. "You have, in fact, met my mother and sister, yes? Gabriel always made it a point to arrive far later than fashionable, merely so he would miss Mother's grand entrances. And that was *before* Davina was in society."

She tutted, unimpressed with my explanation. "It's a masquerade; a certain amount of pageantry is to be expected."

"Remember that sentiment when you see her," I cautioned.

But Celine, ever skilled with reading between the lines, tilted her head, parsing my expression. When she settled back a little on the settee, I could see that she knew that my worries about the ladies upstairs were not the entire source of my agitation.

"I ran into Parker and Beaumont—at the club," I explained, my hands dancing in front of me, tight and sharp in their movements. "There were some... insinuations bandied about."

"What did they say?"

"Nothing fit for a lady's ears."

"I was married to your brother. I've heard a great many things not meant for a lady's ears," she insisted.

I nudged the rug with my toe. A strand had come loose and would need to be seen to. "There was an implication that I would be... better able to secure a wife if I feasted on a lady's... flower the way that I feast on a man's... well, you know. Then there was the generous offer to demonstrate the proper technique on Davina."

Returning their vile words to the air brought the disgust and rage burning back up to the surface.

When Celine demanded to know which of the men said it, I waved the answer away. She was bold enough to give the cut, which would only lead to Beaumont knowing he'd managed to needle me enough to mention it to her.

"Does it matter? They may be the only ones brave enough to voice it, but they all think it."

Celine made a joke about spreading a rumor involving pustules on the speaker's member, and I was forced to give up the name in hopes of seeing that dream come to fruition.

Several minutes spent in the dispersal of the most intriguing gossip was enough to distract me until Davina returned, pressing herself against the wall to make room for Mother to enter through the double doors of the drawing room—which still were not wide enough, and she had to turn sideways to make her way into the room.

The wig was even more impressive atop her head, adding nearly five hands. Predictably, she caught it on the—intentionally unlit—chandelier, and I rose to untangle her while Dav and Cee hid their mirth poorly.

Also predictable was the struggle to fit Mother, her gown, and her wig into a carriage. Cee and Dav left in one, and Mother and I in the other in darkness—lanterns were too risky with the wig. I traveled scrunched and half smothered beneath layers of skirts and panniers. Astonishingly, the drive to the club was so unpleasant that I was actually relieved to arrive.

Four

WAYLAND'S, LONDON - JUNE 5, 1816

TOM

THE *TON* HAD RISEN to the challenge Michael set forth when he opened his gaming hell to all and sundry. Ladies and gentlemen alike poured into the infamous octagonal walls where fortunes were won and lost, all desperate for the opportunity to see and be seen.

Michael, at the behest of his wife, had agreed to host a masquerade for the *beau monde*. The ladies, in particular, seemed to delight in the opportunity to peer into the forbidden world of their fathers, brothers, husbands.

Juliet's hands were all over the night's festivities, from the chessboard dance floor abutting the wall opposite the bar, to the gaming tables pushed along the remaining walls. She'd clearly given the arrangements some consideration. The beginner tables where one could learn the play were crowded nearest the door, whereas the high stakes tables were pushed to the farthest wall.

Drab, muted browns—to my eyes, at least—swirled like handkerchiefs in the wind across the makeshift dance floor.

The quartet, tucked away in the corner, offered the dancers a lively cotillion.

I had chosen to prop up the bar for the moment. Michael would never invite my mother, and she would never attend a ball hosted in this "degenerate cesspool" even if he had. Kate had almost certainly dragged Hugh into a closet to do whatever it was they did in there. As long as she was occupied, I was free of matchmaking, meddlesome women and I wasn't going to waste the opportunity for a reprieve.

A massive wig towered over the dancers on the floor before cutting a wide swath through them—Rosehill's mother. My heart stopped for a moment and I straightened. Her presence didn't guarantee his, but it did hint to it. God bless the dowager duchess and her penchant for eccentric—and oversized—fashions.

The scotch burned as I accidentally swallowed too large a sip in my excitement and I took a distracted bite of one of Anna's tarts to cut the fire. Those alone might have been worth the effort to dress and attend. The crisp, buttery caramel pastry melted in my mouth, leaving only the sweet, tart nip of raspberry. My eyes slipped closed as I savored the taste of my childhood. The greatest loss to the Grayson household had been when Anna wed Augie and opened her own bakery. Now I had to fight the masses for the treats I once only had to sneak to the kitchens for.

A feminine giggle arose from one of the higher stakes tables followed by masculine groans of disappointment. Peacock feathers streamed over the lady's shoulder, shot out from her waist, and puffed high atop one side of her mask. Or possibly ostrich feathers? It was difficult to see the pattern from behind.

She spun in delight. Tall, statuesque with dark hair—was it Lady Davina? Damn masquerade made everything more difficult. If Lady Davina was here swindling the *ton* of every last coin in a way that would make my eldest brother proud, and her mother was attempting to burn down the place by catching her wig on every candle in a five-foot vicinity, then Rosehill was almost certainly somewhere to be found. Right?

Searching, with less subtlety than I ought, from my resting place with my back against the glass-smooth bar top proved to be a fruitless effort. Although I was the tallest of my brothers, my height was no match against the frippery the ladies had donned tonight. And Rosehill wasn't overly tall, perhaps Michael's height. The dreary swirls of brown in every direction overwhelmed his crisp blacks and whites, if they were present at all.

Or, it was always possible, he'd abandoned his classic style in homage to the theme. Wouldn't that be a disappointment? Devastating, even.

"'Ere, sir." Potter, one of the dunners Michael employed, slid a refill of my scotch across the bar, prompting me to glance at the one in my hand. I wasn't entirely certain when it had been emptied, but I grabbed the replacement.

Attention recaptured by the gaming floor, I took a distracted sip. And cringed. Gin. *Christ I was distracted.* And Potter must have me confused with someone else. Again.

I took a heartier swallow, hoping it would improve with exposure. It didn't.

"Whiskey, please." A short head of dark, overgrown, messy curls turned to me after Potter acknowledged the request.

"Have you seen my sister?" Formerly Mr. Kit Summers, now a very reluctant Lord Leighton peered worriedly into the crowd as he leaned back against the bar beside me.

"In a closet with my brother most likely."

"Well, that is a revolting thought. If she asks, you have not seen me."

I raised a curious brow.

"She's in a matchmaking mood lately. You ought to avoid her too."

"Noted," I said as I tipped my glass in his direction. Once again, I regretted the sip.

Potter returned with an amber glass this time, though I rather suspected it was scotch and not whiskey. Kit nodded at me before wandering off. I lost sight of him after that, but my search continued.

Lustful men gambled obscene sums. Ladies fluttered fans at gentlemen. Kate appeared and captured her brother at some point and was determinedly dragging him about the room to every available debutant. Her Grace's wig was caught in the banister, and she required a rescue. And through it all, there was not a single sighting of Rosehill.

A pointed cough and a flutter of delicately embroidered silk at my side indicated the arrival of Juliet, Michael's wife and tonight's hostess.

"Two glasses of Michael's scotch and just a water for me, please, Mr. Potter." She turned so her back was pressed against the wood beside me. "I do believe this bar is capable of remaining upright. Even without your assistance."

"How confident are you? Your husband did put Potter back there," I mumbled as I tipped my head back toward the dunner fumbling with the good scotch and sloshing it over the side of the glass.

"But he wasn't responsible for the construction. I don't think," she added warily.

"I'm sure the building would have collapsed by now if he were."

"True," she said as she watched a new dance begin. "And really, Tom, you couldn't even bother to don a mask?"

I shrugged, offering her a sheepish smile—earning an indulgent eye roll.

Out of the corner of my eye, I caught Potter handing off

the drinks that were surely intended for Jules and Michael, to another masked gentleman. He spun around and startled when he caught sight of her. Then the man stared, uncomprehendingly, before turning back to pour another glass.

Jules, still surveying the crush, hadn't noticed the foible. Instead, she added, "It's quite crowded in here. In fact, I just sent an old friend of mine who needed a few minutes' reprieve up to Michael's office. I promised to bring him one of those drinks. If you think the bar could spare you, would you mind delivering it to him?"

I glanced down at her upturned face. Something whimsical flickered in her expression that I couldn't quite name.

Potter arrived, appropriate number of amber drinks in hand, and set them behind us before scurrying off without a word. I turned to see him trying to pour the cheap swill Michael kept for those who couldn't afford the good bottle into said good bottle. He spilled more than he managed to get in, but it was certainly enough to alter the taste. Abandoning my post would be for the best. I'd need probable deniability when Michael came complaining about the switch.

"I can do that," I agreed. "Why does my wastrel brother have you fetching drinks anyway?"

"He doesn't know. I just thought he might like another." She slid the water and one of the scotches toward the edge of the bar before pausing and turning back to me. She reached for the beaded reticule hanging from her wrist. Delicate fingers worked the knot before pulling out a domino and offering it to me. "Here, it matches your eyes."

I smiled at my apparent predictability and took the half mask from her, studying the brownish fabric. My eyes were greenish. I knew that. Or I'd been told that. And it *was* almost identical to the muted shade I saw in the mirror.

"Here, bend down," she ordered. She grabbed the mask and stood on tiptoes to reach around my head. Once I understood her meaning, I dipped lower, chuckling a little at the impropriety of it—the action so unlike the prim and proper Juliet I'd first met.

"There, very handsome," she said, smoothing the fabric over my cheek.

"Thank you."

"Now, off you go. And good luck."

I didn't have time to question her before she grabbed two of the drinks and scurried off to wherever Michael was taking the *ton* for all they were worth.

I snatched the last glass, abandoning the dregs of gin on the bar, and skirted along the octagonal wall.

Luckily, I reached the open staircase that curved along the plaster without crashing into anyone and took the steps two at a time. At last, I reached the balcony that ran around the whole second floor. The first heavy oaken door was Michael's. Often unused now that he had turned over the day-to-day running to his second, Augie. The office was more symbolic than functional these days. I knocked perfunctorily before opening the door and slipping inside without waiting for a response.

My heart stopped at the sight that greeted me.

There, in perfectly clear black and white, was Alexander Hasket, Duke of Rosehill.

Five

WAYLAND'S, LONDON - JUNE 5, 1816

XANDER

My hiding place was quite nice—I wasn't too proud to admit it, but I was hiding.

Mother and Dav were in a competition, each determined to see who could expose themselves to the most ridicule in a single evening. Mother was winning, but only by the smallest of margins.

I *should* be chaperoning Davina—well, Mother ought to have been chaperoning Davina but she required a chaperone of her own. And I was just... exhausted. I felt absolutely every one of my thirty years and then some.

Annoyance hung around my shoulders like a particularly inconvenient cloak. Neither of them *meant* to add to my difficulties—at least not seriously. It was simply that they failed to think of me at all. I loved them both with all of my heart, and Celine, too, but I was attending a masquerade ball hosted by a woman I once intended to wed. And none of them had paused for a moment.

Juliet was proper and amiable as always, and kind—she

was unfailingly kind—even when forcing my hand. But with continued whispers of my long-broken engagement and lingering stares from Beaumont's speech yesterday, my already precarious situation felt at a cliff's edge.

So when Juliet offered a safe haven, I snatched the opportunity with the desperation of a man dying of thirst and offered water.

Far from sparse, Wayland's office featured a cozy fireplace surrounded by massive dark green leather chairs, with a drink cart against the wall between the door and the hearth. The opposite end featured an oversized mahogany desk. It was obvious he no longer made frequent use of the room. Matching empty shelves that surely once held ledgers lined one wall, and the desk was entirely bereft of paperwork.

At Juliet's urging, I helped myself to the drink tray and poured a finger of the fine scotch. But before I could settle into one of the chairs to enjoy the relief of solitude and watch the dying embers until guilt at abandoning my family to humiliation and ruin overtook me, a sharp knock sounded.

I spun to face the door. The itchy sensation of trespassing lingered low on my spine even though I had been invited.

When the ornately carved wood swung open without allowing time for a response, breath abandoned my body in a rush leaving me lightheaded and fluttery.

The man was... lovely. There was no other word for it. Tall with a long, lean frame that was perfectly muscled. In the firelight, his hair shone a dark auburn. It was styled, but a few pieces escaped from the pomade to brush his forehead. A sharp, ruddy complected jaw with the barest hint of growth was visible below his domino. An impossibly soft and full lower lip was topped by a thinner but still enticing upper lip. But his eyes... They were a shade even I could not name. Not green, not blue, but so perfectly matched—enhanced—by his mask. The effect was breathtaking.

And he was within grabbing distance. I could catch his arm, pull him to me, and drag his lips to mine. I hadn't had such a visceral reaction to a man since I was a green boy. When his throat bobbed, it took everything inside me to hold back a groan.

"Your Grace," he said in a musical, honeyed tenor. So distracted was I, by thoughts of licking that throat, that it was a full beat before I made the connection.

He knew me.

That wasn't surprising. Most of the *ton* knew of me. But I didn't know him, and that was a travesty I could not abide.

"I'm afraid you have me at a loss, Lord…" My voice was higher pitched than I'd like, shrill.

The edge of his lip quirked up, and his gaze left mine, finding the drink in his hand. He raised the glass and took a sip, and I caught my first sight of his hands. Long, elegant fingers ending in blunt tips with well-manicured nails caressed the glass. The back of that hand was wiry—but strong. Christ, what could a man do with hands like that?

The glass slipped away, leaving a droplet behind on his burnished copper lip. He was trying to kill me—it was the only explanation.

"Mister," he replied.

"Mister?" I repeated dimly.

A soft chuckle left him as he stepped back against the door, leaning against it just to fluster me further. "I do not know if I should be insulted that you find me so forgettable, or pleased that you've managed to forget what an arse I made of myself."

"I beg your pardon." The words escaped as one in a disgruntled rush.

"We've met."

"Surely not. I would remember."

"Apparently not," he retorted before imbibing another sip.

His impossible eyes were bright, amused when they met mine over the glass.

Usually, I loathed that, when people poked bemused fun at my generally flustered nature. But on him... it didn't read as him laughing at me but more as though he found the situation diverting.

More concerning though, I'd met this man, this perfect specimen, and forgotten entirely. *How? And why? And how?* It should not have been possible.

"Remind me?"

He tipped back the last of his drink before inhaling through his teeth. "I don't think I will. How often in life are you gifted with a second first impression?" There was something in his tone—a playful tease?

"I assure you, you make an exceptional second impression. Certainly enough to overshadow any forgotten first." The statement was bolder than I usually would have allowed but still held a hint of plausible deniability.

With a thoughtful hum he pressed off the door and strode confidently to the drink cart where he helped himself to a rather fine scotch with ease.

"How are we to converse if I don't know your name?" I added.

"We seem to be doing well enough at present." He stepped over to one of the chairs and turned it to face the other before the fire. Wordlessly, he sat, legs stretched out in front of him. Those legs should have been too long to settle casually, but he managed it gracefully, with one straightened before him, and the other crossed over at the ankle. "Make yourself comfortable," he added, gesturing toward the other chair with one elegant hand.

Eagerly, I clambered to sit before realizing I was angled toward the fire and not this man. With an awkward, rocking shuffle and a harsh scraping sound, I turned the chair to face him. It was entirely the opposite of his confident maneuver and I felt a flush curling up my neck.

"I really must insist on a name."

His head cocked to the side with a secret smile. "You are not used to being denied, are you?"

I considered that for a moment. It was true, most material things that I wanted, I received. Usually in triplicate. But the real things, the important things, the most essential thing... That I could never, would never have. But *that* hadn't been what he meant.

"Not really, no. Which is why you must tell me."

"Tom," he said simply.

I felt every bit of the intimacy when I asked, "Mr. Tom..."

"Just Tom. It *is* a masquerade. I won't be the one to ruin the mystery."

"I can hardly call you Tom while you address me by my title."

"I'll call you whatever you'd like," he said, a pleased lilt in his voice. He couldn't possibly mean... Surely, this was just an amusing conversation for him, not anything more.

I'd had a dalliance or two on the continent before my brother passed, visited a molly house once or twice, but I hadn't been brave enough to try anything in town. In nearly a decade, I hadn't had so much as a flirtation.

And never with someone who looked like *that*.

"Xander," I said, opting for a casual tone, steering us toward slightly safer waters.

"*Xander*," he repeated. And, oh was I wrong... These waters were too deep to stand, the current too sharp to tread. No one had ever said my name with such dulcet reverence. I wanted it breathed into my neck between kisses.

"Perhaps not," I choked, desperate for distance.

"Too intimate?"

"Yes."

"Very well, *Your Grace*." Somehow that might have been worse. A bit of lusty gravel layered his tone now.

"Xander it is," I half shrieked.

The effort earned me another chuckle. "If you insist. Lady Juliet sent me to bring you a drink. It seems she quite forgot about the presence of the drink cart."

I was so distracted by the grin he'd finished the speech on that it took a moment to grasp the implication. Juliet. But she had instructed me to make full use of the cart. Which meant...

She had been Lady Juliet Dalton still when I told her my secret. She was, perhaps, the only person alive who knew for certain. My mother and sister suspected. Cee too. But I'd told Juliet in a fit of desperation when I could not offer her the release from our engagement that she'd begged for. She'd been unexpectedly kind when she learned the truth, at least before she forced my hand and left me no choice but to end it.

And she had sent this man up to the office in what I was beginning to suspect was an ill-considered matchmaking contrivance...

"Perhaps she thought I could use a friendly face," I supplied, flailing for any other explanation than the one I was staring down.

"Something like that."

"I should return downstairs. If you know who I am, then you know my mother and sister are surely wreaking havoc."

"Ju—Lady Juliet will see to your mother. And I passed Lady Davina on my way up. Lady Grayson was trying to arrange a match between your sister and her brother."

"Well then I certainly need to return."

I couldn't force my legs to obey my commands, to stand. Not when he was so close, and his eyes had tiny flecks of amber in the center.

"There are worse suitors. He won't do anything untoward," he said.

"It's not him I'm worried about."

His head tipped back into a laugh, a giggle really. It was so unexpected, so endearing a sound, that I couldn't help but join him.

"I had a similar thought when I saw them. But if he's anything like his sister, he's more formidable than he looks."

It was all the excuse I needed to do precisely as I wished, which was to sit and bask in this man's presence.

"So you know Lady Juliet well enough for her to entrust you with errands. And you speak with familiarity about Lady Grayson and her brother."

"This again? Come now, Xander. It's a masquerade. Do not spoil the fun."

I'd heard that my entire life. Dav was always complaining that I ruined everything. But after Gabriel was killed and father passed, one of us had to be responsible. And it certainly wouldn't be mother or Dav.

Tonight, though, for one night, with this stranger... It *was* a masquerade. I could be someone else, someone carefree, someone I had only ever dreamed of becoming.

"All right. Tonight, I'm Xander. Just Xander. Only until the unmasking."

"Agreed, just Xander. Until midnight," he said in that same tone that sent chills up my spine. And then he leaned forward and held out his hand between us.

By the time I finally realized what he intended, he'd started to pull back. In a rush, I caught his bare hand in my gloved one and tightened my fingers around his. A gentlemen's agreement.

Six

WAYLAND'S, LONDON - JUNE 5, 1816

TOM

I'D NEVER HATED a scrap of fabric more. Well, it wasn't a scrap. It was certainly a piece of ridiculously expensive silk. Most likely spun entirely by a single worm in Japan that was watered only with the tears of an angel. Then stitched by a dauphine with thread made of actual gold taken from the place settings at Versailles. Such facts didn't make me loathe the black glove any less.

It had taken a moment to decide whether I was more amused, relieved, or devastated that he didn't remember our first meeting. That he hadn't recalled any of our other interactions wasn't a surprise. Those had involved me staring at him desperately from behind a convenient pillar. But the first, our only conversation—humiliating though it might have been—had meant everything to me.

Still, his poor memory did afford me an opportunity now, one I was eager to seize.

Xander didn't remember me at eight and ten.

But I could ensure that tonight was unforgettable.

I had him flustered, that much was clear. He was making those vexed, flailing hand movements with every sentence. The ones he so often made when his sister was being particularly troublesome. I shouldn't find them so charming, but I did. I had a lot of shouldn'ts where Xander was concerned, and not a one of them had prevented me from years of lustful pining.

None of those shouldn'ts waivered even slightly when one gloved hand reached behind his head to tug at the ribbon and pull his own domino free. There was something intimate about the gesture, private. And I was greedy for more.

A glance at the clock above the mantel confirmed what I already knew. We didn't have enough time. Twenty-seven minutes until midnight. And that was only if the clock was right.

"Well, if my time with *Xander* is limited, I suppose I should take advantage."

"Take advantage, how?" he asked with an irritated divot in his forehead. His brow was heavy, some might say overgrown, but I liked the way it contrasted with his pale complexion and the way it drew my gaze to his dark eyes. They were brown, but so dark I was almost certain they were actually brown and not some other color that only looked brown to me.

"I want to know you."

"Again, I ask you, how?" His hands danced in front of him while he spoke. I adored the way he did that, as if every single word from his lips deserved the emphasis of a gesture. Nothing he said was unimportant.

"If I ask you something, will you be honest?"

"Absolutely not."

His affronted tone had a laugh ripping from my chest.

"If I promise to answer the same?" I asked between chuckles.

"Irrelevant. I have much more to lose here," he insisted, annoyed.

"That is true," I agreed, dragging the final word along for a beat. "Very well, you've left me no other choice. I'll have to ask my questions and wonder if you're being honest."

"Very well," he said and tipped back his drink.

I used the opportunity to study the long lines of his neck, peeking out from above his cravat. This man... He was every bit as intoxicating as he had been the first time I met him. As mesmerizing as he had been every time I'd studied him since. This night, these twenty-seven minutes in this office... It was everything I'd wished for from the moment I first set eyes on him.

"Well?"

My tongue darted out between my suddenly dry lips. "If you could wish for one thing, what would it be?"

"That?" he sputtered. "That is what you want to know? I thought you would ask me my favorite color perhaps, or worse, something scandalous."

"I already know your favorite color—not that I particularly care about colors anyway. And I'm saving the scandalous questions for when you've finished more of your drink."

"And what, precisely, is my favorite color?"

"Black."

"Wrong," he retorted, twisting his lips to one side thoughtfully. Everything about him was fascinating. He was so expressive. I wanted to memorize each change to his visage, to learn what they all meant.

"What is it then?"

"No, you had your chance for that answer." He stretched out, legs reaching toward the fire. A sardonic curve slipped across his lips. "I would wish for Gabriel."

My stomach dropped, twisting with jealousy. Desperate to press the knife a little deeper into my heart, I asked, "Who is Gabriel?"

"My brother."

The evil demon that had momentarily taken root inside me loosened its hold, replaced with a swirl of relief. His heart wasn't already claimed—at least not by Gabriel.

He continued, "The title should have been his."

And then the true extent of my doltishness revealed itself. His brother was gone.

Guiltily, I asked, "You were close?"

"Oh, Lord no. And to be quite honest, he would've been a terrible duke. At least before he married Cee. She tamed him a bit." Now I remembered. Lady Rycliffe—the French widow Michael had taken up with.

"Then why would you—"

"Wish for him? I suppose it's not really a wish for his presence as much as a wish for someone else to be me. For Mother and Dav, even Celine, to be someone else's responsibility. To walk away from it all. I'm the second son. I wasn't built for a dukedom."

"I don't think it works like that. Firstborn sons are not born with innate leadership qualities." At least, Hugh hadn't been. Not that he was father's firstborn. But he was the first legitimate son.

"I know, but sometimes it's all I can do to stay here, chaperoning the chaperone, shuffling Mother away from the worst of the gossips, paying Davina's way out of whatever mischief she's found today. Gabriel was a notorious gambler and a degenerate. Years before he died, he won an estate in Scotland off some baron or other. And he gifted it to me, as a present with some flimsy excuse. I've never even laid eyes on it, but some days I wake up and I can almost taste the crisp Scottish air."

He'd gone wistful, far away.

"Is the air in Scotland particularly crisp?" I asked, drawing him back to me.

"I've no idea. That's hardly the point."

"No, I know. I just... I understand what you mean. My family is less prone to scandal—actually, no. That's a lie. They are merely less frequent with it. But my elder brothers, oil and water. I've spent my entire life—until recently—acting as an amicable buffer. And my mother... Well, at least yours means well."

"Do you ever want to run away?" he asked, leaning forward in his seat and propping the empty glass on his knee. One corner of his mouth was pulled up curiously.

"I hadn't considered it before. I'm lucky, I suppose. I have bachelor lodgings. But my brothers both found wives."

"And you don't like their wives?" he asked.

"I adore their wives. But they're sickeningly happy. And I want that. I want to fall in love. I want to be able to reach out and brush a lock of hair off the forehead of the ma—person I love. And my brothers, they know they're lucky, that they don't deserve their wives. But they don't realize what a privilege it is... A gift, to wake up every morning next to the person you love. And not everyone receives such a gift."

"And you don't think you'll have that?" His question was barely a breath.

"I cannot."

"You're young—how young are you?" Now he wore a scandalized tilt to his brow.

I leaned back, chuckling a little. "Younger than you."

"Rude," he said with a pinched mouth but with no force behind it. "And I was trying to be reassuring."

"That is not the reason."

"What is?"

I considered for a moment. I didn't *know*. Not truly. But I *felt* it. Something about Xander called to me—to the place deep inside my chest, the one that ached when I lied to my family and the *ton*. The nagging tangle in my chest that tightened painfully every time I half-heartedly agreed when Hugh made a jest about the evenings I spent at the theater. That part of me sensed a kindred spirit in Xander.

My gaze caught his as I finally settled on, "You know."

His eyes widened and he practically fell back in his seat. "I assure you, I do not."

A knot began to form in my throat, twisting, tightening. "Right then. I suppose it's just me." My voice was a pathetic croak.

Xander's lips parted, almost as if he wanted to take it back. But that was likely wishful thinking, desperation brought on by a dream rapidly fading to nothingness.

Floundering for a way out, my gaze fell on the black mask resting on his knee. "What *is* your favorite color then?" I tossed out. I wouldn't be able to appreciate it, but it wasn't likely to add to my heartache.

He glanced away, to the mantel clock. My gaze followed. Thirteen minutes.

"Prussian blue."

"That is... oddly specific."

"It's a deep shade of blue with hints of green."

"I wouldn't know."

"You're wearing it," he explained.

My eyes dropped down, searching for something I wouldn't be able to see.

"Your mask," he interrupted my futile search.

My hand found my cheek and made to pull the domino away before I remembered myself. I had a secret to maintain—more necessary than ever with his rejection—and I wouldn't be able to see his world anyway.

"You're really not going to take it off?"

"I'm not that easily fooled. And it wouldn't matter anyway," I retorted with a teasing grin.

"Why is that?"

"I don't... I can't see colors—not the way everyone else

does anyway. The best I can tell, they look to me the way browns look to you."

"Really? All colors?"

"No. Reds and greens are the worst. I cannot tell them apart at all. But a blue with hints of green—I probably wouldn't see it the way you do."

"That is... quite sad, really," he murmured.

"It's not. Not truly. I do not know any different. Though I do find your clothing a refreshing change—even your waistcoats. I always know what color they are."

He dragged a hand over the aforementioned waistcoat, drawing my attention to the angle of his waist. "I'm glad to be of assistance. Most find them dull. Or intimidating."

"I like the way you dress. Can you... Your eyes, they're brown, right?" It was impertinent and inappropriate and I couldn't live another second without confirmation. To know that I saw him as he truly was.

"They are. A rather dull shade, I'm afraid."

My breath escaped in a relieved sigh. "No, not dull. Everything about you—" I caught myself just in time.

"Everything about me, what?"

"I apologize. That was... too far." A sideline glance showed the truth of it. Two minutes until midnight. I'd wasted my twenty-seven minutes.

"I lied," he said—blurted.

"What? Your eyes aren't brown?"

"No, they are. I just—I knew what you meant. Before. I understand." His fingers twisted, one hand tugging at the seam of the other glove.

Elation warred with frustration. The minutes were gone. Only seconds left. But I hadn't been wrong. Far from wrong; I'd been right. "Why now?"

"I-I don't know. It's a terrible idea to reveal it. But I just... needed you to know."

"Thank you. For telling me."

"You're not going to tell anyone else?"

"Never," I vowed.

"Ten... nine..." The world outside the door broke in. Shattering our last seconds.

Without a word I grabbed the domino from its perch on his knee. He stood to meet me. He was shorter than me, half a foot perhaps. I pressed the mask to his cheek and one of his fingers came up to hold it in place. The fastening ribbons were fine and black. I traced them until my fingers met behind his head. Inky, silken strands brushed my skin as I retied the knot.

Task complete, I allowed myself one last indulgence. I dipped down and pressed a kiss to the place on his cheek where mask met skin.

"Good night, Your Grace. It has been a pleasure."

"I... You're really not going to tell me who you are?"

"The real world is calling, Your Grace," I said before grabbing my glass and striding over to the drink tray.

He sighed before replying. "Good night then."

The door creaked angrily when he opened it. The raucous cheers from the crush spilled into our sanctuary. When the latch clicked back into place, the roar dulled. And our sanctuary was mine alone.

Seven

RYCLIFFE PLACE, LONDON - JUNE 6, 1816

XANDER

CELINE HAD LOST her damned mind. It was the only explanation.

I had gone to sleep anticipating a bit of a lie in, only to be ripped from dreams of entrancing blue-green eyes and sensual, graveled whispers at half eight by Godfrey with news that my sister-in-law had arrived before dawn. I found Celine rummaging like a peculiar rodent, unchecked, through my ledgers.

Now, she sat across from me holding a file of secondary ledgers that my brother had apparently used to track his illegal activities before his death. His involvement in enough illegal dealings to require a second set of books wasn't shocking, but that she had the foresight to steal them was. Furthermore, Celine was absolutely insistent that William Hart had murdered Gabriel. *William Hart.* Bookish, bespectacled solicitor and vicious, bloodthirsty killer. The claim was incongruous at best.

Gabriel's death had changed Celine down to her very

marrow. That kind of grief, nursed with that kind of care, over that many years—it could do little else. But I had thought she'd retained at least a small fraction of her sanity. She was *supposed* to be the easy, biddable, respectable lady in the Hasket family.

Something had happened between her and Will last night at the masquerade, and that something had shaken the foundations of Celine's carefully managed world. Good for Will.

Except that her evidence, flimsy and circumstantial though it may be, was also the tiniest bit compelling. The beloved son of my father's steward, Will had always had a seat at the family table at Father's insistence. I remembered the night he first saw Adriane LaMorte, whose family let the house next door. His bright eyes had been awash in instant adoration. With perfect clarity, I could recall the way she toyed with his affections before turning her eerie gaze to Gabriel with the obvious purpose of tormenting Will. I could absolutely believe that Gabe had compromised Adriane—I was almost certain he had.

Celine's tale wasn't that far-fetched—a man who fancied himself in love would seek vengeance for the lady's ruined life.

"Wouldn't you?" Celine insisted. "If someone hurt someone you loved? Not just hurt but destroyed. Imagine if it were Davina."

She needn't have twisted the knife; she knew without a doubt that I would do anything for Dav. I had, on more than one occasion, endured great expense and humiliation in an effort to spare her the same.

"All right, say I believe the motive. You have no evidence."

She handed me a simple scrap of parchment, yellowed at the edges with smeared ink, but the words were still legible.

Hyde Park, 6:30
W

I should have been grateful that she didn't want to immediately hand Will over to the authorities with her "evidence." But her plan to investigate the man was utterly absurd, and, in the very unlikely event that she was right, incredibly dangerous.

With a sigh, I reluctantly agreed to assist her, if only to prevent bloodshed. Christ, I hoped this wouldn't end in Will and Mr. Summers refusing to help me with Davina's nonsense in the future. It really was damned hard to find a competent and discrete solicitor able to keep my sister from ruin.

∼

THERE WAS a little alley beside the offices of Hart and Summers, Solicitors. Three windows lined the wall on the first floor.

"Which one is his?" Celine demanded. I tried to picture the interior of the office. Will and Mr. Summers each had their own room at the back with lines of clerks up front. There was a room on one side that I'd never been in. Typically, I spent more time in Mr. Summers's office, and I couldn't recall a window there at all.

I pointed to the farthest window. "That one, I believe."

She stepped across the gutter stinking of something I didn't wish to consider. She then snatched an empty milk crate from nearby and upended it beneath the window I had indicated. When she rose to stand on it, I could only stare.

To think, I'd once thought her my most sensible relation.

"Remember, enunciate," she ordered in a harsh whisper.

"I cannot believe I am doing this..." I muttered, mostly to myself, as I slipped out of the alley to approach the offices.

There was a little bell atop the door. I was so familiar with its distinctive clang that my eye twitched instinctively at the sound. The majority of my visits were to enlist one of the men in rescuing Dav from some scandal or other—never pleasant.

Mr. Summers's door was closed, but Will's was wide open. He was visible from the entry, behind the row of clerks. He gestured me into his office with a greeting and rose to close the door behind us.

My heart fluttered in distress. If Celine couldn't hear—that would be the end of it. She would insist on "investigating" on her own if she couldn't overhear our conversation and she'd get herself or someone else killed. "Morning, Will. Oh, there's no need to close the door," I blurted. "It's a bit warm today. I could use the airflow. In fact, would you mind opening that window?" I gestured toward the one beside him.

His bright eyes narrowed suspiciously, but he performed the task without comment.

Every time I saw him, I was reminded again how striking he was. In fact, his eyes and impossibly sharp cheeks had featured in a number of youthful fantasies. It would be an absolute travesty if Celine were right. Handsome men ought not to be murderers.

As he turned back to the desk, something behind me caught Will's attention. Cee wouldn't... would she? I spun only to be faced with the sight of a gentleman peering around the corner from Mr. Summers's office.

It took a moment to place him, the youngest Grayson brother. Tim? His hand was raised in an awkward wave. "Sorry, Will. Didn't realize you had a client—Oh, Your Grace!" He broke off, wide-eyed, his cheeks flushing. The hand, frozen in a wave, remembered itself and crept behind his head to rub at the back of his neck as he straightened in the doorway. There was something expectant, wary perhaps, in his expression. "Repurchasing your sister from the pirates?" he asked.

Terror shot through my spine. "What? She's been

consorting with pirates again? Which ones?" I demanded, my tone too shrill.

He chuckled as he stepped back and rested his backside against the nearest clerk's desk. The man offered him a disgruntled glare that—Tim? Tom?—failed to notice. "That was a joke. She's been kidnapped before?"

"Why would you jest about something like that?" I snapped, still on edge as my pounding heart refused to slow. He truly was a gangly thing, wrapped in an absolutely atrocious waistcoat—had he purchased it in the dark? Citrine, juniper, and apricot swirled through the fabric in abstract lines. Hideous.

"Well, I thought it was too absurd to have happened before. What are you doing then?"

Panic surged back through me. Celine and I hadn't considered that part of the "plan" before sending me into a murderer's office. My mouth answered before my head had a chance to agree. "Oh, I was planning to do a bit of traveling and I wanted Will's advice first."

Perhaps I should consider speaking first and thinking later more often; it was as good an excuse as any I would have thought out.

"Where are you going?" Mr. Grayson asked. He leaned forward with interest, bracing his palms behind him against the edge of the desk. His legs were absurdly long; they half spilled into the doorway—though, his thighs, those were quite muscular, even underneath the revolting reddish umber of his trousers.

"I don't know. Yorkshire? Scotland? I'm still considering my options. That's why I'm here." Why was he so interested? I'd seen the man several times in society, but I wasn't entirely certain I'd ever actually spoken to him.

"Right, apologies. I'll leave you to your considerations," he said and stood, his tone just pitiful enough to leave me with that sinking, gnawing, guilty sensation in my stomach. "Kit, see you tonight," he directed toward Mr. Summers. The bell clinked again as he strode out the door and my eye gave another twitch.

Even though his presence had been thoroughly disconcerting, his absence was more so. I was left even more tetchy and on edge.

Mr. Summers peered his head in to let Will know he would be leaving early. "Tom thinks Jules is expecting, and Kate wants the whole family there for the announcement."

For several seconds, I struggled to process that information.

When Mr. Summers disappeared back into his office, Will returned our conversation to my flimsy excuse for a visit.

I was still peevish over Mr. Grayson's nosy questions, flustered over Cee's plot, and preoccupied by the mysterious man from the night before. I shouldn't have been surprised when my mouth answered for me again.

"I've been meaning to travel for some time. And I expect I may settle more permanently at one of the estates." As the words formed, they became truth. They flowed freely, as they had with that gentleman last night. I wanted it, desperately. To be anywhere but here, somewhere free. *Scotland.*

A sharp cough came from the alley. Right, Gabe's murder. "I would need to set up provisions for Mother and Davina. Gabe traveled a great deal. Did he have anything in place?"

Will's gaze narrowed again with suspicion. "Not that I'm aware of," he drawled. "But I was not his solicitor, your father was still alive, and your sister still a child. I imagine the arrangements were somewhat less complicated."

Damn... My mouth dropped open, and I waited, breath baited, for it to save me again. Seconds passed before I realized no salvation would come. Floundering, I replied, "It's been so long, I nearly forgot. I'm so forgetful. You were friends, right?

You and Gabriel." It was stilted, to be sure, but I managed to keep the focus on my brother.

A glance to the side revealed a hint of blonde hair in the window. *Damn it all, Celine!*

"*Friends* is a strong term... Why are you asking me about your brother?" Something about my gaze must have drawn his own, because he trailed off with a puzzled expression directed at the window.

"Oh, you know, just reminiscing," I blurted.

He shook his head, turning his attention back to me. "You mentioned Yorkshire and Scotland? If you're looking to make improvements, I would recommend the Scotland property. It could use some work and I think it would be well worth your efforts. If it were in better repair, should you choose to take a wife, you could summer there. Or you could sell it at great profit."

Outside the window, there was a commotion, a man shouting, "Bonjour, Madame," clear as a bell.

A sharp crack rang out, then the distinctive *thunk* of someone bracing themselves against a wall to prevent a fall. A feminine lilt in the falsest Scottish accent ever uttered replied, insisting she was not who the person claimed her to be. Masculine protests followed, slipping farther away.

Will rose to peer out the window, and I called out to him —dragging his attention back to me.

I rose and backed out of the room slowly. He stared, expectant, as I made my escape. "Well, that was strange. You've given me a great deal to think on. I should be going now." And once again, my lips spoke from my heart instead of my head. "Do you think you can draw up some paperwork to keep Mother and Davina from bankrupting us if I travel for an extended time?"

"I can... You're really not going to address that?" he asked, nodding toward the window.

"I have no idea what that was about. Some poor Scotswoman accosted on the street."

"Right... I'll draw up some paperwork. Perhaps daily and weekly spending limits with the most likely culprits, modiste and the like. You go see to your poor Scotswoman."

"Thank you!"

"Yes. And, Your Grace?"

"Yes?"

"Next time, come alone?" His voice tipped up at the end, as though it were a question, but it was so obviously a statement, an order, that I abandoned my pathetic guise.

"All right," I said and slipped out the door. The damned bell offered one last grating ding as I backed onto the street.

As soon as I was out of view of the glass door, Celine grabbed my arm and yanked me a few feet away. "Well? What did he seem like? Did you notice anything circumspect about him?"

"Celine?"

"Yes?"

"Never again," I stated, then turned on my heels and left her to trail after me, protesting all the way back to Rycliffe House.

Eight

40 BLOOMSBURY STREET, LONDON - JUNE 6, 1816

TOM

HE HADN'T RECOGNIZED ME. Again. My lips still tingled from kissing his cheek and I was nothing to him.

It was, perhaps, even worse than our first meeting. Our first meeting had been brief; Rosehill was distracted. I hadn't spent the entire night before floating on a delicate cloud of joy, hope, and wonder—with a little lust for good measure.

My chest ached as I strode the five or so minutes to my apartments at a clip. The air was too muggy, remnants of last night's rain lingering in city soot.

There had been a split second when I saw him, recognized his frame from behind, when my heart had stopped in giddy delight. And then he sent it all crashing down.

What was it about me that was so forgettable?

I was generally good at this sort of thing—speaking to people, putting them at ease. Hell, I'd spent my entire life sheltering one brother from the verbal impact of the other.

But something about Xander—Rosehill—turned me into

a bumbling fool. *Kidnapped by pirates*? Truly? Could I have said anything more absurd?

And he planned to travel. If he chose Scotland... he would be gone until spring at least. It was preposterous to feel an ache in my chest at the prospect of a man I'd had one—admittedly life-altering—conversation with preparing to travel for a few months.

The familiar black door creaked as I pushed it open. My apartment was small, just a kitchen and dining area, a closet-sized study, a pitiful drawing room and bedroom. In fact, I employed only a part-time maid whom I shared with the doctor who lived above me.

I collapsed in a heap on the bed, lamenting almost immediately that I would need to rise if I wished for a drink. Worse still, if I was to be even close to timely for dinner at Grayson House, I needed to leave in an hour—though the thought exhausted me.

The inclination to wallow in my own self-pity was strong. That was a Grayson trait I wasn't overly proud of. Even Michael, who hadn't inherited the name, had a tendency to disappear into depression and drink when the walls crumbled in.

Xander had been so perfect last night—flustered in the best possible way. His dark gaze had flicked up and down my form, leaving me aware of my musculature, of my own skin, in an entirely new way. He had been open, so devastatingly honest that I was breathless for more. I would remember last night for the rest of my life, the same way I would Hugh's wedding.

I rolled to one side, facing the door. An internal war was waging between duty and apathy, and I wasn't certain which would win when a glint of light caught my gaze.

Sitting on the bedside table, a delicate little snuffbox shot the setting sunbeam back into my eyes. Sometime after I moved out of Grayson House and into this place, it had migrated from the drawer below to a place of honor on top. And every night, I fell asleep staring at it like a pathetic milksop.

∼

Mother had feigned a megrim, which was a key ingredient in a pleasant supper. Of course, I had a megrim of my own brewing behind my eyes, which had made it even more difficult to leave the comfort of my bed and return to Grayson House.

More than two years ago, Kate hosted her first family supper with only Mother, Michael, Hugh, and me in attendance. The addition of Juliet and Kit tended to put Mother off, though she had warmed to Kit with the new title. Mother was a fickle creature.

What a difference two years made. Far from the stilted supper where Mother tossed barbs at Kate and spit venom at Michael while I tried to act as shield for them both, now the conversation was animated and jovial—at least when Mother absented herself.

"So truly, none of the ladies caught your eye the other evening?" Kate asked her brother.

"Kate..." he warned in a low growl.

"I'm not allowed to inquire any longer?"

"You were never allowed to inquire."

"Well perhaps if you would tell me what you were looking for in a lady I might be able to narrow my search."

"Any lady you introduce me to now would have scoffed at me a year ago."

"Kate, leave him be. He's young," Hugh said, trying to save his brother-in-law.

"He's older than you were when you married me."

"Yes, and he was too young to marry," Michael added with a laugh. "Not every gentleman can have Hugh's unearned good fortune."

Kate considered Michael for a moment, weighing the implied compliment against the attempted foiling of her schemes.

I took a sip of the wine to help choke down a bite of the goose. The new cook had nothing on the recently retired Mrs. Hudson, and that was a loss for the entire family.

"How is little Henry faring? Still teething?" Juliet asked brightly. My chuckle was difficult to trap, but I managed it. I was good at deflecting uncomfortable conversations, but Juliet was a *savant*. Nothing would distract Kate like her son.

"Yes, I'm afraid. He's been miserable, the poor dear."

Hugh cut in, adding, "He said his first word yesterday. *Papa*."

"Don't be ridiculous," Kate retorted. "He said *pa* twice."

"Precisely. Papa," Hugh explained proudly.

"So he said a nonsense syllable twice in a row?" Michael's smirk was pleased. His wife caught the edge of her lip between her teeth, biting back her own an amused grin.

"It was *papa*."

"I think his first word was *Kit*," the man himself explained. "He said *ki* last week. That's clearly a reference to his favorite uncle."

"Take that back," I replied with no severity. In truth, I could not be more pleased that Henry would have his pick of favorite uncles, all worthy of the title. Though, of course, none so worthy as me.

"Yes, you're all wonderful uncles," Jules added. "But I think the important part is that there is no question of who is the favorite auntie." Once again putting an end to what was sure to have been a half-hearted but not entirely unserious argument.

I tipped my glass of wine toward her before taking a sip. She shifted in her seat, a prim, silent acknowledgment of my compliment.

"At least until one of those two finds it within himself to bring home a wife," Kate added.

"You think anyone could replace me as Henry's favorite auntie?" Juliet asked in mock offense. "Nay, that would be impossible."

"Of course not. Besides, he'll probably be a man grown before either one of them deigns to offer for a woman."

Juliet's bright sapphire eyes met mine with something like discomfiture. Not for the first time since the masquerade, I wondered how much she knew. "I, for one, would not adore either of them a jot less for it." Her gaze flicked to Kate. "You should not try to rush these things."

"I'm not."

"I saw you at the masquerade. You were very much doing precisely that."

"I wasn't! I could not even find Tom," Kate complained.

If Juliet were so inclined, she could have given Michael a run at the card table. A sharper than usual blink was her only tell. "It was a successful evening, do you not think? Even if it didn't end with any additional sisters-in-law," she said.

"It certainly was," Hugh added. "Do you think you will repeat it? Perhaps next year?"

"I wouldn't be opposed to it. Though we may not be in a position to..." Michael said, trailing off with a significant glance at his wife as he caught her hand in his.

"We do have some news to share," Juliet added quietly. "I am with child."

Cheers of delight erupted around the table. The couple's previous losses had been a poorly concealed secret, and there wasn't a person present who could contain any pleasure for the couple.

I was ecstatic for them, truly. But there was also the sharp twinge in my chest when I caught the way they looked at each other—the way my cool, perpetually unaffected brother stared at his wife with naked adoration always left a confused swirl in my chest. A little sliver of envy crept in. A longing for a great love of my own that tarnished my joy just at the edges. I hated that part of myself.

My hand itched for a waist to settle upon affectionately, possessively. My lips longed for a private, special smile to share. My forehead craved a temple to rest upon, a place to lend strength.

And the man I wanted every single one of those things with didn't even recognize me. That was the painful knot I had to swallow as I wished two of my favorite people in the world well deserved joy.

Nine

RYCLIFFE PLACE, LONDON - JUNE 13, 1816

XANDER

THE LIGHT WAS FADING TOO SOON, and I still wasn't precisely sure what was wrong with my landscape. I preferred the morning light of the room I chose for my studio, but the afternoon was close on morning's heels.

The painting wasn't quite right. The early dawn sky was too bold, and the grass wasn't muted enough.

For days, the watercolors had refused to do my bidding, each work a greater disappointment than the last.

I wasn't an artist, not by any means, though I did fancy myself a connoisseur. That meant I had more than enough understanding to know precisely how far I was from being an artist—a true artist. But I was rich and idle. And painting was something to pass the time. Something to avoid the unpleasant thoughts of recent days.

My shoulders met the wall as I stepped back to take in my work. The fired orange and honeyed reds swirling in the sky and kissing the edges of the clouds were more vibrant than I'd intended. It was too much, cloying. It also wasn't a problem I'd ever had before.

I enjoyed watercolors for their gauzy, soft qualities. There was a dreamy note in them—the world as though beneath bedsheets, in that hazy place between waking and sleep.

But ever since the masquerade—since that night, everything felt wrong. My skin stretched too tight on my frame. The stitching on my shirt chaffed my arms. Food was under seasoned and uninteresting.

And my nights, oh my nights. Long, lithe fingers caressed my skin as husky whispers promised to shoulder my responsibilities if I only let go. Prussian eyes traced my form, looking not to judge but because doing so brought him pleasure. Increasingly filthy words were whispered by soft lips against my flesh. It was maddening and wonderful at the same time.

Consumed within a lovesick melancholy for a man I didn't even know. Utterly absurd.

A knock sounded, interrupting me as I was wiping my hands on a rag—Godfrey, my valet.

"Your Grace?" A tentative, pitchy quality laced his tone. Which only meant one thing.

"What has she done now?"

"Your mother sent a note that your sister is missing. She requests your presence at Hasket House."

A sigh broke from my chest. "Is that all she said?"

"Well, Her Grace used more words than that. And a scented parchment."

My fingers found the bridge of my nose where an ache was already forming. I pinched away the more pleasant thoughts of my nighttime paramour.

"It all smells like that."

"Of course, Your Grace."

"Thank you, Godfrey. I should dress."

"Yes, Your Grace."

A change of clothing followed by a brief stop in my study to locate my purse, and I was off.

When I arrived at Hasket House, Mother had taken to her chambers in a fit of histrionics, as was her usual way.

I found her in her dressing room, curled on the floor beside her shoes with a very distraught—and new—lady's maid trying to coax her to a nearby settee.

The girl fled eagerly at my dismissal.

"Mother?"

"Oh, Alexander! It is too wretched to conceive. Your dear sister has relinquished, forsaken, discarded all the comforts of this dazzling abode. She is lost to us, to all amiable society henceforth. How should I be expected to endure such a grievous loss? Another precious babe, taken from me prematurely!"

My head gave a disgruntled throb behind my left eye. Mother was moments from a full episode. They'd become more frequent after Gabriel's death, and more common still after father passed. But they were no less dramatic for their frequency.

If I could not produce my sister, and soon, Mother would be bedridden for weeks with ailments ranging from megrims, fatigue, and nervous flutterings to vertigo and aching in her joints.

I helped her to the chaise, one arm around her shoulder to guide her. She threw herself on it, face first, and collapsed with a dramatic wail.

"How do you know she is gone, Mother?"

"My darling Davina left a missive, but she neglected to convey the rest of her stratagem." She cried into the fabric, so shrill and loud that I could make out every word.

"She left a note?"

"That is what I said."

I refused to begin yet another argument over semantics with Mother. "Where is the note?"

"I abandoned it on the vargueno when its contents overtook my sensibilities."

Leaving her to sigh pathetically on the chaise, I strode over to find the slip of parchment in Dav's messy scroll. It contained the usual sentiments. *I want to go on an adventure. London is dreadfully dull.* Then I found the details of this specific misdeed. *I've learned of a third-rate naval ship docked at the port. I plan to board and sail to the East Indies. By the time you read this, I will be long away.*

How the devil...

No matter. It was more information than she often left.

I turned back to my mother's feigned sobs. "Mother, I need to retrieve her. Can I have anything brought to you for relief?"

"Yes!" she cried. "Procure my precious babe, my dearest, beloved daughter."

"That is my intention. Is there anything else? A cup of tea?"

"No, not a thing. I shall not take nourishment until she is returned."

"I'll be off then," I replied, desperate to escape.

I froze on the entry steps for a moment, considering—I could go to the docks, try to find Dav on my own. Or perhaps it would be more efficient to go straight to Mr. Summers and have him try to lessen the effects of whatever crimes she had committed in pursuit of entertainment.

In the moments I wavered, a boy, no more than twelve and wearing a blue coat, ran past. Oh good lord. He was here for me. He made it another full house before he realized his error and doubled back.

The ship's boy skidded to a stop, panting in front of me with one hand on his side.

"M'lord," he wheezed out. I wasn't about to correct him.

"Are you here about Lady Davina?" I asked, urging him to sit on the steps. A knock on the door produced Mother's butler. "A glass of lemonade, if you please." He nodded his affirmation and slipped back inside.

"M'lord," the boy tried again. "I was supposta find you at Rycliffe Place. But your butler said you'd be here. M'lord, it's your sister," the grubby boy broke off, wheezing. The butler returned with the glass, holding it out with thumb and forefinger as though it were dirty and not its recipient.

The child took it eagerly in both hands, not so much drinking as pouring it down his gullet.

"I take it she was caught?"

"In a lieutenant's coat an everythin'."

The place behind my left eye throbbed. "She is unharmed? Safe and still in England?"

"Yes, m'lord. But the Master at Arms is sayin' he wants her punished. He don' believe her story an says he thinks she might be spyin'. Esponge, he says."

It took a moment for my head to translate his meaning. *Espionage.* My stomach jolted. Surely they couldn't... not a lady.

"Why are you here? If he didn't believe her?"

"Your sister. She said you'd pay the gentleman who assisted in her release." The boy straightened his spine, tugging on the lapels of his coat between wheezes.

I slipped a hand into my pocket and placed three guineas on my outstretched palm. He grasped one coin between both thumbs and forefingers with an expression of pure awe. "They're all for you, lad. And there's another five in it for you if you can keep her from being arrested until I can get there."

His grey eyes widened in a way that would have been comical if I weren't oscillating between letting them arrest my sister to serve as a lesson and joining my mother in a panicked, inconsolable heap on the chaise upstairs.

"O'course, m'lord. Anything you need, I'm your man."

"What's your name, lad?"

"John Taylor, m'lord." There was a sense of pride in the way he announced it.

"Very good, Mr. Taylor. And your ship?"

"The HMS *Grampus*."

"All right. Mr. Taylor, I need to meet with my solicitor. I want to be sure we are prepared for any legal troubles that Lady Davina might be facing. Can you give the Master at Arms this card? Tell him I'll be there to sort this out right away." I pulled my card from the other pocket and handed it to him.

"Yes, m'lord." He nodded eagerly before pulling off his boot and stuffing the coins in the toe. He slipped it back on and rolled his ankle experimentally. There was a soft jingle, but nothing that would be of note.

With both arms, he pushed off the steps to stand and set off at another run, back toward the docks, my card clenched in his fist. Hopefully it would still be legible when it arrived.

I stepped into the waiting carriage and set off toward Hart and Summers, Solicitors.

∼

THE DAMNED BELL was as unnerving as ever.

Will peered out from his back office with a concerned expression. I offered him a wave before gesturing toward Mr. Summers's office. "Davina is making a nuisance of herself again," I said by way of explanation. "As I understand it, her problems are Mr. Summers's to solve."

That caught the man in question's attention and he stood from his desk and rounded the corner.

Will replied, "Of course. If you have a moment afterward, I've done some of that investigating we discussed."

I nodded and turned to Mr. Summers and his questioning gaze. "She was caught trying to board a ship dressed as a lieutenant."

"Right, I'll leave that to Kit... Good luck," Will called out.

Mr. Summers's countenance shifted to something paler, more sickly as he ushered me into his office.

"So Lady Davina has boarded a naval ship?" he asked in a shaky tone as he returned to his seat behind the desk. I hadn't thought her behavior could shock him any longer.

"So it would seem."

"Right, I just... She could be hurt. The obvious dangers of ship life, of course, but also... all the lonely men."

My stomach dropped. I hadn't considered that.

"Surely they wouldn't. They're men in his majesty's service."

Mr. Summers swallowed. "I pray they would not. If the ship has left, there's nothing that can be done but pray and follow her to their next port."

"It hasn't. She managed to convince a ship's boy to locate me. She's being held by the Master at Arms, who isn't convinced of her identity. The boy said something about espionage."

He swallowed thickly. "Right, well, she is a stowaway... There's a fine. And possibly hard labor, I cannot recall. They certainly wouldn't sentence a lady to hard labor anyway. Espionage... It's not my expertise. Shockingly. But I suspect proving her identity will go far in convincing him of her innocence."

"We should go at once."

"No, no. Her reputation—we need to keep this as quiet as we can. A duke's presence will only draw more attention. I'll hurry over there and see what can be done."

"But... You're an earl."

"Barely. And I look like a solicitor."

"You're certain this is the best course?"

"Positive. I'll get her back, Your Grace. I give you my word."

"Very well. Whatever you need to do, anything you need." I handed him the entire contents of my pockets, coins and banknotes alike. "There's a ship's boy, John Taylor. She's being kept on the HMS *Grampus*. I owe him five guineas if he brought my card to the Master at Arms."

Kit raised a brow at the sum but nodded. I'd authorized him to offer whatever was necessary. Of course I would pay the lad what was promised.

"I'll be off," he said, then jumped up and strode toward the door.

"And I'll just be here. Looking like a duke," I muttered, unable to entirely erase the irritation in my tone. The day, once so promising, had been overtaken by waves of panic leaving me tetchy and snappish. My head throbbed in a way that only Davina could cause. And I was rendered entirely superfluous except for the contents of my pocket.

As soon as that thought took hold, it refused to leave. It whittled away until all that was left was a needling question that seemed to have no real answer. *What, precisely, was I doing here?*

My feet carried me to Will's office without my head ever giving the order.

He invited me inside and gesturing toward my usual chair.

"Come in, come in. Everything sorted?" he asked.

I shrugged, still perturbed. "Kit is going down to the docks."

"Better him than me. I've had some time to look at your property holdings."

"Scotland—is the place inhabitable?"

His head tilted questioningly for a moment before righting itself. "Your steward seems to think so. How long are you planning to stay? You may wish to arrange some improvements if you're to be there the rest of the summer."

For a moment, I hesitated. Then I recalled why I was still here, rather than at the docks helping my sister. My sister who was managed perfectly well by others at Wayland's. My sister, who was, at this very moment being rescued by Mr. Summers. Without me.

I forged ahead. "That was one of the things I wanted to review. I would like to settle there. For that to be my primary residence."

"Pardon?" His brow shot to his hairline.

"I would like to move. To Scotland. Permanently," I repeated.

"But, with all due respect, Your Grace—"

"It's Xander, Will. You've known me forever."

"What about your mother? And your sister? And a wife?"

"Will, I think we both know the answer to that last one. And why it's time for me to leave."

His bright eyes met mine with something like sympathy in the set of his brow. He cleared his throat, then asked, "And the first two?"

"That's why I have you. I need to set up provisions for Mother and Davina, and Celine, too. How much control are you able to give Celine? She's the only one with a lick of sense. I'll need everything that isn't entailed to be split between Mother and Dav if anything were to happen to me. However, I do not think they would do well with immediate, unfettered access."

"Well, the Yorkshire property belongs with the dukedom. The Scotland property is yours outright, though it doesn't bring in a great deal. The houses here in town I'll need to look into. The Rycliffe house, at least, should not be entailed with the dukedom. But, Xander, are you certain this is what you wish to do?"

"I have a great many wishes. Unfortunately, wishes cannot change reality. I expect you know that better than most." My throat tightened, the memory of Prussian eyes and long, elegant fingers seeming so far away now.

"Right, well, you're young. You should have many years before the entail becomes a concern for your family."

I bit out a laugh, more a scoff, if I was being honest. Gabriel had years to live as well, and a wife too. "I was never intended to inherit. If I do not wed and have children, the dukedom will go to some second cousin. Is the income from the un-entailed estates sufficient to support Mother and Davina? I do not want to rely on a second cousin's goodwill."

He hesitated, catching his lower lip between his teeth. It was unbearably attractive. "Any other mother and sister I would say yes, more than. Yours..."

After a sigh, I replied, "That is what I feared. Is there any way to take income from the entailed estates and set up accounts for them now that cannot be accessed unless something were to happen to me?"

"Well, the dowries should be untouchable."

"Who, exactly, do you think will be willing to marry Davina?" I asked with a laugh.

His grin was a sheepish acknowledgment. "I'll need to review and determine exactly which properties are entailed to see what will need to be done."

"Very good. Can you look into dowering Celine as well? Obviously we could not guarantee it if the title changes hands. Still, while I'm able, I would like to offer her that option. She has her own funds, but I do not want her limited in her choices. Also, can you determine what authority she could be granted to manage things?"

He glanced away, his gaze flicking out the window to where Cee once hid. How much did he know, anyway?

"The dowry should not be an issue. Authority may be. I also hate to be the person to bring this up, but... Davina? I cannot imagine she will stop her adventures when you are away."

"Mr. Summers will be given carte blanche to use whatever funds necessary to get her out of whatever scrape she has gotten herself into. As he has done today. Though that is one of the things I am hopeful Celine may be able to manage in my absence. And, if my sister is still getting into mischief after my untimely demise, she will have to find her own way out of it."

"Well, you've given me a great deal to consider. To be quite honest, I thought the trip was a ploy to get into the office, so I haven't been as thorough as I ought." His boyish expression should have been ridiculous on a man of his age, who wore his years of struggle in the lines of his face—it wasn't.

Nor was it his fault. I wouldn't have taken my request seriously either. "Ah yes, I owe you an apology for that."

"Unnecessary. It was certainly amusing."

"Well, apology issued, nonetheless. My departure does not need to be immediate, but I should like to be settled in Scotland before the weather starts to turn."

"I will have answers to your questions by next week and contracts drawn up just as soon as we discuss my findings. Would that suffice?"

"Perfect. Thank you, Will. I could not trust just anyone with this. I appreciate that I can trust you. Now, do you suppose I should head down to the docks and retrieve my recalcitrant sister?"

"I'm certain Kit will need an extra set of hands. Good luck!" he offered as I stood to leave.

∼

THE IRRITATED CRUNCH of every pebble in the roadway echoed in the furious silence of the carriage.

Poor Mr. Summers seemed to very much regret accepting the ride from the docks. He ran a hand through increasingly disheveled hair as he stared out the open window with panted breaths. The desperation in his expression was reminiscent of a jailed man watching the freedom of the horizon.

Davina, on the other hand, sat across from me, lips curled into a pout and arms crossed over her chest. Every half minute or so, she would let out an annoyed huff and give me a glare. A glare that I matched at every turn.

One shoulder spilled out of her navy coat and she crossed her ankles primly in her boots and breeches. Her dark curls had been tied back, but they had escaped the ribbon's confines and now spilled across the velvet. Still, her absurd tri-corner hat tipped jauntily to one side, swaying with every rut in the road. Who on God's earth could have mistaken her for a man?

No sooner had we jolted to a stop outside the offices than Mr. Summers tumbled out of the carriage, tossing his thanks behind him as he lurched toward the door.

I snapped the window shut as we set off before rounding on my sister. "What in the hell were you thinking?"

"I explained that quite well in my note, thank you very much," she replied with a note of false piety.

"Mother is beside herself. Did you even consider that?"

She rolled her eyes. "Mother is always beside herself."

"Because you're always running off on whatever dangerous whim has caught your eye in the moment."

"Mother has been beside herself for longer than I've been alive. If it wasn't this, it would be something else."

"Which is why you should strive to keep her calm," I insisted.

"I should, should I? And you? Have you succeeded in keeping her calm by following every single rule—including the ones you've fabricated for yourself?"

A sharp jolt hit my chest at the slight. Christ, it was unfair, the way I carefully cultivated my life, the way I had to stuff myself into a mold of what society wanted—and fail at every turn. But my sister could flout every expectation with impunity and leave me to clean up her mess—untouched by the hateful words of the *ton*.

"Damn it all, Dav, think of the future for just once in your life! What if your plan had worked?"

"My reputation would have been ruined? I would never marry? Oh, no." Her expression was one of careful, sarcastic vacancy.

"It would serve you right, to face ruin for once in your life."

"That is the point!" she shouted.

It took a moment for comprehension to settle, and when it did, it knocked me back. "What?"

"I don't want to marry! I never want to marry."

"Well not now, but—"

"Never. Not ever."

"Davina, I..." Her shouted words rang through my mind, bouncing against the walls there until a brand-new picture formed. My sister, surrounded in a new light. "Is that what all of this has been about?"

She melted, anger seeping from her frame. "Not entirely— I do enjoy my adventures. But, if I were ruined and deemed unmarriageable... Would that truly be so bad, Xand? Is marriage truly all I'm good for?"

One of my earliest memories had been passing by a shop window and spotting a porcelain vase painted with cerulean entwining florals. It was exquisite—and I desperately needed my mother to have it. I remembered presenting it to her, pride filling my small frame. She cooed her gratitude and settled it in a place of honor in the entry. And I remembered my father returning home that night and asking why Mother had purchased such a hideous vase. I couldn't recall her response, but I did know that the vase remained in the entry for years, new roses filling it every few days—long after Mother rid the house of every other blue decoration.

And I would never forget the moment when little Davina, running everywhere and nowhere in particular, refusing to sit still for a moment, jostled the table leg.

Her words today left my heart shattered in precisely the same way that the vase had.

Marriage—marriage to a person I loved—was a dream so precious and so impossible that I couldn't allow myself to consider it. Of course Davina would casually knock it over—accidentally so I couldn't even blame her. And she would ask about it precisely the same way she had when she'd mumbled, "*You love the vase more than me.*"

And just as I had then, I asked, "What? Of course not! How could you even think that?"

"You're always so worried about my reputation."

"I'm worried about your safety! You could have been hurt. You could have been killed! And yes, I do not want you to be shunned by the whole of society. Is that a bad thing?"

"No..."

The carriage shuddered as we arrived outside of Hasket House. Davina leapt at the opportunity to escape the uncomfortable confines and conversation. I caught her wrist as she brushed past.

"Dav, I promise that I will never, ever force you to marry against your wishes. I may suggest it, I may even cajole, but the choice will always be yours. And I will do everything in my power to ensure that it remains yours no matter what. You do not have to work to ensure that no one will want you."

Her lips pursed on a swallow as her eyes welled up. *That* was entirely too much sentiment for either of us to manage.

"Besides, you needn't work at it; no one would want you regardless." I paired the insult with a teasing smirk which earned me an, "Ugh, Xander!" that had it turning into a real smile.

Davina pulled her wrist free and stepped into the house. I ought to go in with her, see to mother, but I just couldn't bring myself to in that moment. Instead, I knocked on the ceiling and called out, "Rycliffe Place," as I moved to the forward-facing seat.

I allowed my head to hinge back and stared at the dark silk covering the roof of the carriage. Davina wouldn't stop her adventures—nothing could slow her down as a child, and I knew her too well to think anything would change now. Still, the understanding was a relief, even if I still wanted to throttle her.

Of course Davina would throw away something I wanted desperately. The memory of cerulean eyes surrounded by matching fabric, a teasing smirk, and long limbs flashed behind my eyes. What would it be like? To flirt with intent, to flirt with the possibility of something more, something real, with a future?

I shoved those questions to the back of my mind. Wishing for the impossible brought nothing but pain.

Better to focus on possible dreams. Scotland. Scotland was real. Scotland grew more tangible with every day. Scotland could be my future.

Ten

WAYLAND'S, LONDON - JUNE 15, 1816

TOM

I PREFERRED Wayland's to every other club, but certainly to White's. Though I may have been a touch biased.

In the near fortnight since the masquerade, Michael's club had been returned to its usual state, where gaming tables ruled the land and there was no dance floor to be found. My brother nodded toward his office before stepping past to knock on Augie's door.

I slipped inside and shut the door behind me. It was precisely as I'd left it and a wave of warmth rushed over me. For a few moments, I could be the man I'd always wished to be. I could flirt and smile, laugh and tease a handsome gentleman. And the world didn't end.

Michael barged in with a stack of paperwork.

"What are you doing with all of that? I thought you handed most everything over to Augie."

"I did. But the ball was Juliet's idea. He didn't want to deal with the nonsense of it, so I agreed to manage that piece."

"Why did you?"

"We had just lost the babe. Jules wasn't feeling herself. And... she gave up a great deal to be with me. She asks for so few of the luxuries of her former life. Someday you'll understand. When the woman you love asks you for something within your power to give... There's nothing to say but yes."

"It seems unlike her, as well."

He sighed, then dragged a hand through his hair while he strode to his desk and settled there. I took the chair opposite it, rather than one by the fire. Those were special.

"She's a lady. They like to wear fussy gowns and dance on occasion. Or so I'm told."

I hummed and stretched my feet up atop the desk before me in the way Michael loathed. He glared at the intrusion but bit back the complaints.

"You can go play, if you wish. I saw Lord Haxburg down there. He's abysmal at hazard. You can take him for a tidy sum."

"I think I'll stay here for a bit, if it's not an intrusion."

"You're always welcome," he replied. The way he said it, so matter of fact, I could believe it—this Tom, the one who adored actresses and opera singers, and slung his dirty booted feet across the desk, he was always welcome.

But the Tom I wished to be... Would he always be welcome? If anyone were capable of it... it would be Michael.

I swallowed the knot in my throat. "Hugh and I were at White's the other day."

His gaze shot up, brow furrowed. "The brothel?"

"The club," I replied incredulously. "There's a brothel called White's?"

I received a chuckle for my naivete. "It looks better on the ledgers. Easier to cover one's tracks."

That was... rather ingenious. "Well, we were at the club. I loathe it."

"Why did you go with Hugh then?"

"It was something to do... And I was looking for someone." My breath caught, though I'd given him nothing.

"Oh?"

"A gentleman. I thought I might try to strike up a friendship." Deep in my chest, my heart froze.

"A friendship? With whom?" Michael set aside the quill and stood to attend to the drink cart. He raised an empty glass with a questioning brow. At my nod, he poured two.

When he set one before me, he knocked my feet off the desk with a sharp hand. The gesture shocked my lungs back to working.

I swallowed against my dry mouth. "Rosehill." I tried for simple, unaffected. But there was something strained in the word.

Michael straightened before me and froze there for a beat. A second. Before moving back to his chair with his drink.

"A friendship. With Rosehill."

"Yes," I choked out.

His tongue darted out, wetting his lips, before he took a careful sip of his drink. Michael was always comfortable in his skin, always. But this effort was studied.

"Rosehill is a good man," he said carefully. At my nod of agreement, he continued. "I wasn't happy with the way he handled Juliet's request to end their engagement. But I understand his reasons and I cannot fault him for them."

"You do?"

"Understand his reasons? I do." Michael ran a hand through his dark waves—so much more like mine than Hugh's long strands. With a fortifying breath, he forged on. "And I'm beginning to suspect that you do as well."

I swallowed, numbness settling into my extremities. "I believe that I do."

"Tom..." He drew out the word, letting it hang in the silence. His mouth slipped open and he started before aborting the effort. He repeated that effort several times before he finally managed. "Anything you need, or want. Juliet and I... we are here for you. Unconditionally."

Tears filled my eyes, entirely without permission. But the weight on my chest was gone. The air was thick, nourishing. I could breathe again.

"I— Thank you."

"There is nothing to thank me for. Jules and I... If it were possible to choose who to fall in love with, I wouldn't have my wife. But, Tom, you understand the implications of what you're telling me?"

I shook my head, curls brushing my ears. "There's nothing to tell. And there's every chance there never will be. But I just..."

"Wanted to tell someone?"

"Precisely."

He pressed his lips together in a thin facsimile of a smile. "I'm glad you did."

"Hugh..."

That gave Michael pause. They'd worked at their relationship in recent years, forming a bond that, while not like the one he and I shared, was respectful. "Hugh has a title. And a son who will inherit that title and all the responsibilities that come with it. He doesn't have the freedom that comes with vast wealth and a deep loathing of polite society."

"I know that—I do."

"Hugh has surprised me before. He could do it again. If you want him to know... You have my support in whatever you decide. To be honest, I might need to explain a few things to him first. He's still painfully naive." Michael broke off with an amused chuckle. "I do not know what he's told you, but if *you* require a diagram, I'm afraid I've no practical advice to give."

I had no idea what he meant, but he seemed to be laughing at Hugh's expense, which was usually deserved.

"You're not planning to tell your mother, are you?" he asked suddenly. "Because that might be the condition to the unconditional support."

"Are you certain? Because that may actually give her the megrim that kills her."

"Christ, you're right. Please tell her."

I settled back in my chair, matching his laughter with my own.

⁓

THE HOURS SLIPPED by in idle chatter, swirled signatures, and topped off drinks. Dawn was just beginning to crest when the door swung open, interrupting the hard-won ease.

"Augie, we've discussed this," Michael chastised with half-hearted irritation.

The man in question strode into the office and gave a performative knock on the desk between Michael and me. My brother, used to such behavior from his second, merely raised a brow.

"We've got a problem."

"A problem without fifty ledgers to sort through? What a delightful turn."

Augie waved to someone I hadn't noticed lingering in the doorway. The gentleman was rail thin with clothing so mismatched, even I could see it. The trousers were too short, with shoes too large. Thin arms crossed over a properly fitted shirt, though it was covered with a black-and-white waistcoat several sizes too big. A familiar waistcoat.

My gaze shot to the gentleman's face. It was then I recognized the heavy—if slightly more delicate than her brother's—brow of Lady Davina under the outdated powdered wig.

Laughter burst from my chest with no warning.

"Damn it all, I told my wife this would happen. The club is too much temptation."

Lady Davina huffed. "Oh yes, it's irresistible. That's precisely why I'm here."

"Well, why are you here then, Miss…"

"Why should I tell you?" she asked tartly.

"Lady Davina." I supplied. The lady herself wrinkled her nose at me. "Rosehill's sister," I added when presented with his blank stare.

A low curse escaped Michael. "How much did you lose?"

"She didn't," Augie cut in.

"She didn't what?"

"Lose."

"She won?" Michael asked, incredulity heavy in his voice and in his eyes.

"Of course I won," she crowed.

"Well how the devil did you manage that? How do you even know how to play?"

"Gabriel taught me," she snapped.

"Oh. So he taught you how to cheat," Michael extrapolated.

"I didn't cheat. He taught me to play properly."

"Baldwin was watching the play tonight," Augie interjected. "He didn't notice anything untoward until Beaumont accused her. Once he saw her up close…"

"Who let her in?" Michael asked.

"Potter…"

Michael dragged a tired hand across his face. If there was a problem at Wayland's, it was always Potter. But while he was a bumbling, inattentive fool, he was a kind bumbling, inattentive fool. And Michael had a soft heart—no matter how much he protested the contrary.

"How are we going to cover this?" he asked. "Her reputation will be in tatters."

"Oh, he didn't accuse her of being a lady. Beaumont accused *him* of being a cheat," Augie clarified.

Laughter escaped Michael and me at the same time. From afar, in the dim light of the hall, she could be mistaken for a gentleman. But now, in front of us, she was every bit a lady. It was in her carriage, her movements, her heart-shaped face and delicate rose complexion.

"Where is the daft fool?" Michael asked.

"Wearing a hole in my rug," Augie said. "He's refusing to pay her."

"How much did he lose?"

"He didn't lose. I *won*," Lady Davina insisted.

"It's a fair point," I added.

"You, hush or go home," Michael scolded. I hushed as I had no interest in returning home now. "How much?" he asked.

"Three," Augie said.

"Three pounds?" I tipped my glass toward her in a toast.

"Three *thousand* pounds."

The scotch caught in my throat, slid into my lung, and burned there until I coughed it up.

"No wonder he's refusing to pay. He doesn't have it," Michael said. "Did he know who you were? Or that you were a lady?"

"No," Lady Davina insisted. "I spoke like this," she added in a feigned masculine growl.

I managed to bite back my laugh. Michael wasn't so successful. Lady Davina huffed as she yanked her wig off in a fit of irritation and flung it onto Michael's desk in a spray of white powder.

Michael apologized between what could only be described

as giggles. "Augie, pay her from house funds. We'll sort it out with Beaumont later."

The man nodded, plucked a key from his pocket, and slipped into the hall.

"You're going to pay me?"

"Of course. You won. You claim you played fair. None of my dunners saw anything questionable. Though it is something of a concern, frankly, that they didn't notice your gender. But I'd pay any gentleman in such a situation. Why would I not pay you?"

"Because I'm a woman..."

"Honestly, I adore it when anyone beats Beaumont. That it was a lady, and a titled one at that, makes it all the better. If I thought it wouldn't cause more problems, I'd have you in all the time."

"You do not care?" she asked.

"I care in as much that your reputation is at stake. And that I've caused your brother enough problems to last a lifetime already. But... Shall I tell you a secret?"

She nodded and stepped forward eagerly.

"Cee is an exceptional hazard player as well."

Her eyes widened, excited. "Cee came here too? When?"

I watched as the realization washed over my brother. His eyes widened and his lips parted as he tried to work out an appropriate explanation for why her sister-in-law spent time in the club. The actual explanation was far too scandalous for a lady, after all.

"Rycliffe—your brother—he taught her to play here," I supplied. I owed Michael tonight. And it would be a shame if Xander was forced to call Michael out before he got to meet his child.

Augie slipped back inside before Lady Davina could ask follow-up questions. Her gaze held none of the intrigue from before my explanation, so it was possible she believed it. Or at least wouldn't examine the details too closely. Her brother had almost certainly passed well before Michael built the club if my math was correct.

"Here," Augie said, thrusting a bank draft at her.

"This is too much," she protested. "I only won three."

"I like watching Beaumont lose," Augie replied. "Now, I need to get home to Anna and Emma."

"Right, and we need to get her home as well," Michael added.

"I'm *right* here. And Mr. Summers always sorts these things out," Lady Davina said.

"It's already sorted," Michael protested.

"But... When I have a problem on one of my adventures, he fixes it." It was a fact to her, that much was clear. Whenever she got into mischief, Kit was there to solve it. I had to catch my lower lip between my teeth. Apparently she had no idea what to do when the mischief sorted itself.

Michael caught the bridge of his nose between two fingers. "Augie? Would you have time to stop by Hasket House and alert Rosehill to the situation before you go home?"

He agreed, gestured toward the door with a thumb, and made his way from the room.

"Rycliffe Place," Lady Davina called after him, correcting my brother.

I caught the edge of Augie's nod before he shut the door behind him. It was only when the latch clicked that I recognized my missed opportunity. *I* could have been the one to alert Xander. *I* could have been the hero. But I was too distracted by the absurd situation.

"All right. Let me see if I can find a maid to act as chaperone," Michael said, then followed his friend out.

"I do not need a chaperone," Lady Davina said to the closed door. "I do not need a chaperone," she repeated to me. I rather thought trapping me in here with her was more improper than the lack of chaperonage. But I'd had more glasses of scotch than I could count, hadn't slept a wink, and couldn't bring myself to care overmuch. After all, her presence in this building, in such attire... If anyone found out, her reputation was in ruins whether she was in a closed office with me or not.

"Let him fuss. He still feels poorly about what happened between Jules and your brother."

She hummed, disinterested in the explanation. Instead, she grabbed my nearly empty glass and raised it to her lips. Her eyes caught mine and held them. Only when she was sure of my attention, did she tip the glass back, finishing the drink. She swallowed, then dipped her tongue out to catch a wayward drop of scotch.

It was an effort designed to entice. And were I anyone else, it probably would have worked. I let my gaze drop back to the desk.

Then I felt the brush of fine fabric against my wrist. I turned to face her as she made to sit on the arm of the chair. I shot up, backing away from the chair.

I scrambled for the drink cart and rolled it between us. There, I tipped a heavy pour of scotch into a new glass and downed it in one swallow.

From her perch on the arm of the chair, Lady Davina studied me. Her head tilted questioningly.

Before either of us could speak, Michael returned with no maid in tow. "They're all off until a more reasonable hour. We'll have to risk it. Gather your things. We'll leave out the back entrance."

"But Mr. Summers..." she protested.

"We're going to Mr. Summers. I need to discuss what to do with Beaumont anyway."

"Oh, all right then," Lady Davina replied, more agreeable than she had been all evening. She pulled the neck of her shirt back and tucked the bank note into some undergarment I wasn't interested in considering too closely. Then she snatched the wig off the desk, and another cloud of old wig powder settled atop the wood.

Without being asked, I followed them from the room. If they were going to Kit's, then that was where Rosehill would be. And, pathetic though it might have been, I wasn't about to miss the chance to see him again.

Eleven

HART AND SUMMERS, SOLICITORS, LONDON - JUNE 16, 1816

XANDER

Sleep had proven a fantasy in recent days. Instead, I rose hours before the sun and padded down to my little makeshift painting room. Far from a landscape, my newest inspiration was... different.

In the candlelight, with wishful brushstrokes, I brought him back to me. Dark curls caressed his forehead, escaping the attempt he'd made to tame them. Thin lips pressed together in a pleased smirk—lips that had brushed my cheek. His teasing eyes, the ones haunting my dreams, peered back at me from behind matching silk. Something about them wasn't quite right. I'd stared at them morning after morning and failed to capture the essence of him—*Tom*.

A sharp knock interrupted my evaluation, and I rushed to toss a bedsheet over my work—hoping it was dry enough for such efforts.

"Come in."

One look at Godfrey's expression was all I required.

"What has she done now?"

"A Mr. Ainsley for you, Your Grace."

My head hinged back on a sigh. Sororicide was frowned upon. Even if she really, really deserved it... Was it not?

Less than half an hour later, I found myself flinching at the damned bell at Hart and Summers, Solicitors once again.

Will rose to greet me, another gentleman trailing him out of the office.

It took a moment to place Mr. Grayson. His face bore at least a night's growth, his hands had destroyed any order he'd once tamed his hair into, and his cheeks bore the ruddy flush of liquor. More distracting, he wore only his shirtsleeves and waistcoat. The sleeves of his shirt had been rolled up to reveal masculine forearms with a dusting of auburn hair.

In short, he was so distractingly handsome that I quite forgot my intended purpose. When had the gangly lad learned to look like that?

Fortunately, Will reached me, pulling my distracted gaze from the beautiful, disheveled man before me.

At this point, greetings were unnecessary. "Is she in there with Mr. Summers?"

"And Wayland. I'm sure they'll be out in a few moments," Will replied.

"She was gaming at the club then?"

"So I'm given to understand. I believe she won, at least. Have a tart and a seat—catch your breath," he added, gesturing to a side table ladened with tarts. Tarts and Mr. Grayson's derrière where he leaned back against the table. He rose with two tarts in his hand and urged me toward the office.

He flopped into the chair by the window, leaving the other free for me. As I sat, Mr. Grayson wordlessly passed one of the tarts in his hand to me. I tore off a piece and savored the sharp bite of raspberry and the buttery softness of the pastry.

"So," Mr. Grayson started. "I was wondering something."

There was a hopeful note in his voice. I knew precisely what the next words would be. I'd heard the tone more than once when Dav first entered society. Before she'd set down every gentleman to try to win her favor.

"You need her permission," I replied simply.

"What?"

"You need Davina's permission. To court her. The Lord himself could not force her into a courtship she did not wish. I'm certainly not going to attempt it." I ripped free another bite of pastry and plopped it in my mouth to ease the sting of my brief moment of attraction.

After another bite with no response, I tipped my gaze up to his. There was something familiar in those blue-green depths, underneath the glaze of alcohol.

"I wasn't going to ask to court your sister," he said. There was a hint of incredulity in his tone, as though the thought were absurd.

"You weren't?"

"No! I envy the men brave enough to court Hasket women. I'm not one of them." His glance toward Will was significant and I had to bite back a grin.

"Well, what do you want then?" The question burst from me, the hand free of pastry dancing in front of me.

"I was just wondering where you decided to go for your trip."

I snagged another bite of the tart. "My trip?"

"You were planning a trip the last time I saw you," he said. His lower lip was trapped between his teeth and the image was giving me entirely indecent thoughts.

Shaking them away, I finished the last morsel of tart. "Oh, I'm for Scotland."

"Scotland... Highlands? Lowlands? For how long?"

I was missing the tart now that the conversation had turned into an interrogation. "Near Edinburgh. I'm planning to make it my primary residence. Why do you have so many questions?"

His expression shifted into something I couldn't name. "I... you... Nothing. Just making conversation."

"Right, sorry. I'm a bit... distracted at the moment. What with my sister." I tipped my thumb toward the wall shared with Mr. Summers's office.

"Of course. When... uh, when do you leave?" he asked, picking a piece of fluff off his waistcoat—this one was less unfortunate, a simple dark grey with leaves of various lighter grays scattered across it.

"That depends on what Mr. Hart has managed to find out for me. Hopefully within the next few weeks.

"I suppose I should leave you two to it then," he said, tipping his head toward the main area.

I turned to Will, who was watching us with a queer expression.

"I have answers for some of your questions," he began. "Surprisingly enough, neither the Rycliffe residence nor Hasket House are entailed. Only the Yorkshire property. If you wanted to sell the Rycliffe residence after your departure, you could, and the money would be yours to do with as you see fit. It would be untouchable by any heirs. You could stay with your mother whenever you return to town."

My heart leapt. "I can sell that house? You're certain?"

"Yes. Your father treated it as though it were a part of the courtesy title. But it was only purchased by your grandfather for your father."

"I don't have to live there? Where he died?" My chest felt lighter than it had in nearly a decade. Until precisely this moment, I hadn't realized it bothered me to live in that house. But now—with an alternative before me—I wasn't certain I could abide another night.

"No. If you would rather, you could use the funds to

purchase a different house in town. I did not realize you wished to give it up. I deeply regret that I did not look into that earlier."

"No," I said, brushing the apology away. "Thank you. Thank you so much."

He raised his hand to brush the back of his neck uncomfortably. "Yes, well. Lady Davina's dowry, such as it stands, is untouchable, even if she remains unwed. I could set up anything additional you wish to add to it for her to have access to at an age you deem appropriate. Normally, I would suggest twenty-five. But…"

"Thirty? Do you suppose she will mature by thirty?"

"It's possible. You can also have it released to her in installments rather than as a lump sum. You may wish to do the same with your mother."

"Yes. I can dower Celine from those funds as well?"

A flush bloomed on his sharp cheeks. "Yes, if you wish."

I couldn't help myself when I asked, "And what do you wish?"

"I beg your pardon?"

"I heard an interesting rumor last night. You are staying at Cadieux House?"

"I-I am…"

"Mr. Grayson claims not to possess the bravery necessary to court a Hasket lady. Do you?"

"Whether I possess the bravery is neither here nor there. I believe she has determined that I am to court her. I've simply chosen to accept my fate."

He could not possibly have answered that question in a way that would satisfy me more. In a few sentences, Mr. Hart had made it clear that he understood Cee in a way few others ever did.

"Good man. Is she able to manage some of the funds?"

"Yes…"

"You do not sound certain."

"As long as she remains unwed, she can manage the funds. If she were to take another husband, they would become his. We could write the contract so that it would terminate at that time. But that would leave you with the same problem you currently face. No one to manage your mother and sister."

"Why is that the case?"

"When a woman is born, she exists under her father's identity. When she weds, she and her husband become one in the eyes of the law, and that person is him. It is only if he precedes her in death that she becomes her own person, legally speaking. If she weds again, she accepts her new husband's identity."

"Well that is patently absurd," I blurted without thought.

"I cannot disagree with you."

"And there is no way around it?"

"A vote in parliament..." He lifted his shoulders in a shrug paired with a sympathetic press of his lips.

Damn. "Oh, well, there is no problem then."

"You could still manage everything by post. There just may be some difficulties. What those might be, I have no way of knowing."

I considered that for a moment. Would Cee even wish to wed again? A few weeks ago, my answer would have been a vehement no. But now, with Will's flush...

"Right. Let me discuss selling the house with Celine. She should have a say as well. Do we need to have a purchase in place to draft the documents?

"No, I can get them started and we can determine what funds should be placed where before signing."

The other office door creaked open and its three former occupants peered around the corner.

Wayland was the first to break the silence. "Rosehill, I trust you are well." It was stilted in the way he always was with me. I was never able to discern if it was due to the business with Juliet ending our engagement. Or if he *knew*. Regardless, he was never cruel, simply uncomfortable.

"I am," I replied.

"Good, that's... good." Seeking an end to the uncomfortable conversation, he glanced around. When his gaze found Mr. Grayson, he sighed. "Tom... off the furniture. How many times must we have this conversation?"

Mr. Grayson made no move to rise, instead asking, "Everything sorted?"

"It is. Let's go home."

The man rose in an ungainly pile of limbs and trailed after him. And then the clang of the damn bell announced their departure.

Dav stomped into the room and flopped into the chair beside me with an irritated huff.

"I assume you two need to have a discussion," Will asked Mr. Summers.

"Only if you're finished. It can wait."

"I believe we're sorted for now. Do you want to use my office?"

Mr. Summers settled into Will's vacated seat before asking the other gentleman to stay.

"So, Lady Davina won some £3,000 off of Mr. Beaumont. Michael is determined to pay his debts. However, Michael is equally determined that he cannot have young ladies sneaking into the club dressed as young men."

"It would serve you right, you know. If Mr. Wayland had you arrested for public indecency," I snapped at my sister.

"He would never! He still feels badly for stealing Lady Juliet from you," she spit back, entirely unrepentant.

"A person cannot be stolen. She made the choice that would make her the happiest and I am glad for them both. You are not to exploit any feelings he has on the subject. Do you understand?"

She crossed her arms in a familiar pout. At my unmoved countenance she finally added a quiet, "I understand."

Mr. Summers continued. "We can set up an account for her personal use. It will be under your name, of course, if you agree."

"Her own account? Is that necessary?"

"It might be good practice," Will offered.

"She also won £575 from Mr. Wesley Parker and £250 from Lord Thurston Lucas," Mr. Summers added.

The space behind my eyes throbbed in irritation. "Davina…"

"Why are you scolding me? I did well!"

"You could just as easily have done poorly. Did she bankrupt anyone else? I thought Parker was more fond of the tracks than the tables."

"No, Beaumont was the most substantial gain," Mr. Summers explained.

"All right, have the accounts drafted I suppose. I'll call for the carriage." Pointing to Davina, I added, "You stay right there."

Just to be difficult, she stood and leaned against the desk in defiance.

The carriage took but a moment, and I marched Dav from the offices with a distracted wave straight into the carriage without so much as a glance up the street.

She settled across from me, arms crossed with a pout.

"Davina Rosamund Hasket, are you trying to get yourself killed? Because men have been killed for smaller sums."

"Oh, they were hardly going to kill me. And if they'd called me out, I would have revealed my identity. No one would have actually shot me."

Frustration racked through me anew. "Our brother was stabbed on the steps of his home. Over what was very likely gaming debts. Do not ask me to burn another dining table, Davina. I wouldn't survive it."

Across from me, she shifted, arms uncrossing. "You burned the table?"

"He died there. I could hardly break my fast there any longer."

"Oh... I didn't know that," she said, quietly contemplative.

"Well, now you do. Davina, this nonsense has to stop. I thought we discussed that."

"It's just a bit of fun. It's not nearly like whatever Gabriel was involved in."

"Davina... You're probably right. Given your status, you're unlikely to be killed. But we *just* discussed your reputation."

"I was thinking of *yours*," she insisted.

"I beg your pardon?"

"He was talking about you—Mr. Beaumont. So I goaded him a bit."

"Davina..."

"He called you... Well, you know what he called you."

A knot formed in my throat, and swallowing around it was nearly impossible. "I do. But, Dav, it's not your responsibility to worry about that."

"Ugh... Xander!"

"Yes, yes. Ugh me. I need to discuss something else with you." Something about voicing my plans to Davina made them real in a way they hadn't been when I discussed them with Will.

"No one was hurt. And the fire didn't even have a chance to spread!" she blurted.

"What fire?" My hand flung nearly halfway across the carriage entirely of its own volition—fueled by exasperation with Davina.

Her spine straightened into that of the prim debutant she

was capable of being on very brief, very rare occasions. "Oh, what was it you wanted to discuss?"

"No, no. Fire first," I insisted.

"If you didn't know about it, then clearly it wasn't worth worrying about."

As much as I loathed to admit it, she had a point. Some things I was better off not knowing. And all her limbs appeared to be intact. "Fine. I've been considering, for some time now, making a change."

"A change?"

"The rumors are getting worse, have been for some time. Beaumont and others like him aren't going to stop. The longer I'm here, attracting their attention... It will impact your prospects, Mother's invitations..."

"What are you saying?"

"I'm leaving town."

"You're what?"

"There's a property that Gabriel won before he passed. He gave it to me. I'm going to make it my permanent residence."

"You're leaving me?" The genuine hurt in her voice astonished me. I'd expected mischievous glee. Or distracted indifference as she plotted her next escapade.

"I'm leaving *for* you. For mother. And for me as well. I'm tired, Dav."

"I'll stop! I promise. I won't go on any more adventures."

As much as I'd wished for that very promise for years, I hated the desperation with which she threw it toward me. "I cannot believe I am about to say this. And I will deny it to my dying breath, but don't stop. You wouldn't be you without a cloud of chaos around you. Just like Mother wouldn't be Mother without her histrionics."

"But..."

"Maybe be more careful with the adventures you choose, though," I added.

"Then why are you leaving?"

"Because I haven't been me. Not since father passed. Not since Gabriel died. Maybe not ever."

"And you can't be you here? With me?" she asked.

"You know that I cannot."

"But you can wherever the property is?"

"Scotland. And no, probably not, but I won't have to hide so carefully either," I explained.

"Who's going to look after me?"

"I'm giving Cee some authority over the accounts. And Mr. Summers will continue to come to your rescue, he just won't have to wait for my say-so. But I would very much like it if you went easy on them. At least until they accustom themselves to the responsibility."

"I just don't understand why you have to do this."

Because I'm a superfluous liability whose one wrong move could ruin this family forever. "If you really wish me to stay, I will."

She studied me in silence. Whatever she was searching for she must have found because she simply said, "Go. We'll be all right."

Twelve

40 BLOOMSBURY STREET, LONDON - JUNE 17, 1816

TOM

It was something of a habit, even when I was away from my brother's house, to sit on desks and stare at the paintings behind them. For years, in Grayson House and Thornton Hall, my father's portraits had hung, judgmental and imposing, behind the desk.

Michael loathed my habit, but staring at the swirls of paint on canvas depicting a man I hardly remembered helped me think.

Henry Grayson hadn't been a particularly good man. And he'd been an abysmal viscount. But for most of my life, I *thought* he'd been a good father. It had taken years to see what he'd done, or allowed to be done, to Michael and Hugh. The way he let my mother pit them against each other. The opportunities she stripped from Michael as our father stood silently by. It turned out, he was a terrible father too.

Which was honestly a relief. Because when I'd thought his haughty stare above me meant something, that his judgment was worth a damn, I'd felt the weight of that stare.

THE SCOTTISH SCHEME

The study at the apartments I let on Bloomsbury Street featured a different, almost certainly equally horrid, deceased relative. And though it wasn't *my* horrid deceased relative, the effect of the crooked nose and beady-eyed stare was the same.

Because I knew now that this man, whoever he may have been, was just as lost as I was. Only time and paint made him seem like he had the foggiest idea of what he was doing.

A knock came from the door behind me. And to my astonishment, behind the maid's shoulder was Juliet.

"Come in, come in," I insisted. A quick glance at my desk confirmed that it was shamefully empty. My instinct to stack and shuffle pages and ledgers to make room for her was entirely useless.

She settled across from me with her usual grace, dropping a basket of pastries on the desk between us. We each reached for a tart and tucked in.

"I'm afraid I don't know what pleasure I owe this visit to," I said, finally breaking the silence that had been filled with the fruit and cinnamon taste of comfort.

"You did this for me. Once. I only wanted to be sure you were all right."

"How did—Did Michael tell you?"

"He told me enough to confirm what I already suspected."

"So you did send me to Michael's office…"

Her cheeks darkened. It was probably a fetching flush to others, but it was a mere darkening to my eyes. "I am afraid I must confess. I am as shameless a matchmaker as Kate. I had hoped…" She dropped her gaze to her lap. "I do not know what I hoped. It seems I made precisely the wrong choice. And for that I am truly sorry."

"Don't be."

Juliet merely met my gaze with an intrigued expression.

"It was the best night of my life," I finished.

"Then I take back my apology. I understand… That sentiment... There was a time when Michael and I seemed impossible. And I wouldn't have given back our stolen moments for the world. Even if I had to live off them for the rest of my days."

And that was it. My regret wasn't the masquerade. It wasn't the conversation. I regretted that I would have to live the rest of my days with the memory of nothing more than the brush of my lips against his cheek. Why hadn't I been bolder?

"And if they're not enough? What if there aren't enough... stolen moments to sustain me?"

"The masquerade, it was not your only meeting. Was it?" she asked.

"Only one of note. He didn't even remember our first meeting." The petulance in my tone didn't phase her.

"But you do."

"We first met at Hugh and Kate's wedding breakfast. I'd suspected there was something... different, that I wasn't—that I didn't..."

"Understand the appeal of the fairer sex?" she supplied.

I shrugged. It was better than I could have done. "But I saw him. And everything that had always been confusing made sense. He made sense."

"And he did not remember you at all."

"Precisely."

"What happened next?"

"It was Mother who introduced us. Given that she had just lost Hugh to 'a conniving harlot,' she was angling for a match between Lady Davina and myself."

"I may have to tell Kate that your mother called her a conniving harlot. She has finally learned to take pleasure in Agatha's displeasure."

"Oh, I'm well aware. She even encourages it on occasion." I laughed, Juliet's joining mine.

When the echoes of our mirth faded, I continued.

"Meeting Rosehill changed my life. And he didn't even remember my name."

"So your first meeting was a mess. I assume the masquerade went well?"

"Yes." I could feel the flush rising up my chest, neck, and cheeks.

"Well, then... What seems to be the problem? Aside from the whole of society, of course."

"Yes, just that little thing. Also, he's leaving."

"He is?" she asked.

"He has property in Scotland. He plans to make it his primary residence."

"Oh, Tom," she said softly. "What are you going to do?"

"What can I do?"

"Well, it seems you have two options. You can stay. Or you can follow."

"Follow and do what? With what?" I asked, stuffing a bite of tart into my mouth.

"*Make* him remember you."

"I'm entirely dependent on Hugh and Michael. I have no money, no house, nothing of my own. I can give Xander nothing."

"I did not realize you felt that way. You are absolutely wrong, of course. But I hate that you feel that way."

"Oh, I'm wrong?"

"Tom, I was penniless when Michael and I wed. My reputation was in tatters, the title was worthless. In fact, it cost Michael thousands of pounds to clear my father's debts. Do you think Michael ever, for one second felt that way about me?"

"Of course not. You're perfect for him."

"Precisely. Rosehill has no need of money, or titles," she said.

"But I don't *do* anything. I helped Hugh when funds were tight, but now..."

"Tom, you are the glue. You hold everything together. You always have. And this family will absolutely be worse for not having you near. But you have done your duty your entire life. If you need to find your own branch of the family to hold together, we can manage in the meantime. You have taught us well."

"But..."

"Just promise you will come back. Do not fall so in love with *Scotland* that you forget the rest of us."

"Jules..."

"You are my favorite brother, you know. I always wanted one. I know I should not pick favorites, but... I cannot help myself."

"Well, with such competition as Hugh..."

Her laugh was bright and free. "He improves upon closer acquaintance."

"He improved after Kate yelled at him."

"You had no need of improvement, and thus you are my favorite," she insisted.

Thirteen

HUDSON'S BAKERY, LONDON - JUNE 17, 1816

XANDER

Telling Mother of my plans had been... less than pleasant. And I was in need of the strongest drink money could buy. Unfortunately, it was but ten in the morning, so I was forced to settle for pastries.

I pressed open the familiar red door and settled at the table by the bay windows. Behind the counter, Mrs. Ainsley nodded in my direction and raised her index finger while assisting a maid intent on filling an entire basket to the brim with various delights.

Hudson's Bakery, owned by the former Miss Hudson now Mrs. Ainsley, was beloved by all in the two years since it opened. The air inside swirled with scents of flour, butter, and spice, hints of cinnamon and berries lingered on my tongue.

Though the shop primarily catered to those wishing to take their pastries with them, Mrs. Ainsley had placed a few intimate tables scattered across the shop floor. The bakery had quickly become a popular location for the lords and ladies in the first blush of a courtship.

In an hour, perhaps two, I was certain it would have been all but impossible to find a table.

The maid swept toward the door, arms ladened with two baskets nearly overflowing. I rose and opened it for her, while she nodded a distracted thanks.

"Your Grace," Mrs. Ainsley called from behind the wooden counter. "Your usual?"

"Yes, please," I replied and settled back at my table. I wouldn't risk losing my favored spot.

She nodded and set about fetching tea from the back room.

Through the window, I could watch merchants going about their day. None of them cared a lick for my title. Oh, they would address me with deference, but behind these panes, I was nothing of interest. And that was refreshing.

A soft brush of skirts at my side drew my attention to Mrs. Ainsley's presence. She placed the perfect cup of tea on the table along with a plate with an almond tart and slice of Shrewsbury cake. "Thank you. It looks delicious as always."

"You're welcome. Do let me know if I can get you anything else." She slipped back behind the counter.

I nodded and sank my teeth into the tart. The fruit flavors were the most popular; it could be difficult to find the raspberry or lemon tarts because they sold at first light. Once when Mrs. Ainsley had been out of the lemon, I tried an almond as a last resort. And it was now a first resort—heaven on a plate.

So preoccupied was I by the decadence before me, I didn't notice anyone strolling past my window, and I was in far too committed a relationship with my pastries to be distracted by such trifles as a door opening beside me.

In my periphery, I caught a gentleman and a lady walking over to the counter. "Raspberry, as usual, Anna. You know how he is," a soft feminine lilt replied to the proprietress's request. The transaction continued, only occupying a hint of my attention.

A moment later, I was interrupted from my tart worship by a visitor in a delicately embroidered gown that matched her bright eyes. Lady Juliet.

"Good morning, Your Grace."

I shot to my feet and pulled free the chair beside me. "Lady Juliet, what a pleasure."

Delicate as always, she dropped to the chair and allowed me to adjust it to her liking before settling back beside her.

"I'm afraid I cannot stay. I just wanted to say hello," she said.

"I'm so glad you did."

She leaned closer, nothing scandalous, just enough so we wouldn't be overheard. "I also wanted to apologize for the masquerade. I fear I was a bit... presumptuous."

"Oh... no. I had a... pleasant time."

She straightened considerably. "Well then. I'm pleased that you enjoyed yourself. I do hope you know you'll always be welcome. *Always.*"

"I... Thank you for that."

Behind me, I heard a tentative, "Jules?"

Her gaze flitted past me while I spun awkwardly in my seat.

Damn.

"Your Grace, have you met Mr. Grayson?" Juliet asked. There was a hint of something in her tone, but I couldn't read it. Not as distracted as I was by Mr. Grayson—suddenly everywhere.

"I have," I replied, swallowing thickly.

Mr. Grayson merely nodded, looking anywhere but at me.

"Oh! I just remembered!" Juliet cried and shot to her feet. "I have something to pick up at the modiste. Tom, I'm afraid I must leave you here. I'll just have Anna pack up my tarts."

"Jules..." he said in a low tone. An overly familiar tone.

She peered up at him, her eyes wide and innocent. There was a subtext between them that I wasn't privy to, and it was a nagging irritation. "Please, take my seat. I'm sure His Grace will not mind. Right?"

I rather did mind. Mr. Grayson left me on edge, unsteady, and flustered in every one of our interactions.

"Of course not. Please," I said, gesturing to the vacated seat.

With a nod and a grin, Juliet flounced to the counter. Leaning across, she whispered something to Mrs. Ainsley.

Mr. Grayson shifted on his feet for a moment before carefully sitting. His back was rod straight, and he balanced right on the edge of the seat. His overlong legs tucked beneath the chair, but it was clear it would be too small for his frame even if he sat properly.

His gloves were tucked in one hand and he draped them across his thigh. A rigidly coiled thigh that flexed enticingly beneath his tan breeches.

"Thank you," he croaked out, then cleared his throat. After settling one hand on the table, he stared down at it as if it held the answer to all of life's secrets. With his thumbnail, he traced the grain of the wooden table. His fingers were long, elegant, but clearly possessing strength if the veins along the back of his hand were any indication. There was something beautiful, enticing about those hands.

Juliet returned, bag in one hand and plate and teacup in the other. She set the tart covered plate in front of Mr. Grayson before freeing her finger from the handle of the cup as it joined the tart. "She's out of raspberry. I brought you blackberry."

"What's in the bag then?" Mr. Grayson asked.

"Nothing to concern yourself with," she replied smoothly.

"Oh, so definitely not the last of the raspberry tarts."

"Certainly not. I would never."

"Open the bag, Juliet," he ordered. But there was a smile on his face and in his tone.

"I am a lady and as such, my honor is unimpeachable."

He scoffed. "You lie as easily as breathing. It's just a miracle you choose to use your powers for good."

Her hand found her chest in exaggerated outrage. "I would never."

"Jules, you complimented my mother's perfume last night."

Oh no, that was possibly the greatest lie ever told. I'd worried, during our engagement, that she wouldn't hold up well to life in the Hasket household, that she would wilt under the strain of it. Now... Well, whether she would or wouldn't wasn't really of concern. She had Wayland's ring on her finger.

"Yes, and it distracted her from calling Michael a spiteful wretch. So I rather think it was a worthy sacrifice."

"You're not the one who will have to be around her every day. She's going to use so much more of it now," he whined.

"It is hardly every day. You visit once a week, perhaps twice."

"Yes, and now I will have a megrim every time. I'll have to follow her lead and take to the bed for days to recover. Which is why you should give me one of the tarts you're hiding."

"You are right. I am in possession of the last raspberry tarts. You cannot have them. Goodbye." She clutched the bag to her chest and started backing away. "Your Grace, it has been an absolute pleasure. I am so sorry I cannot stay."

"Lady Juliet," I replied as she twirled out the door in a flurry of skirts.

"Thief!" Mr. Grayson called after her. The affectionate grin hadn't left his lips for the entire exchange. When the door shut behind her, he chuckled silently, his chest rising and falling as he shook his head fondly.

And then he turned his gaze to me. In the light of the window, they sparkled a bluish green with a grey ring around the edge. Just around the pupil was a hint of a greenish brown. It wouldn't even be visible were his pupils wider. But in the edge of sunlight caressing him through the window, his eyes were breathtaking.

An enticing finger clasped the teacup and lifted it to where his thin upper and full lower lip met.

"Apologies, Your Grace," he grumbled into his cup before taking a sip.

"For what?"

"That was an unseemly display," he explained, ruddy cheeks darkening.

"You witnessed the chaos my menace of a sister made the other day."

His response was a strange mixture of a shrug and head tilt and in doing so, he sloshed a dollop of tea on the table. As he rushed to wipe it away with a napkin, his flush deepened.

I chose to ignore his fluster. There was something charming about it—and me being the one less flustered. "Remind me, how are you so familiar with Lady Juliet?"

"Oh, I assumed you knew. It's a poorly kept secret. Michael—Wayland—is my eldest brother."

A memory shifted into place. Somehow, knowing that Wayland was the late viscount's bastard hadn't translated to recognition that Juliet would be Mr. Grayson's sister by law. Which was... dim-witted of me to say the least.

"Well, that explains your presence for Dav's latest escapade. You seem... close. You and Lady Juliet, I mean."

"Yes. Jules and I... We have an understanding."

My brows nearly hit the sky.

"Oh! Not that kind of understanding. No. No. Absolutely not. No. We just..." he trailed off, gesturing between us as though that would clarify. "We're the family peacemakers. A shared talent for placating volatile tempers."

"I see..."

"Oh you wouldn't. And be glad for it. I actually— I owe you another apology," he began before breaking for another sip of tea.

"Whatever for?"

"You wouldn't know it, not from our interactions. But I'm usually less... I'm the eloquent brother, believe it or not. But for some reason I just keep offending you. I assure you, I do not mean it. And I wanted to apologize—the other day, I was prying and I upset you. It wasn't my business, and it was inappropriate to ask."

The majority of the speech had been directed toward the blackberry tart, but at the very end, he glanced up at me, hesitant, beneath dark lashes. The very tips of them were dusted with a rusty red. It should have been a childish, sheepish expression. But instead, it was an enticing look. One that brought to mind contexts far away from pastry-scented bakeries and apologies.

"How old are you?" I blurted, so busy trapping other thoughts behind mental doors that I couldn't restrain that one.

His brow furrowed while he tipped his head to the side. "One and twenty. Why?"

Something about that number was both a relief and a frustration. Far too young—not that there was anything to be too young *for*. But also... not. Because Juliet had been considered halfway to on the shelf at the same age when I proposed. Not that it was relevant.

"Just curious," I said, brushing the thought away.

He shifted back to sit properly in the chair, though his legs remained tucked up under it—too long for anything else.

"I suppose I owe you more than a few probing questions. After all, I started it with my impertinence."

"You don't need to, by the way."

"What?" he asked.

"Apologize. It wasn't—"

"Don't say it wasn't improper. It certainly was."

"Oh, it certainly was. But I overreacted. Davina has a tendency to do that to me."

A smile bloomed across his lips before a huffed chuckle rumbled from his chest. "I've noticed."

"She vexes me on purpose," I explained.

"I'm almost certain that you're right. As a youngest sibling, I must inform you that it is our life's purpose to vex the elder at every available opportunity."

"Oh, it is?"

"Yes, there are few things in life I enjoy more than vexing Michael or Hugh. Though in fairness, Hugh is just as often the one to vex me as I am him."

"Not Wayland?" I asked.

"Michael isn't easily vexed. Though he does loathe when I use furniture improperly. A foot on the desk and his eye begins to twitch. And he rarely has the time to vex me in earnest."

"The furniture seems to be a struggle even when he isn't present." I nodded toward his legs, still tucked ungentlemanly under the chair.

"Chair is too small," he replied, finally taking a hearty bite of the tart before him.

"Legs are too long," I retorted.

He swallowed the bite heavily. "It is a daily struggle. It seems every chair in London is too small. And don't even let me tell you about the doorways."

"Were you teased as a boy?"

Something about the question had him flushing again. But he pressed forward. "Not about that. Though your sister did call me a cricket once. I can only assume it was in regard to the legs."

My palm found my face as it so often did in regard to Davina. "Oh good lord. When was that?"

"Hugh's wedding. The day we met." His tone was soft, tentative. And behind his eyes, there was a significance I wasn't catching. "I think you were distracted. She'd wandered off, I suspect," he added.

"I don't—I'm sorry."

"Don't be. It was a poor showing. Unfortunately, life rarely offers a second chance for a first impression."

Memories flashed through me like lightning. Eyes the color of the sky peeking through the forest, that time behind a domino of the same coloring. My heart stopped and suddenly I could taste the caramel burn of scotch, smell the remnants of a dying fire, hear the faint chords of the quartet. *Him.*

"Tom..." I breathed, incapable of anything more significant. My heart began again, the rhythm faltering, unsteady.

Those damned beautiful eyes widened and his tongue dipped out to wet that plump lower lip.

It was obvious. So obvious. Blatant to anyone paying the tiniest bit of attention.

"Yes," he answered, his voice a silken caress. It could have been brushed aside as a question. But we both knew it was a confirmation. "Yes."

"You..."

"Yes." He didn't explain. Didn't clarify his meaning. It was entirely unnecessary. We both knew what it meant. Yes, it was him. Yes, he meant it then. Yes, he meant it now. Yes, he wanted what I wanted. Whatever I wanted, if the way his gaze flicked over my form was any indication.

"How? Why?"

"I cannot answer the how. Except to say that I made a pitiful first impression. You thought my name was Tim Gregerson, if I recall correctly. As far as the why? That night... It was perfect. Or the closest thing to it I've ever touched. But it was an intermission. A reprieve. We both knew that. And sans mask, I returned to the usual, embarrassing form when faced with you."

This time, when he brought the cup to his lips, his eyes held mine.

"It wasn't—there was nothing embarrassing about it," I protested.

One side of his mouth curled up in a self-deprecating smirk.

Rather than respond to that assurance, he forged ahead. "So, Scotland."

It was somehow so much harder to force out the single syllable. "Y-yes." It caught in my throat for a moment before freeing itself.

"When do you leave?" His voice had the same strained quality as mine.

"July, weather allowing."

His silence was heavy, accompanied by a single, solemn nod.

"It was you, actually, who gave the idea form."

A bitter huff escaped. "I'd gathered that. I cannot decide if it would have been better for the idea not to have taken root at all. But that would erase that night. I don't, I cannot regret that for the world."

"I don't regret it either. It is just... time."

"Well, for what it's worth—which is probably nothing—I will miss your company."

My heart gave a jolt, rapturous even over the ache. "That is worth far more than nothing."

His answering expression was inscrutable, merely a tightening of his mouth. Whatever thoughts lay hidden behind that motion, he shook them away. "Tell me. About your home there. What is it like?"

"I have... absolutely no idea. I've never been. Gabriel, my elder brother, won it in a game of hazard. And, well, I was the second son. I suppose he wanted me to have something of my own. It was a half-considered gesture, of course, but it was possibly the nicest thing he ever did for me. I think he knew that I would need..."

"Somewhere quiet?" he supplied.

"I suppose. And now, well, it has been my haven—if only in my head—for a great many years. My expectations are modest though. I cannot imagine it will exceed them."

Something dark settled across his face, though I could not account for it.

"Uncle Tom!" A feminine voice cried out—startling us both out of our moment. A stout, ruddy-cheeked woman materialized beside Tom, a suspiciously babe-shaped bundle in her arms. Her fiery hair, now peppered with grey, was tucked back under a cap.

"Mrs. Hudson." Tom rose, warmth in his tone, and offered the woman a one-armed hug. "And Miss Ainsley," he added, brushing a large hand over the red curls that escaped the bundle. "How are my two favorite ladies this morning?"

"Charm away, lad. The raspberry tarts are all gone."

"Even for me?" His smile was bright, charming.

"Especially for you."

He pulled back with a gasp, clutching his chest in false pain. "You wound me!"

"More people ought to say no to you, then it wouldn't be so distressing."

"Mrs. Hudson! I cannot believe you to be so cruel. And in front of the child!"

"Yes, yes. Speaking of the babe..."

Tom's smile grew even as he rolled his eyes. "Hand her over."

"It's only that the new lad Anna has hired..."

"Isn't playing with a full deck," he supplied, reaching to take the girl.

"It wasn't I that said it."

Tom settled the babe against his chest with one long arm. "Go, supervise."

She cupped his cheek. "Good lad. There's a raspberry tart in the oven for you if he hasn't burnt them all."

Tom's eyes widened as he tipped his head toward the kitchens. "Go! Go quickly! Go now!"

He watched as the woman rounded the counter in a flurry of skirts, then met Mrs. Ainsley's mouthed *Thank you* with a nod before he turned back to me.

After he settled back into his chair, feet again tucked awkwardly around the legs, I offered a dry, "Uncle Tom?"

His answering flush was endearing. "Mrs. Hudson was our cook. And my mother—well, anyone would've been better. But there isn't anyone better than Mrs. Hudson. Besides, I'm already little Henry's favorite uncle. I need to win over Miss Emma here as well."

The girl in question snuck a hand out from the blankets. Tom quickly supplied a finger for her to tug at. When he peered back up at me from beneath lowered lashes, my heart gave a disgruntled tug. He presented an impossible picture, but all the more breathtaking for it.

I swallowed the knot in my throat. "I do not suppose I shall ever be an uncle—at least not while Davina continues to be... herself."

"Family is what you make of it. After all, in Scot—" A great crash from the direction of the kitchens echoed throughout the room. Before I'd even recognized that he'd moved, Tom was out of his seat and halfway to the counter with the babe still in his arms, now offering a displeased cry.

Mrs. Ainsley wore a torn expression and wavered between the line of startled customers and what was surely chaos beyond the closed door.

Wordlessly, Tom shooed her toward the door and turned to the line of customers while still balancing the babe in one arm. Mrs. Ainsley hesitated only for a moment before disappearing into the kitchens.

Tom, on the other hand, soothed the infant back to quiet while fetching a requested pastry. He had to pause to check the cost from the little slip of parchment on the window before taking the gentleman's money.

The sight was so odd, so unexpected, that it took several moments to comprehend. Tom was just... selling pastries. With an infant on his hip. He was slow, clearly unpracticed, and he struggled to manage the work one-handed. The queue was lengthening by the moment. But he was muddling through.

There was something unbearably appealing about the sight, the way he directed the small turmoil into something neat and orderly. No one questioned his authority or his presence. The very evidence of his competence left me with a flush curling up to my cheeks. What would it be like—to have someone to silently step in, share the load, carry the burden for a few short minutes? It would be intoxicating, addictive. I was certain of it.

This man, *this man* was flustered by *me*. It was a heady thought, one that left my stomach twisting with delight.

I was so entranced by the display that I didn't even recognize his need for assistance before Mrs. Ainsley and Mrs. Hudson returned. The elder took her granddaughter from Tom's arms. He murmured something to her and she disappeared back into the kitchen before returning with an overflowing bag. A hint of guilt welled in my chest, I had been exceptionally unhelpful.

"I've got the raspberry. If you've never had them, they're my favorite. There's a few almond as well." He explained as he pawed through the bag, distracted and looming over my seated form.

"Those are yours. You earned them."

His eyes were darker than I remembered, a stormy sea, when they met mine. "And if I want to share them, that is my right."

"But I didn't do anything," I protested.

"You don't need to *do* anything. Except eat a tart. Take one with you if you wish." Tom swallowed, his throat bobbing enticingly. "One last tart before you leave them behind." Something about the note of his voice was puzzling, but I could find no explanation for it in his expression.

I wanted to say yes. It was tempting to accept anything he had to offer. But I knew Davina would find some way to steal it for herself. Or mother would declare herself on a reducing diet without warning and order every sinful treat thrown from the house. Somehow, some way, it would be ripped from my grasp. And that would be worse than never having had it at all.

"I couldn't possibly."

Tom only cleared his throat in response, the sound settling low in my spine and hovering there, meaningfully.

With a short, solemn nod, he rolled the top of the bag down and snatched his gloves off the table. "Well, then. I suppose I should leave you to your day. I've monopolized more than enough of your time. I hope your haven is everything you wish and more." His tone was dull and flat, nothing earnest or sensual to be found.

"Tom..." I floundered, wondering precisely where I had gone wrong.

"Have a wonderful afternoon, Your Grace."

"Mr. Grayson," I replied with a sad nod. I watched, silent, as he slipped out the door and passed by my little window. Far from the peaceful quiet before his arrival, the space around me now felt heavy... He'd taken the peace with him. Tom left behind a disquiet that couldn't be sorted.

Fourteen

GRAYSON HOUSE, LONDON - JUNE 17, 1816

TOM

ANOTHER NIGHT, another ball. At least this was Kate's and she had been able to guilt Mrs. Hudson from her retirement to cook for the event.

Hugh regretted his poor performance during the first ball his wife hosted so he had a tendency to glue himself to her side during these events. Which left the study for Michael to commandeer until the lure of his wife became too great.

Kate's guest selection tended to include those she generally liked, regardless of station, so the company was nearly always better than it was at other events. My only concern was her propensity toward matchmaking.

If I hid in the study drinking jovially with Michael, Kit, and Augie... Well, that was an hour or two less for Kate to throw me at her unwed friends.

But when Mr. Hart arrived, Michael made quite a mess of *that* interaction. It was too painful to watch, and I was forced to abandon him to his shame.

A quick glance in the ballroom confirmed I had no

interest in any of what was happening there. Instead, I trailed listlessly down the halls, then climbed the steps unnoticed to the family wing.

Mine was the second door on the left, as it had always been. There was the familiar nick in the oaken wood beside the brass handle where I had drunkenly attempted to unlock the already unlocked door with a penknife at sixteen.

The absence of dust over the mahogany dresser and clean grey bed linens reflected the addition of several members of the staff with the improved financial situation of the estate. But the fundamentals were unchanged. Small writing desk below the window, too-large wardrobe beside it, dresser across from the too-small bed—all precisely as I had left them.

Absently, I traced a finger across the dresser, obstructed only by a few knickknacks. A cufflink box that contained precisely one cufflink, the other lost to the ages. A tin soldier, half melted in an ill-conceived experiment with Hugh and a magnifying glass. A wooden token Michael once allowed me to win off him in a game of hazard. The old penknife responsible for the nick in the door—father's.

Whispers of the orchestra below floated along the corridor and up the stairs, offering the suggestion of an evening's occupation.

Disinterested, I flopped down on the bed. As always, my feet hit the board, even with my knees bent. Christ, I really was a damned cricket.

I curled up on my side facing the window. The moon was bright and low, just kissing the roofs of the homes behind us. It was a lovely night for Kate's ball. At least she would be pleased. There was no threat of rain to dampen the evening, nor wind to muss hair and gowns.

Crickets or grasshoppers—I suppose as a cricket myself I ought to be able to differentiate, but I couldn't—joined with musicians below. The effect was surprisingly lovely. I was content to listen to the strange, beautiful amalgamation of man and nature and watch the moon rise in my too-short bed. It was a more pleasant fate than what awaited me downstairs. Hours of pointless chatter with ladies whose hopes I would dash—no, I would delay that as long as possible.

The night was so still that I actually startled when one of the small treetops swayed. Just the one...

It was a significant enough change to have me unfurling from the bed in favor of whatever intrigue was happening below.

A jolt went through me. Awareness, hot and live, danced along my spine. Rosehill, in all of his orderly perfection, leaned heavily against the very tree—barely more than a sapling.

I was halfway out the door before I realized I'd made the decision. The servants' staircase was a safer bet than the main for such an endeavor and I slipped out through the kitchens.

It was the work of but a moment to turn the corner. And there he was, even more handsome without glass and distance between us.

His head was tipped back, crown resting against the thin trunk. Above him, deep in the branches, a bird released a little two-note song.

I crossed the small lawn to him.

"I already feel ridiculous, you do not need to laugh at me," he muttered under his breath.

My feet planted in the damp grass, parsing the previous moment for any hint of laughter.

The bird let out another little high-low chirp and understanding dawned. Its song did sound like laughter.

I cleared my throat. The effect was instantaneous. Rosehill jumped perhaps half a foot in the air, his hand jolting to his chest as his gaze snapped to mine.

"Sorry," I whispered sheepishly.

"You!" It was too loud to be considered a whisper, but the tone was there.

"Me?"

He shook his head, hand dragging along his chest and stomach before finding his side. The effect was entirely too enticing to have been an unconscious maneuver.

"You do not know this yet, but once you reach a certain age, you're at risk of one good fright stopping your heart entirely and it just not starting again."

"I'm almost certain that's not true." I took another step toward him, keeping my movements slow so as not to startle him again.

"Well, it certainly feels that way."

There was a hint between his words about how it was my presence that made him feel that way. It was certainly true of his effect on me. But we weren't there—not yet.

"I didn't mean to frighten you. I had no idea you were in attendance."

"I wasn't supposed to be. I sent my regrets because I thought to be finalizing my trip. But then..."

"Then?" I breathed.

"Then this morning."

Nothing in the world could have restrained my smile, nor another step halving the distance between us.

"Is your sister off causing mischief somewhere?"

"No, she is actually quite cross with me. I told her I could not attend and mother was otherwise occupied. I expect she'll never forgive me when she finds out. We can only hope I'll be safely in Scotland by then."

"So you're here alone." It was a redundant statement, but Christ, I wanted to hear him say it. "No other responsibilities?"

"Oh, I have plenty of responsibilities. I'm just neglecting all of them in favor of... this."

Another step. It was too close for propriety and I'd never cared less.

"Good."

His gaze flicked to the French doors opening off one of the retiring rooms. "Someone could come out."

"I'd offer my room upstairs. But I expect you'd say no."

"I would, but it would be a hardship to do so." His fingers twisted into a knot in front of him. I was so close that a knuckle brushed my stomach. The muscles danced in answer.

"Damn. I should have asked." I caught one of the gloved hands in mine, then pulled him to the side yard opposite of the kitchens. Urging him toward the little wrought iron table that abutted a backless bench. It must have been Kate's addition because it hadn't been there in my youth. *God bless Kate.*

"There, we'll have warning if anyone slips outside." I pressed him down on the bench, not releasing his hand. I threw a leg over the bench and plopped down beside him as though astride a horse.

"You're much bolder tonight," he commented.

I shrugged. "You know now. The motivation of all of my fumblings is readily apparent."

"And that was all it took to erase the fumblings?"

"You're here. You're here to see me." I felt the smile overtake my face, wide and bright, deepening when he groaned, his head tipping back to the sky.

"Don't," I said, tugging at the hand I'd claimed. "I'm glad you came. So, so glad."

His head hinged back up to meet my gaze. His lips were tipped to one side, hiding the smile beneath.

For no other reason than because I wanted to, I caught the tip of his forefinger and dragged the glove down. Then the middle. The ring. Littlest. Thumb. I caught his gaze, waiting for protest. When he was silent, I worked the glove off of his hand and dropped it on his knee.

Bare skin met for the first time in weeks as our fingertips touched. My heart was set to explode. Was this what he meant before—about a heart stopping and never starting again? It would be worth it.

A glance at his face showed he was just as infatuated with the sight and sensation of our fingers as I was. And when his fingers slotted with mine, it trapped my breath in my chest. When those fingers closed on mine, and our palms kissed, the breath escaped in a rush.

"I cannot believe you're here," I said.

He shook his head and a lock of hair escaped his precise grooming efforts. "I shouldn't be."

That strand—it called to me. With my free hand, I brushed it back to join the rest while my heart clenched on nothing. "Don't say that. Let me have tonight—let *us* have tonight. Be a duke tomorrow. Be with me tonight. One more night."

His tongue darted between his lips. "All right, tomorrow."

"That was easy."

"I said I shouldn't be here, not that I didn't want to be."

With that confirmation, I set about removing the other glove with far less hesitance than the first. Though, performing the task entirely with my left hand slowed the process slightly.

"I've been thinking," he began, "about what you said that night, about how you see the world? I think it's probably a little like right now. The dark, with only the moon—it washes away the reds and greens. It leaves the blues and grays behind. It's not perfect, and it's hard to keep my head from correcting the color on its own. But it's my best guess of what your world is like."

"It is?"

He pointed to the house. A few new rose bushes bloomed against the wall. "Those are red, I'm almost certain. Mostly because Lady Grayson seems to have a preference for red roses. But they're kind of brown in the blue moonlight."

"Dull, isn't it?" I teased.

"Not at all. It's rather... enchanting."

"Well, that's unreasonably kind."

"I paint. With watercolors. I've been working on a landscape for weeks that just wasn't quite right. And now I know why. It needed a brush of moonlight."

"You paint?"

"Not with any particular skill. But it passes the time," he said, brushing away the thought with his free hand.

"I'm absolutely certain that isn't true."

"Oh, it is. I've seen the greats. I own a few myself. I have an excellent understanding of my own talents and they are middling at best."

"I'd like to be the judge of that."

"Oh, absolutely not," he said, rearing back, incredulous.

"Now I'm dying to see something,"

"No one sees my work," he insisted.

"Why?"

"Because it's not very good. I've told you."

"That's a subjective measure."

"It is objectively not very good. And it's not false modesty. I've been reliably informed that they're nothing special."

"By whom? You just said no one sees your work."

His eyes slipped shut as he tipped his head back, lip trapped between his teeth. Just as suddenly, all the tension escaped in a great sigh. It was completely ridiculous to find that as arousing as I did. But thoughts of other situations where he might release such an explosion of tightness came without bidding.

"My father. So you see, if my own father could find nothing worthy of praise within them, they are truly not anything worth viewing."

It wasn't the first time I'd wanted to throttle a dead man, but it was the first time that man wasn't *my* father. "My father found nothing worthy of praise in Michael. Father allowed him to be mistreated by my mother and Hugh. And when my father died, Michael cleaned up the mess he left behind, far better than he could have managed on his own. Fathers don't know everything."

"What?"

"Father left the viscounty with nothing. We were weeks, perhaps days from losing it all. And in a few years, Michael brought it back to a thriving estate, all in Hugh's name. When Hugh came of age, Michael handed it off without a word and built Wayland's. Then Hugh, the heir, the true-born first son, ran it back into the ground. Tell me, was my father right?"

Xander's brow furrowed, considering me. "I... I had no idea."

"No one did. Once Hugh sorted up from down in the mess of ledgers, we had to borrow from Michael again. Hugh and I have been able to make some improvements to the estate, but it will still be some years before we can begin to repay him. Not that he will accept, of course."

He'd never said as such, but Michael had an odd sort of pride. And as much as he enjoyed bankrupting the titled, he would never allow the loan to be repaid. He had created a separate account for me after Father died. It gave me the means to live independently, even after everything fell apart. I had no doubt he'd begun doing the same for little Henry and any other babies Grayson that came along.

"I can see now why a lady would prefer scandal with Wayland to a respectable life with me."

It took a moment to grasp his meaning, but when I did, it was with a laugh.

"If I'm honest, you two might have suited each other. You may have been happy together, at least as happy as it is possible to be under such circumstances. But those two... Well, Hugh and Kate got on like oil and water when they first married. But Jules and Michael? They complement each other, make each other better. I'm sorry to say, but once he gave her a book it was only a matter of time."

"I could've given her a book," he murmured defensively under his breath.

"I should also apologize for my part in it."

"What part?"

"In my defense, I urged her to consider carefully before choosing Michael. But... I can't say that I encouraged her to choose you either. And I certainly provided moral support when she decided to take a torch to her old life."

"Oh, so it is you I should blame for my humiliation?" he grumbled. In spite of the overtone, I could hear the smile beneath.

"I accept full responsibility for my part in it. But how could I be expected to encourage her to wed you? I was aflutter with boyish feelings. I couldn't very well see you married to another."

"Oh, I'm sure."

"That I couldn't see you wed to another? It would have been devastating. It will be devastating, one day."

"Tom... This isn't—"

I couldn't bear to hear him finish that sentence. To tell me that this—whatever it was—wasn't worth being devastated over. "One thing I never understood. How did it come about? The engagement?"

His eyes slipped shut and he shook his head. "Oh, that. Only the worst thing I've ever done. Would you like a list of my other sins as well?"

"Honestly? Yes. I want to know anything you'll tell me."

He passed over that opening, instead rushing to explain. "There have been rumors of some form or another for as long as I can remember. It probably started when I was in school. I don't rightfully know. Regardless, once Gabriel passed and it was clear Cee wasn't with child, Father demanded I wed. There were brief courtships. Nothing serious enough to be noteworthy by the *ton*. Then there was Lady Charlotte."

"Lady Charlotte James?" That must have been before I was moving in society. "Was she less of a shrew then?"

"She wasn't—hasn't... Her father—She hasn't had it as easy as everyone thinks. Her father is cruel. Rumors must have made it back to him because when I went to speak with her father, he made it quite clear that he would never consent to a match with a molly. And that I wasn't to speak to his daughter ever again or he would expose me."

"So you never spoke to her again?"

"What else could I do? A few weeks later, she was wed to Lord James. And quite clearly unhappy about it. She may have been after me for my title and wealth, but I was using her as well.

"After that, the rumors only got worse. I'm not—I don't behave the way a duke ought. I'm titled and wealthy, but I'm not popular. People are happy to gossip. And somehow Westfield, desperate for cash, heard the gossip. He came to me with an offer—an ultimatum. Wed his daughter, pay his debts, and he would keep his trap shut.

"It seemed that once she had finished caring for her stepmother's illness, he no longer had a use for Juliet. She was another mouth to feed and a dowry to pay—one he had gambled away. He thought to use me to kill two birds with one stone. And Juliet... You're right, we would have suited. A marriage to her would solve my problems as well. And until she came to me to end the engagement, I'm afraid she wasn't a person so much as a solution to a problem.

"I'm not proud of it, if you were wondering. I'm ashamed."

"I didn't mean to imply that I thought you were. And she never, not once, blamed you for the situation."

"She wouldn't. She's far too kind to survive in my family. Mother and Dav would've walked all over her. Cee, too, probably. Though she would've been nicer about it." He chuckled at the thought.

"She's stronger than most people know. Her father..."

"Yes, that was a shock. I honestly thought she'd run to Gretna Green before she'd do something like *that*."

"Oh, she certainly would have. But Michael was licking his wounds in the silver hells," I said, grinning at the memory of my scotch-soaked brother learning of his future wife's plan.

"Well, I suppose she allowed me a little more dignity than the alternative."

"What do you plan to do then? About a wife? And an heir?"

"Nothing. The estate and title will pass to some second cousin or other. I hope to outlive Mother and see Dav settled. But I've arranged funds for them if that turns out not to be the case. Cee as well, though I think Will may have been offended at the notion. And he's the only contender for her affections in years."

"So just... nothing at all?"

"Precisely. I've ruined one lady's life and nearly done the same to another. I think that's more than enough for one lifetime. I do not need to devastate a third."

"And your legacy?"

"Legacy is hogwash made up by people who've built nothing, earned nothing, saved nothing, done nothing worthwhile in their lives. All to make themselves feel better about the utter banality of their existence. Look at them in there," he said, gesturing to the house. "They were placed where they are by luck, happenstance. They were born to privilege and power by chance and think they've earned it.

"My father wasn't a good man. He wasn't intelligent, or benevolent, or kind. He was manipulative and cruel. He was an utter simpleton who happened to be born the eldest son of a duke. And me? I wasn't even born to be a duke. But here I am, merely because my elder brother couldn't be convinced to stop fixing races. I don't have some innate ability to lead because of it."

He spoke with passion, with conviction. His hands danced to emphasize his point. I could watch him speak for hours about nothing and still be fascinated. There was a grace to his movements that was purely masculine. Nothing was delicate or tentative but smooth and sure. I wanted more, anything, everything he had to give me.

My stunned silence must have lasted too long because he flinched. "That was too much, wasn't it? This is why I don't speak."

"No! No," I insisted. "I'd never considered it. But you're not wrong. My family is more than proof of that. Hugh is learning, and some day he may be a great viscount. But it's not natural to him the way it is Michael."

"I... There are a lot of things that society deems as the natural order. And things they've decided are unnatural. I think it's mostly twaddle."

"I can only disagree on one point."

"And what's that?" he demanded.

"I think you're a great duke. At the very least, you're a great brother and son."

He scoffed. "Davina runs roughshod over me. Of course she likes me."

"I suspect she would run roughshod over everyone."

"Almost certainly. That doesn't make me a good duke. At least not any better than anyone else would be in the role."

"You've managed to keep her alive. And out of the hands of pirates. Mostly," I added with a grin.

"You do that a lot."

"What?"

"The way you tease me. No one does that."

"I'm... sorry?" I replied, half in question, half apologetic.

"Don't be. I like it—at least, now that I know you're not mocking me." He shrugged, lips sliding all the way to the right side of his face in an oddly contemplative expression.

"Two decades of preventing bloodshed with humor. It's... When I'm nervous, it's how I... it's my way."

"So I make you nervous..." There was something light, pleased in his tone.

"This cannot be new intelligence," I grumbled, glancing away.

"Oh, but it is. I'm seeing our every interaction with new eyes. It paints you in a far more charming light."

"That's... good?"

"I make you nervous," he repeated with a pleased little seated dance.

"You do," I agreed. It was impossible to argue when he was so delighted at the possibility. And it was the truth, regardless. "It's just that, when I'm in the presence of such a wealthy and powerful duke, you know..."

He rolled his eyes.

"Handsome too."

"Your eyes don't work properly," he retorted before his hand caught his mouth. Wide-eyed, he stared waiting for my anger.

If anyone else had said it, I might have been, not that I would have done anything about it. But a tease back from him... That was ecstasy. I held back the laugh as long as I could before it burst free.

"You're not very practiced at teasing, are you?" I bit out between chuckles.

His laughter joined mine and the tension in his form dissipated with every huff. "I'm quite good at being teased."

"You are. You can practice on me—truly—any time you wish."

Xander nodded, considering me.

"While you're still here, I mean," I added.

He didn't say anything, just continued his study of me. What he was looking for, I couldn't say. There was nothing cruel in the expression. The only thing I could read was interest.

And when our eyes met, it was different, somehow, than any time before. There was nothing of secrecy between us. We both knew the clock was ticking on this evening and that it was likely to be our last.

Then Xander leaned forward, just the tiniest bit, imperceptible to anyone not studying him. But the movement was there, and my breath caught in my chest at the thought.

My answering lean was stilted and aborted too soon when nerves overtook desire. Fortunately, Xander had no such qualms. My motion was his permission.

His hand, soft and warm and too large to be anything but male, caught my jaw, holding me where he wished. When his eyes searched mine one more time, he found whatever answer he needed. Because in the space between one breath and another, he closed the distance, and his lips met mine.

Fifteen

GRAYSON HOUSE, LONDON - JUNE 17, 1816

XANDER

It was a simple press of the lips. For a long moment, that was all it was. Perfectly lovely with the appropriate fluttering of nerves and excitement in the chest.

Tom was still, allowing me to brush my lips against his once, twice, a third time, but offering no further response. Satisfied with a pleasant enough kiss for our goodbye, I pulled back.

Our lips didn't have the chance to part. Instead, a desperate sound ripped from the back of his throat. His hand found my neck and yanked me back in.

There was nothing perfectly lovely about the kiss now. Nothing pleasant enough. He surged forward, lips capturing mine, parting them with his tongue. Long, elegant fingers curled around my neck, his palm cradling my face. His other hand slipped inside my coat to catch my waist while he devoured me.

It was awkward; he was still astride the bench while I faced forward. The angle was all wrong. His movements were inelegant and limbs ungainly as he dragged one palm down my chest and carded his fingers through my hair with the other.

Tom was incapable of deciding what he liked. Instead, he seemed to try everything, everywhere, all at once. Every thought he'd ever had about kissing, he experimented with them all. It was entirely obvious that this was his first kiss—at least the first that he'd enjoyed. It *should* have been wretched.

And I'd never been more aroused. This man, far too young and inexperienced for the likes of me, moved with the wild hunger that only came from years of repressed feelings. And he had my heart ready to break free from my chest and my cock ready to rip a hole in my trousers.

It was impossible to keep up with him, impossible to predict his next movement. I surrendered to the reckless, wanton caresses. And I let him take what he needed as I tried desperately to hang on. The heady fact was, what he wanted—needed—was *me*.

His frustrated whimper tugged at my heart when his hand tangled in my cravat, unable to undo it one-handed, with his eyes closed. And clearly the other hand was unwilling to abandon the strands of hair it had curled itself into.

I pulled as far away as he would let me, mumbling into his lips, "Sweet— slow down. You're going to choke me."

Those words seemed to penetrate the haze of lust and he pulled back. Eyes wide, he stammered, "Fuck, I-I didn't mean to—"

"Not that I'm entirely opp—never mind—" *Too soon, far too soon.*

"I'm sorry. That was... not my first time. But the first one that..."

"—Was with a man? Yes, that was readily apparent." I fought to keep the smile from overtaking my swollen lips.

"That felt like *that*," he corrected. His expression reflected none of the irritation of his tone. "And yes, with a man. And it certainly... confirmed a few things. One of which is that I should not have encouraged you to learn to tease."

"Tell me more about this confirmation," I instructed, my hand reaching for my tangled cravat. His eyes followed my movement as I found one loop and pulled the end through and free. Then they snapped to meet my gaze, heat darkening them to a stormy navy blue—just barely visible in the moonlight. I found where the fabric looped back over and tugged it under still one-handed. His throat bobbed as his attention flitted back to my movements.

With my free hand, I made a go-on gesture.

"Can you repeat the question?" he asked, tongue darting out to taste his lower lip.

He'd managed to knot the cravat quite thoroughly. And perhaps I was drawing this display out—just a little. But I couldn't recall the last time a man looked at me with such hunger. It was flattering, and more than a little arousing.

"You said our kiss confirmed some things. I want to hear about the things."

He blinked slowly, still distracted by my hand that was still untangling the last loops of the cravat.

"Why are you undoing your cravat?" he asked, entirely disregarding my question.

"It was in your way. And strangled by my own neckerchief in Grayson's yard isn't the way I'd like to go."

"I don't—" He cut himself off, straightening. "I'm not entirely clear on what the objection is. Is it the strangulation itself, the object used for it, the location, or the owner of the location that displeases you?"

"All of it, to varying extents. And you're dodging my question."

His lips turned down into what should have been a frown but somehow read as a smile. "Until I met you, I had a suspicion or two. But I thought... I wasn't capable of those feelings, the ones all the poets write about. Or perhaps they were all made up, that... attraction, was just a lie everyone told themselves to get through the day. But when I saw you, I knew that it wasn't a lie. And just now... I'm positive the rest isn't a lie either."

"The rest?" I pressed. Now finished with the cravat, I left the ends to hang loose around my neck. The better for him to grab onto—at least now that the risk of death by overeager lover was mitigated.

He sighed. "The buttons on my falls are sure to give up their efforts any moment now. Are you happy?"

"Yes, very," I whispered, closing the gap between us once more. It seemed as though whatever mania had overtaken him before was dimmed. But the enthusiasm was still there.

His lips were soft and gentle against mine, but sweet, pressing back, melting under my tongue. Tom opened for me so beautifully. Meeting my every move with one of his own. A heartbreakingly beautiful dance, at least when I remembered that we would only have tonight to perfect it.

At last, his hand found the loose ends of my cravat, tugging on it with just enough possessiveness to remind me of the wiry strength I'd admired in his forearms.

I could admit it now, if only to myself, I was attracted to Tom Grayson in a way I hadn't been attracted to anyone in years, perhaps ever. He was too young, too inexperienced, and too male—in every way that could be interpreted—to be appropriate. But my body could not have cared less. Not when my hand raked through coarse, unruly curls.

His chest was firm, not broad but defined under the layers of fabric. And delightfully sensitive if the groan that broke from his chest as my free hand brushed over a nipple beneath the linen was any indication. That sound tasted good on my tongue, warm amber scotch and something sharp and herbal that I couldn't name.

Tom's lips slid from mine, tasting along my jaw with something like a whimper.

"What?" I breathed, trying to catch his gaze.

He shook his head, lips finding the hinge of my jaw with a shaking breath. There he worked magic, nipping—just sharp enough to have me gasping—before soothing with lips and tongue. The effort was enough for thought to abandon me, until my entire world became the places we touched. His lips on my neck. Mine on his shoulder through coat and shirt and waistcoat I was too overwrought to pull aside. My hand on his cheek and still trapped in close-cropped curls. His on my jaw. And still I wanted more.

My mind, lost in sensation, took a moment to comprehend the shudders running through Tom's form.

I pulled away but his fist in my cravat caught me short. With the hand on his cheek, I tugged him from my shoulder. "Tom?"

His shuddering breath was harsh in the night air. "I don't know." A pink tongue darted out along swollen lips as he dragged a frustrated hand through tangled curls. "Too much. Not enough. I'm burning. If we keep going, I'm going to combust. But I never, ever want to stop."

I could recall the feeling of overwhelm, though not as affecting as it seemed to be for Tom. The first quick fumblings that held the possibility of *more* were long forgotten memories from some hazy Mediterranean night. Surely, I had been physically overwrought, but this... this was something different. Precious.

Something in my gut twisted painfully. Tom was a second son, a second son with a healthy and whole elder brother with an heir of his own. Tom could have his own tour, and there he could find a gentleman who could give him more than a quick fumble outside a party. They could have a precious forever together.

I swallowed the knot in my throat. "We should stop. This isn't the time or place for this."

There. I'd said it. And he would never know the cost. My own insides were as tremulous as his hands. My breath, steady on the face of it, ripped a hole in my chest. This man needed me, wanted me. I was important to him. And I was a greedy man, desperate to take whatever precious pieces of himself he wanted to bestow on me. Take them. Keep them. Lock them away to keep me warm during the lonely nights sure to come. But they didn't belong to me.

His only response to the insistence that cost me everything was a groan as his forehead hit my shoulder.

"There is a ball inside," I added, strengthening my argument. Whether that was for his benefit or mine was irrelevant.

"Kate is used to me missing the entirety of her parties."

"Someone could see or hear."

"They haven't," he protested, his hand catching my chin and trying to drag my lips back to his.

"Tom, we can—"

He won the battle, his mouth claiming mine again before nipping at my lower lip. I wasn't a saint. Not even close. If he offered me the things I wanted, who was I to say they weren't mine to take? This time, it was my fingers tangling in his cravat, working at the knot with blunt nails.

"Tom, are you out— Oh..."

Ice filled my veins and my stomach sank at the masculine tone. Tom was frozen as well, too still even for breath.

I pulled back slowly, willing this to be a hallucination, a dream, anything but the irate viscount I was sure to find when I turned.

But it wasn't a figment, it wasn't a premonition, it was Lord Grayson standing before us. His mouth twisted in such a way that it would've been amusing in another situation, like he'd swallowed a frog.

"Lord Grayson," I croaked out. Perhaps I was the one who'd gnawed on a frog.

"Your Grace." His voice was dead, leaving nothing to indicate his thoughts on the situation he'd stumbled on.

"Hugh!" A feminine voice cried from the door. Juliet raced around the corner, slipping on the grass as she rounded it. It was the least graceful maneuver she'd ever made, at least in my presence.

He spun to face her, moving to cover her eyes with a hand. "Inside, Juliet," he commanded.

"But..."

"Inside. Keep everyone inside."

"Perhaps Michael—"

"No. Inside. Now."

She turned to head back with a sag in her shoulders, but flashed an expression of sympathy in our direction before she rounded the corner. Something about her movement must have jolted Tom out of his shock. He snapped to his feet, throwing his leg back over the bench and striding forward, hands outstretched. An attempt to placate the viscount.

It took a moment to comprehend, to recognize. But he'd thrown himself between me and his brother. And though it was an entirely inappropriate thought, I rather wanted to kiss him again for the effort.

"Hugh..." he began. Seemingly, it was all he'd managed to plan out because he hung on the name, dragging it out.

"Sit, Tom," he said, crossing his arms.

"No, Hugh. Please... It's not—"

"What I think? Please, enlighten me, Tom. Because I'd love an explanation beyond the obvious."

"I..."

There was something about the single letter, barely a word. The desperation, the hurt, the fear, all wrapped in that syllable that cracked my heart, the fissure creeping along until the greedy, underused, muscle gave way. It broke, leaving that same, ill-considered noble sentiment that had been quelled by Tom's lips, tongue, teeth.

I clambered to my feet. "It was me."

Hugh's only response to my outburst was a raised brow.

"I seduced him," I added.

"What! No! He—I—no!"

"I did. I seduced him," I insisted. Tom turned back to me, eyes full of something distressingly close to betrayal. I swallowed the instinctive guilt. Someday he would thank me. When the day came that he was grateful for the love of his family.

"Explain," the viscount demanded.

"Hugh, he didn—"

"Damn it all to hell and back, Tom. Inside. I can't even look at you right now," Lord Grayson hissed.

Silence crashed over us. The naked anguish on Tom's face splintered whatever was left of my heart.

"Go," I whispered.

Wordlessly, he turned back toward the house.

"The back steps, Tom," Lord Grayson added.

His retreating form shrank still further, as though he'd been crushed under the weight of his brother's disapproval and my confession.

Turning back to Lord Grayson, I steeled myself for the inevitable fist.

Instead, I was met with a stern slash of a mouth and inscrutable grey eyes, but his fists remained clenched, stacked underneath crossed arms.

"Are you trying to get him killed?" He laid the horrifying question between us with an eerie calm.

"No! Of course not."

"Really, because your complete lack of discretion indicates otherwise. How long has this been going on?"

"Tonight. Just tonight."

"Do not lie to me," he said, tone blade-sharp.

"I'm not lying."

"I saw—we saw—you at White's the other day. And, in retrospect, his reaction was not that of an unaffected bystander."

My instinctive wince did nothing to soften what I now knew as icy rage in his furrowed brow and slate gaze.

"It was tonight, truly. We'd spoken before, but nothing more."

"And tonight you decided to seduce him."

"Yes."

"Why?"

I hadn't considered this part. The part where I would need to play the merry rake. The part where I would have to cheapen a moment that had been sweet. Precious. I called forth the memories of Gabriel's misspent youth, rocking back on my heels. "I'm leaving town. It seemed like an entertaining way to spend an evening."

Lord Grayson's jaw clenched but he said nothing.

"I was tired of footmen and valets. In the mood for a challenge."

He sighed, dragging one hand through his hair before nodding to the bench behind me. "Sit."

My body obeyed the command instinctively and plopped back on the bench with no grace.

"If you were not such a terrible liar, I would be calling for my small sword."

"But—"

"You have induced my brother to disregard his safety and potentially his life. Convinced him to forsake, not only his reputation, but mine, my wife's, my son's as well. And then you try to claim blame for what was clearly a very consensual seduction, if a seduction at all. I am going to need you to explain this to me. Because I do not understand it." The viscount paced through his speech, pausing to stare at me briefly before resuming his efficient, practiced strides.

The moonlight glinted off my hessians as they swished back and forth, cutting divots through the grass.

"Do you love your wife?" I asked.

"What has that to do with anything?"

"Just... do you love her?"

"Of course. My love for her... the risks you have taken with her reputation. It is one of the reasons I am so tempted to run you through. But if I did that, I would certainly have to abandon her in exile. And thus she is also one of the reasons that I have refrained."

I swallowed the knot.

"And before her? Women in general, you appreciated their form? Enjoyed their flirtations?"

He shrugged a single shoulder, then settled his arms back across his chest.

"I don't... When a woman flirts with me... I don't *feel* that."

"I did not either. Not until Kate. Perhaps Tom just has not met the right lady."

"It's not like that. Not for me. I don't know about To— Mr. Grayson." A sharp glare had me retreating to formality. "All the pleasant things the poets write about. I feel them when I look at men—some not all."

"So, when you look at me, you feel..."

This conversation could not possibly be going more poorly. Although it could involve more weapons. "You're a handsome man. In general, I don't allow myself to consider such things. But if I did..."

He shifted back a half step.

"I'm not going to seduce you. Christ, I'm not explaining this well. You, presumably, find many ladies handsome. But you do not desire them the way you do your wife? It is the same for me."

"But you desire Tom. In that way."

Did I? I wasn't entirely sure how Lord Grayson felt about his wife. But I'd made a mockery of this conversation thus far. I couldn't very well question him further on his sentiments toward his wife. "Yes," I settled on.

"And he... desires you in the same way."

"You would have to ask him."

"And these *desires* are strong enough to risk your reputation, your family's reputation, your title, your life?"

"Not historically, no. Tom is very... Imagine, for a moment, that you weren't married to Lady Grayson. That you could never marry her. Ever. That you could never share a life with her. That you couldn't offer her the protection of your name and your body. That you would have to spend every day for the rest of your life dreaming of what it would be like if only you could press your lips against hers. And you would know that nothing would change. Every day would be the same torture, until the day you die. That even wanting to touch her would lead to your ruin, your family's ruin, her ruin. And you knew she felt the same, that being apart from you was causing her the same anguish it was causing you."

He swallowed, jaw flexing. With no response forthcoming, I continued. "Now, swear to me that you wouldn't slip up. Ever. That your eyes wouldn't meet across a crowded room and cause your will to break."

For a long moment, he considered me, silent and still. Without warning he jolted forward, turning to sit beside me. His elbows met knees with his head bowed.

"I... That must be difficult," he said to his shoes. "But you must know I cannot allow this. We—I am not a duke. I have nothing like your wealth. There are things that the *ton* might be willing to overlook from you that they will not forgive Tom for. And I cannot allow that to happen to him."

"I *am* leaving. Truly. I am bound for Scotland and I do not anticipate a return. I'll leave. And he will forget me. He's young."

"He is the same age I was when I wed Kate."

"Precisely, far too young," I teased gently.

"I think you should go. There is a back gate through there," he added, gesturing toward the other side of the house. "I will make your excuses if anyone asks after you."

"All right. Would you, can you pass a message on to T— Mr. Grayson for me?"

His gaze met mine for the first time in several minutes. There was a sorrow to his molten silver eyes. "I do not think that would be wise. A clean break, I think, would be best."

My stomach sank but I nodded. "Very well."

I stood and made my way to the indicated gate, legs heavy with pooled blood.

"Good luck in Scotland," Lord Grayson whispered behind me.

I nodded, not bothering to face him, as I slipped the rusted latch free. The gate didn't swing open; instead, it groaned with disuse both opening and closing. My heart joined in its protest.

Sixteen

40 BLOOMSBURY ST, LONDON - JUNE 30, 1816

TOM

The fervency with which I was avoiding Hugh was truly impressive.

It used to be a regular event—avoiding one or the other of my brothers. But not like this.

I hadn't left my apartments in days, instead pacing, drinking—tea and whiskey in equal measure—trying and failing to read, and reliving the life-changing moment when Alexander Hasket, Duke of Rosehill's lips met mine. And cringing when I reached the end of that memory and Hugh's shocked, horrified voice washed over me like frozen rain.

How was it possible to have your greatest wish and your worst nightmare wrapped into one shining, rotting memory?

The kiss—it had been the culmination of weeks, months, years of moments between Xander and me, coincidental and contrived. And it had been everything I'd ever wanted. It was heart and heat, sweet and sensual, raw and restrained. And Hugh, stodgy, proper Hugh, destroyed it.

After he'd ordered me inside with all the lofty, formidable viscount he could infuse in his tone, I slipped out of Grayson House and into the night.

No word of a duel between an imperious viscount and an unlikely duke appeared in the papers—so at least their conversation hadn't come to blows. And Mother hadn't seen fit to grace my humble abode with her presence—presumably he hadn't told her either. Perhaps Hugh was content to never see me again. Or more likely he had reverted to his former problem-solving method which involved ignoring the problem until it resolved itself or exploded in his face.

I hadn't bothered with the grey curtains that morning, or any of the others. Daylight peered in around the edges, threatening me. Last evening's drink left me bottle weary and I doubted today would be the day I braved the curtains.

The collection of empty tumblers and teacups on my table was beginning to disgust even me, though I still left one or two unused—perfect for at least another day or two.

As the second son of an impoverished viscount, I didn't employ a valet, and my maid had been caring for an unwell mother for some weeks. She'd likely quit when she returned and saw the state of the place.

The chamber pot was calling me but the thought of moving was exhausting. Instead, I watched the light spilling in from above the curtain spread in an ever-lengthening semicircle across the ceiling.

My bedding was unmade and smelled of sweat and whiskey, and the scent wasn't improving my stomach. Tea would help, but I'd have to make it first—and that was an unappealing thought.

With a sigh that would have been performative if I had an audience, I rolled to my side and curled my knees up. There, on my bedside table, lay a metallic snuffbox—the one I'd stolen from the Duchess of Sutton like a desperate child because Xander's fingers brushed mine when he handed it to me on Hugh's wedding day.

With the curtains drawn, the light couldn't reach it, didn't caress the delicate facets sending fractals dancing around the room. That, more than anything, had me considering the curtains with more seriousness.

Before I had worked up the will to move, a heavy knock in the entry rattled the door in its frame and my stomach dropped.

I rolled over, silent, desperately praying Hugh would assume I was away, but another few pounds sounded from the hall.

"Tom, open up!" a masculine—distinctly not Hugh—voice called. I was all astonishment when I placed the voice of Kit.

Kit and I got along well enough at family dinners, but we weren't what anyone would consider close—certainly not visiting each other's homes close. Which meant one thing. Kate had sent him.

It was an interesting strategy, I had to give her that.

"I know you're in there—I can smell you from here."

With a sigh, I rolled to seated, grabbed a shirt from the end of the bed and gave it a tentative sniff—damn. He probably wasn't lying.

I dug a fresh-ish one from the wardrobe and tugged it over my head before padding to the hall barefoot.

"What?" I demanded as I yanked the door open.

"Christ..." His gaze flitted up and down my sad form.

"That bad?"

He nodded. "And worse, I have to admit to Kate that she was right to be worried. Do you know how insufferable she is when she's right?"

"She's only insufferable to you. She's sweet to everyone

else." I turned and trod back down the hall, leaving him to follow.

"Precisely... Did something die in here?" he asked when we reached the dining area where the majority of my cups were perilously piled.

"Tragically, no."

He hummed thoughtfully before beginning to collect the glasses in the crook of his arm.

"Leave that."

"Absolutely not. Katie would have my head if I left it like this. And don't bother glowering at me, you're not nearly as terrifying as my baby sister. Go—wash up, get dressed. I'll manage this."

"Why?"

"I shoved Will off on his honeymoon and I need an extra set of hands at the offices," he explained.

"Don't you have clerks for that?"

"Astonishingly, a few of them quit when their office nearly burnt to the ground." It was a shock when someone attacked Will Hart outside of his offices and set them alight. Though Will's injuries were relatively minor and no one else save the perpetrators were injured, I could understand the reluctance to work out of a half-ash office.

"No one has any work ethic these days..." I quipped.

"I know, such an inconvenience. Don't think you're distracting me—get dressed."

I sighed, then wandered off to my bedroom and left him to my beverage receptacle collection. By the time I returned, he had them in an orderly stack by the sink for the maid.

"I'll see if Katie can spare anyone for a day or two—you cannot live like this," Kit muttered, eyeing a teacup warily before perching it atop the rubbish pile.

"It doesn't bother me."

"Well it should." He finally glanced up at me, now mildly

more presentable after a few moments at the wash basin and a pair of fresh breeches.

"Why are you here, Kit?" I pressed.

"I told you, Katie sent me."

"But why?"

"I don't know. Didn't ask."

"You just came all the way over here on your sister's instruction with no further questions?"

He shot me a look. "You're family—even if it's by way of your arse of a brother."

"But—"

His head tipped toward the hall, and as I started down it, his hands made a shooing motion, urging me along. "This is what you do for family. I know yours hasn't been strictly... functional. But I promise, Katie and Lizzie have both done this for me a time or two. And Will as well. Now, come make yourself useful. I'll buy you one of those little cake things from Hudson's on the way."

"I prefer the tarts," I explained as we spilled onto the street and turned toward his law offices.

"Blasphemy!"

"Do you— Does Kate know— Did Hugh tell— I don't even know what I'm trying to ask."

"I gathered that," he replied, a sardonic note in his voice. "And probably—Kate always knows everything. But she was only worried after you—nothing else."

I turned to meet his gaze, trepidation slowing my steps. "You sound as though you know something."

His lips pressed in tight together, as though he were biting them shut from the inside. "I know nothing, and even if I did, it wouldn't change a thing, Tom. You're still by far the most acceptable of Katie's relations—save Jules, of course." He clapped me on the shoulder and squeezed before shoving me forward along the pavement.

"Of course," I agreed, quietly considering the implications of his words. "More acceptable than Michael?"

Kit shrugged, considering. "Yes, but do not tell him. His club is our biggest client by far."

"To the grave," I agreed.

He nodded. "To the grave."

Seventeen

KILMARNOCK ABBEY, EDINBURGH - JULY 15, 1816

Dav,

I have arrived in Scotland. Please assure Mother that I am well. Also, please send a new pair of hessians. Possibly two. The cordwainer has my sizing.

Warmest Regards,
Xander

XANDER

THE CARRIAGE MADE excellent time as it trundled away from the wreckage I'd made of Tom Grayson's life. Guilt, it seemed, was trundling along with me. It hadn't lessened in the slightest over miles of rolling hills, wet moors, and continued even as we lumbered through the peak district. The guilt, and perhaps a bit of longing.

For a few brief moments, I'd had what everyone else took

for granted—an illicit moment in a darkened corner, a sensual tryst in a moonlit garden, a sweet flirtation over a pastry.

And it had been easy, so easy, when his lips met mine, tasting of scotch and freedom, to forget the consequences. They were distant, vague, inconsequential things that didn't bear consideration with long fingers running through my hair and sliding down my waist, and a hot groan caressing my ears. Entirely amorphous, right up until the moment Lord Grayson's voice cut through the haze of affection and lust.

I shook away the memory and pulled back the curtain. The hills had increased in frequency and size, and shifted from rolling, gently sloping things to ragged craigs in the last day or so. The most recent coaching inn, I had been assured, would be the last before we reached Kilmarnock Abbey.

The view was scenic. A pretty little cerulean pond—certainly not the precise shade of Tom's eyes—the far bank dotted by a small copse of beech, oak, pine, and ash trees. The path ahead, though, was unkempt. More grass than gravel. As we continued, a house came into view. Nestled pleasantly among the trees, it had surely once been an impressive manor. Now, it had fallen victim to age. Half-dead vines crawled and dug into the lines of mortar, threatening to reclaim the tan brick facade for nature. The windows that weren't yet boarded up were broken or cracked. It was unfortunate that such a well-situated property had been so poorly cared for.

We turned, following the pond's bank, and my stomach dropped. Surely—certainly not. It couldn't possibly be—

The carriage shuddered to a halt, and I released a sigh of relief. We'd made a wrong turn. Any moment now it would lurch forward and turn back to the main road. Perhaps they needed to consult a map or—

I caught the sound of a disgruntled bleat from ahead. Sheep?

"Godfrey?" I called out the window.

"Yes, Your Grace?"

"Please tell me that we're lost."

"Wishing I could." There was a wariness in his tone I didn't like.

"We're trapped by the sheep, right? That is why we're not back on the road?"

With an unsteady hand, I opened the door. I stepped out on shaky legs, only to feel the unmistakable sinking, slipping sensation—and scent—of a boot meeting feces. My eyes slid shut for a moment before I could brave a look.

I wasn't an expert in sheep by any means, but the bleat I heard from just beyond the carriage was striking in its similarity to human laughter.

Bracing against the open carriage, I made a valiant effort to scrape the dung off my hessian and into the grass as Godfrey spilled out of his seat and over to my side with a distressed cry for the leather.

Ignoring his fussing, I called out to the driver. He, in turn, vaulted off the seat and rounded the carriage.

"I cannae get ye closer than this, Yer Grace, not without upsetting Fenella something fierce." He was tall, with a medium build and thinning hair, though what was left of it was an overgrown reddish blond. His nose was hooked and his blue eyes were clear and too small, and a thick beard, the same shade as the hair on his head, covered his jaw.

"Fenella?"

"The sheep," he clarified, as if that made the comment less absurd.

"The sheep is named Fenella?"

"Yes, Yer Grace."

"And you cannot upset her?"

"No."

"Listen..."

"Lochlan Ramsay," he supplied.

"Mr. Ramsay—"

"Lock, if ye please."

I sighed, tightening my hands into fists at my sides. This was a new start, and I couldn't—wouldn't—let my feelings be so obvious here. "Listen, Loch—"

"Lock—Loch is my wee cousin."

Too short fingernails bit into my palms. "Those sound exactly the—never mind. Lock, there must be some sort of mistake. This is not Kilmarnock Abbey."

"But it is, Yer Grace."

"Then there is another Kilmarnock Abbey—like there are numerous Lochlans."

"Afraid there's only the one, Yer Grace."

"Is there a Kilmartin? Or a Limarnock perhaps?"

"No, just Kilmarnock."

"Which is just behind this ramshackle ruin..." I gestured at the crumbling architecture before me.

"No, Yer Grace."

"You mean to tell me that this—" My hands flung up from my sides, gesticulating wildly toward the entirety of our surroundings, from the collapsing hut to the recalcitrant sheep. A tightness grew in my chest, leaving little room for air. "Is my inheritance."

"No, Yer Grace."

"What do you mean?" I was shrill. I could hear it, recognize it, but I couldn't stop it for anything.

"The sheep doesnae come with the property. She's just a bit stubborn. It's best to let her do as she wishes."

"Your Grace, if I may," Godfrey cut in. "Perhaps the interior is not..."

"Disintegrating?"

"Precisely. And I should like to get to work on this boot right away."

While I appreciated the sentiment—and ordinarily would

have agreed—I rather thought the boot was the least of my concerns at the moment.

Warily, I stepped around the carriage—carefully searching for more gifts from Fenella. She made another sound of amusement—if sheep were capable of such a thing— as I rounded her slowly.

"Is there no staff?" I called back to Lock.

"Did ye hire a staff?"

"Most assuredly, I did. I've been paying a housekeeper, butler, gardener, stable boy, and several maids since I took over management."

Lock caught us as we approached the door—shockingly still attached to the frame. It was worn, with several layers of peeling paint in shades of blue, red, and white.

"I dinnae ken who ye were paying, but no one's worked here in a decade, perhaps longer."

"I beg your pardon?"

"Which word was confusing, Yer Grace?"

"The order of them was the concern." I was flailing now. The shameful display of my agitation that I couldn't have contained for anything was accompanied by a dramatic twisting of my brow. "You mean to say I've been fleeced? For years?"

"Seems as much."

"And a Mr. Douglas McAllen? Can you take me to him?"

"Dinnae ken a Douglas McAllen."

"He's a steward—based out of Edinburgh," I said with a desperate note in my voice.

"I can take ye to Edinburgh. But I dinnae ken a Douglas McAllen—as I said."

"But your boot, Your Grace!"

"Godfrey... one more word about the damned boot and you're sleeping here tonight. Lock, I have an address."

The man shrugged. "Horses need to rest a while. Then we can head off."

A sigh broke free. With no other occupation for the next hour or so, I forced myself to turn the knob.

I was relieved to meet with the overpowering scent of age, rather than something more revolting. The movement of the door distributed dust and soot into a swirling, perilous cloud of irritants.

It was slow to settle, but eventually it dissipated to reveal an entry hall. Straight ahead was a set of stairs. Certainly, they were once fine, but the ornate railing leaned threateningly in places. The stairs, a quality mahogany, were intact by all appearances at least.

One side opened to a drawing room—the wallpapering was yellowed and moth-eaten, peeling at some edges, hanging off the wall in others. Outlines of rectangles marked where paintings had once hung. It seemed unlikely that they had been properly stored—such a waste.

The furnishings had, at least, been covered by a sheet, but they hadn't been saved from the ravages of time. Now that the dust had dispersed, I caught the scent of rot and feces—though I expected the latter was from my boot.

With a sigh, I bent awkwardly to pull it off, unwilling to risk sitting on the covered settee or chairs. Wordlessly, I handed it to Godfrey, who pinched it before wandering back outside.

"Godfrey?"

"I can say with absolute certainty that anything I find in *there* will not be an improvement on lake water and the polish I brought with me, Your Grace."

I followed him out, unable to face any more horrors. Instead, I plopped on the stoop and let my head fall to my hands.

"Yer Grace?" Lock asked.

"Just see to the horses, if you please," I retorted into the gravel beneath my one booted and one stockinged foot.

Without additional commentary, he sidestepped me, footsteps quieting as he went.

I could feel the tightness of sorrow and frustration welling in my chest, but they refused to provide the relief of a sob. Instead, my breath was harsh and jagged.

For years, Scotland had been my escape. This promised magical estate away from everything and everyone who knew me. A place I could begin anew, if need be. I funneled money into the estate every month—extra in the winters for firewood, more for the gardener in spring and summer. Ten years of pounds and shillings—all sent in the hope that this, Kilmarnock, would be there when I needed it.

Much as I loathed the way I left London—the devastation I'd made of Tom's life—I had been excited to start anew, hopeful even. In Scotland, I could be someone other than the fussy, too-particular dandy with the *ton*'s worst-kept secret.

Instead, I'd been swindled—Hell, it sounded as though even Gabriel may have been swindled if this place had been empty for more than a decade. My late brother was many things, but easily taken in was not one of them.

Perhaps it had been a cruel joke—Gabe certainly wasn't above such things, nor was he unwilling to wait for years for a payoff. But this... His schemes usually resulted in a flush pocket—not my devastation. Father might have been responsible as well, but his punishments were more direct and efficient.

But I wasn't even certain Father had been aware of this acquisition. I was but two and ten when Gabe had returned from Scotland and handed over the paperwork with a conspiratorial grin. No... he'd assured me that it was a place I could go beyond Father's reach.

A furious *maaahah* followed by Godfrey's answering

screech drew my gaze from the ground. The man skittered around Fenella, spinning so he was always facing her. Once he rounded her, he backed slowly toward me.

The sheep was large, at least ten stone, with large, curved horns, a black face, and formerly white wool. It seemed primarily content to munch on the foliage lining the front drive—only expressing irritation when someone came too close. I couldn't blame Godfrey for his wary steps.

Once he arrived before me, he spun around and presented the boot proudly. I had to admit he was skilled with a boot brush. I let him help me into it and pull me to my feet.

Together, we passed the sheep, giving her careful consideration, before reaching the carriage.

"Can we be off?" I asked Lock.

He nodded. "Horses are fine to get to the city. We can change there if ye want to return tonight."

"I assure you, I do not. Roxburgh Street, please."

Without waiting for a response, I poured myself back into the carriage, fortunately missing Fenella's gift in the process. With a quick knock on the roof, we set off again, back toward the path and civilization.

I let my head rest against the glass window as I watched the scenic cragged landscape pass with something like dread.

Time passed in a daze, and before long we turned onto cobblestone streets. My stomach had thoroughly twisted in on itself by the time we stopped in front of an unassuming stone house. Its three stories were oddly arranged, with two sets of three windows to the right of the door and a third row with a single window—unaligned with the rest—above them. A mismatched drainage pipe ran vertically along one side. There were three smaller windows randomly dotted above the black door and a bar of windows in the black-painted attic as well. Nothing of symmetry or style to be found in the facade.

Godfrey opened the door and I stepped out, checking for

surprises before planting my feet. Ten steps were all that stood between me and the man who'd seemingly been swindling me for years. I hadn't considered the possibility that he would not be in residence—I hadn't the slightest idea of what to do in that event.

I was no stranger to the anxious knot in my chest, but the cause was entirely new. The steps were worn and dipped in the middle with use. At last, I reached the door and knocked before I had a chance to panic first.

It took a moment, perhaps two, just enough for my heart to begin to pound and my fingers to twitch with the urge to fidget.

And then it swung open.

The girl was young, certainly not twenty, with a sturdy, feminine frame—just barely rounded with child. Her eyes and hair were a rich deep brown. And her brow...

There was no mistaking a Hasket brow. Grandfather's was white and overgrown in bushy bristles. Father's had been a dark, thick shock before finally streaking with grey a few years before he passed. Davina's chocolate arch required more manicuring than she would admit to. My own heavy black lines plagued me. And Gabriel—Gabriel's had been a lighter walnut brown, but still heavy and unforgettable.

This girl—this was Gabriel's daughter. I would stake my life on it.

"Can I help ye?"

Eighteen

HART AND SUMMERS, SOLICITORS, LONDON - JUNE 30, 1816

TOM

Half of "Hart and Summers, Solicitors" was a charred-out husk. The other half was untouched.

Clearly Kit had been hard at work. I knew Will's injuries had prevented him from providing much assistance. All the paperwork from Will's old office was stacked precariously along the far wall of Kit's.

The walk over had been quiet, punctuated only by a stop at Hudson's for a tart for me and a "little cake thing" for Kit. Both of which had been consumed in the few steps between the bakery and the law offices.

Kit quietly directed me to sort the paperwork in one stack by client in alphabetical piles. He set about doing something with a stack of ledgers and a pile of paperwork at the desk, leaving me with only the floor as a workspace.

The slight didn't particularly bother me—it was, after all, more practical for my task—but I was constitutionally incapable of allowing it to pass without comment. "Earls can't sit on the floor?"

Kit glared at me before returning to the documents before him. "Not an earl."

"I'm not sure that's how that works."

"I'm a solicitor. I've worked my entire life to be a solicitor—and a damn good one. People died—people I love—and now everyone thinks I'm an earl. 'M still just a solicitor."

It was quite possibly the longest speech I'd ever heard from him—and clearly a sore subject.

I turned back to the paperwork, abandoning my teasing in favor of actually sorting. If I had to be awake, vertical, and tragically sober, I might as well make myself useful. The work was slow. Some of the documents had been burned in the fire, soaked in the efforts to put it out, and then dried in wrinkled clumps. For five minutes, we worked in companionable silence before I could stand it no longer.

"Why, precisely, am I doing this? There is no possible way these documents could still be considered legal."

"I need an inventory of which accounts were burned. And you agreed to do it because Katie pestered me and I pestered you to make her stop and agreeing was the only way to make me stop."

"I sincerely doubt this is what Kate meant when she asked you to check on me."

"She was nonspecific as to how. And she forgets that some of us are employed. Besides, I've managed to coerce you into bathing and sitting upright. I'm certain Katie would consider it progress."

I honestly couldn't deny the truth of it. No sooner had I turned back to my crumpling, ashen stack than Kit's grumbly tenor washed over me. "Do you want to talk about it?"

"Absolutely not."

"All right then—back to your paperwork. And, if anyone asks, you were never here—confidentiality."

I bit back a smile and set to work. The next several

minutes were spent attempting to separate two pieces of parchment that were so fused together they may as well have been glued.

With a quick glance at Kit to confirm he was otherwise occupied, I crumpled them into a ball and tossed them toward the rubbish bin with a flourish.

"I didn't bring you here to throw away my work." I shot around, pinching my neck in the process. He hadn't even looked up from his desk.

"Whatever it was, it was lost to the fire."

"Already, I regret helping you," he muttered.

"Then perhaps I should return home and get on with my day."

"You haven't worked off your tart just yet."

With a grumble, I turned back to the fragile stack. My hands were long blackened with soot, and each touch left fingerprints lining the legible areas of the parchment. A piece disintegrated in my hand, giving way to a document relating to Michael's gaming hell. The astonishing number of zeros was yet more evidence that my eldest brother made far too much off men with infinitely more money than sense.

But God, that night at his club. An hour, perhaps a few minutes more. One hour hidden away in Michael's office—away from the glamour and drama of the masquerade ball. One hour in delicious, brave flirtation with Alexander Hasket. One hour where—behind the anonymity of a mask—I could be exactly like every other gentleman at a ball, flirting with the most beautiful person I'd ever seen.

And now he was gone—off to some estate in Scotland—never to return.

"Would you stop sighing?" Kit mumbled, then flicked a page in irritation.

"I offered to leave, you're the one who insisted on dragging me here. I was perfectly fine."

"You were still soused from last night."

"As I said, perfectly fine."

"Just sort the documents—quietly."

I created a pile for the club, and the next several documents were all associated with Wayland's.

After throwing a few more into the bin under the watchful glare of Kit, the next document, with another familiar name, had my heart stopping for the space of a breath.

There was a flourish on the *R* in Rosehill. Alexander Hasket's name and title in perfectly legible glory. Of their own volition, my fingers brushed around the script pathetically, smearing a loop of soot around the letters. I was a milksop, through and through.

Shaking away the instinctive longing, I began a new pile. It quickly became apparent that there were a great number of documents pertaining to Xander in my stack. His estate, his sister, his mother, his—now former—sister-in-law. Every facet of his life was reflected in these pages.

The man had money that nearly put Michael to shame— that much was clear. And he'd meticulously managed the funds to ensure that every single person in his life was cared for. Including his sister, who was apparently determined to see herself ruined if even half of these exploits were truthful.

"What?" Kit asked.

I turned to meet his gaze, his head cocked to the side in curiosity.

"Pardon?"

"You hummed. Did you have a question?"

"No... Yes—no."

"Which is it?" he demanded.

"I have an... inappropriate question."

"Yes?"

"Did Lady Davina truly invest in a whiskey company founded by pirates?"

His lip quirked in the corner in what I was coming to understand was his version of a smile. More than two years I'd known the man, and I couldn't recall a single genuine, teeth-baring smile. This expression might have been the closest to one though—there was a crinkle in the corner of his dark eyes.

"Still does—though she thinks no one knows. And when I first learned of it, she insisted that it be known—they're lady pirates. I'm not entirely certain why the distinction matters but who am I to question a lady?"

A fond note tinged his voice that had me biting back a smile.

"And the rest of these?" I asked, lifting up the stack in reference.

"All true, every last one." He said it with a hint of pride in the curl of his lip.

"She's a bit of a hellion then. The night at the club was nothing, it seems."

"An absolute menace," he agreed before turning back to his paperwork.

Dismissed, I returned to my own. Page after page, I unraveled a tiny bit of the mystery that was Alexander Hasket. Charitable landlord, deliberate landowner, caring brother, and doting son—his heedfulness was written in these pages.

And then I found it. On a page buried near the bottom of my original stack was an address. An address in Scotland. My heart tripped before rushing to catch up for the misstep.

It was wrong. It was entirely inappropriate. Kit would be furious. But God himself couldn't have stopped me from carefully folding the parchment into fourths—quiet as a mouse—and slipping it into my pocket.

Trembling, I returned to my sorting with a renewed vigor it didn't warrant, soot fingerprints littering the pages.

At last, around the time my back began to make a serious protest, Kit suggested we clean up and dine at a nearby pub.

Hours that felt like weeks later, I returned to my apartments with a pleasantly full belly and a promise to limit myself to no more than three glasses of scotch and assist at the offices again tomorrow.

I had no intention of keeping either promise, of course, and once I locked the door behind me, I slid down to the floor and pulled the parchment from my pocket—thankfully unharmed for my efforts.

Several glasses of scotch later, I fell into bed, entirely forgetting about the letter I'd written and addressed—abandoned atop my writing desk.

Nineteen

KILMARNOCK ABBEY, EDINBURGH - JULY 15, 1816

Xander,

I am wonderful. Thank you for asking after me in your last letter. The devastation of missing your sister is etched in every line.

Mother is fretting that you've been replaced by a changeling and they wrote your letter. I tried to explain that you're far too old and unfortunate looking for a fairy to bother with, but she would have none of it. When I reminded her that a changeling would have written a more informative and polite letter she was soothed.

I hope you like the hessians I've selected. I agonized over the choice. I am curious though, why did you not pack any?

Best Wishes,
Davina

XANDER

Time and the grief of his passing usually left me feeling rather wistful when I thought of Gabriel. But Christ the man had made a damn mess of everything he touched.

Years ago, he'd returned from Scotland with the deed to Kilmarnock and handed it off to me with a grin. I'd discovered after his passing that the acquisition hadn't been strictly aboveboard—instead the estate was won in an ill-considered card game. A practice I was astonished to learn was legal. Apparently, he'd had an even more eventful time in Scotland than he'd let on.

The woman before me was Gabriel in a delicate feminine frame—sharp jaw, heavyset brow, pale skin, straight nose—an exact match for his before it'd been broken in a tavern brawl. And she was staring at me as if I'd grown a second head.

Slowly, she made to shut the door in my face—a fair reaction to my slack-jawed stare.

"Wait—"

"Oh, are ye intending to speak, then?" She even sounded like him, voice low and throaty.

"I—" This wasn't the time, nor the place. I brushed away my astonishment for the moment. "I'm looking for a Mr. Douglas McAllen."

Her eyes widened, and she made to slam the door in my face. Instinctively, I nudged my boot against the frame—a choice I regretted immediately when door met boot with shocking strength. Biting back a curse, I caught the door and pushed it back open.

"Mr. McAllen. Now, if you please."

She even narrowed her eyes in irritation the same way my brother had. "Leave, or I'll call the constable."

"By all means, I expect the constable will be very interested to learn of my situation with Mr. McAllen." I gestured inanely toward the place a constable would stand should one exist.

"Mr. McAllen isnae home."

"I'll wait."

"Dinnae expect him for quite some time."

"I've quite literally nowhere else to go."

Slowly, she opened the door with a wary glance up and down the street. "Fine, but I warned ye."

I stepped forward, backing her in before she turned and led me down a hall and up the stairs to a little drawing room. It was decorated in rich jewel tones and decent—though not opulent—furnishings. I had a strong suspicion that my payments went here instead of Kilmarnock.

Without waiting for direction, I claimed one of the wingback chairs near the fireplace. Quietly, she took the opposite, her eyes finding her boots beneath the hem of her dove-grey dress.

"Your name?"

"Sorcha." Her gaze never left the brown leather boots—the juxtaposition of brown against grey irked me more than I liked. "Ye must be Mr. Hart."

I merely hummed.

"He will be surprised to find ye here. I ken Mr. McAllen was waiting for ye to write when yer employer planned to visit."

"Was he?"

"I just said as much."

"Indeed."

Her feet swished back and forth against the carpeting. "He's been awaiting yer letter."

"I'm certain he has."

"Is there a reason ye didnae write?"

I stretched my feet out in front of me, grasping the chair

arms to keep from my usual overwrought gestures. "Shall we dispense with the ruse?"

"I beg yer pardon?"

"There's no Mr. McAllen—I wouldn't be surprised if there never has been."

"No—he'll be back, just not for some time."

"Of course. You should know, though, Mr. Hart was injured and has been indisposed. That is why he hasn't written to announce my arrival."

"What?" Her head finally shot up, her gaze meeting mine.

"I'm Alexander Hasket—I expect that name is familiar to you."

Suddenly, Sorcha's eyes turned sharp and assessing. They dragged along my form before finally catching on my brows—dark and overgrown just as hers were.

"Yer Grace, I—"

"Swindled me out of truly astonishing sums? Yes."

"I didnae—"

"Mean to? I find that difficult to believe."

"I—"

"What I am struggling to understand is why?"

Her lips curled into a familiar smile, equal parts bitter and wry—the same one Gabriel always wore around father. I'd hated it on him and I hated it now.

"Truly? Ye dinnae know why?"

"Fine, I know why. But you could have written—if I had known of you—you would've been cared for. I didn't know you existed."

"Why should ye? I'm no one to ye."

My stomach dropped and realization crashed over me. She didn't know. Of course she didn't—how could she?

"I—forgive me. I thought—assumed. I thought you would know." My fingers itched with the urge to explain. They always worked faster than my words.

"Ken what?"

"Nothing, never mind." I waved away my previous comment, desperate to avoid this conversation. "Where is your mother?"

"Dead." Her expression, her affect was flat. There was something impossibly sad in that. Not to mention how much more difficult it would be to explain my relation to this woman.

"I am sorry for your loss."

Shrewd eyes narrowed at me once again. "Why did ye not ask after my pa?"

"I—no reason."

"Or my husband—I'm with child as ye can clearly see."

"Do you have a husband?" My curiosity suddenly peaked. I didn't know if a husband would make everything more or less complicated, but it was certainly her best hope to avoid scandal.

"No, but ye dinnae know that. Why would ye have cared for me? Because I'm with child?"

"Yes," I supplied with no real thought beyond moving past that topic. "Can we return to the reason you've been fleecing me?"

"Should've thought that would be obvious. I needed the coin."

"How long?"

"Me or Mam?"

"Your mother, too, then?"

Miss McAllen nodded.

My hand slipped free from where it was clutching the armrest to pinch the bridge of my nose. "Both, I suppose."

"Seven years, or near as much. Ma started after Pa died. I only continued the practice."

So she had a father. Perhaps I was wrong and she just bore a striking resemblance to my brother. There were other overdrawn brows in the world, other ladies with striking jawlines and chestnut hair and eyes. Just because this one happened to be around the right age to have coincided with my brother's visit didn't mean she was his.

"And the money? Is there any left at all?"

And then she dipped her chin in the same defiant manner Gabriel always used when father was lecturing him. Something twisted in my belly at the sight—whether it was longing at the mannerism or chafing at the unfamiliar sensation of relating to my father was impossible to tell.

"No," she replied sharply. That was a yes then.

"How much?"

"Are ye right in the head? I just said there wasnae any left."

"You'll have to forgive me if I do not take your word for it. Besides, I've been sending extra for improvements before my arrival. And clearly Will let you know I was intending to visit —you've been squirreling it away."

Her glare was pure Gabriel. She may have had a father—but he wasn't blood.

"Yer daft."

"And you're a thief."

Strong arms crossed high on her chest—overtop her growing belly. My eyes caught on the delicate curve. Gabriel's grandchild was growing inside her. Something ached in my heart at the realization.

Thief she may be, but she was also my niece. One last living piece of my brother—complicating life even from beyond the grave.

I sighed. "If you return what you still have, and pay back what you stole, I won't involve the law."

Her smile was sarcastic and accompanied by an unladylike snort. "If ye think I can pay ye back in this lifetime, yer dimmer than I thought."

It was an impulse, the one that kept rearing its head—

abandoning London for Scotland, seeking refuge in an empty office at a masquerade, kissing Tom Grayson. I knew, even as I made them, that they were poor choices. Ill-considered and ill-conceived, every last one. And this one—this would be even worse. But I could no more have trapped the next sentences behind my lips than I could force my heart to stop beating.

I rose and stepped toward her. "You're not going to pay me back with shillings and pounds."

"We're in agreement, then."

"You're going to help me repair the estate."

Miss McAllen blinked, eyes wide and owlish. "I beg yer pardon."

"You heard me. And you're going to help me."

She stood, mirroring my position with hands on her hips. "I think ye'll find that I'm not."

"If you do not wish to give birth on the open sea—which I promise you, you do not—I think you'll find that you will."

"They'll not sentence me to exile." Dark eyes rolled back.

"You're correct. They'll sentence you to death and if you're very, very lucky, they'll exile you instead. I'm a duke, remember. The law doesn't take kindly to crimes against nobility. And the sum you've stolen..."

"I cannae help ye. I dinnae know anything aboot fixing up a house."

"Neither do I. We'll have to figure it out together."

Her expression was wary and calculated as her gaze flicked up and down my form. Her eyes caught on my pocket. I had little doubt she'd rob me and disappear as soon as she found an opportunity. "And ye'll not call the constable."

"As long as you do not do precisely what you're contemplating—I won't call the constable."

Her glare was penetrating and awash in irritation, brow furrowed, lips curled in a snarl. "How would ye know what I'm contemplating?"

"So you weren't planning to pick my pocket and run to Lord knows where, forcing me to return to London—destitute—never to be seen again."

"I hadnae thought quite that far."

"You would've gotten there eventually."

"Such faith..." The sneer belied the words.

I shrugged. "You... remind me of someone I used to know. It's what he would've done—maybe not the pickpocketing—but he sent more than one gentleman penniless back to wherever they came from, head hung in shame."

Miss McAllen huffed out an irritated, bitter chuckle. "Can I make an arrangement with him instead?"

"You can try, but you'll have to ask the devil, himself. Or perhaps he *is* the devil... No way of knowing."

"That's unfortunate. He sounds like much more fun."

An assessment shared by nearly everyone acquainted with both Gabriel and myself. It had vexed me in my youth—but it had ceased to bother me in the months and years after his demise.

"You're not wrong—too much fun, perhaps. But, alas, you've only me to deal with. And since my estate isn't in any condition to live in, I'll need to stay here."

Overgrown brows shot so high, they hit the treetops. "Oh, no, ye'll not."

"Oh, but I will. You're not leaving my sight until my home is in perfect order."

"That could be months!"

"A generous estimate, I expect." At some point, entirely without my notice, I'd lost control of my hands, and they danced about before me, gesturing to nothing in particular. The effort only served to betray my agitation. I clenched my fists at my sides in what was certain to be a futile effort at restraint. "Perhaps you should have considered it before you stole from me!"

She let out an "Agh!" before spinning on her heels in a manner that was so perfectly reminiscent of Davina that I was forced to bite back a laugh. My sister directed that sound to me on such a regular basis that I almost considered it a term of endearment.

I padded down the hall after her—I was serious about not allowing her out of my sight—even if my reasoning hadn't been the entire truth. We reached the kitchen and she dragged a ceramic cannister across the worktop, pulled off the lid, and snatched a roll of bills from inside.

Miss McAllen thrust her fist toward me with a huff. "Here—ye can go now."

A quick flip through the bills revealed one hundred pounds. It was a struggle to keep my feelings off my face. The sum was rather impressive and reflected decent—if slightly immoral—sense. I wasn't fool enough to believe that was all of what she had stowed away. But it was certainly enough for her to live quite comfortably on for some time if she was frugal.

"And the rest?" I demanded with a raised brow.

"That's all of it."

"Do you take me for a fool?"

"Yes, if I'm honest."

"I admire the honesty. But I'm certain you've at least double this hidden away."

There was a judgmental, assessing quality to her gaze and the set of her mouth, her upper lip curled just slightly. "In my room."

"Lead the way."

Her steps were heavy as we turned back down the hall and ascended a flight of stairs. She paused outside a rickety door. "Ye cannae come in—a lady's room is private."

"You're no lady."

"It wouldnae be decent."

She wasn't quite as skilled as Davina—scheming and

adventuring was in my sister's very marrow. I suspected this was a muscle Miss McAllen hadn't had to flex very often. But I knew without a doubt that she planned to escape out the window.

At my nod, she whirled into the room, then shut the door in my face. Quietly, I slipped back down the stairs—fortunately in good repair so there weren't any loose boards. No sooner had I stepped outside where Godfrey and Lock leaned against the carriage, than I caught the familiar drag of a window opening.

I stepped between the men, leaning against the carriage with my arms crossed. The sensation of being watched crept over me as their curious gazes dug into me. My eyes, however, were fixed on the second-story window farthest from the door.

From my new vantage, I watched as a dove-grey-skirt-covered leg slipped out the window. Then a hand escaped, wrapping around to catch the drainage pipe. Finally, a dark head appeared, focused on the pipe.

"That doesn't look particularly sturdy..." I called out.

Her attention shot to me with a curse, audible even several feet away.

Two sets of eyes flicked from me to the window and back again, each man utterly befuddled.

Slowly, Miss McAllen tucked back into the window and I stepped back into the house.

"I'll be a little while," I called back over my shoulder to the waiting men.

"Seems like it, lad."

Twenty

DALTON PLACE, LONDON - JULY 5, 1816

TOM

My week continued in the same vein—dragged off to Hart and Summers, Solicitors, to half-heartedly assist in some manner, then return home to drink until I could sleep.

Kit and I hadn't spent any significant time together before, but he was easy company—reminding me a great deal of my eldest brother in temperament and wit. While the work was messy—I'd left covered in soot every single day—I could see why Kit enjoyed having an occupation and was reluctant to give it up. This work offered a small sense of purpose I hadn't known before.

On Saturday, I woke to a now expected knock—to find not only Kit, but three familiar housemaids from Grayson House who bustled in without explanation and set about cleaning without a word.

"What..."

"I told Katie you would need at least three. Do not worry, they've been very well compensated for the extra work."

"But—"

"No. You're disgusting."

"Thank you."

His only response was a raised brow and a nod toward the door. Dutifully, I followed him on what had become our ritual. First, a stop at Hudson's, followed by the practiced walk to the offices.

Hudson's was bustling, as it always was, but Anna waved with a smile from behind the counter when she saw us before returning her attention to the patron at the front. While I missed having the exclusive access to her pastries that I had enjoyed when she served as maid at our family home, I was pleased at the evidence of her success.

Kit and I joined the back of the line, content to wait our turn with the knowledge that our usual selection was already set aside for us.

My eyes slid shut as I inhaled. The air in the bakery was always sweet and buttery, with varying waves of whichever fruit tart was currently in the ovens—I suspected apple this morning, but I wouldn't stake my life on it. The scent was comforting, as familiar as it was mouthwatering.

"Brother," a familiar voice washed over me.

I opened my eyes to find Michael, bag in hand, an unfamiliar expression on his face.

"Can you spare him this morning?" he added, turning to Kit.

The man merely nodded, too focused on the proximity to pastry to devote much attention to anything else.

"Walk with me? I need to get these back to Jules before the craving passes." He raised the bag, presumably full of some delectable treat or other.

"Pardon?"

"Apparently women with child have cravings. And husbands are expected to fulfill those cravings. I do what I'm told," he added with a shrug.

I turned to follow him before recollecting myself. "Do not forget my tart. Whichever is currently in the oven, please," I said to Kit.

"You'll get whatever she has saved and like it," he retorted without turning.

Rather than argue, I sighed as I followed Michael out. Any tart was better than no tart—and was certainly delicious.

As soon as we stepped out of the crowded shop and onto the street, Michael cleared his throat uncomfortably. We turned toward his home while he waffled for a moment before finally settling on, "How have you been?"

I merely shot him a raised brow.

"Right, dim question. Juliet has been fretting something fierce over you. Been pestering me about calling on you damn near every day."

"She needn't worry after me."

"My wife is rather fond of you. And it's a privilege to be worried after by her—do not squander it."

I could not restrain a sigh. "I'm quite fond of her as well. But I cannot stop her fretting."

"That is not what I meant, and you know it."

"What do you wish for me to stay, Michael?"

"Something, anything."

"There is nothing to say. It's over."

He caught my elbow, stopping our progression and pulled me beside a building. "Tom, I—"

"I'm fine, Michael. I'll be fine."

"You don't look it—you look like I did when—"

"I'm not you, Michael."

"No, I know." I couldn't read that expression either. It was an unfamiliar sensation. I'd always been able to read Michael and Hugh both—it was a necessity of survival in my youth.

"Are we finished? Kit needs my assistance."

"No. Juliet will feel better for having seen you with her own eyes."

"I hope you have an extra tart in that bag."

Confusion fell over his expression and settled in the lines of his brow. "Didn't you request one from Kit?"

"I fail to see how that's relevant."

A chuckle escaped him and he clapped me around the shoulder and shoved me back toward Dalton Place.

At least the weather was fine and I was less bottle weary than previous days—the walk was not entirely unpleasant.

No sooner had we set foot in the house, than he caterwauled, "Jules?"

"Drawing room," she called back, much more sedately. If Juliet Wayland was ever anything less than the perfect lady, I couldn't name the instance.

Perched on the new settee in the refurbished drawing room, she was hard at work over an embroidery hoop. I didn't fully grasp the intricacies of ladies' finery, but her work was always lovely.

"Oh, Tom!" she exclaimed and pushed off the settee with both hands as she abandoned her work. Her belly had grown round in the weeks since I had seen her. There was no hiding it now, she was certainly with child. "I am so glad you're here. Come, come. The gazebo is fine this time of year."

"I brought you the tarts you requested," Michael interjected.

"That is nice, dear. Thank you."

His shoulders fell on a sigh. "The craving has passed, hasn't it?"

Juliet's expression was sheepish, a lip caught between her teeth.

"Mine has not," I added.

Michael glared at me but tossed me the bag without comment. It was possibly sacrilegious to handle Anna's tarts with so little care. But as the recipient of such good fortune, I wouldn't call him out on it.

"Leave me a raspberry one," he mumbled before turning to where I knew the study to be.

Juliet took my arm, arranging it in such a way that it looked to any outsider as if I had offered it, then she tugged me outside in a perfectly elegant manner.

What was once a small plot of overgrown weeds and dead plants had been transformed into a lovely little garden. The gazebo was new to my eyes and fit well in the cultivated wilderness blossoming in the heart of the city.

"When did you have this built?"

"Last spring." She led me up to the wrought iron bench in the center and urged me to sit silently before releasing my arm. "Tom, I need to—I apologize for not coming to see you earlier. I should have made the effort."

"There is nothing to apologize for, no reason to visit."

Her smile was soft and accompanied by a self-deprecating scoff.

"Juliet, I—"

"How are you?"

"I beg your pardon?"

"I wish to know if you are well."

"I'm perfectly well, as you can see." I gestured to my person—well attired and groomed more than I had been in recent days.

Rather than comment on my appearance, she tucked her arm through mine and pressed her cheek against my shoulder.

Something about the gesture left my throat too tight and my eyes burning. "He left," I choked out.

"I know," she whispered, something thick in her tone too. "I know."

"I just— Have you ever had one of those moments? The kind where your entire life can be divided into before and after? And the you that you are at the other end of that moment is fundamentally different from the you you were before... I'm not making a lick of sense."

"No, I know what you mean. I have experienced a few—mostly with Michael."

"I've had three—and two of them were with Xander. And this version of me—he doesn't know how to go back to living like the version who hadn't ever kissed him. I didn't know anything could be like that. And now I'm expected to spend the rest of my life never experiencing it again—only now I know what I'm missing."

"He did not run away from you—surely you know that. It has been his plan for months—years."

"Yes, but he made those plans before me. Our kiss—to him, it was just a kiss. He was precisely the same Xander before and after. It—*I*—wasn't enough."

"I saw the two of you, and that was not the expression of an unaffected man."

"Just not affected enough."

"It's not as simple as all that. You know that—you told me as much once. When you're kissing the man you love, it all seems so simple. But the truth is, there are consequences to forsaking society, for both of you. Are you prepared for that?"

My heart answered for me. "Yes."

She offered me a closed-lipped smile. "Then I am afraid I have to give you some wretched news." Her tone belied her words, lighthearted and easy.

"What?" I was half trepidation, half laughter.

"Men in love are deeply, deeply foolish. You'll probably have to go all the way to Scotland to retrieve your man."

"Do you suppose I'll need to have anyone arrested?"

Her laugh was bright and infectious.

"Lord, I hope not. It's quite the overdone thing, you

know." Silence settled over us for a moment. "Are you planning to eat that tart? It's actually quite tempting."

"Ye—wait, didn't you send Michael to fetch it because you were having a craving?"

Her expression turned sheepish again, a blush coloring her pale skin. "I may have received some intelligence that you'd been at the bakery every morning at around ten... I cannot possibly help it if my craving struck at precisely the same time and I absolutely had to send my dear, doting husband out for it."

I bit back a smile as I pulled the tart from the bag, tore it in half, and handed her the larger piece. "You're quite the schemer, Juliet Wayland. You act all innocent and ladylike, but if you put your mind to it, you could take over the country."

"Only the country?"

"For a start. I wouldn't want to limit your future endeavors."

She tipped the tart out like a glass. I tapped mine against hers before we took a simultaneous bite.

"To my inevitable future rule."

"Long may you reign."

∽

It was dark by the time I escaped from Kit's offices. I was entirely astonished when I returned to a brand-new apartment —entirely free of rubbish and clutter.

I would need to find a time to thank Kate—and I wasn't yet willing to brave Hugh so it would require some careful plotting.

Instead of reaching for the scotch, I set the kettle on for tea. Absentmindedly, I tugged on the knot of my cravat as I wandered over to the writing desk in the corner of my sitting room.

I couldn't recall precisely where I had, in my drunken state, put the address I'd borrowed—certainly not stolen—from Kit. I pulled open the drawer and flipped through pages for something covered in ash and half-burned.

At last, I found it in the very last drawer. I tugged it free, settled it atop my desk, and reached for a fresh piece of parchment. As I did, my gaze caught on the address—Kilmarnock Abbey.

Memory washed over me. The drunken waves of longing spilling across the pages by candlelight. Folding and addressing the missive in my infinite soused wisdom.

Fuck.

The chair smacked angrily against the floor when I shot to my feet. I grabbed a drawer, and the contents spilled free in a pile across the floor.

My knees protested when I fell to the wood and began sifting pathetically through the wreckage for a letter I knew I wouldn't find. Because deep in my gut, I knew. One of the maids had taken it.

I barely had the forethought to pull the kettle off the stove before I rushed out the door for Grayson House at a sprint.

Twenty-One

KILMARNOCK ABBEY, EDINBURGH - JULY 3, 1816

Dav,

    These boots are brown. Literally every piece of clothing I own is black, which you well know. You are a spiteful little hellion and I am glad to be rid of you.

    Tell Mother that the only creature I've had the misfortune of meeting is a particularly recalcitrant sheep named Fenella. The sheep makes it a point to defecate precisely in the places I most frequently step. Godfrey has threatened to give notice if he is asked to clean my boots one more time.

    Scotland itself is lovely. The house is in need of a few repairs, but I am certain it will be in perfect order shortly.

Warmest Regards,
Xander

XANDER

AFTER A NIGHT with little in the way of rest, I woke with the sun. I directed a much more well-rested Godfrey to locate Lock and seek out recommendations for laborers. And then to find a pallet, a cot, anything in the realm of a bed for Kilmarnock.

Miss McAllen—either having not attempted or having failed in her efforts to escape in the night—rose much later. She grumbled in precisely the same manner Davina did when one of her plans had been foiled so I rather suspected it was the latter.

She set about making breakfast with a practiced efficiency, lighting the fire and setting the kettle to boil. Without a word, she cut a few slices of bread and set them over a hot stone to toast.

It wasn't until, at last, she settled before me with a singular plate and a singular cup of tea, that I realized the purpose of the entire performance. Her eyes met mine overtop her teacup as she sipped, slurping pointedly, before setting it back on the saucer with a smirk.

The subsequent display involving the toast, butter, and jam, was equally involved and I had little doubt that she was imagining my head when she chomped into it.

"Charming."

"Were ye hungry, Yer Grace?"

"Not at all," I tossed back, ignoring the gnawing sensation in my stomach. I hadn't eaten supper yesterday either. But too many years with Dav had taught me better than to rise to the bait. Miss McAllen may be skilled at needling, but there wasn't a soul on this earth more capable of driving one to madness than Davina Hasket. My patience was forged in fire and blood, its strength tested hourly for nearly two decades.

Miss McAllen ate purposefully, taking small, almost sarcastic bites of the perfectly browned bread. Each sip of tea was accompanied by a dramatic slurp, and her gaze almost never left mine. It was a challenge, a gauntlet.

It seemed she had formed a plan in the night, and that plan was to make me wish I'd never been born. I had to respect it, to be perfectly honest. Most men, men who hadn't been raised by a hateful father and a self-indulgent mother, who weren't preceded by a gambling, lecherous brother and followed by the most troublesome sister in existence, would be brought to their knees by her—I had no doubt of it. But Miss McAllen hadn't the slightest idea who she was dealing with. And it would be her downfall.

It took her nearly half an hour to finish two slices of toast, and I was certain her tea was long cold before she finally emptied the cup with a final, overloud gulp, topped with a dramatic *Ahhh*.

"As soon as Godfrey returns, we'll be heading for Kilmarnock. I suggest you pack a bag, you'll be away for awhile."

"I willnae!"

"I suppose you needn't pack a bag if you do not wish to. But I rather think you'll regret it. Godfrey and I do not possess a single frock between us."

"I'll nae go with ye. It wouldnae be proper."

"You're already with child and without a husband. I rather think propriety is the least of your concerns."

Her glare was sharp, her overgrown brow furrowing above dark eyes. "How do ye know I'm without a husband?"

"You said as much yesterday."

"I lied yesterday."

"Yes, about a great many things. That wasn't one of them."

"How do ye ken that?" she asked.

"Ah, I think it best I kept that intelligence secret a little longer." In truth, I wasn't certain. There was just *something* in her countenance that reminded me of Gabe when he was pulling the wool over someone's eyes. And the tell hadn't been there in that moment. "Best see to packing if you don't wish to wear that dress for the foreseeable future," I added.

She huffed as expected, crossing her arms before stomping off toward the room she'd tried to climb from the night before.

"You'll need a different route if you hope to escape," I called after her.

Godfrey returned shortly after her departure with pastries. They had nothing on Hudson's, but they were tolerable. The buttery pastry sparked a memory—Tom Grayson at my side in the bakery, a tart crumb caught on his lower lip in a way that left me desperate to lick it— This wasn't the time for such thoughts.

By the time Miss McAllen finished her purposeful dawdling, it was nearly midafternoon.

Godfrey loaded her trunk while I shooed her toward the carriage.

"Lock—meet Miss McAllen. Miss McAllen—Lock. Not to be confused with Loch."

"Quite right, Yer Grace. Pleased to meet ye," the man agreed with a jovial grin.

She raised a dark brow before turning to enter.

"Not so fast. Lock, you should know that Miss McAllen is a dangerous thief. As such, she is not to be allowed near horses, sheep, goats, donkeys, medium-sized dogs or large numbers of small dogs, any livestock large enough to ride or pull a cart, nor any conveyance, whether it be two- or four- wheeled or not wheeled at all. Nor is she to be allowed on walks, jaunts, strolls, parades, stretches, hikes, or turns about any place. She is allowed to assist in the repairs to Kilmarnock and nothing else. Agreed?"

"Seems a bit harsh, Yer Grace."

"She's stolen hundreds."

He choked on nothing, before adding, "Perhaps not harsh enough, Yer Grace."

"Indeed."

"Do ye intend to speak as though I'm nae here with everyone?"

"Yes." I resumed my shooing motion to the carriage.

She climbed in with a huff and we were off. I settled across from her on the black velvet cushion. "What, exactly, is yer plan in all of this?"

"I hadn't worked out the entirety of it. But for now—to keep you where I can see you."

"Brilliant."

"It's no worse than yours."

"It wasnae mine. It was my ma's. I just kept it up."

"Tell me about your mother," I demanded.

"Why do ye want to know?"

"You keep asking me that as though I'm not the one who has been fleeced for years. You are free to assume that I have my reasons and that they are private."

"She was my ma. I dinnae ken what ye want to ken."

"What was she like? Was she from the area? How did this scheme come about?"

"Pretty—she was pretty. With light hair and eyes. Small, too, fragile. I think she was from town. And if she had any family, she never mentioned them. I think she was a widow before she married Pa."

Miss McAllen was quite pretty herself, but not in any of

the ways she described her mother. She was tall, and her frame was sturdy—not large, but not petite either.

"And this scheme…"

She rolled her eyes. "It was after Pa died. He was a steward —yer steward. And rather than starve or be forced to wed again… I dinnae ken. She used to say yer family owed her—us. Never ken'd what she meant by that—I always assumed ye were underpaying Pa. When she passed and I took over, that didnae seem right."

I knew precisely what her mother meant. With each word, I was more certain of the girl's parentage.

"Your father."

"What about him?"

"What was he like?"

"Sickly, always sickly. His hair was always falling out and he had a cough my whole life. Don't miss finding clumps of yellow hair all over the house. But he was good, I suppose. Honorable."

"When did he die?"

"Seven, maybe eight years ago. I dinnae remember exactly."

"And your mother?"

"Six months ago." There was a sorrowful note in her voice at that.

"I am sorry for your loss."

She scoffed. "No, yer not. That is just what yer supposed to say."

"Both things can be true at the same time. Do you have any brothers? Sisters?"

"Nae."

"And the father—of your child—where is he?"

"I dinnae want to talk aboot him." Her arms folded across her chest as she turned to the window.

I was honestly astonished I'd gotten as much information

out of her as I had, so I left her to her sulk until we arrived at Kilmarnock.

With great relief, I noticed that Fenella had seemingly moved on to greener pastures as we pulled up around the pond.

Kilmarnock looked no more impressive for a night's rest—if anything, it seemed to have disintegrated further.

Miss McAllen's gaze widened at the sight of the ruin.

"Didn't realize the extent of your efforts, I take it?"

She said nothing, but ripped her eyes from the abbey and, instead, focused on a loose thread on her glove, picking at it.

"Nothing to say?"

"I dinnae know what ye want me to say."

"Nothing at all." I sighed and spilled out of the carriage to hand her out.

When I turned toward the house, I realized that in my haste to leave the wreckage of my scheme behind, I'd neglected to shut the door—or it had abandoned the pretense of its function entirely and collapsed in on itself; either way I regretted my return.

"Come," I insisted, leaving Miss McAllen to trail after me up the drive. Weeds sprang up amid the gravel and there was something irresistible about stepping on as many as possible, grinding my foot with every step.

Finally, I reached the open doorway. Whether a breeze or time had blown it in, I had no notion, but the door hung in pathetic resignation halfway swaying back and forth—surrendering to its inevitable demise.

I stepped inside and turned to the drawing room to find that the breeze must have blown the coverings off a table. It, at least, seemed to be in acceptable shape at first glance. The sheet was piled on the floor, gnawed to holes by something I didn't wish to contemplate further.

"Christ..." Miss McAllen muttered behind me.

"Precisely."

I turned and made my way down the hall. Nearly half of the floorboards creaked with each step, a depressing symphony as our parade marched on. Yellowed wallpaper hung in moth-eaten sheets, clinging desperately to relevance.

"Are you certain you wish to stay here tonight, Your Grace?" Godfrey called out from near the door, his voice filled with trepidation.

"Wish to? No. Will? Yes."

"I believe I shall wait out here for the gentleman with the beds—he assured me they would be delivered before nightfall." I'd be damn lucky if Godfrey didn't give notice.

I strode forward, past a music room, an office, and a dining room—all in a similar state to the drawing room.

Just as the weary exhaustion settled into my bones, I heard it. A familiar, wretched bleat.

Before understanding could make itself known, I felt the familiar squish under my boot.

I bit my lips together, holding back every curse I knew as I tipped my head to the ceiling—darkened with a depressingly suspicious stain.

"Yer Grace?"

I turned slowly on my heels, facing her. "Yes, Miss McAllen?" I spit between gritted teeth.

"I think ye stepped in something."

"Really? What on earth gave you that notion?"

"Just a sense I had."

"Perfect, then you can use your impeccable senses to go first." I grabbed her by the shoulders and dragged her around in front of me. "Careful of Fenella. I'm given to understand she has a fearsome temper."

"Fenella?"

"The sheep."

She rolled her eyes before turning down the hall. A few steps more and the *meehheh*s grew louder.

And then we reached the last room in the hallway.

"Christ!" Miss McAllen shouted, hand pressed against her heart.

"What?"

Silently, she pointed to the cloth-covered dining table.

There, standing atop the table, was Fenella, chewing on the edge of what was once surely a beautiful floor-length velvet curtain but was now a dust-covered treat for the sheep.

"It's a bleeding sheep!"

"I told you it was a sheep."

"I thought ye meant it was a wee little lamb! Hell, yer city folk—could be a large dog for all ye know. But that's a whole damned sheep!" She spun to try to get behind me, but I refused to budge from the doorway.

"No. You'll be the one to remove Fenella from the house."

"I think ye'll find I'll not be doing that."

"I think you will."

Fenella took that moment to defecate directly atop the table while staring at me with something like malice in her beady gaze.

Miss McAllen caught her snort of laughter behind a hand, but her shoulders shook with silent glee.

"Remove the sheep. Or I call the constable." I turned back down the hall, refusing to watch yet more destruction of property. Besides, I rather thought Miss McAllen and Fenella would get along splendidly. They were both stubborn she-devils.

I bumped into Godfrey partway down the hall. He sniffed the air for a moment before his gaze found my boot.

Horror washed over his face.

"Your Grace?"

"Yes?"

"Please consider this my notice. Effective immediately."

"You are joking."

"I am most certainly not. But I do wish you the absolute best of luck." With that, he turned and strode out to the drive.

"Godfrey—wait!"

I spilled out onto the front steps, tripping after him in my shit-stained boot.

A large wagon was parked out front where laborers were pulling a simple metal bedframe from the back.

"Gentlemen, I'll be returning with you to town, if you don't mind," Godfrey explained to the disinterested men.

The one that seemed to be in charge looked to me. "Where do ye want these, then?"

Behind me, a familiar bleat rang from the doorway.

"Oh, ye'll want to keep Fenella oot of the house. She's nae trained," he added.

"You know Fenella? Where does she belong? I will pay you double if you can make her be elsewhere."

"Wishin' I could. But Fenella does what Fenella wants. Besides, ye'll be needing a new bed in a week if she's decided yer house is her house. Dinnae need the extra."

"Can you bring the beds inside at least?"

"Aye. Just as soon as Fen moves oot of the way."

Dread filled me as I turned. There in the doorway stood Fenella. It was clear from her expression and her frame that she hadn't the slightest interest in moving forward or backward, regardless of Miss McAllen's half-hearted shooing gestures and gentle coos.

My head tipped back toward the sky as I shouted, "Fuck!"

Unfortunately, the satisfaction of the gesture was somewhat lessened when my curse was covered by the sound of Fenella's bleat.

Twenty-Two

GRAYSON HOUSE, LONDON - JULY 5, 1816

TOM

I WAS TOO frantic to wait for a hack. It wasn't until I was halfway to Grayson House that I began to lament my choice to run through the streets of London at full speed and recognized that my efforts might be—not necessarily overly dramatic—but fruitless. If one of the maids had taken the letter with the intention of posting it on my behalf as I suspected, then the five minutes I saved by sprinting, shouting my pardons over my shoulder as I brushed past lamplighters, servants, and gentlemen alike, would not be the five minutes they posted the letter.

By the time I reached the black double doors under the sharp archway and Grecian columns, I was breathless, sweat-soaked, and disheveled. That was the moment I recognized I hadn't bothered to grab my coat or retie my cravat but raced through London half undressed. I could only pray Mother was not in residence as that lecture may actually kill me.

One hand braced on my waist, panting, I banged on the door. Weston's face shifted from irritation to astonishment at the sight of me and he ushered me inside. If he said anything, I couldn't hear it over the rushing of my ears and my harsh breaths.

Kate's soft soprano successfully cut through the panic. "Tom, good Lord! Are you well?"

She reached my side, her tiny hands grasped my shoulders, soothing down them before turning me around. It took me a moment to understand she was searching for injury.

"Letter," I wheezed.

"Pardon?"

"Letter—"

"You received a letter? Good lord, is it Michael? Juliet? Did something happen to the babe?"

I could only manage a continuous headshake through heaving breaths at her frantically peppered questions. She did stop fondling me so at least I'd convinced her of my physical health.

"I," gasp, "wrote," gasp, "it—"

"You wrote a letter?"

Irritation finally overwhelmed the lack of air. "Would you let me finish?"

She nodded, eyes still frantically casting over my form.

"I had a letter on my writing desk. It's gone. Do you know if one of the maids took it to post?"

"All this over a letter posted? I've no idea. It is that important?"

"Kate, look at me. Do you suppose I would look like this if it wasn't important?"

Her gaze flicked over me. "Right. I'll go ask—shall I?"

"Please."

"Kate?" *Damn.* "Tom? What on earth happened?"

I turned to face my brother for the first time in days. "Hugh."

"Are you well?"

"I believe he's physically unharmed. He said something about a letter, I'll go check with the maids," Kate supplied.

"Letter? Is it Michael?"

Unwilling to repeat the entire conversation a second time, I added, "I wrote it. I'm physically fine. As far as I am aware, Michael, Juliet, and the babe are all perfectly well."

"Good, then you and I have a few moments to speak." Neither his expression, somewhere in the vicinity of his usual frown, nor his tone, indicated his mood.

I could have chosen to be difficult, avoided the conversation as I wished, but frankly, avoiding my brother was exhausting. I trailed after him, dragging my feet all the way to his study.

Inside, he gestured toward the chair across the desk from his own while he filled two glasses with a generous pour of the scotch he favored.

The leather was cool against my overheated back and thighs—so much so that it would have been a relief were I not faced with the stony visage of my father. Something about his portraits, which still hung in the studies of both the London home and the Kent estate, never failed to leave me weary and on edge.

Whether either of my brothers or I matched my father's precise coloring would forever remain a mystery, but there were pieces of him to be found in each of us. The way he stared down, however, his haughty expression cast in oil—an insect in amber—was entirely his own.

"I was considering commissioning something new," Hugh said conversationally, nodding toward the painting.

"Yes?"

"I thought, if you were willing—and Michael, of course—the three of us." That was enough to rip my gaze from the painting.

"You want to include Michael?"

"He *is* our brother."

"*I* know that. *You* refused to admit it for years."

Hugh shrugged. "He belongs up there, beside us."

I took a moment to consider my brother, truly observe him, as I hadn't in years. The Hugh I once knew never would have included Michael in our ranks—our baseborn brother, in spite of everything he'd done for the family, hadn't been considered worthy of the name. Now, Hugh wanted a portrait of the man.

"You've changed."

He held the glass of scotch up to the candlelight, turning it first one way, then the next, considering it. For an impossibly long moment, I wondered if he would dignify my observation with a reply. At last, he settled on. "For the better, I hope."

I nodded. Hugh wasn't perfect, no one was. But he *tried* in a way he hadn't before. Something about that realization made me want to be brave, vulnerable—honest.

"Do you have questions?" I asked.

Hugh gave me the honor of responding truthfully himself, offering no confusion as to my meaning in his shrug.

"I assume this letter has something to do with Rosehill?"

I nodded again, overgrown curls brushing against the rumpled collar of my shirt.

"I am trying to understand, Tom. Truly, I am. I need you to know that above all else."

There was a truth to his words that I felt in my bones. Hugh had two methods of managing circumstances that made him uncomfortable. Kate had encouraged him to face those situations head-on with generous assumptions. But Hugh's natural inclination, born of years in our mother's company, was suspicion and avoidance.

"Michael tried to explain it. Well, Rosehill made the first attempt, then Michael.

"You spoke with Michael about this?"

"At first, I spoke with him hypothetically. When it became clear that we were both trying and failing to discuss you without actually discussing you, we dropped the pretense."

"Lovely, I'm ever so glad I was able to provide entertainment."

"Tom," he sighed. "You know that is not what I meant. And besides, you were gone to the wind—I haven't seen you in days. When, and how, was I meant to gather my answers?"

I hadn't the slightest notion of what to say to that. I took a heavy sip of my drink instead, buying time.

Hugh took the bait and continued, "I used to believe I knew nearly everything, and everything I didn't know could be readily discerned using my impeccable judgment. But I've learned I know almost nothing. And regardless, Michael has accidentally become the person I go to with such questions."

"Often have questions about such things?"

"More often of late—but he proved to be quite the artist when I had questions about pleasing Kate."

"Artist?"

"He drew me a diagram—there were instructions. It was… illuminating."

"May I see it?"

"Do you suppose you'll have need of a diagram with instructions on how to please a woman—a wife?"

"No, but I still think it would be amusing."

"You think everything is amusing."

"And I'm usually right."

"You are," he agreed quietly. "So, Rosehill?"

"What about him? He seduced me, remember?" My tone had shifted, the memory sparking something petulant and unkind.

"Oh yes, you were well and truly seduced by the time I happened upon you."

An irritated huff of laughter escaped.

"Will you tell me about it? What you feel? How it happened?"

A second laugh escaped, still under my breath and restrained, but genuine. "We met at your wedding."

"I beg your pardon?"

"Mother introduced us, in point of fact."

"I... do not..."

"I believe she intended for me to wed Lady Davina, in truth. Make amends for your failure to secure a suitable wife." That comment earned me a growl in spite of the jest in my voice. "I looked at him and suddenly... everything made sense. The world that never seemed quite right, always a little chaotic, a little unwieldy, was ordered and tidy and everything that I was told you're supposed to feel when faced with a beautiful lady—I felt it the second I looked at him. The butterflies, the heart palpitations, damp palms—all of it."

"And you've never felt that? For a young lady, I mean."

"No. There are beautiful ladies, but it's an abstract beauty."

"And Rosehill felt the same?"

"Christ, no." At his glare, I corrected. Kate was still a vicar's daughter. "Lord, no. He doesn't recall our meeting at all. Which is almost certainly a positive thing, I was a bit of a mumbling dolt. I did steal a snuffbox from your wife's aunt, though."

He sighed, thumb and forefinger pinching his nose. "Do I wish to know?"

"No."

"Very well then. What you feel for Rosehill... It is love?"

"I've never been in love before."

"Sometimes when Kate smiles at me, I forget to breathe."

A little chuckle escaped me. "I don't think Xander knows how to smile. But when he speaks—you know the way he does with his hands—my heart forgets to beat."

Something in my brother's expression was wistful, his lip quirked at one corner. "Do you wish to do anything with those feelings?"

"What do you mean?"

"Do you want to be with him? If there were no obstacles, and your feelings were reciprocated—do you wish to build a life with him?"

I nodded, swallowing the harsh knot in my throat at the thought.

Hugh's tongue darted out between his lips, moistening them before downing the entirety of his glass in one swallow. "You understand the consequences? It's not done often, but the law—you could be hanged, Tom."

I mirrored his actions with my glass. The fortification was necessary for the rest of this. "Wouldn't you? If it were Kate?"

He sighed, his head falling to the desk with a soft thump. "I wish everyone would stop mentioning wretched things happening to my wife by way of explanation. I am capable of comprehending the feelings and sentiments of love without the demonstration."

The chair creaked as I leaned forward to offer a conspiratorial whisper. "Did you not say a few moments ago that you required a diagram?"

My ear rang for a moment after Hugh clipped me round it.

"I need you to be serious for once in your life, you ingrate," he muttered. At my sobering nod, he continued. "There are very, very few things I would not do for you. You know that, I hope. But this, if it goes poorly, I very much doubt there would be anything I could do for you. And if there were things I could do, I'm nearly certain that doing them would imperil Kate and little Henry—and those, alone, are the things I will not do. Rosehill will be shielded, his title all but ensures it. If you're discovered and they wish to make an example of someone... I couldn't bear it."

"There is nothing to discover. Xander is gone to Scotland."

"An impassable distance, so I understand your willingness to forsake the love you spoke so passionately about. Orpheus went to hell for Eurydice, but no one could expect a man to go to Scotland."

"What are you saying?"

"You know what I'm saying."

"You..."

"I do not wish for you to go, to be clear. And I will absolutely fret over you in a manner that will surely be embarrassing. Mother will certainly have my head if she finds out I encouraged you. But as you said... if it were Kate..."

My heart comprehended his meaning before my head, swelling in my chest, leaving no space for anything else, not even air. "Hugh..."

"Be safe about it? Please?"

"You're really suggesting this? You understand?"

"Not the mechanics of it—and please do not explain. But if there's one thing I know, you cannot help who you fall in love with. If I could have, it never would have been Katie and that would be the greatest loss of my life."

"Hugh..." My voice was thick and overwrought. That would not do. My brothers and I did not share sentiment. I shook off the emotion. "Thank Kate for me?"

"For what?"

"Everything. You were unbearable before her."

"I'd cuff you around the ear again if I didn't agree with you. You will write? And come back when you can?"

"Of course. You'll let me borrow the carriage?"

"For weeks? Absolutely not. You'll take a coach."

"But they're so uncomfortable."

"Orpheus never complained."

"Orpheus never had to ride in a post coach for days."

"You are not having the carriage. Bother Michael."

A soft knock interrupted our lazy debate. Kate popped her head in. "Tom? It seems as though your letter was posted. Sara said it was already addressed."

"I thought as much. Thank you for confirming."

"You seem... more relaxed."

"I am. Say, Kate, do you suppose I might borrow your carriage?"

"Of course!" she replied at the same time that Hugh interjected with, "Absolutely not."

At his wife's confused expression, he added, "He wishes to take it to Scotland."

Her head tipped to one side, considering me, before she seemingly made a decision. "The weather is fine, we can use the curricle. And if the weather turns, I'm sure Michael and Juliet will have no concerns with us borrowing theirs."

When I turned back to him with a smirk, Hugh had thrown his hands up in exasperation. "No one mind me. I'm only the viscount, it's only my carriage."

"Oh, good. We shan't," I retorted, knocking back the last dregs of scotch. "If you'll both excuse me, I have packing to do."

"When will you be back?" Kate asked. "Before it snows?"

"Perhaps," I murmured, rising to stand.

"He's in love," Hugh singsonged in a tone I'd never heard from him and hoped never to hear again. "He's off to win hearts." I shuddered, rounding the desk to cuff *him* around the ear before making for the door. His laugh followed me until I reached his wife's side.

"Oh Tom," she whispered, reaching up to cup my cheek. Once I recognized her intent, I had to dip at the knees so she could reach. "Supper, tomorrow. I'll invite everyone—well, do you wish for your mother to attend?"

"Not particularly."

She gnawed on her lower lip, wavering. "Oh, you should see her before you leave."

I dropped a kiss on her cheek. "I'll take tea with her. Spare everyone else the pleasantness."

"My favorite brother," she called after me as I made my way down the hall, much calmer than before.

"I'm certain you say that to all your brothers."

"I do!"

Twenty-Three

KILMARNOCK ABBEY, EDINBURGH - JULY 15, 1816

Xander,

    I am enjoying the season. Your concern for my well-being is truly touching.

    You should have specified the color of the boots if you had a preference. I cannot read minds, you know. If you'd like black, you'll need to return and purchase them yourself.

    Mother has now been convinced that you've taken up with a boggle and are set to wed them. Once I explained that no self-respecting boggle would have you, she calmed.

                       Best wishes,
                         Davina

P.S. Whatever Mr. Summers has told you is a gross exaggeration.

XANDER

I MANAGED to coax Godfrey into continuing his employment at double his current pay. To be quite honest, I rather suspected it was a bargain given what I was putting him through. Especially when I learned that he'd also been to the market that morning while he was out.

The three of us had managed to shoo a displeased Fenella from the house while the men set up the beds in the drawing room—no one thought the stairs were sturdy enough to support several burly men in addition to the beds.

Miss McAllen and Godfrey worked to rig a door from one of the large cloths covering the furniture—one Fenella hadn't pissed on.

Meanwhile, I located a dilapidated garden shed. It took a bit of maneuvering to open the rusted door and once I did, I immediately regretted it. The distinctive sound of something skittering into the shadows sent a shiver down my spine—I was only grateful no one was nearby to hear my pathetic whimper. The sunlight caught an infinite collection of spider webs, some with beasts still inside them, lining every available surface.

When I could finally bring myself to look again, I found a shovel hung against the wall—whether that was by a hook or webbing was anyone's guess.

The time it took to weigh my desire to sleep in a home without piles of sheep shit against my desire to never set foot in the infested hell before me was shamefully long. With a fortifying breath, I toed a boot into the shed. The wooden floor creaked in irritation but held. I shuffled another inch forward, then another. One foot remained firmly on the safe grass outside—as though that would save me.

At last, my fingertips brushed the handle—the least cobwebby part—and I nudged it toward me. It swayed, banging against other tools I didn't know the names of. I shuffled a tiny bit deeper inside and managed to catch the thing, knocking it off the wall and onto the floor with a clang.

More skitters echoed in response.

I leaned down to grab it, a wretched mistake, because when I rose again, prize in hand, I backed into a spider web. Instinctively I turned and was then smacked in the face with another.

In my haste to remove it, I dropped the shovel directly on my foot.

Fenella once again bleated out my "Fuck!" as I hopped about, trying to dislodge the webbing while not putting weight on my surely maimed foot. Her *mehhehhehe* still echoed very much like laughter.

I rounded on her, still teetering on one foot. "Fuck you too!"

"What are ye doing?" came a feminine lilt from the house.

"Praying for death to take me."

Miss McAllen padded up next to me, head tilted in curiosity. "Does that have anything to do with the spider on yer forehead?"

My squeal was anything but masculine as I brushed furiously at my head, desperate to dislodge wayward arachnids, and jumped in pain every time I accidentally set my injured foot on the ground even as I danced about.

Her peals of laughter bled into Fenella's, an indistinguishable cacophony of self-satisfied mockery.

"It's just a wee thing. Ye dinnae need to panic."

My desperate, fortifying breath wasn't enough to ease the terror entirely. "Is it gone?" I ground out, moving my lips as little as possible to prevent the beast from climbing in.

"Yes. It was a harmless wee jumpy one, probably dead under yer boot now. Honestly, ye'd think it was a man eater the way ye were flailing aboot."

Summoning the dignity I'd lost somewhere between stepping in Fenella's shit the first time and shuffling into the shed, I limped to the house without a word. Miss McAllen trailed after me and, while she didn't say anything, I could sense the mirth emanating from her very being.

"What happened to ye, lad?" Lock asked when he caught sight of me.

"Spider," Miss McAllen filled in.

Ignoring them both, I flung the curtain to my home open, and stomped inside to remove Fenella's gifts, leaving them free to snicker behind me.

I'd never actually used a shovel before, but fortunately the motion seemed instinctive. What I did lack was a pail of some sort to put the excrement in. Instead, I was forced to carry it throughout the house at the end of the shovel and wait for Lock to lift the curtain so I could fling it outside. The process was repeated no less than three times because Fenella was nothing if not prolific.

Eventually, the pain of my humiliation overtook the pain in my foot and my task was finished. I flopped on the front step, finally pulling my—horribly scuffed—boot off. Godfrey was going to have a fit at the sight.

I wasn't able to pull off my stocking without taking off my breeches, but beneath the white silk, a purplish bruise was forming. The swelling, however, seemed minimal and after poking it a few times, I was fairly certain the damage was superficial.

"Ye all right, lad?" Lock asked

"No, but unfortunately, the injury seems unlikely to kill me."

"Cheer up."

"Oh, of course, how could I forget to be cheerful? Fenella left me such lovely welcome gifts."

"Ye got a letter from home at least. I set it on the table—

the one Fenella left untouched. Why dinnae ye see aboot supper after ye finish yer letter and the lass and I will see aboot a tether for Miss Fenella."

"Ye want me to what?" Miss McAllen asked, her tone full of incredulity.

"Help me with a tether for the sheep," he repeated, slowly.

"That is a wild animal. And I'm with child—I couldnae possibly risk it."

"Yer with child? My felicitations!"

"What did ye ken?"

"I didnae ken, too many cakes?"

A hint of laughter bubbled up in my chest.

"Ugh!" Her grumble was accompanied by a petulant stomp of her foot—so perfectly Davina that the laughter did break free, delirious and giddy. I slumped against the doorframe, tears streaming down my face in between giggles.

"I think he's off his head..." Lock mumbled, grabbing Miss McAllen by the arm and dragging her away. I couldn't exactly disagree with him.

Gently, I pulled my boot back on, wincing as I did so. Bracing against the doorframe, I pushed myself up and limped down the hall toward the kitchen. It was a slow, painful trek, but blessedly free of feces.

In the kitchen, I found Godfrey, sat cross-legged in front of one of the box stoves whispering words of desperate encouragement to the pathetic flickering flame inside.

"Godfrey?"

"Your Grace, forgive me. I'm not overly familiar with this sort of thing."

"You wouldn't be, besides you're doing a damn sight better than I would."

"I think the wood is damp," he explained, tipping his head toward the pile in the near corner. The kitchen itself was spacious, with a scullery just off one side, and a separate larder off the north wall. The walls might have once been a pleasant goldenrod, but between fading, grease, and peeling paint, it was only a guess.

"What can I help with?" I added.

"Oh, I couldn't possibly—"

"I've damaged my boots again. Consider my assistance payment for the inevitable fretting."

He turned to shoot me a glare. "Again, Your Grace?"

"Yes, but if it will make you feel better, I've already decided to replace them entirely. So you need not fuss at all."

"I suppose that is some small measure of comfort."

The small fire in the stove wavered ominously, drawing his gaze back as he fed it more twigs. "You can chop the vegetables, they're on the table."

I turned to see carrots, onions, celery, and potatoes piled high on the scarred oak table in the center of the room. "Right, yes—chopping." What I did not see was a knife, which I suspected was an essential tool for chopping. "Er... have you seen a knife anywhere in your preparations?"

Godfrey merely pointed with the twig in his hand toward the far counter. Since there was nothing visible on top, I was left to open drawers until I located a knife.

After returning once again to the vegetables, I considered them with a wary eye. How was one meant to chop round vegetables without them rolling off the table? How big should they be?

The celery seemed the most likely to stay put. I ripped off a stalk and lined it up in front of me before wrapping both hands around the knife handle and slamming it down. The celery rolled out from under the knife and shot across the kitchen.

"What the bleeding hell?" Godfrey exclaimed, clutching the back of his head where the vegetable had smacked into it.

"I am so sorry. It got away from me."

The man humphed, eyeing me with trepidation before turning back to his task.

Having learned from my first mistake, I snatched another stalk and put it in my left hand, keeping the knife in my right. I was about to bring the knife down—

"Stop right there!" Miss McAllen shouted from the doorway. "Put the knife down before ye lose a finger."

"What?"

"Shoo—Stepping in the dung was amusing. Losing a finger is not." She pried the knife from my hand by the handle before pointing at a nearby chair. "Sit there and dinnae touch anything."

Cautiously, I followed her instructions as Lock strode in with fresh firewood, moving to assist Godfrey.

"Do not, under any circumstances, raise a knife like that with yer hand down below again. Do ye understand me?"

"I tried to keep both hands on the knife, but the celery went flying."

"Oh, is that why it's on the floor?" Lock asked.

Miss McAllen sighed. "Can ye bring me a chopping board?" she asked Lock before turning to me while he did as bid. "Come here, stand behind me."

"I just sat—"

"Just do as I say." When I stood to peer over her shoulder, she grasped the celery in her left hand, just as I had.

"That's what I did—"

"No. Stop talking. Listen and watch. Don't splay yer fingers aboot so they're easy to chop off. Tuck them under so they're harder to cut. Then, hold the knife like this and rest the tip against the board." She *was* keeping it much closer to the chopping board. "Rocking motion, not hacking motion or whatever the bleeding hell it was ye were doing."

Carefully she rocked her hand down, slicing through the

celery into even chunks. "See how I'm not cutting a finger off? Maybe consider that way."

She turned, offering me the knife, handle first. "Ye try."

Dutifully, I took it and tried to mimic her efforts. I was met with substantially more success than my first attempt, and Godfrey's head remained unscathed. While my pieces were not nearly as fine or even, they stayed where I put them.

"Good. Where are the knives?" I nodded toward the open drawer. She returned to my side with a knife and board of her own, and reached for a potato.

"When they're round—how do you..."

"Keep them from rolling off the table?"

"Yes."

"Cut them in half first. Finish the celery and I'll show ye the magic of the onion—it'll be a revelation."

"Thank you," I murmured.

Lock announced he was going to go do something with the chicken that I didn't understand and didn't wish to contemplate while Miss McAllen did indeed demonstrate the mystical chopping of the onion.

"Yer a wee bit helpless aren't ye?" she asked, peeling the carrot while I carefully sliced through my half of the onion.

"A bit, I suppose. I'm certainly not equipped for this sort of thing."

She considered me thoughtfully, head tilted to the side. "Ye remind me of someone but I dinnae know who."

I rather suspected the person I reminded her of was herself. But that wasn't a conversation I was willing to have yet. "Is that a good thing?"

Her brow furrowed thoughtfully. "Not sure."

"You'll let me know? When you decide?"

"Aye."

EVEN A SIMPLE SUPPER of stew was far more involved than I had ever imagined, but it was astonishingly good, especially given my empty stomach. After eating, Godfrey, Miss McAllen, and I settled into the drawing room and Lock went to wherever Lock went when he was not here, with a promise to return in the morning.

To be quite honest, I was fairly certain the only reason the driver was still wandering around was because he found my situation unbearably amusing. Regardless of the reason, he was helpful and I wouldn't be the one to send him away.

The beds were less beds and more pallets on the floor, but they were better than whatever we would find when we eventually risked the second floor. I knew that much. Someone had outfitted them with clean bed linens and lit a fire in the hearth. All things considered, it was not the most uncomfortable I'd ever been.

No sooner had I sat on the edge of my pallet bed than Miss McAllen added, "Oh, Yer Grace, a letter came for ye while ye were fussing with shovel. It was an express."

I limped over to the table she indicated and brought it to my bed by the fire to read as the other two tucked under the covers, turning to sleep.

Far from the expected elegant swirls of Celine, the overdone flourishes of mother, or the distracted scribbles of Davina, the handwriting was an unfamiliar, sloppy, unembellished script.

I worked the paste open, carefully unfurling it.

My heart knew the writer long before my eyes dragged down the page to find Tom's name at the bottom. There was no one else it could have been.

The handwriting was clumsy and inconsistent, and I rather suspected the product of several drinks too many.

Xander,

I hope Scotland is everything you hoped it would be and more. And another, more wretched part of me hopes that you're miserable—both because I wish you would return and because you left me. It was so incredibly easy for you to leave me.

For a few, too brief, kisses, you gave me everything I ever wanted. Then you took it away with you. I'm left here to long for feelings I'll never know again. It is a kind of cruelty that defies sense, strains logic.

When I'm near you, the world makes sense. But when you're away, the world is a dull, unfeeling thing. Was it a figment of my imagination? Were you there with me, filling me with hope and lust and, dare I say it, love?

I could have loved you. Sometimes I think I always have. Late at night, I worry that I was made for you—that God took a piece of my heart and gave it to you for safekeeping. But he forgot to give me one of yours. It is the only explanation —the only thing I can think—it is why I can barely breathe in your presence. And it is the reason you are so entirely unaffected by me.

The moment we met—the moment I saw you —changed my life. And that moment was so inconsequential to you that it didn't even spark a memory. And in the cruelest of ironies, I was blessed to know you, touch you, kiss you for a few *years, weeks, minutes. Those seconds, hours, eons, will live in the scar where a piece of my heart once resided—a beautiful agony I can never—do not wish to—rid myself of. But you, your heart is intact and overfilling with mine as well—those memories will have no place inside you, no room.*

You upended my life and you set it alight and all I wish to do is beg you for more. If you were here I would, on bended knee, but you are gone—away from me with no word, no hint, no hope of contacting you.

That I made an opportunity of my own does not negate your neglect. If you had but asked, I would have come with you—begged to do so. Instead, I'm left to nurse the wound in my heart, the one that will never, cannot ever close.

Though I will never send this, I suppose I must wish you well, for it is the only way for the piece of my heart to experience joy.

Your drunken lovesick fool,
Tom

For a moment, I thought the ceiling was dripping—it wouldn't be out of character for the house—but the drops were falling from my eyes.

I thought I had done well, made the right choice. A clean break would be easier for him—for us. Three conversations and I'd set fire to the whole of his life. Leaving, hastily and unceremoniously, was best for him and his reputation.

He didn't know—hadn't the slightest idea—what it was when the rumors began to swirl. When the cruel looks became cruel whispers that became cruel words. It wasn't long then before those wretched words could turn to hate-filled actions. I had the shield of title and wealth. Tom had neither. His only protection was the cloak of secrecy. And rumors stalked me like a wildcat. Leaving him was the only gift I could offer him.

But he had seen my gift as a lack of caring, of compassion. That fact, more than anything, was devastating.

My throat ached with the effort of holding back the deluge of tears. I wasn't in love with him—certainly not yet—but I could have been. If the world were a different, better, place, if it hadn't beaten me back at every turn, I could have been the kind of man who could have loved Tom Grayson as he deserved to be loved.

But I had to live in this world. This world with its invisible rules and lines, the ones that others saw innately but I tripped over until I was smacked back often and hard enough to learn where the lines were and how to toe them. Love was not a luxury afforded to us all.

Tom's heart was sweet, gentle, and precious—and full of teasing mirth. And I had done the right thing in protecting it.

One day he would see it too; one day he would thank me. That understanding would need to keep me warm tonight. The fire, seemingly growing dimmer by the moment, certainly wouldn't.

I rolled to my back, watching the dying light dance along the ceiling in ever smaller circles as I desperately struggled to ignore the ache in my chest. My body was exhausted, bruised and beaten, but my head refused to yield to the promise of rest. Once beautiful memories of Tom Grayson's lips swirled in tainted understanding—a new layer of self-loathing.

Why did he have to be so damned beautiful, his sharp, enticing angles softened by kind eyes? I didn't deserve kind eyes, especially when I knew now that I'd made them sad. It was an unfamiliar expression on him, and I couldn't quite picture it. Affable, teasing Tom should never have sad eyes—but I'd done it.

I shut my eyes in what would surely be a futile attempt to find rest and curled on my side. Sleep was often a reluctant friend—that was a natural result of a mother and sister determined to ruin themselves at every available opportunity. Often, counting breaths would work, the dullness of the activity sufficient to distract from valid worries. Tonight, sleep resisted, and only after I'd reached more than a thousand did I begin to drift away.

Twenty-Four

KILMARNOCK ABBEY, EDINBURGH - JULY 16, 1816

Davina Hasket,

I've received no correspondence from Mr. Summers. What have you done? At least assure me that the house is still standing and your reputation remains in the same tarnished but more or less intact state as I left it.

Assure Mother that I am well. I did encounter several spiders, but they possessed no mystical properties that I could identify. The sheep continues to vex, though. It may have some magical jumping abilities, but I cannot confirm that as I am not overly familiar with the skill set of common livestock.

Warmest Regards,
Xander

P.S. Tell Cee to withhold your pin money as

punishment for whatever mess required the intervention of Mr. Summers to sort out.

XANDER

THE BLACK-AND-WHITE CHECKERED *dance floor was overcrowded, people tripping over hems and backing into each other with every turn. My place, long ago defined, was on the sidelines. The violin was out of tune with the rest of the quartet—discordant and disconcerting.*

The couples parted for the briefest of moments, and there was Mr. Grayson—Tom, eyes hot on my form. He truly was lovely. I wasn't certain how I hadn't noticed before. Even with his brow furrowed and his lips pressed tight together, there was no mistaking the defined cheeks and breathtaking eyes. Long, muscular legs filled out his trousers in a way that left little to the imagination.

A tiny sprite of a lady appeared at his side, drawing his penetrating gaze away from me. I couldn't hear the words they exchanged, but they slipped onto the dance floor—waltz already in progress. They fit together, her small frame against his masculine one, moving as one.

This was his future, the one I had purchased for him with my absence. He might not have appreciated my leaving now, but he would when he had this.

Beaumont approached from one side, clapping Tom on the shoulder in a jovial gesture of friendship, earning a crooked, boyish smile.

My chest ached at the sight. Even from the edge of the floor, it was clear that Tom was made for this world in a way I wasn't. With an impossible effort, I ripped my gaze away, finding the floor before me.

A soft breath found my ear and my eyes shot to my side.

Tom, clad in what I now noticed was an absolutely revolting red-and-orange waistcoat, caught my hand—how had I missed that waistcoat? Wordlessly, he tugged me onto the floor as couples parted with scandalized gasps.

"We cannot!" I hissed.

"We can." Surprisingly muscular arms pull me into his space, arranging my arms to his liking.

"People will see!"

The single, formerly discordant, now tuned violin broke into the oppressive silence with a decisive sliced note. "Yes."

"But—"

"Xander, I won't allow anything to harm you." Tom's arms found my waist and he stepped into me just as the rest of the quartet joined the melody. "I can give you everything you want," he breathed into my ear as he pulled me even closer. "Everything you've ever wanted. It's all I've ever wanted too." I shuddered at the gravel in his voice, in perfect contrast to the sweet high notes of the quartet.

"How?" I begged, breathless, gasping in his cedar scent through parted lips.

"Trust me." His hand tightened around my waist, pulling me scandalously closer. That was the moment I realized other couples had joined the dance, swirling around us—paying not even the slightest bit of attention. "You have to let me in. You have to be brave."

I pulled back, meeting his heated gaze. "Tom, I—"

Tom's lips caught mine, interrupting me. This kiss was soft, sweet... loving. Long fingers traced my cheek when he pulled away. "We'll make a world of our own, together. All you have to do is love me."

"Tom..."

His gaze snapped to something behind me. "That is for you," he said simply.

"What?"

"You'll have to sort that out for now."

A rustling sound cut through the sweeping notes of the quartet. I spun, finding nothing. I turned back, only to find an empty space where Tom had been. A hollow clank sounded through the gaming hell—

∽

I SHOT up with a start just as the sun was beginning to kiss the sky. It was the work of several moments to remember where I was and several more before I caught that same rustling sound again.

The fire had died out during the night, leaving an unfamiliar damp nip in the air. Through the cracked window, the sky had lightened to that inky slate shade that promised dawn. The swishing sound returned, but without the firelight, I couldn't see the source.

Again, it came, and I localized it toward the door.

My heart knocked about in my chest, my breath too light and too quick. The events of the day and the contents of Tom's letter had left both my body and my head aching.

Another crepitation, the sound of—fabric? fur? against something. It was louder now, more insistent. The instinct to screech, to wake the others, warred with the need to ensure that it—they—did not realize the element of surprise was gone. Was it a bear? Did they have bears in Scotland? Perhaps a wildcat or a brownie? Mother had included both in her repeated diatribes about the perils of the Scottish Lowlands.

Again, I heard it. And then I watched, scream trapped in my paralyzed throat, as the sheet covering the door moved again. For a second, I was almost able to blame the wind, but then I identified a distinctive lump in the fabric.

The sky continued to lightened with every passing moment. The man, spirit, or beast pressed ever more determinedly against the fabric. A sharp snuffling sound rang out in the silent room, punctuated only by the heavy breaths of my companions. A beast—certainly an evil loch creature—come to destroy us all.

Sensing a weakness in the fabric trappings, it shifted its efforts toward the left side of the fabric, reaching ever closer to the edge. Snort, rustle, snort, rustle.

I caught the edge of a horn peeking between the fabric and the door—a sign of the devil if there ever was one. Silently, I shuffled to the end of the bed and reached sightlessly for the iron poker that stood beside the fireplace.

It wasn't precisely where I thought it was and my fingers met air. I flailed, grabbing out, only to catch metal with the edge of my fingertips—knocking against the tool.

Clang!

The poker smacked against the hearth with an echoing clatter. My heart smacked against my ribcage as Godfrey and Miss McAllen shot up with a curse and a wordless shout. At the same moment, the beast poked its head between the curtain and the door.

Fenella's beady gaze met mine, something vengeful in the black of her eyes.

"What are ye doing?" Miss McAllen demanded, hair stuck up on one side of her head and smashed down on the other. The side that jutted upright reminded me of the way Gabriel's had.

"I thought it was a bear. Or a wildcat." I offered pathetically, leaving the fairy folk out of my list of suppositions.

"Ye thought Fenella was a bear? Ye considered bear before the sheep that's tied up and determined to shit in here?"

"She didn't show herself until just now."

"I promise ye, if it were a bear, a poorly hung sheet wouldnae stop it. Nor a wildcat."

"I forgot about the sheep!"

"Ye forgot aboot the sheep? Ye didnae do anything except complain aboot the sheep yesterday."

"I made stew as well!"

"Ye almost cut yer hand off! That's not making stew, that's making a mess."

"Well, I wouldn't have had to make the stew or clean the sheep shit if you hadn't fleeced me for years!"

"Well, I wouldnae had to fleece ye if yer brother hadnae left my ma with child and abandoned her!"

The fight seeped out of me in a puddle. "You know?"

"Of course I know. I'm not a bloody idiot. Look at ye! Look at me!"

Godfrey took that moment to sidle out of the room, shooing Fenella out of the hall and back outside before following her in his bare feet. The discomfort of witnessing this conversation was surely greater than the pain of frostbite.

"But I thought... You spoke of your father—"

"Lending his seed didnae make that man a father."

"But..."

"It was the least yer family could do. When Pa died, Ma and I had nothing. And yer family had—has—everything. Ye owed us."

"Did he know?" I asked, my voice small.

"What?"

"Did Gabriel know?"

Something about my question softened her a little and her shoulders shrank. "I dinnae believe so. Ma never said, but she was proud—she wouldnae write him."

Relief flooded me in a way I couldn't explain. It wouldn't have been at all out of character for Gabriel to have had a child and not have told us. But I couldn't have thought he would lie to Cee about it—and knowing her, she had certainly asked outright.

"Why didn't you write?"

"And say what? My mother was yer brother's grass widow? I'm his natural daughter? I've no proof. How was I to know we'd look alike? And why did ye not say anything when ye realized?"

"Astonishingly, they do not discuss how to have those conversations at Eaton."

"They teach ye how to complain aboot sheep?"

"There was some discussion on the management of livestock," I replied with a shrug. "Miss McAllen... I—"

"Sorcha."

"I beg your pardon?"

"I think ye can call me Sorcha now."

"Sorcha, I—you have to know that he would have done the right thing. He wasn't a good man—not really—but he would've at least seen you cared for."

"Ye just said he wasnae a good man."

"He had a code. It was one of his own making. But it was a code. Honestly, he'd be proud that you managed to take so much and keep the ruse up for so long."

"Did he—do I—are there any others?" Her eyes were wide and her expression wavered between nervous and hopeful.

"Not that I'm aware of. But I didn't know of you either. I have a sister about your age—Gabriel was much older than us —you remind me of her."

"The brows?"

I nodded. "And everything else. She once invested in a whiskey distillery run by pirates."

A little chuckle escaped her. "I think I'd like her."

My foot ached as I rose and moved to sit on the bed beside her. "She'd like you too. My mother as well."

"I assume—yer duke—so my grandfather..."

"Gone. But you wouldn't have liked him. Mother was the only one who did—and even her I'm not certain. Gabriel hated him."

"And my father? What happened to him?" There was a guarded vulnerability in her expression, the furrow of her brow, the curve of her lips, the hollow look to her gaze.

"Gabriel was killed in a gambling scheme gone wrong. His murder was just recently solved by his late wife."

"So he did marry."

"Yes, Celine. I think you would like her too."

"And they never had bairn, ye said?"

"No, they were never blessed."

Her gaze fell to her fingers, picking at a cuticle. "So it's me then, just me."

My heart clenched painfully in my chest. "Not just you. You've an aunt, Davina, and a grandmother. And there's me, I suppose."

Dark eyes found mine, brow lifted. "I dinnae even know yer name."

"Alexander—Xander. My name is Alexander Hasket, but I prefer Xander."

"Xander. So yer my uncle?"

"I suppose I am. Never been an uncle before. I'm not certain I'll be any good at it."

"Davina disnae have any bairn?"

"Davina is determined to never marry."

"I hate to be the one to tell ye this, but marriage isnae a requirement for bairn." She gestured toward the curve of her belly with a sardonic smile.

"Speaking of, the father?"

"As I said, lending seed disnae make a man a father." There was something wry in her tone.

"Who is he?"

"Just a boy, vicar's son. Said he'd marry me an' take care of me and I wouldnae have to worry about money again. But he was a liar."

"The vicar's son? Where does he live?"

"What are ye going to do?"

"Force him to take responsibility, obviously."

"I dinnae wish to marry him. He wasnae kind."

"What do you wish to do then?"

She blinked at me, seemingly startled by the question. "Hadnea gotten that far. I planned to fleece ye until the babe was born and then forevermore until yer solicitor wrote. Then I was just hoping to fleece ye until the bairn arrived and I could move somewhere new—claim to be a widow. But then ye arrived."

"I'm left with the absurd desire to apologize for upsetting your plans even though your plan was to steal from me until I died."

"Ye should. It was a good plan."

"It actually was. Much more well considered than most of Dav's."

"Thank ye."

"We should discuss this further, but I find myself famished. And Godfrey's probably prepared to turn in his notice again by now."

"Cannae say I blame him," she retorted, rising from the pallet and padding toward the kitchen, leaving me to retrieve Godfrey from the jaws of Fenella.

∼

Lock arrived just after breakfast—a more successful endeavor on my behalf than supper had been—with a gentleman.

The ruddy cheeked man was a master builder. Burly, with hair the color of mahogany and dull grey eyes, he lifted one peppered brow at the sight of the place.

Silently, he stalked through the first floor of the house, making notations in a ledger here and there. I was left to trail after him, sharing befuddled looks with Godfrey as we struggled to read his countenance.

Eventually, he crept up the stairs, studying each one closely before placing weight on it and stepping over others entirely. I followed his path with careful consideration, praying they would hold my weight. When we reached the landing, I was left to follow him aimlessly from room to room. Six bedrooms, two with separate sitting areas for the lord and lady, lined the hall. Each oaken door was carved in a simple but elegant design of vines—those seemed to have held up well, though they were overtaken by cobwebs.

The furnishings had fared worse. At some point, the roof had clearly leaked in several places overtop beds and carpeting, leaving the scent of mildew caked into the very plaster. Sounds of skittering followed from room to room and I struggled not to give the sound consideration.

Paint and wallpaper peeled and chipped in equal measure in every room we ventured into. Most of the windowpanes, too, were cracked, some of them completely overcome by long-dead vines outside. Floorboards creaked ominously with every step, protesting the weight after so many years of disuse.

I followed the man as he carefully measured his steps down the servants' staircase and into their quarters. Those rooms were slightly better, having no visible water damage, though much of the bedding was ravaged by insects and time.

When we finally circled back to the kitchen, Lock, Sorcha, and Godfrey all perked up with interest.

"Not good," the builder muttered.

I bit back an *obviously* and instead asked, "But it can be fixed? Right?"

"I dinnae have the time."

"But you know someone who does?" My hands danced as I filled in his sentence.

"No."

"But you can make time for the right price?" I wasn't delusional, I knew the house wouldn't be fixed quickly or affordably, but not at all? It was unfathomable. If there was one thing in the world I knew, it was that everyone had a price. Everyone.

"No."

"But—"

"No, lad."

Panic began to rise in my chest, settling there, tightening, shoving out everything, until nothing was left but terror. I could feel my gestures tightening, shifting from smooth flowing motions to harsh jerking ones.

"What do you propose I do then?"

"Move."

"Move?"

"Aye, move."

"I cannot— That is not— I'm not moving."

"Didnae say ye have to. Just said that ye should."

"Why can you not help?"

"Nae just me. Everyone is working on Dalkeith."

"Dalkeith?"

"Palace," Lock filled in. "The duke is having it remodeled."

Which duke? *I* was a duke. What good was having a damn title if I couldn't throw it around on occasion? If it could not get me what I wanted as I wanted it?

"What am I to do?" I repeated inanely.

The man shrugged. "Dinnae ken. But ye'll not find good help." With that, he set off, out through the door and into the yard. I heard Fenella bleat him a greeting from her place tied up to a different—hopefully sturdier—tree.

Sorcha had the decency to look chagrined. Godfrey's expression remained stoic, while Lock seemed to waiver between disinterest and amusement. I wasn't entirely certain what the man was still doing here. But, given his ready assistance, I wasn't willing to begrudge his presence.

My chest was knotted painfully tight, each breath a struggle on both inhale and exhale.

In silence, we sat around the scarred table. I was waiting for someone to pipe up with an idea—presumably that was everyone else's design as well. The morning's breakfast settled like a rock in my belly, plopped there like a lead cannonball, sinking down, down, down.

At last, I could stand the silence no longer. "Any suggestions?"

"No, lad," Lock retorted. Sorcha shook her head, at least feigning a contrite expression.

"You and I return to London?" Godfrey supplied.

"I cannot, you know I cannot."

"I know no such thing."

Before I could change the subject, I heard the familiar sound of hoofbeats through the open—broken—window.

My stomach twisted warily. There was no indication that it was bad news, none except the dearth of good news in recent days.

No sooner had I stepped out the front curtain than a carriage rounded the corner. It was an older model, but well cared for, and I did not recognize it.

I waited for it to drive past the wreckage of my life, but instead it turned around the pond. The driver stopped short, avoiding Fenella's irritated bleat.

Something settled deep in my spine, an awareness, perhaps a recognition. Whatever it was, it felt like hope.

When the door opened, I wasn't surprised to meet with Prussian eyes and the teasing smirk of Tom Grayson.

Twenty-Five

KILMARNOCK ABBEY, EDINBURGH - JULY 16, 1816

TOM

THE JOURNEY WAS LONG, and dull, and astonishingly fast. When the driver informed me that the changeover would be my last, I was nowhere near ready to face him.

I wouldn't have been disappointed if those last few miles took years. It had all seemed so simple in Hugh's study. Travel to Scotland, confess my feelings, kiss Xander until neither of us remembered the purpose of air—mere trivial concerns. But as the distance between us shrank, my nerves grew.

Scotland was a novelty to me. The lush forests and clear skies were lovely—even if I couldn't make out the precise shade. The air out here was crisp and bright—as Xander predicted—and lacking the stench of London.

Though I longed to stretch my legs outside of this blasted carriage, I wasn't prepared for what came next. For the entire journey I had considered what I might say upon arriving at Xander's doorstep.

I'd considered excuses and fibs. I'd considered a declaration. I'd considered abandoning this idea as folly and returning to London, hat in hand.

Butterflies danced in my stomach as they had for the best part of my trip to such an extent that I could hardly eat.

As we passed a small woodland abutting a little pond, we rounded a bend onto an overgrown gravel drive. Just beyond the pond was a ramshackle brick house. At one point, it had certainly been fine, but time and nature had reclaimed it. So I was all astonishment when we slowed to a stop in the drive.

In place of a front door, a curtain hung along the frame and I couldn't help but wonder what had happened to the original.

It fluttered for a moment before it was pulled back. Alexander Hasket's dark head peered out before the rest of his broad frame spilled onto the drive. My heart gave a delighted jolt. In his shirtsleeves and waistcoat, hair jutting every which way, he was still the most beautiful man I'd ever seen.

Unable to restrain myself, I slipped open the door and stepped onto the gravel and weeds below. He was too far away to make out his expression, but nothing about his countenance or the way he held his frame indicated irritation.

Tentatively, I stepped toward him on wobbly knees. Christ, I really was a cricket. My legs were too long and too ungainly to be relied upon.

Muehheheh! A sheep called out in my direction, drawing my gaze from Xander—the beast had prevented the carriage from traversing any farther up the drive.

A heavyset thing with a white body, dark face, and impressive horns, it gave another irritated bleat. I stepped forward, offering it my wrist for a sniff. It gave a weary huff before allowing me to scritch it behind the ears with a quieter *mehheheh*.

"Hullo there. What's your name?"

Suddenly, a huffing breath sounded at my side—*Xander*.

He was even lovelier up close, impossibly long lashes framing dark eyes overtop full lips and a stubbled jaw—I remembered those lips, so soft against my own, the perfect contrast to the bite of his half-considered beard.

"Don't"—wheeze—"touch"—wheeze—"her," he panted, hand pressed into a stitch in his side. I liked him breathless, even if I wasn't the cause.

"Why not?"

"She's evil. She'll attack."

The sheep offered a tentative bleat, nudging its—her—snout into my palm. My fingers curved instinctively, scratching along her chin.

Xander stared at us, gaze flicking back and forth between me and the ruminant beast, his jaw slack and eyes astonished.

"What?"

"She's not trying to— What do you know about sheep?"

"Almost nothing. Why?"

"She's been nothing but trouble since we've arrived. Threatening to charge anyone within range, sneaking into the house to defecate, making a general nuisance of herself. But you—"

"I think you're attributing a great deal of malice to a sheep."

"No, that is a malevolent hell-sheep." He gestured toward the thing with his usual irritated gestures. The sight made me smile. It was so lovely, so Xander, that my heart was entirely full with it.

"Well, she seems to like me well enough."

"So she does..." he muttered, then turned to face me. "And, I suppose I should ask, why are you here?"

My amusement faded, leaving behind nerves and nausea, tinged with the tiniest hint of hope.

"I... uh... I do not know. I just..."

His expression was unreadable, brow furrowed, not in irritation, but not in pleasure either. "You just..."

"Wanted to see you." My tongue darted between my suddenly dry lips, wetting them. "I just wanted to see you.

"You wanted to see me?"

I swallowed, desperate to shove the rising nerves back down my throat. "Yes."

He turned back to the curtain, searching for something. Whether he found it or not, I didn't know. He grabbed my wrist and pulled me behind him, calling back to my driver, "Stables are on the north side."

The man grunted and set off to rest the horses. I stumbled after Xander. He was astonishingly difficult to keep up with in spite of my longer legs. We rounded the house, if it could be called that, and stepped into a side yard.

He tugged and suddenly I found myself pressed against the house. The tan bricks damp with the remnants of morning dew. And then his fingers slid into the messy curls at my nape and pulled my lips down to his and I could think of nothing else.

The fabric of his waistcoat was fine, with a subtle texture beneath my fingertips as my hand found his waist. My other hand found his cheek, the silken strands of his hair kissing my fingers as his overgrown stubble bit at my palm. His lips and tongue and teeth stung and soothed as well.

Christ, this was better than I remembered. How was that possible? That first time, he'd allowed me the chance to explore, to discover. Apparently, he was done with that. He maneuvered me as he liked, kissed me the way he wanted, touched me the way he desired. The efforts left me weak-kneed, breathless, and hungry.

His lips ripped off mine, traced the line of my jaw as I pathetically, helplessly, fingered the buttons of his waist coat.

"Why are you here?" he growled in my ear. "You shouldn't be here."

Alone, the words would have crushed me. But combined with the hardness pressing against my thigh and the play of his tongue along the tendons in my neck, they lost a great deal of their sting.

"Why did you leave me?" I shot back, grabbing his chin in both hands and yanking his mouth back to mine with a nip to the swollen flesh of his lower lip. He mumbled something against my mouth and I just grabbed the back of his neck and pulled him harder to me.

He tasted of Earl Grey, strawberry jam, fire smoke, and dust—nothing like his previous herb and forest scent and malty scotch. But I liked it all the same. I rather thought he could smell and taste of anything and I would love it.

Blood rushed through my ears, drowning everything except the deliciously sinful slick of our lips, the sensual rustle of fabric, and the lewd harmony of our moans. Lord, his groans—there was something about the masculine note that settled in the base of my spine and left me panting with want.

"Left you for your own damn good," he muttered, nipping at the knot of my throat as he worked sightlessly at my cravat.

"You don't get to decide what my own damn good is," I shot back, grabbing the back of his head and slamming my lips back onto his.

His tongue fought mine for dominance before he pulled away again, fingers moving toward the buttons on my waistcoat. "I do if you don't have a damn fiber of common sense."

I caught his lower back, pulling him against me, forcing him to feel what he did to me. "There's your common sense."

I felt the laughter in his breath against my neck and the shaking of his shoulders. "I know that's where it went. That's the whole damn problem."

My own laugh broke through the haze of irritation and lust. Xander returned to my lips, kissing me gently as he rebuttoned my waistcoat and straightened my cravat.

He pulled away, whispering, "We can't do this here. Fenella will be by any moment to take a shit."

"What?"

"The sheep."

"I don't...."

"And Godfrey and the others are probably wondering where I've gone off to."

"Who..."

Strong fingers tucked back a lock of my hair before he ran his hands along the fabric of my waistcoat, smoothing it. He nodded, seemingly satisfied with whatever he found, then started off toward the front of the house, catching my hand as he went.

"Wait, your hair—"

"Damn," he laughed, turning back to me. I took my time, enjoying the moment of putting this man back together, brushing a wayward strand of hair into place, straightening his waistcoat. Every sensation was one worthy of luxuriating in.

By the time I finished, his lips were still swollen, and probably a little darker than usual, but he was more or less presentable—less obviously ravished.

He caught my wrist again, dragging me toward the front of the house.

"What happened to this place?" I asked as he lifted the sheet covering the doorframe for me to duck underneath.

"Apparently nothing. For the best part of a decade."

"Truly?" It was an inane question. Anyone with eyes could see the peeling wallpapering and chipping paint. The broken windows and warped floorboards, too, were obvious. And the scent of dust and decay overwhelmed everything else.

"It's a long story..."

"Who was that at the road?" A feminine voice called from down the hall. My heart stopped for a moment. But then I caught sight of the girl who stepped into the hall. She was a little less delicate than Lady Davina and clearly with child, but her dark hair and brows spoke of Hasket blood. "Oh, hello."

"Sorcha, this is Mr. Tom Grayson, a friend of mine. Tom, this is Miss McAllen, my... niece."

Xander was already a duke by the time I met him. Intellectually, I knew he had an elder brother who had passed, but I'd never met the man. It was easy to forget his existence except for how his passing affected Xander.

"Why did you not say you had a niece in Scotland?" I knew he didn't owe me an explanation, but it would've been nice all the same.

"That is also a long story."

"Did ye already eat? There's a bit of bread left if ye wanted to break yer fast." Miss McAllen gestured behind her to where the breakfast area was presumably located.

"That would be nice." It was more for lack of any idea what to say than desire for food.

I followed her down a hall until we reached the kitchens where two other men were seated and having a lively debate over the merits of blackberry jam over strawberry. One was a tall man, with a medium build and light hair and a heavy accent. The other was thin, with dark hair and a hooked nose and the unmistakable put-upon accent of a current or future butler.

The kitchen itself was spacious, with fine equipment—though it was rusted and warped with disuse. I settled at a stool while one man, presumably the valet, brought over a slice of toast and two jams—clearly I was meant to break a tie. With the sole purpose of causing mischief in mind, I took a bite of plain bread. I couldn't identify them by sight anyway, the color was too similar. It wouldn't be a fair assessment. Both men grumbled as Xander took a seat at my side, sliding a cup of tea across the scored table to me.

"Thank you," I whispered.

"What are ye doing here?" Miss McAllen demanded, apparently no longer content to feign propriety. She was certainly a relation of Lady Davina.

"Eating toast."

"And?"

"Drinking tea."

"Ugh!" She stomped her foot and I stifled a laugh.

"I heard Scotland is nice this time of year."

"No ye didnae."

I took another bite, my gaze flicking over to Xander. While my welcome hadn't been everything I dreamed of, it was better than I'd hoped. My blood still thrummed with interest, even as I broke my fast. His expression was one of challenge—he wasn't going to provide Miss McAllen an answer, that was certain.

"I wanted to see the country."

"For how long?" Xander asked, significance heavy in the tenor of his voice.

I shrugged. "As long as Scotland will have me."

"I dinnae know what yer on aboot," Miss McAllen interjected.

"So the house?"

Xander's lips slid to one side, pursing there. "That is Sorcha's doing. She and her mother kept my payments for the best part of a decade."

"Truly? Pulled the wool over Will and Kit as well? They'll not be pleased about that."

"Oh, I hadn't thought—have there been any issues concerning Davina? I left Mr. Summers in charge of her affairs."

"No, at least not before I left. I'd been helping Kit with the offices while Will was... otherwise occupied. I have not heard a word about Lady Davina."

"Good, good."

"Do you have a plan for repairs?"

Xander collapsed onto his forearms, with an exhausted thump.

"So, they're going well, then?"

"There's not a laborer to be found. They're all working on Dalkeith Palace," the mysterious Scotsman added.

"None of quality," the Englishman explained.

I took another bite of toast, chewing thoughtfully. "None at all? Or none worth having?"

"None worth having. Which, for all intents and purposes, is the same thing," Xander mumbled.

"Well, no. A poor mason is still a mason—which, I suspect, is better than none in this circumstance."

"And of course, there are some repairs that can be done without skilled craftsmen."

"What can you mean?"

"Well, I did a bit of carpentry—at Thornton Hall."

"Thornton Hall?"

"The family estate. The dower house was in a similar state to this place. We had laborers, but for the betterment of Hugh's marriage, it was in everyone's best interest to have my mother moved as soon as possible. I learned a few things."

"I—you—you know things?" Xander demanded, adorably befuddled expression on his handsome face.

"Bit of carpentry mostly. Tiny bit of masonry. The basics, of course, but more than none."

"You can fix this?" he gestured toward the entirety of the house.

"No, I very much cannot. But I can do a few things, and also, I very much cannot make it any worse."

"But..."

I rose, grabbing his shoulders. "Xander, what is the worst possible outcome? You have to pay someone to fix what I've done? You already have to pay someone to fix it. And it sounds as though it will be months before you can do so. Winter will be here by then—do you not wish for a door, a real one, before then?"

"And you do not mind?"

Mind an excuse to stay indefinitely by his side? There was no better outcome I could name. "No, I do not mind," I whispered, shaking my head.

"Well, it's decided then, lads," the Scotsman interjected, reminding me of his presence. I dropped Xander's shoulders as if I'd been burned. My stomach jolted uncomfortably as I glanced from person to person. None looked particularly scandalized and I took a deep breath, stepping back.

My blood hummed in that icy, jittery way that happens when you've done something wrong and are about to be caught. But not a one of them looked as though anything unusual had happened. And I suppose it hadn't. Men grasped other men's shoulders. It wasn't a lover's caress—at least not for most men. It felt like one for me though.

I swallowed my panic. "Yes, Mr..."

"Lock—just Lock. Don't ask him to explain, it won't make a lick of sense. He drove the carriage and just keeps returning every morning. I haven't thought to question it because, frankly, he's more helpful than the rest combined." Xander explained.

"It makes perfect sense, ye just didnae pay attention. And I dinnae have anything more amusing to do."

Xander just shook his head before nodding to the Englishman. "Godfrey, my valet. Do not let him near your boots. You'll never hear the end of it if they're ever dirtied again."

The man in question sniffed performatively before casting a surreptitious glance at the state of my boots. They probably did need a good shine, but his seemed to be an overreaction.

Xander was fitted with a string at the best of times. And the state of this house... it was not the best of times. Frankly, I adored that about him. He cared so much, all the time, about everything. I could rarely muster the energy to care about much of anything. But I cared about this. I wanted, itched, desperately, to be the person who could calm him, who could soothe his stress, fix his problems. That his natural state was one of fretting made the challenge greater and more worth doing. I wasn't delusional, I knew I couldn't solve all of life's problems. But this—this I could try to do.

"So what is the first concern? The door?"

Each and every single person replied in tandem, "The sheep."

Twenty-Six

KILMARNOCK ABBEY, EDINBURGH - JULY 16, 1816

Alexander Hasket,

Gloomy weather has my spirits low, but your kind letter brightened my day. I can feel the brotherly affection pouring from your words.

In order for me to inform Celine of my punishment, she would need to leave her boudoir. As far as I can tell, the newlyweds have not yet surfaced for air.

Now you're to wed a ceasg according to Mother. Apparently it is some sort of half-fish, half-human creature. I'm not entirely clear on how it differs from the kelpie. I assured her that your children would be no more hideous with a ceasg wife than a human wife, and she calmed right down. I also reminded her that the last human woman you tried to court had her father *arrested rather than wed you. She agreed that if the ceasg would have you, it was for the best. She does long for grandchildren, after all.*

Best wishes,
Davina

P.S. I asked a friend of mine with some familiarity with sheep. Apparently they come by their jumping skills quite naturally.

XANDER

TOM SENT Lock and Godfrey to town for whatever timber and building materials could be scrounged up before braving the shed. After, of course, shucking his coat and rolling up his sleeves in a way that truly ought not be quite as appealing as it was.

Unwilling to risk the infested hellscape a second time, I waited outside offering helpful encouragement. He was taller than me—at even greater risk of spider attack—but he merely ducked under the doorway before setting a lantern on the floor of the shed and taking inventory of the supplies.

"Was that skittering? I thought I heard skittering."

"Probably a mouse—there are almost certainly mice in here," he said, running a hand through his messy curls with no real concern.

"Are you sure you want to be in there?"

He turned to face me, his smile light and easy. "It's fine. I'm a fair sight bigger than a mouse. And I hate to be the one to tell you this, but there are almost certainly mice in your doorless house as well."

Oh, good Lord, I hadn't considered that and now that I had, I wanted to cry. "There aren't rats—surely?"

"And bats. Snakes as well—we should probably ask Lock if there are any we should worry about."

My whimper was masculine and impressive. Tom's smile was bright and teasing.

He stepped out of the shed and caught my hand in his. "I'll protect you," he whispered, dipping his forehead to press against mine before stepping back into the shed. The display had no reason to affect me the way it did, but I was forced to bite back another whimper for an entirely different reason.

Quietly, he took stock of the equipment before pulling several different saws—or saw-like things—off one wall and setting them on the grass in front of the shed. He forged back inside and brought out a long T-shaped pole with some sort of cylindrical metal bit at one end. Its purpose was a mystery to me, but it, too, was set on the grass.

Seemingly satisfied with his collection, he grabbed the lantern off the floor, blew it out, and returned to my side. He dropped that beside his tools and ran a hand through his hair before brushing off his shoulders.

There was a cobweb in the crook of his neck that he missed. Summoning all the bravery I possessed, I brushed it away with the back of my hand, the other hand mimicking the effort on the opposite shoulder for no real reason other than the pleasure of an excuse to touch him. Of their own volition, my hands slid down his shoulders to his chest. Tom's eyes slid closed, savoring, before they fluttered open again—darkened.

His hands caught mine, trapping them against his chest. "Do you want a sheepfold built? Because *that* is not how you get a sheepfold built."

"What is a sheepfold?"

"Small paddock, but for sheep. They're usually made of

stone, but that would take longer and require materials we don't have."

"How do you know that?"

"Michael. He'd take me sometimes, when he visited with tenants."

"And you know how to make a sheepfold?"

"No, but I can hazard a guess."

I nodded toward his collection of tools. "You know what all of those things are? How to use them?"

He shrugged. "More or less."

"Even that one?" I nudged the mysterious T-shaped tool with my toe.

"Postholer—for holing posts."

"Holing posts?"

His chuckle was soft and teasing, not a cruel note to be found. "Digging holes for posts. Now, we need to see if there are any downed trees—we'll need timber."

"I thought you sent Lock for some."

"I did—but we're going to need quite a bit. And we might as well use what you already have."

"But..."

"Xander, come for a walk in the forest with me." His voice was low and soft, and my body reacted before my head—with a tightening in my breeches and a flutter in my belly.

"Right, yes. Yes." My nod was too enthusiastic, but he didn't seem to notice. Instead, he slung one axe over his shoulder before guiding me with a hand on the small of my back over to the small copse of trees lining the pond.

∼

TOM GRAYSON WAS A TEASE.

A tease that was forcing me to carry half of a massive tree. If I was being honest, massive was an overstatement. But still

—an entire tree—third of a tree—he'd cut it down into smaller pieces first. But basically a tree. While it wasn't terribly heavy, it was sticky with sap. The sensation left my skin crawling as I trailed Tom out of the wooded area.

The unpleasantness of the tacky, viscous goo on my hands nearly outweighed the delightful view of Tom's shoulders straining to carry the tree and the play of the muscles in his bottom as he navigated the terrain. And it was a lovely bottom, firm and round and worthy of admiration—or it would have been if he weren't responsible for the gluey gelatinous substance all over my hands and waistcoat.

Godfrey would have a fit. Rightfully so.

Once freed of the woodland copse, Tom picked up speed, leaving me to stumble after him. He must have sensed my struggle because he turned and caught my gaze before slowing again.

"Sorry!" he called back.

"You should be!"

"I know, I know. It's covered in sap. And sap is sticky."

"I don't like sticky things."

"So you've said."

The words were a familiar reproach. I was whining. He was doing me a favor and I was being difficult and demanding. Ungrateful. Too much. I'd heard all of those things before. While I couldn't hear the admonishing note in his voice, an apology was due.

"I apologize. I'm being rude."

Tom's stop was sudden, jarring. Gently, he set his half of the tree down, and came to my side. His eyes were wide—concerned. "You don't need to apologize. It *is* sticky. I don't like it either."

"Yes, but you're helping. You don't need a litany of complaints while you do."

"What is this about?"

My head hinged back toward the sky, it was lighter, with more grey than his eyes. "I've been told I can be a little... peevish."

"I know. I like it. I like knowing what is upsetting you—so I can fix it. Or try to, I suppose. I cannot fix everything, of course. And I do need your help to carry the wood. But I like knowing what is bothering you. I'm a second son. I've been idle most of my life. It feels good to have a purpose—an easily identifiable problem to solve. Your problems specifically."

"But—"

"And I hate guessing. Michael and Hugh have been butting heads my entire life. I've spent years guessing what was upsetting one or the other and trying to smooth it over. I may be good at it, but it's exhausting, constantly searching for pitfalls, trying to keep myself and everyone else out of them. And most of their problems would be solved by simply talking to each other. But instead, they get in a snit and stop speaking entirely."

"You don't feel I'm ungrateful?"

"Oh, you very much are."

My heart twisted painfully in my chest. "But..."

"But you also feel *right* in a way that nothing else ever has. I don't want gratitude. I want you, complaints and all."

What could I do in the face of such words besides toss my half of the tree to the side and pull his lips down to mine?

His smile tasted like hope, even as his surely sap-covered hands found my waist.

Too soon, he pulled away, glancing behind for observers. Finding none, he dropped one last kiss to my forehead before nodding to the tree. "Come on, if we're going to have a place to keep Fenella before next year, we need to get to work."

He strode back to the other end of the log and picked it up. From behind, I caught sight of the place where my sappy hands had found their way into his curls, leaving behind bits of goo.

Served him right for starting such things with no intent to finish them.

Twenty-Seven

KILMARNOCK ABBEY, EDINBURGH - JULY 16, 1816

TOM

The sheepfold was coming along simultaneously better than I'd imagined but worse than I'd hoped. On the face of it, construction was going well. I'd managed to strip most of the bark using the blade knife with relatively few splinters, but my body was unused to such work and was quickly beginning to protest my efforts.

Xander was still gamely fretting beside me, trying his best to refrain from mentioning his sappy hands. He'd press them together occasionally before remembering the viscous goo and glaring down on them in irritation. It was clear he very much wanted to wash his hands—literally and figuratively—of this entire adventure. But he sat on the grass, occasionally peppering me with questions about various tools—most of which I only had vague ideas of how to answer.

My shoulders and back ached, and my breath was beginning to quicken with the efforts. Fenella better be appreciative of my assistance. The ewe had taken interest in my work, seeming to sense it was on her behalf. She watched with curious eyes, occasionally interjecting with a bleat or a quick bite of grass.

Tired of splinters, I abandoned the logs in favor of the postholer. It was simple enough—and I'd seen laborers use one for improvements to the paddock abutting Mother's dower house. Fortunately, the ground seemed to be soft enough to work with but not soggy, which was likely best.

I rose, brushing off the grass stuck to my breeches—which then stuck to my hands—and held my hand out for Xander. He looked at it askance for a moment before remembering his own were equally tacky and allowing me to pull him up.

"Where do you want the sheepfold?"

"I don't know, wherever they go."

"Is there a flat area near the barn? That is probably best."

He shook his head. "Too many hills."

"Beside the shed then?" I knew that area well enough to know it was flat.

He nodded and shrugged. I took it to mean agreement—and, regardless, it would all be replaced in the near future anyway.

"Do you suppose we can keep it pretty small?"

"Yes, please."

"Here abouts?" I asked when we were beside the shed.

"That will do."

It was a good choice. The area allowed me to use one wall of the shed in place of fencing. "What do you think, girl?" I asked the sheep. "Can you make do with this?"

She offered a bleat that I took to be an affirmative.

With little ceremony, I decided to start beside the shed. I thrust the postholer into the damp ground with all my might before twisting it down. It went about six inches before I began to meet resistance. Again, better than I expected but worse than I hoped.

My struggle to bite back a very unattractive grunt failed as

I turned it. I did not have a laborer's build at the best of times and I'd spent the last weeks either in a carriage or in Kit's office—neither of which improved my physical prowess.

"Is that very difficult?"

"Do you want to try?" I made sure to keep my tone light and teasing. It wasn't a reproof and I didn't wish for him to take it as such—and apparently he'd had more than a few in his life.

His revolted expression made his opinion on my offer exceptionally clear even before his, "Absolutely not."

Xander was beautiful, and opinionated, and he spoke passionately about those opinions, his hands dancing in front of him in a way that left me breathless. I always knew when he had an opinion about something and what it was—except me.

At the very least, he wasn't displeased that I was here. Whether he was as pleased to see me as I was him was anyone's guess. Still, I was glad to find a way to make myself useful—a reason to remain here, with him.

That thought strengthened my resolve and I managed to twist the holer down another half foot. I pulled it out and the earth came with it—as it should. That was a relief.

I tried to remember fences I'd seen in the past and estimated the posts were about five feet apart and eyeballed the distance where another hole ought to go. This was not the right way to go about the work, I was all but certain of it. But the proper way to do it? I hadn't any better notions.

The process was more easily repeated a second time once I knew what to expect, though the grunt was unavoidable.

"So, your letter..." Xander started, soft and tentative.

Damn. I'd begun to hope it hadn't arrived yet, that it had been misdirected or waterlogged or burned.

"Didn't mean to send it," I replied, not meeting his eyes.

"How do you send a letter without meaning to?"

I couldn't have kept the sigh inside if I'd tried. "Short version or long version?"

"I've nowhere else to be."

"Right. I'd been... not well—since that night. A lot of drinking, very little bathing." I felt the shame bubble up and I channeled it into turning the postholer deeper. "I don't know precisely what Kate knows. But she was worried about me. She sent Kit to drag me out of the house. He decided I could be of use helping him clean up the offices after the fire. I—shouldn't tell you this. Promise you won't fire Will and Kit?"

"If I do, it will be because of the state of this house and not because of anything you did. But if I'm honest, he's the only one who can manage Davina even a little, so I'm stuck with them both."

"I found the address and might have... borrowed it."

"Borrowed?"

"I had every intention of bringing it back. Eventually."

"Of course," he nodded with fake solemnity.

I braced myself against the postholer where it was buried in the earth. I would need its support. "So I borrowed the address and proceeded to get exceptionally drunk and write you a letter. I'm ashamed to say I only have the vaguest recollection of its contents. In my soused state, I probably did intend to send it, but the next morning, I forgot about it."

"How did it arrive here then?"

"My maid has been out of town. Kate sent a few over to help. They saw it—addressed and ready to be sent—and very generously took care of that task for me."

"Ah... So you didn't mean it?"

There it was, my way out of this. But there was something in his eyes, the set of his mouth—no I couldn't lie about this. "No, I very much did. I simply didn't wish for you to read it."

He was silent for so long that I moved on, measuring the

next hole. My skin was itchy and uncomfortable and only some of it was due to sap and sweat.

At the same moment I thrust the tool into the ground, he said, "I'm glad you did."

"I beg your pardon?" I shook loose curls out of my eyes to meet his.

"It was beautiful. Heartbreaking and wrong, of course. But beautiful."

"What?"

"It was wrong. I'm not unaffected. It did... hurt me to leave you."

"I... You... But..."

He pressed his lips together in that way he did when he was amused but trying not to show it as he halved the distance between us. Strong fingers found my own and pulled them off the pole to tangle together with only the slightest grimace at their sticky, dirty state. "I did notice—was flustered by you. Leaving you—for your own good, I might add—was painful. I was there—with you—experiencing all of those first flutterings of affection."

"Oh..." It was utterly inane, but there was no word sufficient to express my awestruck adoration and joy—at least none I was in a state to name.

He pressed in closer, seeking a kiss—a gift I was all too happy to bestow. Just as I was to meet his lips, a whinny broke through the clearing. We sprang apart, Xander leaning down and snatching the nearby blade knife to inspect with absurd interest while I drove the postholer into the ground once again with newfound strength.

My heart was still pounding when Lock and Godfrey rounded the corner in a wagon loaded with timber.

"Ho!" Lock called as he bounded off the wagon. "Where do ye want this?"

"What is it?"

"Wych Elm."

"I think the pine here is best for the sheepfold. Best to save that for inside. Do you know, is the door still intact and we just need to replace the hinges? Or do we need to construct an entire new one?"

"Hinges were rusted through. Picked up a few of those and other bits and bobs in town. Also talked to a few folks. Found a carpenter who is free. They'll come by tomorrow," Lock explained.

"Thank you." My gratitude was sincere. I could probably manage the door but repairing the broken slats was beyond my knowledge—and masonry was well out of my grasp.

Xander was still staring at the blade knife in fascination while I dug another hole. It had me biting back a smile.

"Would you two see if there are sawhorses in the shed? I'd ask His Grace, but I suspect the effort would be traumatic."

"Aye, I'll look. Godfrey was to start on supper. Hopefully the lass has finished an inventory of the kitchens at least."

They set off to their respective tasks while I nudged Xander with a shoulder, offering him a crooked smile. Though his lips remained twisted in a pout, he curled one up at the corner for a second to placate me.

I felt it, too, the lost moment. It hung there, waiting to be fulfilled—acted on. But we could not, an oppressive reminder that any future we could have would be peppered with unfulfilled moments, missing kisses, tempered conversations, and longing glances.

Lock grunted from inside the shed, before exiting with two sawhorses.

"All right then, lads. I best be off before my wife has a fit. The two of ye can manage yer log?"

"You have a wife?" Xander asked, all puzzlement.

"Aye."

Xander's expression was one of baffled silence. Eventually, he shrugged when Lock didn't seem inclined to elaborate.

"If ye have problems with the sap, scotch will take it right off."

Filled with relief, Xander started toward the house.

"Not so fast!" I called after him before turning to Lock. "Thank you. Will you be back tomorrow?"

"Aye."

"Send my best to your wife."

He merely nodded. In the meantime, Xander had frozen and pivoted back to face me. "We need to split the log—I'll need your help. Best not to waste the scotch.

Broad shoulders slumped as Xander all but trudged back to my side. "Help me get it up and split and you can go wash the sap off."

"Fine," he muttered. I was fairly certain he was more distressed about the sap than our aborted kiss, and I tried not to take that personally.

In the end, we only got the timber on the sawhorses before light abandoned us. I tied Fenella up in the stables with little faith she would remain there until morning while Xander went to wash the sap off.

As I stepped in the house, it was clear Miss McAllen had done more work than I'd expected. The sheets were removed from furniture and several rooms had been dusted. The kitchen was warm and inviting and the shepherd's pie smelled wonderful—especially given the limited resources.

Xander patted the seat beside him and across from the others at the table, then handed me a whiskey soaked rag as he took a swig directly from the bottle. "Didn't have any scotch."

"I don't recall any instruction from Lock to drink it."

"I've been sticky all day—that you thought I wouldn't require a stiff drink is frankly astonishing."

The rag made quick work of my tacky hands, and I used

the opportunity to follow Xander's lead with a drink of my own. That my lips touched the same bottle his had was a coincidence—it certainly wasn't a thought that made my heart flutter like a lovestruck debutante.

The burn was pleasant and another sip quickly began to soothe my aching muscles. I was both exhausted, bone-deep, and on edge. Xander's presence at my side was painfully difficult to remain nonchalant about. He smelled more like pine than usual but also retained that herbal edge. His warmth burrowed into the side of my body as he bickered, a rhythmic sniping in time with Miss McAllen.

I was too tired and too aware of him to contribute to the conversation. If I truly considered it, the shepherd's pie was surely quite good, but I could taste nothing as I shoveled it down at an unreasonable pace. Presumably I was hungry, but I couldn't feel that gnawing in my stomach. There was nothing, save the humming awareness of the man at my side.

As though it was possessed by someone, something else, my left hand found Xander's knee of its own volition. He stiffened, tripping over his words for a second before I felt him forcibly relax and continue the conversation. The fabric under my fingers was a fine buckskin. Velvet softness over rigid muscle. The thought popped into my head unbidden and I couldn't help but shift uncomfortably as it lingered there. Other, even more desirable, parts of Xander probably felt similar.

I let my fingers trace the seam lining the inside of his thigh and catch on lines and divots of firm, well trained muscle. He must ride—it was the only way a gentleman of his standing would have such thighs. What else did he enjoy that I hadn't known about?

His swallow was loud—but it seemed I was the only one who noticed. A fork clattered to a plate seconds before a warm, masculine palm covered the back of my hand. I froze, making to pull away. Instead, that hand squeezed mine before pressing it more firmly into his thigh and dragging it upward.

My own breeches tightened uncomfortably, my heart racing, as I risked a glance. Xander's jaw ticked, but otherwise he was unaffected.

And wasn't that the way of things? I could barely breathe for wanting and he was not even ruffled. In irritation, I pulled my hand away—only for him to grab and tug it back—not to his thigh—no. Xander placed my palm directly over his prick where it tented his breeches.

My heart threatened to pound right out of my chest. He was hot—hotter even than his thigh. And so hard. *I did that. I made him that way.*

He squeezed my fingers in his once more, then shifted his hips to thrust against my hand before releasing me with a sly look.

At some point, he had bowed out of the conversation, and Miss McAllen and Godfrey had taken over, planning meals for the coming days.

In a desperate attempt toward equilibrium, I took another, heartier, swig of the whiskey before passing the bottle to Xander.

He chuckled quietly and took his own sip, before letting his hand fall between our stools and catch my fingers with his.

I must have flushed because Miss McAllen glanced at me curiously before asking, "Are ye well, Mr. Grayson?"

"I'm a bit tired. I should see about finding some bedding for the floor."

"What?" Xander said at the same time that she replied, "Oh, no, I will go sleep in town."

"Absolutely not," he added, directing his comment to Miss McAllen. "You're not going to run away, Sorcha."

She huffed but said nothing. Clearly I was missing a part

of the story, but I was too exhausted to care about piecing it together.

"One of the servants' beds is still in good nick," Godfrey nodded toward a closed door on one end of the room. "I will take that one."

"Oh, I couldn't possibly ask you to give up your bed. I'll take it," I insisted.

Godfrey looked like he planned to protest before Xander added, "It makes the most sense, Godfrey." There was an eager note to his voice with an unknown source. He accompanied it with a finger squeeze for me to enjoy.

Eventually, the valet relented, slumping back against his stool and the conversation swirled around me.

I couldn't recall a time I had ever been this exhausted or this content. Sleep had eluded me for most of the journey, which had been an irritant—under normal circumstances, I quite enjoyed allowing the swaying of the carriage to lull me to sleep. But from the moment I realized my letter had been sent, I'd been at least slightly on edge. Only once I arrived and assigned myself an occupation did I begin to relax. And that occupation left me aching in places I couldn't even name.

With everyone else, I stumbled to my feet to wash the dishes before Godfrey showed me the servant's room that was still standing.

It was small, but serviceable. Barely wide enough to walk beside the bed, but they had managed to cram a washstand and a trunk in there as well. The far wall was entirely taken up with a window, and I suspected the curtains had been taken down to cover some piece of furniture or other. If I wasn't mistaken, it faced eastward as well—the sun would greet me first in the morning.

"Perfect," I said. Godfrey eyed me warily but nodded.

Soon, everyone was readying for sleep, myself included. The room was warm enough with proximity to the stoves to be comfortable—though I imagined when the kitchens were running to serve an entire household it was probably stifling. The problem with the bed was immediately apparent. In truth, it was apparent before I ever tried to crawl in it. It was the same problem I had at more than one inn during my travels. I was a damn grasshopper and my legs were far too long.

Once I curled up on my side though, I was able to fit relatively comfortably, and I drifted off quickly.

But I woke with a start at the quiet knock on my door.

Twenty-Eight

KILMARNOCK ABBEY, EDINBURGH - JULY 16, 1816

Dav,

    Please, for the love of all that is holy, do not tell me how you know this person who is familiar with sheep and in what ways they are familiar.

    Tell Celine to stop corrupting you.

    As far as Mother's quest for grandchildren, I may have news on that front. I've found a young lady who bears a striking resemblance to our dear brother. She is but eighteen, which aligns with Gabriel's visit. Please do not share this with Mother or Celine until I confirm. I would not wish to upset anyone unnecessarily.

                         Warmest Regards,
                         Xander

P.S. The ceasg would be lucky to have me.

XANDER

THE WAIT for Sorcha's and Godfrey's breaths to even out was interminable. My skin positively itched in a way that had nothing to do with sap.

I had Tom tucked away, deep in a far corner of the house waiting for me.

Finally, Sorcha's quiet snores intermingled with Godfrey's loud, intermittent ones. As silently as I could, I slipped out of bed and lumped the blankets into a vague person shape in case anyone woke. Then I tiptoed down the hall, carefully trying to recall where the loose boards were.

If I were any less libidinous, I would almost certainly be concerned about what I might step in or on with my bare feet, but lust had overtaken sense sometime after the third sip of whiskey, around the moment Tom's hand found my knee.

Christ, he had pretty hands. The distracting feature had been all the more noticeable as he worked today. Sizable palms, with long, elegant fingers. What could those fingers do to me? I needed to know.

At last, I made it to the kitchens and tapped quietly on the door.

After another unending wait, I was met with Tom's bleary face. Exhaustion smoothed off his features at the sight of me, easing the slight guilt that crept up when I noted the pillow creases on his cheeks.

Like me, he'd forgone a nightshirt, instead stripping off his waistcoat and cravat, leaving his shirt open. His braces hung from his waist off dirty breeches—mine were clean. The dirt should have bothered me—it did a little—but my discomfort was more than overcome by the sliver of muscular chest, dusted with the same dark curls on his head.

Tom peered behind me before grabbing my wrist and

yanking me into the room, then turned the key behind us with a decisive click.

His smile was crooked and bright in the moonlight, but I only had a second to make it out before his lips fell on mine. Tonight he smelled of fresh-shaved pine and tasted of whiskey. It shouldn't have been nearly as appealing as it was, but I wanted more of it, everywhere, until it seeped into my pores and became a part of me.

"Hello," I whispered, teasing, when he broke for a breath.

"Hello." His smile pressed against my jaw as he breathed the word.

"I didn't mean to wake you."

Tom pulled back and caught my jaw, forcing my gaze to his. "Always wake me. Always."

Soft lips found mine again, just as his hard cock found my stomach with a significant thrust and a heady groan. I couldn't help but thrust mine against his thigh, the one I'd admired earlier in the day. A wandering hand slipped between us to cup me before sliding over to the buttons of my falls.

Two quick twists of his fingers was all it took before he had my cock in his perfect hand—hot and soft, with just the tiniest bite of calluses on the fingertips. Before I could catch my bearings, Tom was dropping to sit on the edge of the bed as he dragged me, stumbling closer.

"Wait—"

He peered up at me, all blue-eyed wanton innocence.

"I didn't come here for that."

His gaze fell, lips pulling into a frown. "You don't want—"

"No, I do. But I don't expect—I was going to—"

"Xander?"

"Yes?"

"I've spent years dreaming of this. Shut up and let me suck your cock."

My jaw fell open on a vulgar groan. "Right, yes. Absolutely. You just... do that." My nod was too long and too much. Tom merely smiled, bright and pleased, as though he hadn't just offered up the single most arousing two sentences in the English language or any other.

Then his gaze fell to my prick. Gently, he traced it with his fingers, gathered the bead of moisture on the tip, and dragging it down the thick vein at the base. The sensation was unlike any other. Tender, reverent. His touch was nothing like my perfunctory tight strokes and it left me breathless. Breathless and impatient.

"I thought you said you were going to suck it."

He humphed, eyes flicking to mine. "I also said I've spent years dreaming of this. You have the prettiest cock in the whole world. Let me admire it a minute."

"You cannot possibly know that."

"You have the prettiest everything in the whole world." His grin was a bright burst in the dark room.

I should have been irritated by the feminine descriptor, but I was vain and loved a compliment—and everything about his expression was complimentary.

Before I could find more words, he pressed a kiss to the tip of my prick. Whether his groan or mine was louder was anyone's guess. Teasingly he traced his tongue along the same path his finger had taken. Then he pulled back, eyes meeting mine again.

"Do you—Do you know how to—"

He shot me a look that told me I was an utter nitwit before drawing me into his mouth with a groan.

My fingers found the soft hair at the nape of his neck on instinct before I remembered myself. *It's his first time. Don't rush. Don't pressure.* I repeated my mantra with devotion, right until the moment one of his hands found my own on the back of his head and tangled his fingers with mine, then applied pressure.

It took a moment to comprehend his meaning, but gradually I took over, guiding him. I felt his moan along the length of my shaft as his hand left mine to meet the other clenching on the cheek of my bottom.

"Tom," I groaned, unable to form anything longer.

He was surprisingly skilled for someone who'd never had a cock in his mouth before—and like everything else, what he lacked in innate talent he more than made up for in enthusiasm and bravado.

This, just as he had the fence, he approached with a guess and a dauntless determination to try—a willingness to suffer failure. That he was using such charming qualities in the service of my pleasure... It had my heart pounding and my balls tightening. Seeming to sense that my pleasure was rushing to a peak, one hand slipped to cradle them. Release rushed ever nearer as he managed to time his tongue to my thrusts—too rough and fast for much else. My mantra was washed away by the blood rushing in my ears and the filthy symphony of groans and slick flesh.

And then he looked up at me with such an expression of adoration, lust, and gratitude that I lost the tenuous grip on my control with a groan and spilled down his throat—entirely without the warning I intended to offer. My groan mixed with Tom's as his fingers clenched on my arse.

My fingers were slow to cooperate and release Tom's curls. As I did, he pulled back, shuddering as he nuzzled a cheek into my thigh with a sigh. The gesture was so sweet, and the juxtaposition from seconds before left me tetchy and too hot everywhere.

His breaths were nearly as ragged as my own, a tiny windstorm whipping across the hair on my legs. He wore an expression of drunk delight that would've had me ready to peak again if he hadn't wrung every ounce of pleasure from my body already.

My throat was too dry, even after a swallow or two, but eventually I felt certain I was capable of speech. "So…" Whether that speech was worthy of the word was a different story.

I felt his smile against my thigh. "So…"

"Was that— Did you— Was it enjoyable?"

Tom pulled away, gaze meeting mine. His eyes were darker, only the slightest bit brighter than the sky outside caressing the moon. "I believe that's my line."

"No." I cupped his jaw, brushing my thumb across swollen, rose-red lips. "Tell me," I demanded. He could deflect a great many things—but not this. This was too important.

A pink tongue darted between those full lips while his fingertips traced the muscles of my thighs in tandem. "Have you ever had a craving for a treat—a pastry, a cake, something like that? That you've longed for over days or weeks?"

"Yes."

"But when you finally got it, it didn't taste the way you imagined at all. In fact, it was so disappointing that you never wanted it again?"

"What?" I demanded, heart in my stomach.

"This was nothing like that," he added with a cheeky, teasing grin.

"Arse!" I shoved him playfully by the shoulder and he fell back onto his elbows with a laugh.

"Xander," he groaned. "Don't be mad."

"I loathe you," I muttered half-heartedly, pulling my breeches up and buttoning them.

"Oh, well, that is unfortunate. I was looking forward to repeating that. But if you loathe me, I'll have to find someone else to—"

I caught his jaw, pulling him back up to seated. "Don't you dare. You're only allowed to do that with me."

Earnest, wide eyes met mine. "Yes?"

"Yes."

"Now?" he asked, eager hands snaking back toward my rebuttoned breeches.

"No. Some of us no longer have the benefit of youth." I batted his determined fingers away.

"Old man..." he teased.

"Rude," I muttered, guiding him back to lean on his elbow again as I reached for his breeches.

He coughed and pulled back, his expression unreadable.

"What is it?"

His eyes squeezed shut, head tipping to the ceiling. He mumbled something I couldn't make out. Worry slammed into me, and I fought back a shudder.

"Tom, tell me."

"It's too late for that," he said to the ceiling.

"Why is it—oh." It was a struggle to keep the smile off my face as the worry melted away into a masculine pride I had no right to. I didn't *do* anything, I had no right to claim his pleasure as my own.

"Yes, *oh*."

Tom was flushed and still refusing to meet my gaze. I couldn't bear both his shame and our physical distance.

I slipped a knee on the cot, nudging him to turn lengthwise. He grumbled but cooperated, flipped to his side, and curled against me. His legs were too long by half for the cot and we were too wide for it. I lay half on, half off, with Tom's legs akimbo across mine. Finally, he let me tuck my arm underneath his neck and rested his head on my bicep.

I caught a knee with my free hand, caressing it. "Such a cricket."

He grumbled playfully, nudging a cool nose into the fabric of my shirt and inhaling deeply.

"Why are you embarrassed?" I whispered.

"Because I—without you—"

"Mmm, yes, you did." Unearned pride still swirled through my veins; it wouldn't go anywhere soon.

"Ugh." He gave a half-hearted shove against my side. I wrapped my arm tighter around him in response.

Tom was so pretty like this, snug against me, dark curls brushing my cheek—I knew from that afternoon that there was a hint of red in them when the sun hit just right, but in the moonlight, they shone like polished mahogany. His lashes were long and thick, shading his eyes from me. And his weight was warm, solid, and just a little bony against my side.

"Talk to me."

"I-I have stamina—or I did before you. Could almost never... when I thought of ladies." He broke off with a bitter chuckle. "Apparently there was a reason for that because all it took was your cock on my lips and the brush of my hand through fabric and I spilled like schoolboy."

I dragged my thumb across those lips. "Yes, you did."

"Stop," he groaned.

"Why? You brought me to a peak—quite quickly, I might add. Should I be ashamed of that?"

His head popped up. "No, of course not! It was perfect."

"Hmm, and are you not proud that you brought me such pleasure?"

"No, I'll be dreaming of that until the day I die."

"If we're going to do this—and it seems we are—then I want you to experience pleasure in all its forms. Quick and fast like a lightning strike. Slow and drawn out until you beg. Every how, every way, you will know pleasure. Mental. Physical. Too much. Not enough. At my hand. At your own.

Besides, there's plenty of shame waiting for us out there." I nodded to the door. "We don't need to bring it in here."

"All right," he whispered softly. It was a simple agreement, but it sounded like a vow.

"I want it all. Yes? Every thought, every desire, every fear. I want you to tell me them all, show me them all, and know that there's no judgment waiting for you."

He merely nodded, a continuation of his vow. "You're different, in here."

"You make me feel safe."

His eyes slipped shut on a heavy sigh and when they flicked open again, they were so full of devotion that I nearly cried. Instead, I tucked a curl behind his ear.

"There is one thing I've been wanting to discuss with you," I added.

"Anything."

"Your letter..."

Twenty-Nine

KILMARNOCK ABBEY, EDINBURGH - JULY 16, 1816

TOM

I FOUGHT past the instinctive panic. It was safe here, in Xander's arms in this too small bed, in the too small room, in the ruined house, wearing breeches that were rapidly becoming very uncomfortable.

"What about it?" I whispered, hoping the tremor in my voice wasn't too noticeable.

It was, if the way he squeezed my knee was any indication.

"You're wrong. I said it before, and I'll say it as many times as you need to hear it—I have never been unaffected by you, not after the masquerade at least. But you've been laboring under a misapprehension that I don't feel as you do."

My heart skipped at the thought, but weeks of loneliness, of unreciprocated feelings, were not so easily shaken. "But—"

"My body recognized you after that night, even if my head did not. My heart threatened to pound out of my chest. My skin positively itched to meet yours. I was shaken and jittery. And you're not the only one with dreams of lips and cock."

I could only shudder as one hand smoothed down my back.

"No, I was not unaffected. And it was not easy for me to leave, not at all. But I thought it was for your own good. In fact, I'm still certain it was, but I'm too weak to send you away."

"It's not your choice to make."

"No, it's not. But you do not understand the consequences of the one you're making."

I made to protest, but he shushed me.

"You understand it intellectually. But the actual experience—it's not the same. We're different, you and me. Rumors have swirled around me since I was a schoolboy. Something about me, the way I am, people just know. But you, I never suspected. No one would. You could live out your days in town with a pretty wife and handsome children and not a single person would ever question you. You wouldn't risk ostracization and hanging."

"But I wouldn't be happy."

He sighed, the effort raising my chin on his chest. "There is a happiness to be found in security, in anonymity. It may not be perfection—but there is no perfection, not for people like us."

"You're determined then to never strive for perfect happiness?"

"Spoken like a man who has never struggled to blend in. A man with no concerns but his own."

Fury found me in that moment—how dare he presume to know me? I shot upright. It was an awkward maneuver given the undersized, over-occupied bed.

"I have concerns. That you have not taken the time to know them does not mean that they do not exist," I snapped.

"I didn't—that is not what I meant."

"Because I'm not a duke, I know nothing of responsibilities? Because what I am is not obvious to all, it is easy? You are tortured because you are seen by all, but no one sees me, has ever seen me, and that is its own kind of torture."

"Tom, please..."

"I think you should return to your bed, Your Grace. After all, it wouldn't do for you to be found here. It might ruin my reputation."

He rose but dropped his forehead to mine in a way that had my heart clenching even amid the anger swirling in my stomach. "I want to *see* you, desperately. I just could not bear it if you lived to regret me. I'll see you in the morning," he whispered.

With a parting kiss to my forehead, he left. The door snicked shut behind him and I was left alone in the waning moonlight.

~

THE SUN HADN'T YET KISSED the horizon when I was up and out of bed. I found my trunk in the corner of the kitchen —forgotten in the exhaustion of the night before—and changed into fresh clothes before setting out for the shed.

My body still ached, but my mind was finally, blessedly numb. The ax called to me, rusted, and in desperate need of a sharpening, but strong and powerful. Unfortunately, we needed the pine for Fenella's pen, not firewood, and I couldn't manage the pit saw alone.

Instead, I yanked open the shed and set about emptying its contents onto the lawn. Various pieces of farming equipment whose uses I had only the vaguest notion of, small garden tools, twine and stakes, a rusted toolbox, a wooden ladder, hoes, shovels, the lot of it lined the lawn before the sun began to crest.

I found a broom and set to work upsetting the spiders

next, wiping away their hard work from the now empty shed, before sweeping the floor. A mouse hole was left behind and I found a small piece of wood to cover it and tried to remember what the housekeeper at Thornton had used to keep them at bay. Cinnamon, perhaps?

Every time thoughts of Xander brushed against the corners of my mind, I pushed them back. That I'd had this thought yesterday—to clean up the shed and turn it into a private place—when we were interrupted by the return of Godfrey and Lock, was a coincidence.

I had just begun to work on the windows with a rag and spit when I was greeted by a pleasant bleat.

"Hello, Fenella."

She snuffed a greeting, nudging my shoulder.

"We'll finish your pen today. How does that sound?"

There was no reply, but she let me scratch behind her ear.

"I don't know why everyone is so hard on you. You just want a little love, don't you? And that's not a bad thing to want. No, it's the same thing everyone wants. But foolish people think they know what's best for you, don't they?"

My musings earned me a huff, but it was more likely due to the fact that I had stopped scratching.

"They try to keep you out of the house, but you're just lonely. I understand, no one wants me around either."

"*I* want you around." Xander's voice washed over me, soothing an ache I'd been able to ignore thus far.

"I wasn't talking to you," I muttered, not glancing his way.

"That's fine. I just needed you to know. Are you hungry?"

"No." I turned back to the window, clearing decades of grime with the kind of methodical concentration that comes from petulance.

"Do you want a hand?"

"No."

"Would you mind company? Besides Fenella, I mean."

"Go break your fast Xander."

"Tom... You're right. I don't know what is best for you. And you deserve to have everything you want." He was surely waiting for me to turn to him, but I stubbornly refused. "Especially if that is breakfast." When I didn't respond again, he added, "Keep an eye on him, Fenella. And don't shit in the shed."

Fenella bleated her agreement as Xander's boots crunched along the gravel. As soon as he was gone, I lamented his absence. I was aware, on a purely intellectual level, that mine was an overreaction. But it was also yet more evidence that he didn't understand my feelings—not truly.

He might be right, that I didn't know what it was to be ostracized, and I didn't have responsibilities the way he did. But he didn't comprehend the loneliness of confusion either. For years I'd wondered what was wrong with me, why I wasn't quite like everyone else. There was no world in which I could go back to the moment before I'd laid eyes on Alexander Hasket, to return to the darkness of ignorance. I had seen the sun, I couldn't go back to the unending night.

The empty shed was returned to a more or less presentable state—it could use a new window or two. But a glance out on the lawn reminded me that the shed itself represented very little of the work I'd created. Tools that needed cleaning, sharpening, and sorting lined the space in front of the entrance.

Christ, I was a damned fool. I was also starving now that he'd mentioned it, but I was too proud by half to saunter into the full kitchen looking for a slice of toast and a cup of tea. My head throbbed in that way it always did when sleep eluded me and exhaustion staked a claim to my body.

With a sigh, I set about finding a space for the tools. Cleaning and sharpening would need to wait for another day, perhaps a day after Xander sent me packing for acting the part of a petulant child.

Worse still, if I had any hope of completing the recently run-off Fenella's fold in the foreseeable future, I needed a second set of hands to cut the lengths of wood. Yesterday, I'd had the fanciful notion of Xander manning the other side of the pit saw. But now I was certain that wasn't a likely outcome.

The tiny part of my heart that was still hopeful, left a corner of the shed clean and empty. It was absurd. Dukes did not take second sons into tool sheds and instruct them to drop to their knees, no matter what my absurd fantasies might suggest.

The crunch of gravel against boot alerted me to another visitor. Once again, it was Xander, meeting my gaze with a tentative furrow to his brow. In his hands was a small tray with a plate and glass.

"You can be as mad at me as you'd like, as long as you're full while you do it." The words poured out of him in an anxious, nearly indecipherable jumble.

"Thank you," I whispered as he set the tray on an upturned tin bucket. I took another from a stack I'd recently placed beside a shed wall and handed it to him.

"What is this for?"

"Sit. If you want to."

He set it down eagerly, before rounding it and plopping down.

His limbs were too long by far for the bucket.

"Who is the cricket, now?"

Soft, full lips slid to one side in that way that made my heart skip. "Are you going to eat?"

"Yes," I said, grabbing the last bucket and turning it upside down. It was taller than the one I'd given Xander because I was just the tiniest bit petty—and my legs were longer.

He humphed but didn't say anything. *Yes, Your Grace, you may have the second nicest bucket.*

The bread and jam were good once again and the tea, though cooling, did soothe the ache behind my eyes.

"The shed is much improved. Thank you."

"Yes, I evicted all the spiders."

He nodded, clearly for lack of something else to say if his aborted hand gestures were any indication.

Eventually, I finished breaking my fast and downed the last of my tea.

"Is your head improved?" he asked.

"I beg your pardon?"

"Your head, it was aching. Did food help?"

"How did you know my head hurt?"

"You had a little furrow—between your brows. And I caught you rubbing your temples when I found you earlier. Is it improved?"

"Yes, thank you."

"I'm glad."

Breakfast had been a gesture, and a considerate one at that after I refused it, and I felt my resolve soften.

"You were right—I don't know... what it is to be you. I should stop... speaking—making choices—on your behalf." His expression was nervous, and he spoke in fits and starts, hands aborting the steps in their usual waltz.

"I might have... overreacted. I've been feeling indolent lately. And in my youth, I was peacekeeper between Michael and Hugh, more than brother. I served a function. But I wasn't a person. With you, the night of the masquerade, it was the first time I've ever felt... complete, in my own right—and you could not even see my face."

"I meant what I said. I want to see you, all of you. Last

night—before the argument—I've never known anything like it. But I want more than that. I want everything with you, Tom, everything I've never allowed myself to want. Every absurd thing that everyone else gets without a second thought. I want breakfasts and luncheons. I want to nurse you when you're sick, and I want you to do the same. I want to share a bed with you—one that you actually fit in—because I want to know if you steal the bed covers or if your toes are cold at night. I *want* to fight with you and I want to make up with you." He'd leaned forward on his bucket, his hand reaching for mine before getting distracted, swept away with the music that was his beautiful declaration.

"Well, it seems we've had at least a few of those. I've broken a fast with you twice. And we had supper, but luncheon should be easy to manage. My head is much improved thanks to your nursing. And we've definitely fought now."

He must have caught the note of mischief at the end because he swallowed, harsh. "We haven't made up yet, though."

"If I promise to remember that you've been making decisions for everyone for years, do you promise to try not to make them for me?"

His nod was exaggerated and slow and the sight warmed my heart.

"Then I suppose we could consider ourselves made up. You should know, though, my family doesn't much care for that step in the disagreement process. I'm not certain I know how it's done."

His lips were trapped between his teeth, holding back a smile that spilled out into the corners of his eyes anyway.

"I can show you."

"Oh, good."

"I'll need somewhere private to demonstrate a proper

apology. You wouldn't happen to know of a spider-free shed with an unoccupied corner, would you?"

"Do you know, I think I've seen one quite recently." I made no effort to hide my grin. Instead, I set my tray back on the first bucket.

After a surreptitious glance around, Xander's fingers caught the fabric of my sleeve and tugged me into the back corner of the shed. The corner I'd left conspicuously empty, even in my irritation.

My back hit the wall with an arousing thunk at the same moment his lips crashed onto mine. Last night had been soft and sleepy. This morning was filled with the lingering bite of irritation, evident in the harsh grip in my hair and the way I dug my fingers into broad shoulders, belying our teasing words.

I pulled back, desperation for air overwhelming even my lust. Xander had no such needs. He traced the line of my jaw with the edge of his teeth, following it with his tongue in a filthy display that had a curse escaping my chest.

"So convinced you're unwanted. That I'm unaffected," he muttered, thrusting against my thigh. His cock was hard again and impossible to miss even through the thick buckskin of his breeches. "Does that feel unaffected?"

Incapable of words, I shook my head, his fingers tightening even further in my hair.

"I'm aching and you're certain I don't want you."

He yanked aside my shirt, tracing the angles of bone and muscles with sharp nips. "You're so damn beautiful like this—disheveled and wanting. Drunk with need for me. And you think I wouldn't spend every second with you on your knees or your back for me, just like this, if I could? If I had my way, you'd never leave my bed again."

"Xander—"

"You're not leaving this shed until you understand—" his

lips found my nipple and my knees went weak. Only the wall and his body kept me upright. I didn't know—hadn't thought such a thing could feel like *that*.

Vaguely, I was aware that the pathetic whimpers were probably mine. But God himself could be standing outside this shed waiting, and I wouldn't have been able to hush them.

"You made your choice," he muttered, switching to the other side to repeat the exquisite torture he'd provided the left.

Breaking off with a gasp, he dragged the shirt up and off entirely, dropping it on the floor of the shed without a care, before finding my sternum. "I tried to leave, to be a good person. But you followed me."

His fingers worked on the buttons of my breeches with no hint of gentleness, no caresses, just inelegant want, even as he bit the soft skin just below my naval.

"You followed me here. Now you're mine. You're never going to feel unwanted or unseen again. Every single time I want you, you're going to know about it. All day long. I'm going to tell you about it until you're so drunk with lust that you'll let me do whatever I dreamed of, fantasized about. And you're going to thank me for it."

He tugged my breeches down and swallowed my cock like he'd been planning for it his entire life. Dark, hot eyes met mine, throat bobbing, and that was all it took. A second in the wet warmth of his mouth and I spilled without a second's warning.

The world darkened for a moment before returning in little golden sparks. My breath was a harsh, ragged echo in the shed as I fought for air, my lungs seemingly incapable of finding it.

Xander's groan was the only thing that kept the shame at bay. At least until he pulled back, gulping, before whispering,

"Good. Again?" as he traced a finger around the tip of my still half-hard cock. "Say yes."

I nodded, incapable of speech between panted breaths. It was quite possibly a lie, I'd never peaked that hard in my life. But I would have died before giving him a different answer, before disappointing him.

His approach was gentler this time, nuzzling and kissing before he took me back in his mouth. Somehow, the sensation was even more incredible the second time. Perhaps because I had more than a second to enjoy it. The combination of his soft tongue twisting wickedly and the lust in his eyes was quickly enough to bring me back to full stand.

Soft hands traced my thighs, soothing at first, then dragging blunted nails along the skin there as I rapidly approached another peak. One hand slid between my legs to cup my balls before the other rounded the back of my leg. I realized his plan the second before he executed it, but no amount of time could have prepared me for the reality of a finger sliding between my cheeks, tracing a circle around that entrance.

Another peak ripped from me, spilling my very essence into his waiting mouth in great shuddering breaths.

He shushed my whimper at the chill when he pulled back and stood. With uncooperative and sluggish fingers, I reached for the buttons of his breeches. He batted me away, making quick work of them himself. Xander's breaths were even harsher than my own when he grabbed his proud, ruddy cock and began working it in quick, short strokes.

The efficiency was beautiful. I couldn't help but hope that one day I would know how to touch him that well. I could be the one to bring him to a swift climax or draw it out until he begged—whichever pleased us both.

With a shuddering gasp, he came, his seed decorating my thighs, my abdomen, my cock. And then that same hand—the one that had worked his member to such beautiful effect—found mine again.

It was too much, too hot, too slick, too sensitive, too wrung out. My hips moved away of their own volition. "Shhh, let me," he murmured, as he gently painted his spend across my skin.

The sight, the understanding, it was the single most arousing thing to ever happen to me in an impossibly long morning of most arousing things. He finished with a quiet, pleased, "There. Mine," before catching my cheek with his clean hand and brushing away tears I hadn't noticed as he pulled me down for a kiss.

When we broke apart, he eyed me, his gaze heavy as he traced the ruined lengths of me. I was sticky and covered with darkened bruises. My shirt probably draped over a rusty scythe. My breeches were crumpled at my feet. And I could only begin to guess about the state of my face and hair.

"Was it too much?"

I was aware enough—of him, nothing else was capable of penetrating my mind—to catch the slightest note of vulnerability in words. "No—well, yes, but in the best possible way."

A little tension leached out of his shoulders and his forehead found mine. "I should have asked first."

"There's nothing you can do that I don't want, Xander. Nothing you can give me that I won't take and nothing you can ask of me that I won't give."

I felt his eyelashes flutter but when I glanced up, they were squeezed shut. A single tear slipped out and I reached up to brush it away before kissing his forehead.

"You can't rid yourself of me now," I whispered.

Thirty

KILMARNOCK ABBEY, EDINBURGH - JULY 17, 1816

Xander,

I do not understand your concern about my friend with the sheep. They are very fond of their sheep.

Cee does not listen to you any more than I do, so that is a fruitless request.

I find myself adrift at the notion that I may have a cousin that was unknown to me. Fortunately, your gentle delivery has eased the shock somewhat. And I have been positively spoiled by the wealth of information you've provided. I'm left with absolutely no questions to speak of.

Since I was unable to relay your letter in its entirety to Mother, she has become convinced that whisps have led you to your death. We toasted your short, unremarkable life and Mother has set off to *select an outfit for your service. I suspect the veil will be the memorable part of the ensemble.*

*Best wishes,
Davina*

P.S. The ceasg would be lucky to have literally anyone else.

XANDER

TOM WAS A MESS. The linen of his shirt was swirled with rust and mud stains from where it had landed on something I didn't know the name of. His breeches were creased obscenely—though I imagined I would be the only one to know the reason. If I thought too long about those, I would consider what was beneath them and then I'd accomplish nothing for the next week—at least nothing I could admit to in a court of law.

He hadn't bothered with a waistcoat or cravat when he set out before dawn, and his open collar revealed the ruddy, reddish-purple marks I'd left behind, a constellation etched among the smooth skin and auburn hair.

At some point, I'd clearly raked my fingers through his hair, leaving it a nest of mussed curls. And those devilish lips were swollen.

Worst of all, he still wore that awestruck, slightly intoxicated look that had me ready to drop to my knees again, if only so it would never leave his face.

Instead, I straightened the collar of his shirt, hiding the evidence of my efforts from the world. Carefully, I tucked it into his breeches, ensuring I kept my fingers away from his overly sensitive member.

"What are you doing?" His words were slurred with pleasure. It was a travesty that he ever sounded otherwise.

I didn't respond, instead fixing his buttons before smoothing the sides of his shirt. There was nothing to be done about the stains, but it was easily explained away.

His hair took a few moments to smooth into something that was merely disheveled by exertion of a job well done—not the exertion we'd engaged in. Those soft lips were still swollen. My only hope there was that no one had studied him well enough the day before to notice the change. Still, I allowed myself the luxury of dragging a thumb along the lower one. He took it as an invitation to press a kiss there because he was a sweet little grasshopper.

He caught my hand as I stepped back to survey my work. Long, gentle fingers smoothed my hair into something vaguely resembling my usual style. It felt a bit off, but without a mirror, I doubted I could have done better.

Seemingly satisfied, he nodded to himself with a ghost of a smile. "Perfect."

I quirked a brow in answer but restrained a scoff. If he wanted to think I was perfect, I had no interest in correcting him.

When I held out a hand, he took it without question, letting me lead him out of the shed. As soon as we reached the threshold, I had to drop it. Tom offered the mildest sound of protest.

"Where are we going?"

"You need real clothes. Before anyone sees what I've done to you."

"What if I want them to see?"

"Tom..."

"I know, I know..."

"Besides, this version of you is mine."

That sentiment seemed to appease him, and we made our way inside the house—if it could be termed that.

There was no sign of Lock or Godfrey, but Sorcha was, to my great astonishment, once again at work removing wallpaper—this time from the dining room.

"They've not returned yet?"

"Not yet."

I leaned against the doorway, Tom hovering too close to my side, but I was unwilling to offer him a reproachful look. Sorcha was proving helpful. She spared a glance at us, before tugging another strip off—almost in its entirety.

"Ye planning on being any help?"

"No. Tom needs to dress before they return."

"Aye, ye wouldnae want to scandalize anyone with all those spider bites."

"What?" Tom and I demanded in unison—his tone much calmer than mine.

"The ones all over yer chest in a line down to yer roger."

"I— What?" He'd gone shockingly pale and I was almost certainly equally peaked.

"Strange spider—that. I'm surprised ye didnae see it when ye were down there, Xander."

"Sorcha, I—" I started, but in my rising panic, nothing followed.

"Relax. I'll not tell anyone. It explains a great deal, actually."

"What?" I demanded.

"Why yer still here. Why ye came at all. Why yer friend with the too-long legs arrived days later with even less warning than ye did and no plans to leave." She leaned a hip against the wall she was working on, one arm cradling her belly.

"And you'll simply remain silent about this?"

"Yes."

"What is your price?" I demanded

"Pardon?"

"Your price? You want something from me in exchange."

"I'll not say no if ye want to pay me. But I dinnae need anything—not aboot this."

"Why?"

She sighed, her gaze flicking to the floor before meeting mine again. "Ye could have had me arrested—as I said. But ye didnae."

"I'm also keeping you here against your will."

"If ye think I couldnae have escaped last night when ye had yer wee tryst, yer a fool. Or a hundred times before or after."

"You knew about that?" Tom asked.

"Everyone with eyes knew about that. Yer not exactly subtle. 'Oh, I couldnae ask ye to give up yer bed. I'll take the one over here all by its lonesome with a door and a lock...'" she dropped her voice an octave as she mocked him.

"Does Godfrey..." Tom asked, too warry to finish the sentence.

"Probably... I'm not certain," I supplied. "But Lock certainly doesn't—"

"Dinnae worry aboot Lock. We had a wee laugh aboot ye this morning."

"What?"

"If ye dinnae want people to find out aboot ye, ye should be less obvious. Of course ye had to flee the damn country if this is how ye keep a secret."

"I— But— We— You..."

"That's nae a sentence."

"Sorcha, I..."

"Still nae a sentence. But ye should ken, it's illegal here too. Most dinnae care what folks get up to in the privacy of their own beds. Same as London, I expect. But some will. Ye'll need to be a wee bit more discreet." She hopped onto the dining table—entirely free of Fenella's droppings—before scooting back to sit.

"You truly don't intend to tell anyone?" I reiterated dully, dragging a hand through the hair Tom painstakingly righted.

"As I said. I dinnae care what ye do."

"You're remarkably calm about this."

"Mam wasnae exactly a lady. If ye ken..."

A missing piece slid into the puzzle. "But your father was a steward?"

She shrugged. "He was... fond of her. Offered her a bit of security when her circumstances changed. But she dinnae want me ignorant of such things. Though... she neglected to explain that not all men would be kind like my pa."

"And you're determined not to give me a name?"

"Yer not my father or my brother."

"That doesn't mean I cannot call the man out."

"Do ye ken how to shoot?"

Not well enough to stake my life on it. "A bit."

She raised a skeptical brow. "Of course ye do. Regardless, I dinnae wish to marry him. So if ye survive, ye'll have to duel me to get me to wed him. An that much gun powder cannae be good for the babe."

"What are you going to do? When the time comes?" Tom asked, earnest interest in his beautiful eyes.

"I dinnae ken. Yer *friend* upended my plans a wee bit."

"We've time to discuss it," I added.

"Oh, we do, do we?" Sorcha asked in a tone designed to let me know I had overstepped.

"If you want."

"Better. But the two of you'se ought to set yersels to rights before Lock returns. He was bringing a few people from town. Dinnae want to bring undue attention to yersels."

Tom squeezed my wrist before making his way to his room

off the kitchens. I lingered as Sorcha pushed herself off the table and returned to the wall she had been peeling.

"You could stay here. If you wanted."

She turned back to me, lips parted and brows raised. "I've fleeced ye for years. What makes ye think I willnae rob ye blind?"

I shrugged. "It wouldn't shock me if you tried. My sister has as well. And Gabriel would've. It's the Hasket way—seems I'm the odd one out, if I'm honest."

"I'll agree yer an odd one. But sharing a bloodline disnae make us kin."

"Technically it does. But I take your meaning. Gabriel is gone, and I cannot ask him. But I believe he gifted me this place as an escape. He knew someday I would need a place away from society—and father's reach. That he won it in an ill-considered game of hazard and left behind a child in the process so perfectly summed up his life that I honestly do not know what to do besides laugh."

"And ye would just let me live here until what? I've annoyed ye too much?"

"Davina perpetually annoys me and I've not done a damn thing about it except settle funds on her and try to keep her out of ruin."

"I'm not yer sister."

"No, you're my niece."

"And the babe?" She rubbed a hand along the curve of her belly again. It was a protective gesture I'd seen Mother do with Davina.

"Do you want to keep the babe?"

She blinked slowly, something like surprise. "I cannae give a babe the life it ought to have."

"Yes, you can."

"What do ye mean?"

I shrugged. "Well, at precisely this moment, it doesn't look like much—though that is entirely your fault. But a babe could have a good life here. Both of you. If that is what you want."

"Yer willing to let both of us stay here? Indefinitely?"

"With Davina in London, I rather think I might find myself adrift without someone to humble me in every conceivable manner."

"And ye'll just house a bastard bairn?"

"As you've rightly pointed out—I've engaged in less... legal activities this very morning."

Her expression was entirely unreadable.

"Think about it, Sorcha. I do not need an answer today. We can figure everything out. But I'm not your enemy, and this isn't a trick."

I turned to the hall only to find Tom standing a few feet away, refreshed and handsome.

"This is nice," I said, stepping into him and tracing the neck of his slate, floral waistcoat.

"*That* was nice."

"You heard that?"

"I did. And it was very nice." He pressed a kiss to my cheek, his free hand catching the other to keep me there.

"She is my niece, I want her safe and comfortable. Anyone would do the same."

He chuckled, nuzzling my cheek. "No, they wouldn't. Trust me."

That was the moment I remembered his family. "Michael?"

"Mother was particularly cruel. And she encouraged it in Hugh and me as well. I was younger when Father died, and Michael took over the estate on Hugh's behalf. It was harder to reconcile the things she said about him with the way he cared for us and our home. But no, not every family protects by-blows."

"You're not capable of cruelty, Tom."

He hummed, dipping for another kiss. I slipped my hand between our lips. "If you do that we'll never stop." The words came out garbled against the back of my fingers.

"You say that like it's a bad thing," he whispered before kissing my fingertips.

"Lock will be back at any time. We've already been caught once today."

"Fine, if you want to be sensible about it. I need to split the logs for Fenella's fold. Do you want to help?"

"No, but I want to watch."

"You watched plenty yesterday. Come, I need a hand." Tom caught my arm and tugged me along down the hall.

"I'll give *you* a hand..."

"You just turned me down, now you want to?"

"That was before I knew the alternative was woodwork."

He tipped his head toward the sheet. "Come, I'll roll up my sleeves for you."

That was a tempting offer, even in spite of the edge of embarrassment that he'd noticed my appreciation. "Fine, but only if you loosen the cravat too."

"I cannot do that—I was bitten by a rabid spider."

His lips were trapped between his teeth in an effort to restrain his smile, but I could not. Still, I let him drag me out onto the drive where I was greeted with a disgruntled bleat from Fenella, grazing along the drive and leaving piles for aesthetic and aromatic purposes.

Thirty-One

KILMARNOCK ABBEY, EDINBURGH - JULY 17, 1816

TOM

Xander was astonishingly helpful in splitting the wood into usable quarters and in helping me get the posts into the ground. By the time we'd managed that, Lock and Godfrey returned with more timber and a guest.

A young lady hopped off the back of the wagon. A female carpenter? That was interesting.

Xander and I approached her, keeping a conspicuous distance between us. Much as we needed her assistance, I couldn't help but lament the reduction of privacy.

Lock rounded the wagon to perform the introductions. "This here is Miss Isobel Gillan. Her pa is the best carpenter in the city."

"Pleased to meet ye," she mumbled, gaze cast on the ground. She was small, with delicate, freckled features and red curls. Her dress was simple, with a serviceable leather apron overtop.

"Thank you for coming," Xander said, struggling to keep his hands still. "Could I speak to you for a moment, Lock?"

Xander's fingers finally escaped his tenuous control and he snatched the man around the elbow to drag him behind a tree. I suspected the conversation would be an intriguing one. While I could guess his concerns, I also knew that beggars could not be choosers.

The girl was left behind, looking askance at the hole in the house's facade.

"I'm Tom Grayson. I'm just a friend of His Grace's."

"What happened to the door?" Miss Gillan asked, ignoring my introduction entirely.

"No idea. It was like that when I arrived. They keep blaming the sheep, but that seems unlikely. It's propped on the side of the house if you'd like to take a look."

She disappeared in a flurry of practical cotton skirts, pausing only to heave a toolbox off the back of the wagon. It seemed she was not one for small talk.

Xander's mutterings grew more shrill behind the tree, and I abandoned Miss Gillan to her inspection. I rounded the elm to find Xander in a state.

"—and she'll be horrifically injured. She should be at home in front of a fire, not lifting heavy boards and sawing things." His hands danced around searching for words.

"She is the only one available, Yer Grace. It's her or none at all."

I reached for Xander's wrist, catching myself not a moment too soon. "Xander, come now. At the very least, she must have knowledge. She can direct us"—at his glare I immediately corrected—"*me* on how to do the work."

A loud clang came from the direction of the house, and we rounded the tree to see Miss Gillan bracing the door in the frame and adjusting something in the corner.

"What the—" Xander muttered before stomping over. I trailed after him, though I rather suspected I knew what we would find. It seemed Miss Gillan had a strategy to ensure her hire—prove indispensable within ten minutes of arrival.

She was bent over, fussing with the final hinge when I caught up to Xander. No sooner had we reached her side, than she rose and swung the door open and closed once or twice, testing her work.

"You fixed it."

"Rusted pins," she said simply and held her hand out, waiting for him to line his palm underneath. She opened it to reveal several remnants of what I assumed were hinge pins. "The entire hinge needs replaced, but I dinnae have the right size. Can have someone make them for ye in yer forge."

"I do not have a forge," Xander said

"Yes, ye do."

"What? No, I don't."

"But ye do."

"I think I would know if I had a forge." His hand gestures grew larger in his frustration and, as they did, her eyes grew wider and unseeing, her lips thinner.

"Xander," I interrupted.

He turned to me, flustered.

"Why don't we make sure Miss Gillan will have enough to eat?"

"What?"

"I'll help her get settled in. Why don't you see about some luncheon and after, we'll make a list of what needs done."

"But... Fine."

He pressed open the door and turned to stare at it in astonishment before making his way down the hall.

The girl still wore an unsettled look.

"Thank you. For fixing the door. You did nice work."

"Needs a new hinge."

"I'm certain you're right."

"There is a forge."

"All right. Do you want to show me, and we can see what it needs to be functional?"

She nodded, her gaze somewhere over my ear. Before I realized she'd agreed, she began to wander off in the direction of where I assumed the stables were.

"The door looks nice," I added, still trying to smooth over any upset.

She shrugged.

"I'm certain His Grace is deeply appreciative."

Her pace increased and I was left to keep up.

"Xand— His Grace has had an eventful few days. We all have."

No response, beyond her breezy breaths as I panted beside her, desperate to keep up.

We rounded a bend and the stables appeared behind a copse of trees. They could use a few repairs as well but, astonishingly, were in better condition than the house itself. I suspected the use of sturdier, less ornate woods and materials left the structure more prepared to withstand the elements. The last remnants of a path continued over a small hill.

As we crested the hill, a small forge came into view below. It was open on the sides, with a massive hearth, long cold.

Miss Gillan finally slowed as we approached, then reached to drag a hand along the smooth metal of the anvil before inspecting the tools I knew neither the name or use of.

She nodded, mid-toned curls bouncing along her forehead. "This'll do."

"All right..."

We set off back up the hill, the morning's events catching up with me. I couldn't lament last night's lack of rest, not after the events of the morning, but both my body and head had been through a great deal.

Rather than slow as we neared the house, Miss Gillan

strode right over to my approximation of a sheepfold. She made a critical tut before grasping my post and yanking it from the earth in one smooth motion.

"What are you—"

"Ye responsible for this?"

"Yes..."

"Is it intended to actually hold the sheep?"

"Ideally... Is it very wrong?"

"Yes," she said, then snatched up the postholer and thrust it into the ground with surprising force for having such a small frame. She increased my depth by nearly half a foot.

"So, not deep enough?" My hand crept behind my head, scratching the hair there uncomfortably.

"Nae. Ye cut the wood too?"

"Yes... Can I— Would you like help fixing it?"

"Not from ye." Her statement wasn't intended to be cruel —it was simply fact to her—even though the reality of it left something uncomfortable curling in my chest.

Dismissed, and with no other obvious task, I wandered back to the kitchens.

Miss McAllen was seated at a table shelling peas into a bowl. No one else was to be found.

"So we have a carpenter?" she asked as I sat across from her. Without looking up, she slid the bowl between us and moved the peas beside it—she didn't provide instruction, instead raising a dark brow pointedly.

I snagged a pea and, watching her as she returned to her work, followed suit in shelling it.

"It's not my decision. But I don't see why not."

"Then why do ye look like someone shot yer dog?"

"I do not."

"Ye do, though."

"Just feeling a little... superfluous."

Her head tipped to one side as she studied me. "Didnae think ye came here to build a sheep fold."

"I didn't."

"So leave that to her. What is her name?"

"Miss Gillan. And I suppose."

"Leaves ye free to do whatever it was ye came here to do—presumably whatever you'se did in the shed this morning."

"I— You—" My mouth hinged open as I gaped at the woman.

"He didnae look at ye the way he did when ye arrived because ye were good at building sheep folds. Or doors. Or whatever other tasks ye assigned yerself to ensure he'd let ye stay. Nor yer pea shelling, to be sure." She tipped her forehead to the peapod I'd thoroughly mangled quite without my notice. The little beads scattered across the table and onto the floor.

"Right... I'll just see if there's anything else I can muck up."

"Try upstairs. I dinnae believe even ye can ruin anything up there."

∼

THE STAIRS WERE in a sorry state and I hope those made it high on Xander's repair list. It was good that I wouldn't be responsible for mending them—I'd probably have someone falling through within a day.

This place was smaller by far than his London house, and I expected his other properties would astonish me. When I reached the top of the stairs, there were seven rooms. The door at the very end of the hall was ajar. I peered inside, only slightly fearing I'd find that Fenella had snuck passed.

Instead, I found the lord's chambers. The walls were dark

and peeling, and the room gave off a musty, petrichor scent. The room opened to a massive bed with an ornately carved frame—mahogany, perhaps, though I couldn't make out the precise shade. The bed linens were worse for wear, but the rest of the furnishings were also carved with delicate leaves. A large wingback chair in an unknown color called the stone fireplace home. Overall, the room was only probably the work of a day or two before it could be used. Though we should probably check the chimney if the chirping sounds coming from it were any indication.

The bed was set between two large windows that spanned floor to ceiling. They were in need of a good wash but otherwise appeared unharmed. The curtains lining them had not fared as well. The ceiling angled, higher by the door than the windows, by five or so feet.

A large trunk was set at the foot of the bed, carved from a different wood with roses and the initials AJH etched into the locked plate. Unlike the rest of the room, it was free from dust. A glance around showed a few other personal effects. Whether Xander had instructed them brought up, or Godfrey had taken it upon himself to settle them here was anyone's guess.

A second trunk, unadorned, rested on the floor near the door. Beside it was a stack of cylindrical leather tubes of varying lengths. Curiosity piqued, I knelt to open one.

The lid popped off at one end and a rolled canvas slid out.

It was a breathtaking landscape captured in watercolor, the details so soft and intricate I could hardly believe they were captured with a brush. A stone fence framed a series of rolling hills, dotted with various trees. The color was a mystery to me, one that was a frustration. And then, in the bottom right-hand corner, I caught a signature *X Hasket*.

I hadn't known, wouldn't, couldn't have guessed at such talent. My heart beamed with pride even as it cursed the knowledge that I could never appreciate it the way he intended.

With more care than I had ever taken, I rolled it back up and reached for another. What I saw stopped my heart. It was a portrait of a young man, kissed by firelight. Half of the man's face was hidden behind a domino, but his eyes sparkled with mischief, framed by impossibly long lashes. His lips were pressed together in a suppressed smile. I felt my own mimic the position at the sight. Dark hair spilled over his ears in too-long waves, with a lock teasing his forehead.

I'd never seen myself in such a way. Mysterious and mirthful and absolutely fascinating. I was beautiful. And Xander had thought of me—remembered me in enough detail to capture the embroidery of my waistcoat and the freckle on my cheek—the one I often forgot entirely.

And his name was scrawled right where it belonged. Across my heart.

Breathless, I rolled that one back up with even more care before delving into another.

This one was different still. A rose garden at night lit by the moon, the stars, and distant torches. Two lovers embraced unashamedly on a wrought iron bench. The shading on this one was unusual. Somehow, I knew. He'd painted this in shades of brown, grey, and inky black. He'd painted the world the way I saw it, except instead of dull, it was awe-inspiring. How could I have ever considered it anything else?

"There you are." Xander's warm words washed over me. Not even he was enough to distract me from the sight in my hands. And wasn't that incomprehensible? I was holding such beauty.

"Oh, you can put those anywhere. The valuable pieces are all in the drawing room."

"What?" I croaked, finally glancing his way.

"I know they're not particularly impressive. But I do enjoy myself."

"Xander, these are—"

"As I said, the valuable pieces are downstairs."

"Perfect."

He tucked his chin in like a disgruntled turtle before examining the canvas in my hands. "Ah, that one. I was rather pleased with how that one came out. Instead of packing away my things, I spent all night on it. It'd barely dried before we set off," he said before snatching it out of my hands and rolling it roughly to return it to its tube.

I was left with nothing but staccato wordless sounds of protest.

"You'll be pleased to know I hired Miss Gillan. And at what I hope is an appropriate price."

Desperate, I reached for the tube in his hands and yanked it open again before pulling it out with more care. After confirming it had not been damaged in its poor treatment, I rolled it carefully, and slid it back into the cylinder.

"What are you doing?" he demanded.

"That was the most beautiful thing I've ever seen—and you've just manhandled it like a drunkard fondling a three-penny upright."

"It's just a painting, Tom, and not a particularly impressive one. Besides, even if it was impressive, it's not as though I can display it."

"You could, somewhere private."

"Someplace where no maids or footmen will ever stumble upon it?"

"Even if it must be kept secret, it still shouldn't be handled without care," I insisted.

His point might have been valid, but mine was as well.

Something about my tone must have caught his attention because he paused, his dark eyes dancing along my form.

"You're right. You're right." He caught my cheek in a wide palm, pulling my forehead to his. "It is precious."

The tension poured out of me. I hadn't understood what my agitation stemmed from until that moment, but Xander had.

He saw me.

Thirty-Two

KILMARNOCK ABBEY, EDINBURGH - JULY 22, 1816

Dav,

You are never to see the sheep friend ever again.

I would ask you to assure Mother of my well-being, but I know you will not so I will write to her myself. Also, remind her that, while veils may be as long as she pleases in the back, they must be no longer than the floor in the front—it is a safety concern.

The girl's name is Sorcha. She is a feminine version of Gabriel—unfortunate Hasket brow and all. We are both convinced that she is Gabriel's natural-born daughter as apparently her mother was quite forthcoming with her history. She is charming and mischievous and not at all impressed with me—thus proving her relation. In *fact, she reminds me a great deal of you in temperament. If you have other questions, I am happy to answer them, but you will need to actually ask them.*

Home repairs are coming along smoothly with no notable foibles. A friend from town has come to stay for a while and we are enjoying ourselves immensely.

*Warmest Regards,
Xander*

XANDER

With Miss Gillan bunking in the kitchens to save time on the ride from Edinburgh, I had no opportunity to sneak off to see Tom at night. Instead I was left with Godfrey's snores and Sorcha's unrest for company.

But in exchange for the lack of privacy, we had a set of stairs that were unlikely to collapse in on themselves with a wrong step, a sturdy sheepfold for Fenella, who seemed more or less content to stay there during the night—the day was another story—and a functional entry door. I hated to admit it, but I would've made the same exchange again.

"Yer certain ye know the way?" Lock asked as we broke our fast one morning. Tom and I were to set off for Edinburg. Alone. Thank Christ. I didn't even need my mouth around his cock again—I mean, I did, absolutely—but my skin positively itched for even two minutes of uninterrupted kissing.

"I'm certain I do not. But Tom does. You've given him the direction three times."

"There's a pub ye should stop at if ye have time, the Black

Swan off Wallis. I think ye will like it. Tell them my sister sent ye." There was something about his tone I couldn't name, paired with a significant tilt to his brow. I knew I was missing something but hadn't the foggiest guess as to what. And I honestly hadn't known the man had a sister.

Before I could question him, we were interrupted by Miss Gillan and Sorcha descending on the table like locusts—Sorcha especially ate like she'd never see food again.

Then Tom arrived, hair still damp from the wash basin and eyes bright. Two minutes wouldn't be enough time kissing. Would two hours satisfy?

Anticipation curled low in my belly as he tipped his head toward the door with a piece of toast in hand.

"Have a good day," Lock called after us as I trailed Tom outside.

The morning was bright as we set off for Edinburgh in Lock's wagon. We arrived in town two hours after we should have with private smiles. I could safely say that two hours wasn't long enough.

After selecting mattresses and bed linens, we were left in want of a drink. As we turned down Wallis, a memory sparked. And as we drove past the Black Swan across the street, I had Tom stop.

"Lock told me of this place."

Tom shrugged, generally willing to go along with most things, especially with the promise of food.

The door swung open as we approached, and a burly gentleman with light red hair raised a brow.

"Pardon me," I said, slightly confused.

"Who sent ye?"

"I beg your pardon?"

"Who sent ye?" he repeated.

Understanding dawned in that moment and I felt a flush rising up my cheeks. Tom's expression was perplexed as I struggled to remember the precise wording Lock had used. *"Tell them my sister sent ye."*

"My sister."

With a grunt, the man stepped back and tipped his head, allowing us entry. I knew what I'd find based on my brief time on the continent, but Tom was in no way prepared.

There were molly houses in London, but none I'd been brave enough to frequent—not at the risk of Mother's and Davina's reputations and security. If I'd had a bit more warning, I probably wouldn't have risked it here either. But the wide-eyed awe with which Tom glanced around the room, a ruddy flush rising up his chest and cheeks, was enough of a reward.

The environment was tame at the moment, though it would probably get more exciting as the night wore on. I was almost certain he'd never experienced anything like it.

"Molly house," I whispered in his ear.

He nodded distractedly.

And then, with the ceremony it was due, I reached for his hand and laced my fingers between his, before releasing a breath. He startled, glancing down before meeting my gaze. Agonizingly slowly, he brought our joined hands to his lips where he kissed the back of mine.

"Ye'll need to move oot of the doorway." The guard from before muttered, tipping his head toward an empty table. I pulled Tom after me to sit.

We were quickly attended by a man in a dress that would have made my mother weep with envy, a vibrant red silk with more lace than fabric. He'd forgone the stomacher, leaving his front bare for the viewing. "Good evening, gentlemen?" There was a flirtatious note in the tone.

I nodded and replied, "Good evening, sir? Ma'am?"

"Ma'am," she confirmed.

"Whiskey for me. Tom?"

He nodded again, still not managing to form a word.

"First time?" the server asked.

"Yes." His voice was strained.

"Dinnae worry, lad. We'll be gentle with ye."

I hummed. "*I'll* be gentle with him."

"So possessive," she teased, then wandered off with a swish in her step. Tom's gaze flicked over to another table where two men were kissing freely, openly. And I rather suspected a bit more, though I couldn't see.

"Xander..."

"I know."

"I'd heard of such a thing, but I never—"

"I know," I whispered, resting my forehead against his temple, breathing in his fresh scent.

"It's..."

"A lot?"

"Wonderful," he murmured, and I turned to follow his gaze. Two older gentlemen, one with hair mostly gone grey, the other with little hair to speak of, shared a table across the room, simply murmuring quietly and holding hands. I knew the ambiance would be nothing like this in the hours to come, when drink and other substances took hold in the night air. But now, in the late afternoon, it wasn't so different from Gunter's or Hudson's, with happy couples chatting amiably.

A tall, shapely man came over to us with two glasses of whiskey. He wore a black, richly embroidered, feminine corset over his shirt in place of a waistcoat and I heard Tom's quiet gasp at the sight. The man's braces hung around his waist and he'd forgone a coat. Though there was nothing particularly scandalous about the outfit, I could tell that Tom felt something—whether it was intrigue or distaste wasn't entirely clear. At least not until his tongue darted between soft lips.

"There you are, boys."

"Thank you." I waited until he turned back to the bar before questioning Tom. "So, a corset?"

He turned back to me, pupils enveloping his irises. The flush seemed to be a permanent state at this point. "I-I don't—I didn't—"

I caught his cheek and rubbed a thumb along the bone. "I'm not opposed."

His tongue darted between his lips again. I caught them with mine without thought. Tom froze for a second before melting into the kiss.

Before we could become carried away, I pulled back. "For you?" I asked, drawing a hand down his chest with purpose. "Or me?" His eyes widened even further with the second option—as though he hadn't even considered the possibility.

Tom's swallow was thick and loud. "Is both an option?"

"It can be." His answering shudder left me nearly as affected as he was.

"You're just…"

"What?"

"I don't even know. I just—perfect. You're perfect."

"I'm far from perfect."

"Perfect for me," he said, dropping a kiss on my jaw.

"Hmm, you're affectionate today." I tucked a curl behind his ear. It was easy to read in his eyes, the freedom he was feeling. I wasn't looking forward to watching it fade when we left.

He pulled his lips in tight, biting back a smile. "Are there places like this in London? How did I not know about this?"

"There are. They tend to get raided though, so I didn't make it a practice to visit them." I didn't want to dim his light by pointing out that they could usually be found near a pillory.

"Is that why there was a password?"

At my nod, Tom squeezed my hand. "Do you wish to leave?"

No, not while he looked so free, but my well-founded anxieties won out. "We probably should."

I set two shillings on the table after catching the eye of the man at the bar. He wandered over to clear the table. "Ye aren't staying? The evenings are a wee bit more... exciting."

"Not tonight, I'm afraid."

"Just dipping yer toes in the water?"

"Not like that, just—"

"We've not had a raid in months, if that's what yer worried about."

"That, and it's a journey to where we're staying."

"Oh, where are ye staying?"

Against my better judgment, I replied, "Kilmarnock."

"Oh, that wreck. Who did ye anger to find yerself there?"

"You know of it?"

"Aye, everyone does. Is it even fit to be inside?"

"Barely."

"Ye wouldnae need any help out there, would ye? Brennan's a plasterer in need of work. And I think Murray too." He tipped his head to a collection of men I hadn't noted earlier. They sat in the corner playing some sort of dice game.

"They are not otherwise occupied with the repairs at Dalkeith?"

He shook his head. I looked to Tom, whose only input was a shrug and a, "Better than the none we have now." It was a fair assessment. I wasn't enthused about the idea of learning to repair walls.

"Send them over?"

The man nodded and wandered off to the table. Tom turned to me. "I thought we were leaving."

"A desperate desire to avoid further home repair lessons outweighs all other risks."

"But you would've looked so pretty with plaster in your hair."

Before I could offer a retort, the entire table of men arrived.

One was of an indeterminate age—he could be no more than twenty, with tanned skin and bleached hair weathered by sand and sun, or he could be more than fifty and remarkably well preserved.

The second was a young man, perhaps nine and ten, with ruddy everything—cheeks, nose, and hair. If his toes had been visible, I was certain they'd have been ruddy as well.

A woman dressed in dark, masculine cuts was also with them. Her hair was mousy and her face was plain—all except her eyes. Those were bright. The mischievous sparkle reminded me of Davina, in truth.

"Yer hiring?" the sun-worn one asked.

"At present, I'm hiring skilled labor for some repair work. Though I do have need of household staff once repairs are further along."

"Murry," he said, gesturing to himself. "I'm a plasterer by trade—though I've some skill as a painter too. And this here is wee Jamie. He clapped the younger man about the shoulder. "He can paint. An' Kenna, there's nothing she cannae do."

"It is too far to travel every day, and the house isn't in any fit state to... well, house you. Not yet."

"We can sleep in the stables."

"I'm not certain the stables are in a fit state either."

"Xander," Tom whispered, before turning to the folks surrounding our table. "Would you give us a moment?"

"Aye." They wandered back off to their corner to stare with interest.

"We need laborers. They need work," he said, catching my hand. "Why are you fussing?"

"I don't know."

Soft, smiling lips found my jaw. "Something is wrong. Tell me."

"It's too easy." I hadn't known the answer until the words left me, but it settled there in my chest, heavy, crushing.

"What do you mean?"

"I've never... made it a habit to associate with people like me. It has always been too big a risk. And now I stumble in here on Lock's recommendation, of all people, and happen upon an entire staff?"

"Isn't that why you moved here? To shake off some of the trappings of London?"

"Yes, but not this many. This is how rumors get started."

"And then what?" he asked, working his way to the hinge of my jaw, kisses intermingled with the occasional nip.

"What?" It was so hard to focus on anything substantive when he was doing *that*.

"And when the rumors get started, then what?"

"Arrested, noose, shame on both our families."

"That seems a stretch, but all right. What is the alternative?" Intriguing fingers worked on the knot of my cravat.

"Huh?"

"The alternative. Say we're not arrested and hung, and our families live on forever, unashamed. What does that world look like?"

I forced myself to consider, even as he pulled away the starched collar of my shirt to trace lines of my neck with his tongue. "Freedom." A home where Tom and I could be open like this—maybe not precisely like this, this was perhaps a bit too open if the hand tracing down my abdomen was any indication—but we could be together and in love and no one would care—

And that was the precise moment where Tom and love—my love, not his—entered my head in the same context and it didn't feel strange at all. In fact, it was natural, like breathing. And wasn't that an absurd realization to have in the middle of a molly house discussing employment opportunities?

"Exactly," he breathed into my ear, interrupting that nerve-racking trail of thought. "Imagine it. We could share a bed—never having to sneak away before morning. I could kiss you anywhere, anytime I wanted to. I wouldn't have to hide the way I look at you. We could hang your paintings above our bed—hell, I could pose for one. I would never have to bite my tongue to keep from calling you sweet, precious, heart, dear, love... lover. We could have an afternoon tiff in the drawing room and no one would bat an eye, sweetheart."

His honeyed words had my spine melting into the chair.

The vultures in the corner sensed my surrender because they nearly tripped over themselves as they reached the table again, eager for employment.

Christ, it was risky. But then, so was everything else I did with Tom. And at this point, I couldn't, wouldn't, have stopped that for the world.

Thirty-Three

KILMARNOCK ABBEY, EDINBURGH - AUGUST 1, 1816

TOM

ANTICIPATION CRAWLED ALONG MY SPINE. Weeks. It had been weeks since Xander and I had a moment alone that wasn't stolen in a garden shed. Even with our new help, the wait had been agonizing.

Sorcha's room was first. As a gentleman, I completely agreed with that choice. As a man in desperate need of privacy—well, I'd been so devastated by the pronouncement that I accidentally sawed through the dining table. Much to the amusement of Sorcha, Lock, and Murray, who'd been nearby when I lifted the board I'd been sawing to find a lengthy jagged slash in the mahogany.

Then Miss Gillan and Kenna from the molly house needed a room. It wasn't proper for the ladies to sleep in the kitchens, not with all the other folks milling about.

Finally, Xander's room was finished—which was thrilling right up until the moment I realized that I absolutely could not sneak past a host of folks sleeping in the kitchens and drawing room.

And so I was forced to wait another week until a third upstairs room was believably serviceable so Godfrey and Miss Gillan would not question my change of rooms.

It was a cruel sort of torture after the freedom of the molly house. But tonight... I shuddered at the thought.

For some of the staff, Xander's retreat—pleading exhaustion—was an exercise in futility. They all knew what we were about. But there were still a few requiring the illusion of propriety.

Still, Lock had given me a knowing look when I tried—unsuccessfully—to sneak the open bottle of whiskey when I retired precisely twenty minutes after Xander. Once it became clear that I hadn't escaped notice, I grabbed the neck more pointedly and set off.

My blood thrummed through my veins, leaving me delightfully aware of every whisper of air and caress of my clothing.

The echo when I knocked on his door was only in my head.

Xander, clad in shirtsleeves and breeches with braces hanging fetchingly about the waist, opened the door without a word but with a glance down the hall. Once I was inside, he turned the lock with a definitive snap.

"Oh, good. You brought fortifications," he said, taking the whiskey from me. He popped the cork before taking a swift gulp directly from the bottle, followed by a gasping breath through his teeth.

"Are you nervous?" Much as I tried to mask it, my incredulity shone through.

"Of course. It's been years. And it's you," he explained as he handed me back the bottle. The whiskey was cheap, its caramel flavor brief and false before the astringent bite of alcohol overwhelmed my taste buds and clawed my throat on the way down.

"You're supposed to be the confident one in this."

He plucked the bottle from my hand again and took another swig, wincing as he did so. "This is truly terrible. Who brought this? Lock?"

"Murray, I think."

Apparently, it was not so terrible as to prevent him from taking another sip. "Hopefully his oil is better than his drink," he mumbled before passing the whiskey back. "So we're both nervous."

"Yes. We should... talk about it? That seems like the best choice."

The whiskey wasn't any more pleasant on my second drink.

He shrugged. "I'm nervous that you won't enjoy it, that you'll decide it's not everything you hoped for and you will leave me and return to London to marry some pretty, bland debutant and have perfectly gangly children."

"My children wouldn't be gangly," I protested instinctively before the rest of his concerns settled into place. "But you should know, I've never, not once since the moment we met, had a desire to marry a pretty, bland debutante and have perfect, not-at-all-gangly children. In fact, you're the only person I've ever wanted to marry."

He choked on the whiskey and broke into a hacking cough. "What?"

"I know it's not possible. I'm not— I understand. But if I had my choice... If I could choose anyone in the world, I would choose you."

Xander surged forward and pressed his lips against mine firmly, immobile, but passionate all the same. When he pulled away, his eyes flicked to mine before dropping to trace the whole of me. With a tiny, almost imperceptible nod, he bent to set the whiskey on the trunk by the door.

"You would marry me," he repeated in a low grumble.

"Yes."

Broad hands shoved my coat off my shoulders to pile on the floor, landing as a whispered promise of more to come.

"Over anyone else in the entire world."

Deft fingers traced my chest to find the topmost button on my waistcoat. It was only a moment before it joined the growing pile.

"Yes."

Xander's warm hand cupped my cheek while the other settled above my heart. "Christ, you make me want to be brave. It is by far your most irritating quality, you know. I wasn't supposed to fall in love. Not ever. *I* was supposed to marry the pretty, bland debutant. *I* was supposed to have children with limbs of a reasonable length. I was supposed to do my duty by my title. And none of those things required love—in fact, they were the antithesis of love."

The hand on my cheek slipped around to the back of my neck and pulled me into a passionate kiss. I couldn't think, could hardly move. It was all too heady and before I'd managed to sink into him, Xander pulled back.

"But you," he continued. "You barge your way into my life with your too-innocent eyes, too-pretty lips, and too-long legs. And somehow, with one teasing smile, you have me tearing down every guard post, burning every fence. Everything I put in place to protect myself, to fulfill my role is in ashes at your feet."

"Xander..."

His breath was heavy, his chest rising and falling, entirely empty of resistance. "I love you."

"You do?"

"Yes, and it is entirely your fault. You'll have to deal with the ramifications of it."

I felt my lips curve into a closed smile. "And what are those?"

"I am entirely incapable of guile—my face and hands reveal everything. I become easily flustered. I fret about absolutely everything. I'm needy, and in the winter my feet are always cold. These are all now your problems to manage."

I nodded solemnly. "I can do that. Do you know why?"

His lips slid to the left side of his face in his version of an inverted smile. "I do, but I'd like to hear you say it all the same. Because I'm needy."

"I love you too." He surged forward, his arms wrapping around my neck as his lips slipped between mine.

Xander kissed away my nerves, and I could sense the moment—in the tightness of his shoulders, in the arch of his spine, in his responsive moans—when I kissed away his.

He broke away, working my shirt over my head even as he urged me back toward the bed. "Did you have thoughts?"

"Not coherent ones."

His smile was small and easy. "Good to know. About tonight, I meant. Did you want to…"

"Bugger or be buggered?" I supplied in a mocking tone.

The answering sigh was indulgent. "I was searching for a more romantic term. But yes, that was the totality of the question."

"I had thought you, inside me, I mean." His eyes widened in surprise. "But if you had other ideas I would not be opposed to—"

"No, I— No, it's perfect. I just thought you would prefer the other way around."

"Is it wrong? To—"

"No," he insisted. "Nothing we do in here is wrong. Not ever."

I nodded, distracting myself by pulling his shirt over his head and dragging his lips back to mine. I'd grown to love the feel of his chest pressed against my own and tonight was no different. The sensation of coarse hair catching mine had shudders traveling down my spine.

When he pushed me back to collapse onto the bed, the shudders became a groan. Xander found my boot with both hands, tugging off first one, then the other. His soft chuckle when the second came off had my brow furrowing in confusion.

"What?"

"Your stockings."

"What about them?"

"They don't match." My laughter joined his.

"I cannot tell the difference. You know that."

"Trust me, I know. I have to look at your waistcoats all day long."

"What?"

"Oh, yes, they're wretched," he explained, working the buttons on my breeches. "I'll be selecting them from now on. Consider it one of the ramifications."

He nodded at me to lift up at the waist and pulled my breeches and stockings free. Eagerly, I set to work on his.

"Such a hardship," I muttered, as though the real hardship was not that it had been days since I'd had the hard cock in front of me in my mouth—a hardship I immediately rectified.

Xander encouraged my attentions with a groan, carding a hand through my hair in that way he knew I liked. "Look at you..." he breathed. "You look so pretty like this."

My moan had his fingers tightening before he pulled me off with an obscene pop. "Get in the center of the bed," he grumbled, low and graveled.

I scrambled back to follow his instructions, stacking pillows behind my head. It was a luxury, stretching out along a bed. Soft mattresses and new linens welcomed me. And when Xander, now freed from the trappings of his breeches, fell atop me with an eager kiss, it felt like heaven.

We rutted against each other in an inelegant but overwhelming heap of flesh and moans.

"Are you certain?" he whispered against my neck.

"I've always been certain about you."

I felt his eyes squeeze shut against the corner of my neck and shoulder and cradled the back of his head there for a moment. Tenderness washed over me, swirling with the lust.

"All right, that was the last beautiful, sentimental thing you're allowed to say tonight. Otherwise, I might die."

"Of course," I laughed. "Absolute filth from now on. Now fuck me, please."

Xander's answer was half groan, half chuckle. "So polite." He leaned over me, reaching for a chest that was functioning as a side table. "Questions before we begin? Concerns?" He snatched a small glass bottle and a handkerchief off the top. My stomach clenched in understanding at the sight.

"Yes, how long before you cease with the stalling and we begin the fucking?"

"Ugh, you are far too coherent. And impertinent." Amid his complaints, he pulled the decorative glass stopper from the bottle. It was a pretty thing, molded and etched into an elaborate pattern I couldn't make out. It was so absurdly Xander, selecting a beautiful bottle for this. He loved beautiful things. He loved me.

With slick, light fingers, he traced the lines of my cock. "That is not where that goes," I pointed out helpfully.

His smile was wry as he retorted, "So you wanted a dry prick to stroke while I fuck you?"

I shrugged, ignoring the answering throb in said cock. "Valid. As you were."

In a reward for my agreement, he twisted his hand at my tip with a gentle squeeze, before pulling it free.

"Grab a pillow," he commanded.

Sensing his plan, I considered the ones surrounding me for

a moment. I rather thought the pillow would be relegated to this use after I chose. I pressed my hips up and he helped me position it.

He took a moment, dark eyes flicking up and down my body. "I'm going to paint you like this one day." The tone was matter-of-fact, and somehow my body comprehended the words before my head, my belly tightening and my toes curling into the new mattress.

"Yes, please."

The stopper clinked against the glass bottle as he dabbed a bit more oil on his hand, slicking up his fingers. I opened my mouth to offer some insolent comment or other. Before I could, he leaned forward and caught my lips in a kiss that was instantly filthy.

Christ, I loved kissing this man. And I especially loved it when his oiled finger snaked between my legs to my opening. His tongue ravaged, even as his finger caressed. Once, twice, three times he circled before pressing oh-so-softly inside.

The sensation was odd, but not unpleasant, and the understanding of what was happening, and who it was happening with, was more than enough to make it arousing. Enveloped from below in soft linens and covered above by hard Xander, his prick sliding against my own, I was panting and breathless already when he found it.

I thought I understood on an intellectual level—but, Christ, this was something else. Every nerve in my body was connected to this one place and Alexander Hasket was playing it like a goddamn fiddle.

"Not so cocky now, are we?" he asked as I thrashed below him. Thrusting against his finger as I desperately searched for more but found too much.

"Xander, Xander, please."

"More?"

I nodded frantically, but then his finger pulled away and I couldn't help but cry out.

"Shh," he whispered, returning with a second finger to destroy my sanity. "That's better, isn't it?" His fingers settled into some kind of rhythm that was at once more satisfying than my spasmodic thrusting—and more torturous.

"Christ, you look lovely like this. Someday I'm going to do just this until you beg me to stop." He could do this forever. I was certain I would never beg him to stop. I could never get enough of this.

My whimpers sounded pathetic even to my ears, but I wasn't capable of stopping them. There was only one thing that could make this better.

"Are you ready now? You want my cock?"

Between panted "Yeses" and overwrought nods, he must have taken my meaning because his fingers slid out. My whimper turned into a groan when I felt his cock brush my entrance.

"Fuck," he muttered and reached for the oil again. "Forgot."

My shuddered breaths filled the room as I waited for him to slick up his stand. He caught my hand, untangled it from the bed linens, and wrapped it around my prick. "Play with your pretty cock, make it feel good." He said it as though it wasn't the single most arousing sentence ever uttered, chuckling softly as I groaned.

And then he was back at my entrance, pressing slowly, gently, waiting for me to give way. When it finally obeyed my will, it was ecstasy. There was the strange fullness again, but this time I knew what was to come. I waited, tracing the lines of my cock with bated breath as he sank inside me with muted thrusts.

Above me, his eyes were squeezed shut—in discomfort or bliss, I couldn't tell. It was probably a mixture of both, like me. But when his cock brushed against that spot, just once, all thought abandoned me.

And once he found it, Xander was relentless in his determination to drive reason from my body. Sweat dripped from his forehead to mix with my own atop my shuddering form. One hand pulled my cock while the other grabbed at any part of him I could reach as he tortured me with pleasure.

"Are you close?" he panted.

I must have nodded, because his hand found my cheek. "Eyes open, I want to watch you peak on my cock."

"Fuck..." I groaned, hand tightening on my prick.

"You're going to make me climax when you do. And then you're mine forever. Do you understand?"

Apparently my intended yes was incoherent because he added, "Say yes."

"Yes, God yes. Anything. Forever. Yours."

He thrust once more, hard, at just the right angle with a single word. "Peak," he demanded. And I spilled in great shuddering, whimpering breaths across my chest. A second later his eyes squeezed shut on a groan and then he stilled inside me.

It took a moment for anything but the most involuntary movements to return, but eventually I was forced to consciously unclench every muscle and brush away the tears that had escaped unbidden.

Xander, it seemed, had no such problems because he collapsed all at once atop me in a sweaty, satisfied masculine heap. Hot breaths whispered across the hair on my chest. Once I could convince my arm to move, I buried it in his dark strands, keeping him pressed safely against me.

For long moments, we lay there, catching our breaths as sweat cooled in the night air.

"Say something irreverent, please," Xander murmured against my chest.

"I think you fucked the irreverence out of me. I'm entirely filled with reverence."

"That will have to do for present. I'm going to move now, it will feel odd," he explained. He was right. My whimper was pathetic and I was left feeling wrung out, empty. He reached for the handkerchief to clean us both up.

Eventually, he collapsed alongside me once again, tucking into my chest as I wrapped an arm around his shoulders. He traced the hair he found there with teasing swirls.

"I think I need to paint you like this too. Thoroughly fucked—by me."

I hummed. "You can paint me any way you'd like. And you can thoroughly fuck me any time you'd like."

"So it was good?"

"Fuck, Xander. My spine is still soup."

"Soup?" The mirth was clear in his voice.

"You fucked the sense right out of me. I cannot be responsible for my choice of metaphors."

"Noted."

"We have got to find a way to ensure privacy. Because I'm going to want this all the time. Literally."

"Agreed." He murmured into my neck. "All the time. Forever."

Thirty-Four

KILMARNOCK ABBEY, EDINBURGH - SEPTEMBER 13, 1816

Xander,

Your concern over my well-being continues to overwhelm me.

Mother was not soothed by your letter, the first you have written directly to her. She has once again returned to the changeling theory. I suggested we wait to see if the changeling is an improvement over the original before taking rash action. She agreed.

If my new niece reminds you of me in temperament, I am certain I shall find her charming. After all, I am the most delightful person you know.

A friend, you say... It is strange. I heard from Lady Grayson that her brother-in-law packed up and left for Scotland with no warning *shortly after you left. Your friend would not happen to have long, cricket-like limbs would they?*

*Best Wishes,
Davina*

P.S. You're still working on repairs? Just how unsuitable was the place?

XANDER

IF THERE WAS a task in the world more infuriating than hanging wallpaper, I didn't know it. My hatred was readily apparent, a fact Tom found impossibly amusing. It had been a few weeks since Sorcha was at all helpful in repairs—too uncomfortable to manage—but she was happy to provide commentary. Between the two of them, I was ready to throw something.

"That's a wee bit crooked," she commented from the chaise where she enjoyed a glass of lemonade. "A little to the left."

"To the left? I'm not certain. I think it should go to the right," Tom added, egging her on from where he splayed across the floor, trying to measure the strips while I battled with the paste.

"It's perfectly centered. Anyone with the tiniest bit of common sense could see that."

"Is it?" he questioned, an amused note ringing in his voice.

"If it's not, it is because it was cut incorrectly. And that would make it your fault."

"No, the cut looks straight to me," Sorcha said. "Maybe it's yer eyes. Do ye need spectacles?"

"I don't need spectacles," I insisted at precisely the same

moment that Tom said, "You would look handsome with spectacles."

"Agh, boys. Save yer flirting for later. Yer too sweet. Gives me a toothache."

"Well, if you don't want to see it, you could go provide your helpful commentary elsewhere. Perhaps Jamie would enjoy it."

"I dinnae know what yer talking aboot," she said with a huff. As though she didn't duck behind the nearest table or grab the closest cushion every time she saw him. I suspected he wasn't entirely indifferent to her either, given the flush of his cheeks each time he saw her. Some men preferred the company of both men and women, I knew that, but I didn't know him well enough to confirm he was one of them.

"He is sure to notice when there's a babe about. And it's not as though he'll believe Xander or I popped it out," Tom mumbled, one end of the measuring tape between his teeth as he pressed the other end down with a foot.

"'Popped it oot'? How do ye think bairns come into the world?"

Tom spit out the tape and began to cut. "I'm certain I don't know the details. And the few that I do know, I wish I didn't."

"Men," she humphed. "Yer mother didnae teach ye?"

"I do my best to forget absolutely everything my mother taught me. It's in the best interests of myself, everyone around me, and society at large to do so."

He rose to all fours to roll out another length of the silk paper, a silvery grey damask he'd liked. I took a break to appreciate the view. Unfortunately, the paper I was hanging chose that moment to flop off the wall and onto my head.

I was met with nothing but laughter when I finally freed myself from the sticky prison—with no help from anyone else, I might add.

"Ugh! You fight with it." I half tossed the paste brush at Tom's still laughing face.

"That's what ye get for yer ogling," Sorcha called as I stomped out of the room to remove the glue from my hair before it caused irrevocable damage of some sort.

~

Some half an hour later, I returned to the drawing room to find half the panels I had been struggling with hung.

The pattern didn't line up, and I was certain it would make my eye twitch until the end of time, but the gesture was kind and I didn't have to be the one to hang it.

There, on the settee, lay Sorcha. Tom knelt on the floor at her side, a hand on her belly with hers overtop. "Does it hurt? The kicking?"

"Just when the lad hits an organ. He likes to aim for my bladder."

"He?"

"Only a man would cause this much trouble."

Tom chuckled.

"May I?" I interrupted, and both of them turned to notice me. Sorcha nodded and Tom scooted to one side.

I settled beside her as Tom had and she grabbed my hand and placed it on the curve of her belly. Beneath layers of fabric and skin, I felt it. A tiny thump met my hand. Again and again, the babe made its presence known, thumping away. My heart swelled.

I met Sorcha's gaze and, though I couldn't have named it, there was something in her expression.

"Tom, would you give us a moment?" she asked.

He nodded, then climbed off the floor as Sorcha moved to sit upright, offering me half of the settee. The door snicked shut behind Tom, leaving a vacuum.

I settled beside Sorcha, one knee tucked under my leg to face her. She mirrored my position as best she could in her present state.

She swallowed, and her tongue darted between her lips to wet them before she spoke. "I need to ask ye something."

"Yes?"

"This babe. I need him to be yers."

"What?"

"I need ye to claim him, raise him as yer own."

"But—"

"What my pa did for me... It gave me a life, kept me from shame. I need ye to do that for this babe."

Comprehension dawned and I felt my hands rise to begin a defense. "Sorcha, I—"

"A man's trueborn son or daughter, even if there are raised brows, has a far better life than a bastard with no father."

I could feel my chest tightening, knotting. "I intended to raise the child as a ward. Would that not suffice?"

"Ye did?"

"Of course I did. What did you think I meant when I suggested you both live here?"

One hand spilled in front of her, splaying out, palm open. The gesture was one of mine that she either came by innately or learned in recent weeks. Though the habit was irritating on myself, it was charming on her. "I didnae know. I thought ye might like to run a halfway house for fallen nieces."

"Sorcha, if I find a way to claim this child, and I'm not saying it's even possible, but it would be final. I couldn't undo it. As far as the rest of the world is concerned, you would be a mere cousin—to your own babe."

"It's not as though I wouldnae see the babe. That ye wouldnae let me care for it."

"And that would be enough? To help raise a child, your child, but never hear them call you mother?"

"Xander, please. I cannae marry him—he was a liar and unkind. But neither can I imagine..." She broke off with a sigh, shaking her head before forging on.

"The greatest gift my ma ever gave me was marrying my pa. I had a name and a home. No one looked down on me or shunned me. And a babe could have a good life as yer ward. I know that. But I cannae give them a father's name. You could though."

"You've been considering this for quite some time, haven't you?"

"Once I learned that yer not so wretched. Yes. The babe wouldnae have to inherit anything." Her eyes were so wide and earnest.

"That's not the way of things, I'm afraid. Firstborn sons inherit, no loopholes. And any child of mine, son or daughter, would be well cared for."

"Oh, I see." Her face fell, gaze finding the floorboards.

"I didn't mean— I wouldn't object to a child, your child inheriting. I just meant that it's not how inheritances are managed."

"So you would..."

"Consider it," I finished for her. "I would consider it. Give me time to think?"

"Of course. Anything."

"Was that all you wished to discuss?"

"Aye."

"I don't suppose you would help me finish with the wallpaper?"

"I would, but I'm so tired. I need to rest—the babe, ye see."

I hummed, unimpressed, before pushing off the settee to my feet. The wallpapering called to me, with its slightly offset pattern. It was going to drive me to insanity. Sorcha's skirts rustled as she slipped away before I could ask again her for assistance.

The dismay was rising when I felt a warm hand on my lower back. I turned in Tom's arms and wrapped mine around his neck. "Thank you for working on this."

His lips tipped into that upside down smile I loved so much. "I've done it wrong, haven't I?"

"No, it's perfect," I rushed to assure him.

"Xander," he growled. "Tell me."

My head hinged back, eyes squeezing tight to restrain the unreasonable complaints.

Tom squeezed my waist, pressing me, forcing me to meet his gaze.

"All right, yes. It's wrong. And when things are wrong and I cannot see them or do not know what it looks like when they're done properly, it's perfectly fine. But wallpapering should be seamless. I know that and I can see it. And every single seam is visible because the patterns aren't matched. I know I should be grateful because I've already learned how absolutely wretched it is to put up. But it's wrong, and it makes my brain itch."

I watched as he bit the seam of his lips before freeing them, swollen and red. "Do you feel better?" He reached up and tucked a piece of damp hair behind my ear with a tender look in his eyes.

For a moment, I simply took stock. Some of the anxious tightness in my chest and head had abated but not all. The rest was entirely occupied with thoughts of Sorcha's child—possibly my child—and where Tom fit into that entire mess.

"A little. Not entirely. But I'm not ready to discuss it yet."

"Later?"

"Yes."

"I can do that. Do you want to direct me while I try to fix it? Or do you want something to eat?"

"Do you suppose Murray can fix it? Or Kenna?"

"You don't trust me to do it?"

"It's more that I rather think I will drive you from the house, all the way back to London, never to be seen again if you have to listen to me while you hang it."

He dipped to press a kiss to my temple. "Impossible. But I appreciate the sentiment. You're overpaying them, they can hang it."

"I am?"

"Oh yes."

I couldn't bring myself to be too irritated about it. They'd done far more than Tom and I would have managed in several lifetimes.

"Something to eat?" he pressed again.

My stomach answered for me with an angry grumble. Tom's laugh mingled with my own as I trailed him out of the room and down the hall.

I already knew what answer I would give Sorcha. If she was certain, I would agree to her scheme. But Tom, so young and carefree, hadn't chased me from London to play at father to an infant. Would that be the thing that was too much? I could only pray it would not be.

Thirty-Five

KILMARNOCK ABBEY, EDINBURGH - SEPTEMBER 15, 1816

TOM

THIS WAS my favorite place in the entire world. Sunk deep into the feather mattress of Xander's bed with him curled along my side as our sweat cooled in the firelight. I used the opportunity to run my fingers through the hair he would never allow me to muss during the light of day. Every so often, a shudder would run through me when my body remembered the things he did to me, the way he spoke.

His breath was soft against my chest. He traced nonsense patterns in the hair there. Occasionally he froze before returning to the soothing designs. After the fourth time, I caught his hand in mine—the one that wasn't tangled in his silken waves. It was a temptation impossible to resist, and I pulled his hand to my lips and pressed a kiss on his fingertips. A filthy thought crossed my mind when my lips met his finger, but I brushed it aside for another day. I was far too spent for such teasing, so I set him free to resume his drawing.

"Tell me," I demanded, my lazy tone discordant with the contentment I felt.

"What?"

"Whatever is causing that little divot right there," I said, pressing a fingertip to the line between his dark brows.

Broad shoulders rose and fell at my side with his sigh. "I need to discuss something with you and I do not wish to."

"Does it have anything to do with your conversation with Sorcha the other day?"

His stubble brushed against my chest with his nod.

"Tell me."

"She asked me to raise the babe as my own." He left the sentence to hang there, alone, in the crackle of the firelight.

"And you agreed?"

"Not yet. I wanted to speak with you first. But... I should — I would like to if her mind remains unchanged."

My heart clenched and then refused to unclench, and I felt my blood run icy. "I see," I choked out.

"She wants the babe to have the benefit of my name."

The world turned sluggish, moving in slow motion even as my thoughts raced ahead. It was selfish, the question echoing again and again in my mind. *Where does that leave me?* There was a child in question, an innocent babe. I knew what happened to bastard children, I'd seen it with my own eyes. Michael may have made something of himself, but he'd also born the cost of my father's poor choices. It was unquestionably the right thing for Xander to do—give the baby a life.

"When will you—" *wed her* remained unsaid, trapped in my tight throat.

"As soon as I decide, I suppose."

"And it is... legal?" Even as I asked, I knew the answer. By law, Sorcha was the daughter of Mr. McAllen and bore absolutely no relation to Xander.

"Probably not. But I feel confident we can find a loophole of sorts, somehow."

The marriage wouldn't be consummated, I was certain of that. So why was my stomach threatening to revolt?

"I know it is probably not what you intended, when you set off for Scotland," Xander said. "But it would be in the best interests of the child."

"No, of course the child should have a name." My throat bobbed with a harsh swallow.

"So you believe that I should?"

"You are right. It is best for the child." I squeezed my eyes shut against the tears welling up, grateful his head was still tucked into the nook between my arm and chest. "When should I—" my ragged breath broke off the end of the sentence. "Go?"

Xander shot up to face me, hand pressing down on my chest for leverage, grinding away the knot there of his own tying. "Go! Go where?"

"London, I suppose. Or Kent. The weather may cause difficulties."

"Oh, you do not wish to? It is too much?" His voice was strained and his expression unreadable, all wide eyes and angled brows. But something in the words, a note of incredulity gave me pause.

"I cannot watch you with a wife, Xander," I explained, feeling the overwrought exhaustion settle in my form.

"What wife?" His hand flung out in a perfectly Xander gesture before he lost balance, propped the way he was, and it slammed back down on my chest. Whether it was his weight or the words that forced the breath from my lungs, the effect was the same, a breathless, desperate, hopeful inhalation.

"Sorcha."

"Why in the damned hell would I marry Sorcha?"

"To give the babe a name!" I moved to sit up but his hand was in the way.

"You thought... Christ, Tom, I planned to lie! Not bind

myself in holy matrimony to my niece. What the hell is wrong in your head?"

"Well, I didn't think you'd consummate it. How was I to know you were planning to lie?"

"Fuck, did you think I was sending you away?"

"What else was I to think?"

He pressed more of his weight into the palm on my chest. "We've had this conversation. You made your choice! You're stuck with me. I was offering the opportunity for you to change your mind. You're barely more than twenty years old—I wasn't certain you were prepared to act as a father to a babe. But now, I've decided you're staying here with me. You're not allowed to leave."

The pressure of Xander's hand was nothing against the weightless elation seeping into every pore of my body. "This bed? Or..."

Fingers curled possessive above my heart. "Yes, the bed. You'll die here."

"A little death?"

"Thomas Grayson, are you angling for something?" The teasing insinuation, delivered in a low timber had my cock twitching in interest.

"I did not think I was being particularly subtle."

"You were not. But while you are not yet two and twenty, I am thirty and it seems I lack the stamina to satisfy you."

The hair of his forearms was thick and coarse when I clasped it, catching as I dragged my nails along it. "I have no complaints in that respect." I laced our fingers together and brought them together to the headboard. The effort aligned our lips and I stole a filthy kiss.

"You still have my spend inside you and you want more. So greedy..." he tutted when we pulled apart. It was a performative effort, belied by his own rapidly stiffening cock pressed against my side.

The still-dawning relief, his words, our kiss; it all had my heart racing. Xander untangled our fingers and held mine against the headboard in a silent command. Cold air rushed in as he unfurled himself from my side and abandoned our bed.

My whimper was instinctive, impossible to restrain in the face of an absence of contact and an exceptional view.

I watched with concupiscent eyes the smooth, carved marble flesh of his arse as he bent to retrieve some item or other from wherever we flung it.

When he turned with two pieces of cloth, one in each fist, I was unsurprised to find one black and one white fluttering rectangle.

My swallow was loud against the ambient crackling fire and the pad of his footsteps. The bed dipped under his weight and he raised the black cravat between thumb and forefinger along with his brow.

"Yes?"

In lieu of an answer, I brought my free hand up to join the other. Xander's pink tongue dipped between his lips. Then he caught the hand and moved it to the post. Instinctively, my fingers curled around it as he looped the fabric around the wood, then my wrist and tied it off with a simple knot.

The image of his strong, masculine fingers twisting in his fine silk cravat for the purposes of restraining me, keeping me with him forever. It would be etched in my memory until the day I died.

"Comfortable?" He interrupted my nodded response to add, "Words. This only works with words."

His insistence forced a sliver of sobriety and I tested the restraint, first gently, then with a bit of strength. I was positive that if I twisted my wrist the right way, I could free myself. But Christ, I never wanted to be free.

"It's so good."

Those sturdy fingers trailed up the length of my arm with a teasing delicacy that left me breathless.

Without warning, Xander shifted to throw a leg over my thighs, straddling me.

"Fuck!" No utterance had ever escaped me with less forethought. But the sight of his darkening cock beside my own was too much to bear in silence.

His smile was teasing as he repeated his flirtatious trail in reverse up my free arm—still fastened with nothing but a desire to please to the headboard.

Unlike his, my cravat was a plain cotton lawn in an unremarkable white. When Xander finished trussing me up for both of our pleasure, I was left to appreciate the contrast in fabrics.

"That one?"

I tested it. There was no pinching or undue tightness, but the reality of *both* of my hands rendered useless above my head sent my heart fluttering.

"Perfect."

"And your shoulders? Nothing aches?" Even as I felt myself sinking into dazed, sensual fervor, I fought to consider my shoulders.

"No, no pain."

Assured of my comfort, Xander traced intoxicating lines along my chest and stomach. "I finally found the benefit to your long cricket limbs."

The laugh escaped my chest in a single huff.

But then, arresting chocolate eyes found mine and mirth was the farthest thing from my mind. "In twenty minutes, when you're begging, I want you to remember that you asked for this. You chose me. You were made for this, for me."

"Xander?"

"Do you remember that first time in the shed?"

"Vividly." Every moment with Xander was etched in my memory—always.

"You'll remember this vividly too. Now, I need a word for you to say if you wish to stop."

"Snuffbox," I supplied with almost no thought. "But I won't wish for you to stop."

He raised a brow at my choice but said nothing. Instead, he located the oil from atop his trunk. I used the opportunity to lick a stripe along his side while he was close.

When he pulled back, it was with a reproachful look and a familiar vial in hand. The clink of the stopper pulling free—a signifier of ecstasy to come—now drew blood to my cock.

Slowly, Xander trailed a stream of oil over my prick. For a brief second, it was cool before warming with my flesh. Again my cock danced at the sound of the stopper knocking against the neck of the bottle.

My lungs worked too quickly, and half-heartedly, I was left lightheaded with needy anticipation.

Finally, after an eternity, Xander set the oil beside the bed and drew a feather light fingertip along the line of my cock.

Thoughtless, my hand went to reach for his, to curve his palm around my member. When the cravat snapped against my wrist, it took a moment for understanding to burn through the fog of lust.

Xander's smile was pleased in response to my whimper. "I've barely begun, and look at you. Already weeping for me," he murmured as he caught the bead of liquid that escaped my cock.

He brought that finger up to my lips, then dipped it inside when they opened on an astonished gasp. I was intimately familiar with his taste, but I'd never experienced my own. As I swirled my tongue obscenely around his finger—aiming to tempt the man—I could only wonder what we tasted like together.

Christ, he'd made a deviant of me. I'd never had such thoughts before Alexander Hasket had shown me pleasure beyond my wildest imaginings. Now I was depraved, feral, desperate. If there was something Xander could do to or with me that wouldn't leave me begging for more, I didn't know the name of it.

He pulled his finger free, grumbling, "Later," when I chased after it.

My lower abdomen clenched at the thought of his graveled promise. "Like this?" I shrugged so there was no mistaking my meaning.

"Yes."

Apparently having tired of teasing, Xander's mouth found my cock, taking me to the hilt in one practiced swallow.

Both hands jerked against the restraints, frantic for the grounding touch I'd become so accustomed to. His hands, his hair, anything to keep myself tethered to earth. But he'd already done the tethering. Xander had ensured I wasn't going anywhere. No, I was left to watch, helpless, breathless, as he inflicted unendurable pleasure upon me.

The sounds ripped from my chest were pathetic, whiny, and all his. He slid a hand up to tweak a nipple and my hands shook in their bindings. My hips circled in a relentless search for more, harder, too much, too fast, not enough. It wasn't until the fifth time he backed off when I thrust forward that understanding dawned.

"You're a cruel monster."

He pulled off my cock with a soft pop leaving it cold and lonely. "You've just now made that discovery?" With a prowling, cat-like grace, he climbed the length of me to cup my cheek. "You're not in charge here. The sooner you learn that, the easier it will be on you." The tenor with which he delivered the devastating line was a soft, sensual, teasing caress of my mind.

"Xander..."

"Shhh, I'm going to feed you my cock for a bit. Doesn't that sound nice?"

If it was possible to get harder, I didn't know how. I didn't know anything except how to nod for him.

Behind my head, he adjusted a few pillows, ensuring the angle was just right for me to take his—*fuck I was going to die*. My thoughts were sluggish and tinged in a warm, flossy glow. Every single word, every single action, brought me closer to my ultimate state, a babbling, mindless mess devoted to nothing but sucking, fucking, worshiping this man.

Warm hands found my shoulders and squeezed. "Still fine?" he asked, tone different, severe.

He wanted an actual answer. I swam to the surface of the sensual pool I'd melted into the bottom of to consider properly. My shoulders were stiff, tight, but with lust not discomfort. My wrists chafed against the fabric that bound them, but the bite was pleasant. "Yes, yes," I choked out.

"Good, because you're going to look so pretty with your lips wrapped around my cock. And I wouldn't want to be interrupted."

My descent back to the depths of loving depravity began with those two sentences but was seemingly endless. Why did my gut twist and flip in ecstasy every time he called me pretty? And why was it so damn obvious, if his smirk was any indication?

He adjusted so he knelt overtop me, one foot by my ear, the other knee by my shoulder, and his perfect cock *right there*. I strained, trying to reach the hard flesh with mouthwatering desperation.

Hushing me again, his thumbs dragged over my burning cheeks. "Every time I think it's not possible for you to be any prettier, you manage it."

And then, finally, at last, his delicate flesh met my lips. His cock was weeping and I allowed myself a brief revelry in the knowledge that he was as affected as I was, swirling my tongue to gather the evidence.

"Oh, no. We're not doing that. You're going to lay there and take what I give you like a good boy."

Fuck!

Objectively, he was being quite gentle, loving, with me, fucking my mouth in slow, shallow thrusts while he braced against the very headboard I was tied to. But the lack of agency, of control, was intoxicating. My only responsibility was to lay here and allow the man I loved to find his pleasure with and in my body. I was there to be pretty, to be good, for him.

"You're doing so well."

My eyes fluttered shut at the praise, letting it seep into my skin, become a part of me, until it was a fundamental truth of my being.

"Eyes on me," he demanded. They snapped open instantly, eager to fulfill his every whim. "Do you see what you do to me?"

I had been falling, lost in a sea of sensation and dizzy thoughts. But Xander... The telltale splotchy darkening of flesh that indicated a flush, covered every sinewy muscle of his chest, his abdomen, his arms, the lines of his cheek. His eyes, too, were black as pitch, swallowed by his pupils. Those lips, so recently wrapped around my cock, were parted, damp. Sweat glistened at his temple, sliding in rivulets to land on his chest. A few drops were navigating the forest of hair to trail down, down, down. I hoped they would land on me. And his cock, his beautiful cock, was impossibly hard and weeping— for me.

"You see now, you see how perfect you are for me?" He must have sensed my nod because he buried himself to the hilt and paused there before pulling out of my mouth. I chased after him, earning a condescending chuckle that had my cock twitching.

"We'll give your pretty mouth a break. Play with your pretty hole."

The sound that escaped my chest was unrecognizable. My lungs fought for air, but it seemed no matter how great my gulps, it was never enough.

He slid to the side and down my body. Once there, he tapped my knees, not that I needed encouragement to open for him. His hands drew soothing lines down my trembling thighs as he settled between them.

"You don't even need oil, do you? You're still dripping my spend."

"No, no, I don't need it." My voice was rattled and hoarse.

"What do you think, should I fuck you every morning so you can go about each day with the evidence of my desire leaking out of you? Would that help you remember that you're wanted, needed, essential?"

"Yes, God yes!"

He hummed, then slipped a too-light hand along the crevice of my arse. And then, without a hint of his usual warning, he slid two fingers inside.

"Fuck!"

"I don't have to warm you up. You're already stretched for me, aren't you?"

"Yes, yes." I babbled, hips circling as he probed for the spot. The spot that usually left me in this wanton, pleading state. What would it do to me when he located it and I was already there?

On the third stroke, he found it and my heart shot from my chest. My arms wrenched against the headboard in my frenzied thrashing.

Now that he'd struck it, he was relentless in his destruction of my sanity. Whether it was seconds, hours, or days, it didn't matter. Not when he pressed down, rocking his finger there in unceasing, exquisite, agony.

In great shuddering gasps, I spilled across my chest as I succumbed to white pleasure.

The world returned beneath dreamy, sensual waves. First there was the sound of Xander's groan, sending a shudder of pleasure down my spine, then the sensation of his seed joining with my own in the divots of my abdomen. His hand swirled there, mixing it like paint, before he brought a hand to my lips. Instinctively, I opened, savoring the offering on his finger before he pulled it back and cupped my face in a filthy kiss.

I was still lost in the tingly, blissful numbness that always accompanied my postcoital moments with Xander, but this—tonight, it was more. Stronger, brighter, it left me feeling softer, more languid and loose-limbed, in spite of my still-trapped hands.

He was responsible for directing this kiss because I wasn't capable of more than allowing him to take his fill. Our spend, still on his hand, began to cool on my cheek before he finished with me. For one brief moment, he allowed himself the luxury of collapsing against me before he reached for the knots on the cravats.

They came free from the posts, still wrapped around my wrists when I reached for him. My shoulders protested the movement but it was a pleasant ache.

Xander's breath was ragged even as mine had slowed like that of sleep. He wriggled underneath me to rub my biceps, collarbone, shoulders—still leaving a mess wherever he went. It took a moment to identify the additional dampness—seeping from his eyes into the crook of my neck.

"Xander?"

"You're so damn beautiful. Where did you come from? You cannot be made for me like this. It's not possible." His voice was thick and hoarse with overwrought adoration.

I swallowed the knot of emotions. "I was though. I was made for you and you were made for me. And whatever comes next, it will be well."

"Even if I'm making a father of you at one and twenty with absolutely no notice?"

"Even then."

He sighed and pushed himself off me with a weary look at the mess he'd made of us.

"Christ, we're going to need a bath."

"I will not be the one to ask someone to draw it. Can you imagine? We'd never hear the end of it."

"We may not even now. You were a little loud at the end."

"Worth it." My grin was lecherous as I shoved a hand beneath my head. The slight twinge in my shoulder was easily ignored as long as I could luxuriate in the sight of him. Naked and covered in us, I relaxed as he located and then discarded various shirts and handkerchiefs to find a suitable rag.

"There is an obvious solution," I said when he finally returned with a length of toweling.

"What is that?" He wiped, somewhat effectually, at his artwork on my stomach.

"The lake, right outside."

His face twisted in disgust before he consciously fought for something neutral. The effect was rather that of a distraught puppy.

"Not tonight then," I said, laughing. "But you're going to need a bigger rag."

"This was so arousing, essential, when I did it," he whined, gesturing at his chest.

"It was…"

"Remind me of this next time."

"Absolutely not. If you thought I was capable of speech in that moment, you were grossly mistaken. And even if I had been, you could not have paid me to stop you."

"Hmmm." He paused his fussing for a moment, a pleased, self-satisfied smile slipping over his face.

I cupped his cheek and pulled him down to press my lips against his. "I love you," I whispered when we broke apart.

His lips slid to one side in his signature, odd little facsimile of a smile.

"I love you too."

Thirty-Six

KILMARNOCK ABBEY, EDINBURGH - DECEMBER 24, 1816

Dav,

Please send more shirts. My tailor has the measurements. I've ripped a few and the sheep ate one. Black and white only, please.

Mr. Grayson's limbs are perfect—if a little long. It is fortunate that he is so good-natured and was not offended when you first termed him a cricket.

You may confirm the changeling theory with mother. It certainly feels that way, though I think the emotion I am experiencing is called happiness. I am incapable of it, as you know, and therefore must be a changeling.

In a more serious matter, Sorcha is very much your cousin and, as such, is determined to vex me. I should probably also inform you that *she is with child, though unmarried—do not get any ideas. She has asked me to consider adopting the child as my own. Though I haven't the slightest idea how I would go about making that legal, I must admit her argument is compelling. Do not share this information with Mother or Cee. I will write them in due course.*

*Warmest regards,
Xander*

P.S. I may have underestimated the scope of the repairs required when I first arrived.

XANDER

THOUGH THE HOUSE was by no means presentable, it was in a state to be decorated on Christmas Eve. The guest rooms, the billiards room, the library, and the music room were the only ones still in desperate need of repair. With the servants' quarters, the kitchens, the study, the dining and breakfast room, the drawing room, and bedrooms enough for Sorcha, Tom, myself, and a just completed nursery all in need of only minor cosmetic changes.

The scent of fresh lacquer lingered heavily in the air at some part of the house or other on a daily basis. We had little need of Miss Gillan and she had returned home and only visited once or twice a week when her specific skill set was required.

Once the servants' quarters were sufficient to be lived in, we were able to hire a housekeeper in Lock's wife, a valet—Godfrey had more than earned his promotion to butler—a couple footmen, a cook, and some maids. In the spring, we would need to add a gardener, stablemaster, and such, a position Lock had expressed interest in. The Black Swan proved to be an exceptional source of loyal staff who did not bat an eyelash when they found Tom and me in compromising positions. At least, as long as no one paid any mind to subtle adjustments to uniforms or wild flirtations.

Sorcha had looked near to popping for more than a month at this point. And she hadn't wavered in her decision in the slightest. She was resting comfortably—or as comfortably as she was able to at present—on the settee beside the fireplace, directing Lock with the wreath she wanted above it. Murray had proved handy with the evergreen, holly, hawthorn, berries, and ribbon and had fashioned them into a more than passable centerpiece.

Tom was out in the cold, fetching a yule log. Though the winter was colder than I preferred, it was not as severe as I had expected. Snow had been sparse and light, dusting the scenery only to melt with the next day's rain.

Tom returned in a great flurry of fanfare with an impressive pine log he rolled inside. Fenella gave a bleat of greeting from outside to the cheers of our newest staff who hadn't had the benefit of the early days with her. They were all rather fond of her, offering her carrots and other treats on every viewing.

Jamie rose to fetch the sheep something from the kitchens, ignoring my protests entirely.

I met Tom by the door, mostly closed to keep Fenella out, and pulled him close for a warming kiss. There was mistletoe after all...

The tips of his ears were icy when I cupped them, and his nose was the same delightful, ruddy shade he turned all over in our bedroom.

"Aye! Knock it off! I swear the two of ye..." Sorcha complained from her perch.

Her complaints earned Tom another kiss, just to spite her. We were *still* under the mistletoe.

Behind us, Murray hauled the heavy log to the fireplace, now properly festooned. "Are ye ready?" he called.

Jamie came running back and slipped in the hall in his stockinged feet. He had far too many carrots for one sheep to eat clasped in his hands—though I had no doubts Fenella would manage it. "Jus a minute!" He yanked open the door and handed the beast a few carrots that she took with a pleased bleat. Then, from nowhere, he pulled a red strand of ribbon and tied it festively around her neck. The sheep allowed it, never once trying to charge him or shitting where he might step.

The blatant favoritism was beginning to grate.

Token accepted, she set off to her pen, which she had taken to quite happily. The lads decorated it for the holiday with evergreen boughs she had gleefully chewed bare spots into.

"Ready!" Jamie called after shutting the door behind Fenella and joining us in the drawing room.

I shoved Tom's great coat to the floor before guiding him over to the chair I'd claimed. We settled there, in the chair too small for two, wrapped up in each other.

"Ye dinnae want to do the honors?" Murray asked.

I shook my head while Lock's short, red-cheeked wife, affectionately called Missus, brought over two glasses of spiced wine. Tom's neck was a temptation I could not resist after my third—or was it fourth—glass of the stuff. The sweet, spicy combination left me feeling warm and languid, and a little sensual. And the outlet for such feelings was *right there*.

Murray heaved the log onto the crackling fire. It dimmed

under the weight of the addition but slowly, the log caught and began to pop pleasantly.

The staff settled in to watch and play a few rounds of various card games, but I was content to curl up in the chair with the man I loved.

Months ago, the night of the masquerade, we had sat in chairs very much like this one—with several feet between us—and for the first time in my life, I allowed someone to carve a door in the walls that guarded my heart.

Now, we had a home, and a family we were building.

Tom had seen every vulnerable, abrasive, tender part of me, shared his in return, and he loved me. The same way I loved him.

Sorcha made an odd noise on the settee beside us.

When everyone turned to look, she explained, "It's nothing. Just a cramp."

Everyone returned to their games and drinks while she rubbed her belly. Laughter mingled with the crisp sparks from the yule log and the clinks of glasses into a lovely symphony.

"Do you want your present?" I whispered in Tom's ear. He nodded sleepily, polished off his glass, and set it aside.

"Goodnight, everyone," he called, grabbing my hand and dragging me out of the room to raucous jeers.

Before I knew it, we were in our room with the lock snicking into place. "As much as I approve of where your mind has gone, I did have an actual present to give you."

"Me too. But also... after..." His blue eyes sparked with mirth. He must have snapped out of whatever languid haze had washed over us downstairs.

"After. Me first?"

At his nod, I bent to retrieve my gift from under the bed, nerves fluttering. I handed him the flat rectangle wrapped in brown paper and tied with a simple red ribbon.

Tom's expression was one of boyish eagerness even as he carefully, reverently, pulled the ribbon off and pulled the paper away.

It was upside down when he managed to free it, but I heard the catch of his breath when he recognized the familiar shape of a wooden frame wrapped around a stretched canvas.

My cheeks heated as I waited for him to turn it over and when he finally did, I had to look away.

His gasp echoed in the quiet room, hanging there for a moment, two. Then he broke the silence with a ragged, "Xander..."

"Obviously, we cannot display it. But..."

"Are you sure?"

A laugh burst free from my chest, loosening the pressing anxiety. "Yes, it is obscene. And besides, no one else gets the privilege of seeing you that way."

Tom's long finger traced over the brown and grey lines I used to capture his form in watercolor. "I look like this?" he breathed.

"Prettier than that—I'm not skilled enough to capture the way your eyes flicker in happiness or the precise curve of your lips when you're thinking of me."

"Xander, I—" Reverently, he set the painting on the bed, reached for me, and claimed my lips with his own.

Our breaths were ragged when he broke away. I couldn't help but chuckle when he rounded the bed and reached under his side.

The box he pulled free was small and rectangular, wrapped haphazardly in the same brown paper I'd used, but he'd tied it with twine.

"Before you open it, I need to explain. This came into my possession on the day we met. I've kept it with me for years, guarded it like a treasure, because it reminded me of you. I just wanted you to have it—in case you ever consider giving me the opportunity to leave you again. You should know precisely how desperately I clung to the scraps of you I could gather before you were mine."

I could do nothing but kiss him for that speech. After I pulled away, I worked on the twine with shaking hands. What I found beneath the paper was somehow entirely surprising and not at all.

It was a delicate gold snuffbox inlaid with agate surrounded by flowers and vines.

A memory sparked at the feel of the cool metal in my palm. Davina, causing havoc at the Grayson wedding, thieving a snuffbox, and the gangly lad I'd been introduced to whose palm I plopped it into. The gangly lad with the pretty Prussian blue eyes and soft palms.

"Christ," I murmured through a tight throat. "I couldn't even remember your name."

Tom's gasped. "You remember?"

I nodded, then caught his lips with mine again. Tears were slipping down both our cheeks when we broke apart. "You give me this lovely, sentimental gift, and I gave you erotic art of your own arse."

"I know. I think I got the better end of the deal," he teased.

A knock echoed throughout. Tom strode to open it and found Missus there, red-cheeked and wringing her hands.

"Sorry to interrupt, lads. But it's Miss McAllen—the babe is coming. Jamie's run to fetch the midwife."

It took no more than a beat before the instinctual terror flooded through my veins. "Fuck, I don't— Did she want— Is there something we can do?" I babbled.

"I dinnae believe so. She was very explicit when she said not to let either of ye in no matter how much ye fuss."

"But—"

"I dinnae take orders from ye. Not in this Yer Grace."

"Bloody hell. You'll inform us the second we're needed—for anything?"

"Aye. But try to get some sleep. Bairns come in their own time."

Tom and I shared a single look before we silently agreed to pace the hall outside Sorcha's room to absolutely no point or purpose.

~

It was early morning, Tom and I long having flopped down to sit on the floor outside the room, when Missus finally opened the door and whispered, "She'd like family to support her," in my direction. I left Tom curled on the floor with a quick glance at his nodding face.

The next two hours were filled with sights and sounds that absolutely affirmed my preference in gender. Fortunately, after the initial horrors, I was able to keep facing the wall and holding her hand. Seeing my brave, bold niece so frightened and in such pain, kept the vomit where it belonged.

I hated the fact that I was Sorcha's best, only option by way of family. A mother should be here. Or a loving husband. Instead, she was left with her irritating, fussy uncle.

But she was strong and in short order, a pink, wrinkly babe was swaddled in her arms.

A boy.

She traced the lines of his tiny scowling face, complete with a dark brow, her tears mixing with his as she bent to whisper something into his ear.

When she spoke aloud, it was with a strangled voice. "Do ye want to hold your son?"

I met her watery eyes with my matching ones. "You're certain?"

"Yes. Meet Ewan Thomas Hasket." She passed him carefully, waiting for me to grip him under the head and back in both hands before wiping away her tears.

"Thomas?" I asked through my own thick, syrupy throat.

"He should carry both of his fathers' names."

It was impossible to restrain a sob, but I forged ahead between tears. "And Ewan?"

"That was my pa's name."

"Fitting—strong."

"I thought so."

"Ewan Thomas Hasket, Marquess of Rycliffe"

"Oh Christ, not even an hour old and he's got a bleeding title," she joked through more tears. "Missus, can ye send Tom in?"

The housekeeper nodded, then opened the door and dipped her head toward the bed before stepping out. I heard Tom clamber to his feet before he stumbled in, rumpled and terrified. Precisely the way a new father should look.

His jaw dropped as he took in the sight. An exhausted Sorcha, furiously swiping at the tears that refused to stop falling. My own dropping unrestrained on the soft blanket wrapping little Ewan, who was the only one to cease crying and instead released an angry snuffle every few breaths.

"Meet yer son," Sorcha repeated, steadier for the rehearsal.

"A boy?"

"Yes. Ewan Thomas Hasket."

Tom melted in understanding, his hand covering his heart. He approached my side, but didn't reach for the babe. Instead, he found her hand. "Are you well, Sorcha?"

Her laugh was sharp and ironic. "No, but I will be. Little lad couldnae ask for better pas."

"Do you want to hold him?" I asked.

He looked absolutely petrified, brows high and lips parted. There was nothing but sincerity in his nod. When he accepted the bundle, a shocked laugh escaped. "How is it possible that every single one of you shares the brow?"

"Dinnae ken. But I'm glad we do."

I pressed a kiss to her temple while we watched Tom fall in love. It was so plain, so obvious on his face and in his countenance that I wondered how I had missed it all those years. Tom Grayson loved fast, hard, and forever.

When his eyes began to water, we all shared a laugh.

"Fusspots, the lot of us," Sorcha murmured.

"Here," Tom murmured, handing the babe back to Sorcha.

"Oh," she breathed, eyes only for her son.

"Do you want to rest? The two of you? Or we can take him. Whichever you're more comfortable with," Tom said.

"He can stay," she whispered.

Tom and I stepped out and shut the door behind us. He led us back to our bedroom, where he pushed me onto the bed and stripped my boots and his own before he turned me to lay back with the rest of my clothes still on. He curled up alongside me in much the same state.

"How are you?" I asked.

"Overwhelmed. Exhausted. Terrified. In love. Pick one."

"Hmmm."

"You?"

"Much the same."

He nuzzled into my neck and drew a soothing breath. "It will be well, though. After all, the boy just has a little extra love in his life. No one was ever hurt by that."

"No, certainly not," I agreed, leaning down to steal a kiss.

"Just so you know, I am so glad you decided to leave London. We never could have had this in London."

"Not cross with me for leaving you any longer?"

"No. Not when it brought us this—a home. And a life together."

After another sleepy kiss, we settled to fall asleep in our bed that we selected, in the room we made our own, in the house we repaired, in the country we chose. My Scottish scheme had been a brilliant notion indeed.

Outside, a bird gave a two-note chirp as I drifted off, overflowing with love.

Epilogue

KILMARNOCK ABBEY, EDINBURGH - APRIL 14, 1817

XANDER

Tom was on the floor, his back resting against the settee and legs spread with little Ewan propped between them, luxuriating in the evening firelight. The boy had developed a recent proclivity for putting every. single. thing. in his mouth. The only possible reprieve was if something appropriate was already in his mouth. Tom had the most patience for balancing perfectly still and holding the rattle at the precise angle until Ewan tired of it and cried for Sorcha. But with frequent feedings, we tried to allow her to sleep as long and as often as our son would allow.

"It seems the rain is clearing up," Tom whispered, his head resting against my knee as I peered down at them from the settee. "We should try to take him for a little walk tomorrow, if it's not too chilly.

I hummed, giving in to the temptation presented by his dark curls. They were, as always, impossibly soft.

A sharp knock at the door startled all three of us and Ewan

broke away from his rattle with an annoyed cry. Tom pulled him into his arms, rocking and shushing the boy.

As the closest person not currently occupied with a babe, I went to discover the source of the disturbance.

I found a man outside holding his horse's reins. "I've an express for Alexander Hasket."

"I am him." I handed him a few coins from the purse we kept by the door for such unlikely occurrences. He traded me for the folded parchment. "Would you like to come in and warm up?"

"Nae, I'll rest at the inn." Task dispensed with, he mounted his horse and set off again.

Part of me was surprised I hadn't had one or two of these before now, given my sister's proclivity for mischief, but I couldn't help the jolt when I recognized the familiar handwriting.

Not Davina, not Mr. Summers, but the delicate flourishes of Celine.

"Who was it?" Tom called from the drawing room.

"Express from London—Cee."

"Damn," he said, then stepped into the hall with a still fussing Ewan in his arms. "Open it."

My hands were trembling when I peeled apart the paste. Tom sidled behind me to peer over my shoulder, reading along.

Dearest Xander,

It pains me to write this, though I should begin by saying that I have no reason to suspect that she is in very great danger.

Will returned to his offices this morning to

THE SCOTTISH SCHEME

find a note on his desk from Mr. Summers. Apparently, your sister has concocted some sort of scheme and kidnapped Mr. Summers in service of it. He did not know the particulars at the time of his abduction, but he did indicate that it may be of some duration.

 I am devastated to say that his letter was dated a full two days past.

 Your mother has gone to Bath to take the waters for her health, and I will take pains to conceal the truth from her as long as possible.

~

 Since I wrote the prior missive, Will now has reason to suspect their destination and this letter's are one and the same. He traced her steps as far as the distillery, and the ladies there indicated that she had set off in one of their unused carriages with an employee of theirs who was eager to return to family in Edinburgh.

 I will write as soon as I learn more, but I pray their arrival may precede this letter.

 Do try not to fret, Xander. Mr. Summers will not allow her to find too much mischief.

       All my love,
       Celine

"Damn," I muttered. "Would you still love me if I committed sororicide?"

"Yes, but I should be very put out about it." Tom broke off upon seeing Murray. "Oh, good. Would you be so kind as to fetch a bottle of whiskey? We'll need the entire thing. No glasses necessary."

"Right away, sir."

"Tom," I whispered, feeling a little lost as worry settled into my bones, counteracting some of the fury.

"Davina is fine. She is impossibly resourceful, and Kit is there to protect her and temper her worst notions."

"If he had any ability to temper her worst notions, she wouldn't have kidnapped the man in the first place."

"He's never let any harm fall to her before."

"True, true. She'll be fine. They were traveling in a carriage, not on horseback. They'll be here by tomorrow, or the day after at the latest."

"You're right. Everything will be well. It's Davina and Kit. It's not as though he would allow anything untoward to happen."

The End.
The Most Imprudent Matches series will continue with the final installment:
A Lady's Guide to Abduction (And Other Legal Matters).

Read the alternative epilogue at www.allyhudson.com/bonus-scenes.

Support the Author. Leave a review on Amazon

Acknowledgments

Mama, I will never be able to thank you for everything you've done for me. I miss you every day.

Thank you to my incredible critique partner, Laura Linn. I'll never write another blurb without you.

Thank you to my friends and family for your encouragement in this and all my projects.

Thank you to Martha for watching all the period dramas with me.

Thank you, as always, to Bryton for dragging me out of the house on occasion.

Thank you to Mariah for always reading my messy first draft.

Thank you Holly Perret at The Swoonies Romance Art for my gorgeous cover.

About the Author

Ally Hudson is an Amazon bestselling author of steamy Regency romance, crafting captivating tales of love, healing, hope, and family. Her debut series, *Most Imprudent Matches*, weaves together eight unforgettable love stories spanning decades, blending humor and heart with devoted heroes and capable heroines. Ally's stories celebrate the countless forms love can take, each one deserving its moment to shine.

When she's not writing, Ally can be found embroidering, baking, or catering to the every whim of her charming dog, Darcy.

Also by Ally Hudson

MOST IMPRUDENT MATCHES

Courting Scandal - Book One

Michael and Juliet

The Baker and the Bookmaker - Book Two

Augie and Anna

Winning My Wife - Book Three

Hugh and Kate

Devil of Mine - A Prequel Novella

Gabriel and Celine

Angel of Mine - Book Four

Will and Celine

A Properly Conducted Sham - Book Five

Lee and Charlotte

The Scottish Scheme - Book Six

Tom and Xander

COMING SOON

A Lady's Guide to Abduction (And Other Legal Matters) - Fall 2025

Printed in Dunstable, United Kingdom